REDNECK™

CREATED BY

Donny Cates & Lisandro Estherren

DONNY CATES
CREATOR, WRITER

LISANDRO ESTHERREN
CREATOR, ARTIST

DEE CUNNIFFE
COLORIST

REDNECK VOLUME 2. FIRST PRINTING. MAY 2018. PUBLISHED BY IMAGE COMICS, INC. OFFICE OF PUBLICATION: 2701 NW VAUGHN ST., STE. 780, PORTLAND, OR 97210. ORIGINALLY PUBLISHED IN SINGLE MAGAZINE FORM AS REDNECK #7-12. REDNECK™ (INCLUDING ALL PROMINENT CHARACTERS FEATURED HEREIN), ITS LOGO AND ALL CHARACTER LIKENESSES ARE TRADEMARKS OF SKYBOUND, LLC, UNLESS OTHERWISE NOTED. IMAGE COMICS® AND ITS LOGOS ARE REGISTERED TRADEMARKS AND COPYRIGHTS OF IMAGE COMICS, INC. ALL RIGHTS RESERVED. NO PART OF THIS PUBLICATION MAY BE REPRODUCED OR TRANSMITTED IN ANY FORM OR BY ANY MEANS (EXCEPT FOR SHORT EXCERPTS FOR REVIEW PURPOSES) WITHOUT THE EXPRESS WRITTEN PERMISSION OF IMAGE COMICS, INC. ALL NAMES, CHARACTERS, EVENTS AND LOCALES IN THIS PUBLICATION ARE ENTIRELY FICTIONAL. ANY RESEMBLANCE TO ACTUAL PERSONS (LIVING OR DEAD), EVENTS OR PLACES, WITHOUT SATIRIC INTENT, IS COINCIDENTAL. PRINTED IN THE U.S.A. FOR INFORMATION REGARDING THE CPSIA ON THIS PRINTED MATERIAL CALL: 203-595-3636 AND PROVIDE REFERENCE # RICH — 789169. ISBN: 978-1-5343-0665-3

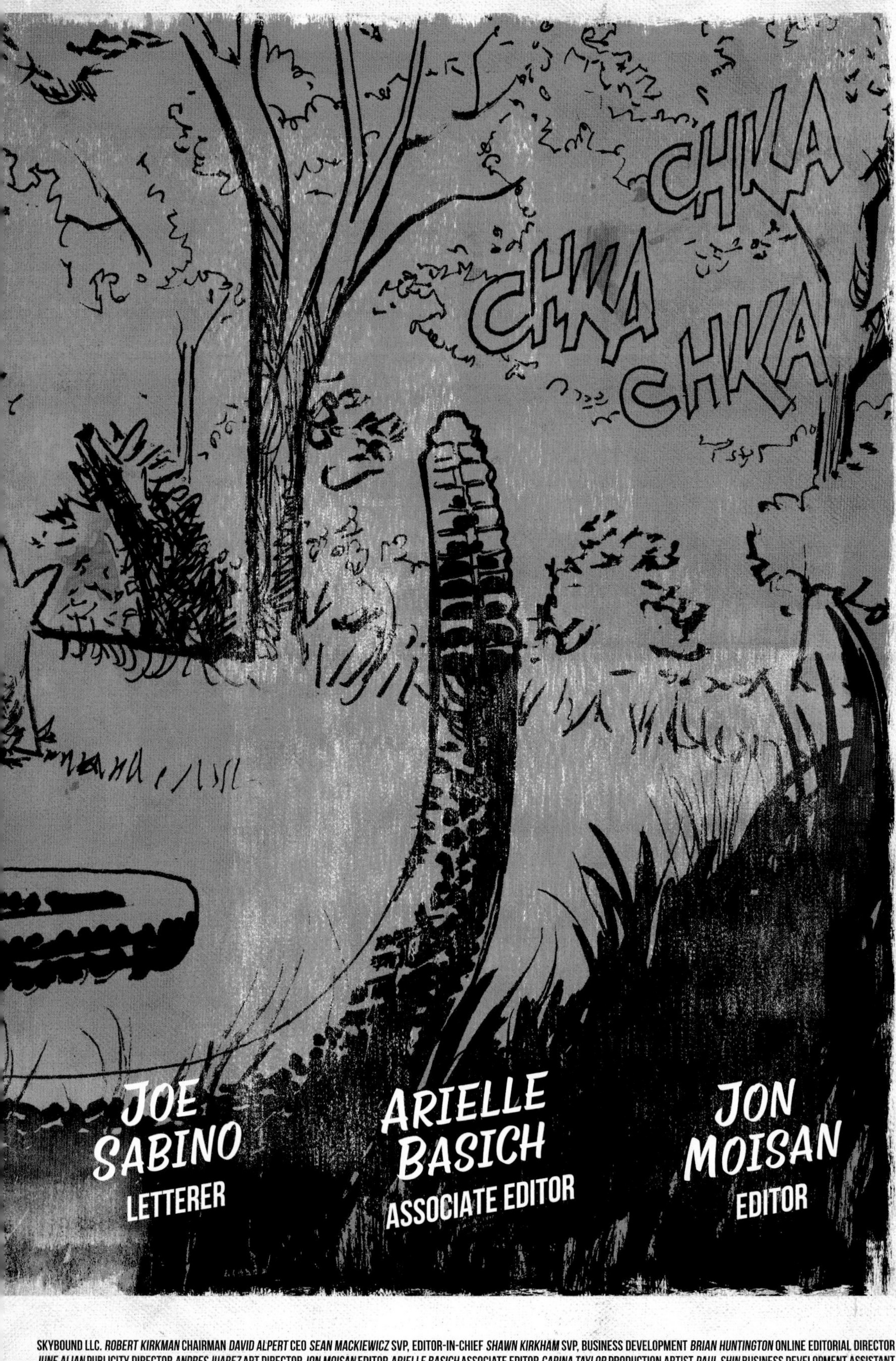
CHKA
CHKA
CHKA
JOE SABINO
LETTERER
ARIELLE BASICH
ASSOCIATE EDITOR
JON MOISAN
EDITOR

SKYBOUND LLC. *ROBERT KIRKMAN* CHAIRMAN *DAVID ALPERT* CEO *SEAN MACKIEWICZ* SVP, EDITOR-IN-CHIEF *SHAWN KIRKHAM* SVP, BUSINESS DEVELOPMENT *BRIAN HUNTINGTON* ONLINE EDITORIAL DIRECTOR *JUNE ALIAN* PUBLICITY DIRECTOR *ANDRES JUAREZ* ART DIRECTOR *JON MOISAN* EDITOR *ARIELLE BASICH* ASSOCIATE EDITOR *CARINA TAYLOR* PRODUCTION ARTIST *PAUL SHIN* BUSINESS DEVELOPMENT ASSISTANT *JOHNNY O'DELL* SOCIAL MEDIA MANAGER *SALLY JACKA* SKYBOUND RETAILER REALATIONS *DAN PETERSEN* DIRECTOR OF OPERATIONS & EVENTS *NICK PALMER* OPERATIONS COORDINATOR
INTERNATIONAL INQUIRIES: AG@SEQUENTIALRIGHTS.COM LICENSING INQUIRIES:CONTACT@SKYBOUND.COM WWW.SKYBOUND.COM

IMAGE COMICS, INC. *ROBERT KIRKMAN* CHIEF OPERATING OFFICER *ERIK LARSEN* CHIEF FINANCIAL OFFICER *TODD MCFARLANE* PRESIDENT *MARC SILVESTRI* CHIEF EXECUTIVE OFFICER *JIM VALENTINO* VICE PRESIDENT *ERIC STEPHENSON* PUBLISHER/CHIEF CREATIVE OFFICER *COREY HART* DIRECTOR OF SALES *JEFF BOISON* DIRECTOR OF PUBLISHING PLANNING & BOOK TRADE SALES *CHRIS ROSS* DIRECTOR OF DIGITAL SALES *JEFF STANG* DIRECTOR OF SPECIALTY SALES *KAT SALAZAR* DIRECTOR OF PR & MARKETING *DREW GILL* ART DIRECTOR *HEATHER DOORNINK* PRODUCTION DIRECTOR *NICOLE LAPALME* CONTROLLER WWW.IMAGECOMICS.COM

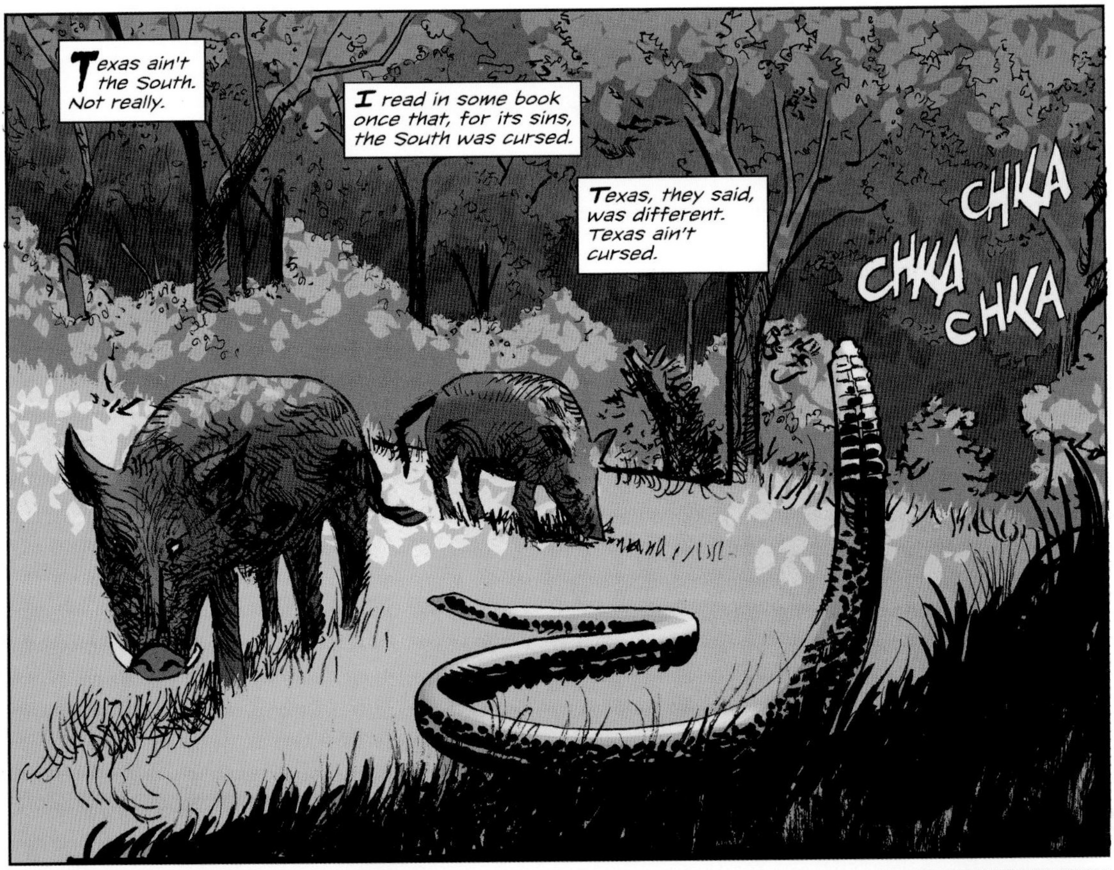
Texas ain't the South. Not really.
I read in some book once that, for its sins, the South was cursed.
Texas, they said, was different. Texas ain't cursed.
CHKA
CHKA CHKA

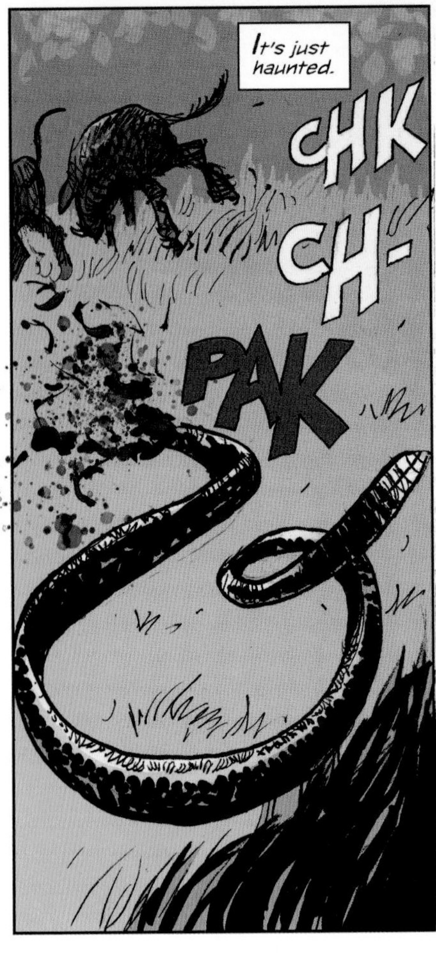
It's just haunted.
CHK
CH-
PAK

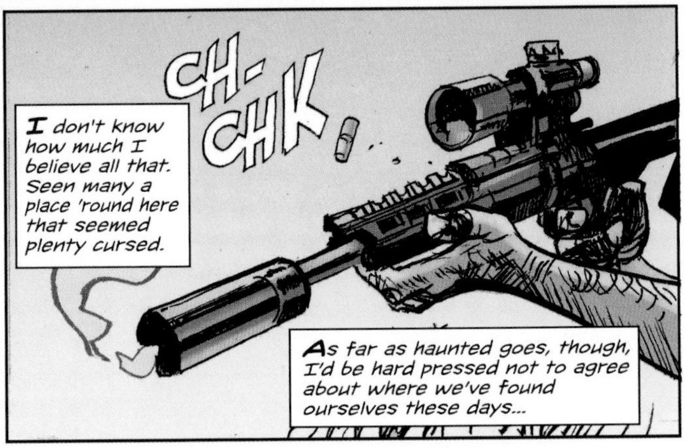
CH-CHK
I don't know how much I believe all that. Seen many a place 'round here that seemed plenty cursed.
As far as haunted goes, though, I'd be hard pressed not to agree about where we've found ourselves these days...

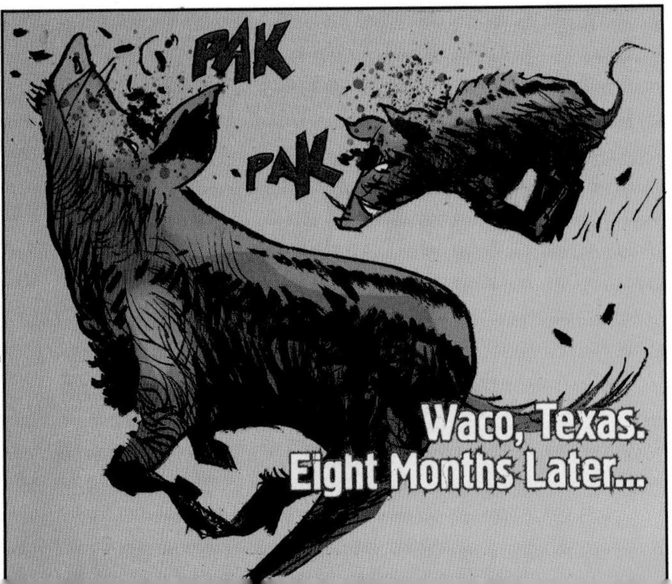
PAK
PAK
Waco, Texas.
Eight Months Later...

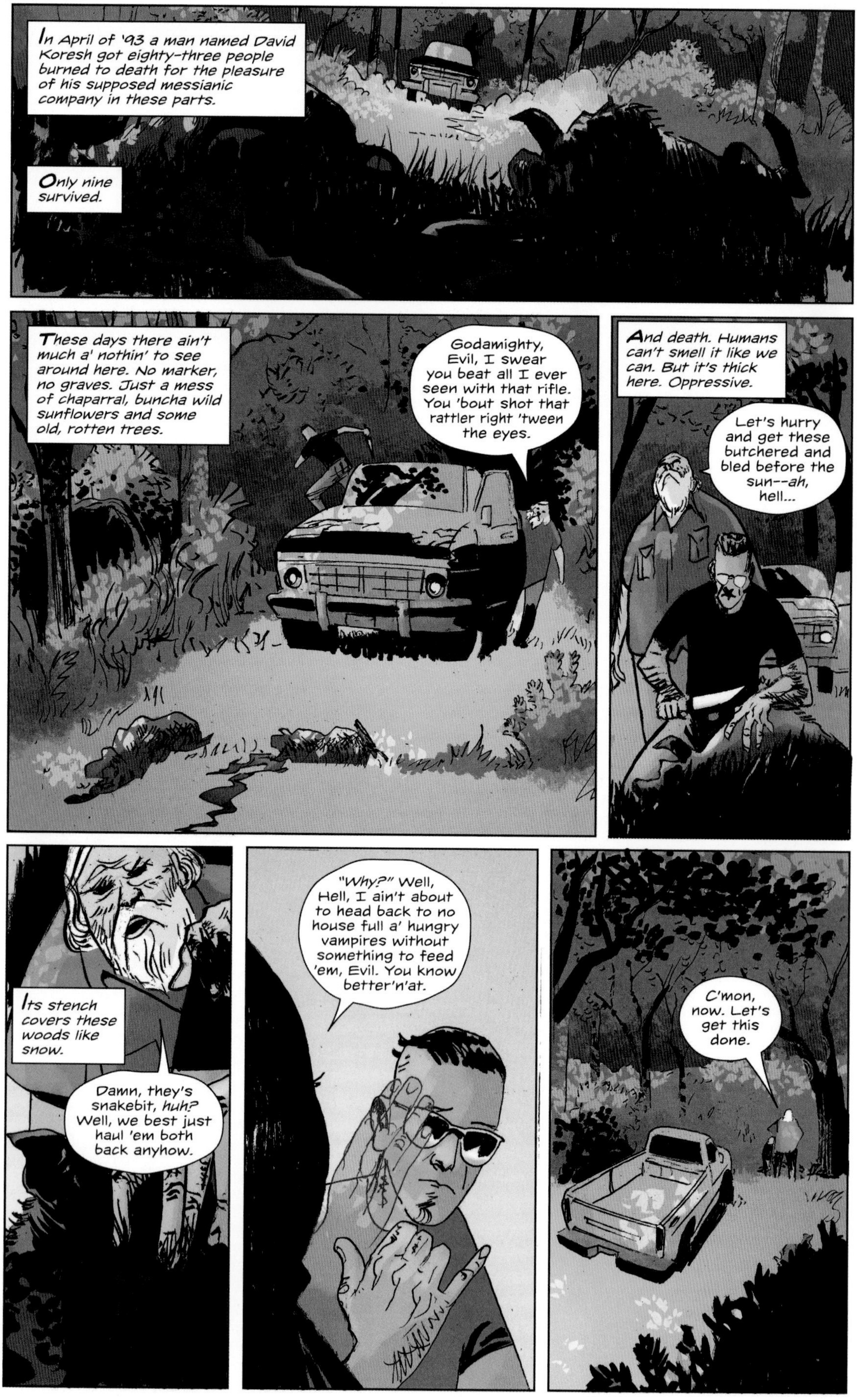
In April of '93 a man named David Koresh got eighty-three people burned to death for the pleasure of his supposed messianic company in these parts.
Only nine survived.
These days there ain't much a' nothin' to see around here. No marker, no graves. Just a mess of chaparral, buncha wild sunflowers and some old, rotten trees.
Godamighty, Evil, I swear you beat all I ever seen with that rifle. You 'bout shot that rattler right 'tween the eyes.
And death. Humans can't smell it like we can. But it's thick here. Oppressive.
Let's hurry and get these butchered and bled before the sun--ah, hell...
Its stench covers these woods like snow.
Damn, they's snakebit, huh? Well, we best just haul 'em both back anyhow.
"Why?" Well, Hell, I ain't about to head back to no house full a' hungry vampires without something to feed 'em, Evil. You know better'n'at.
C'mon, now. Let's get this done.

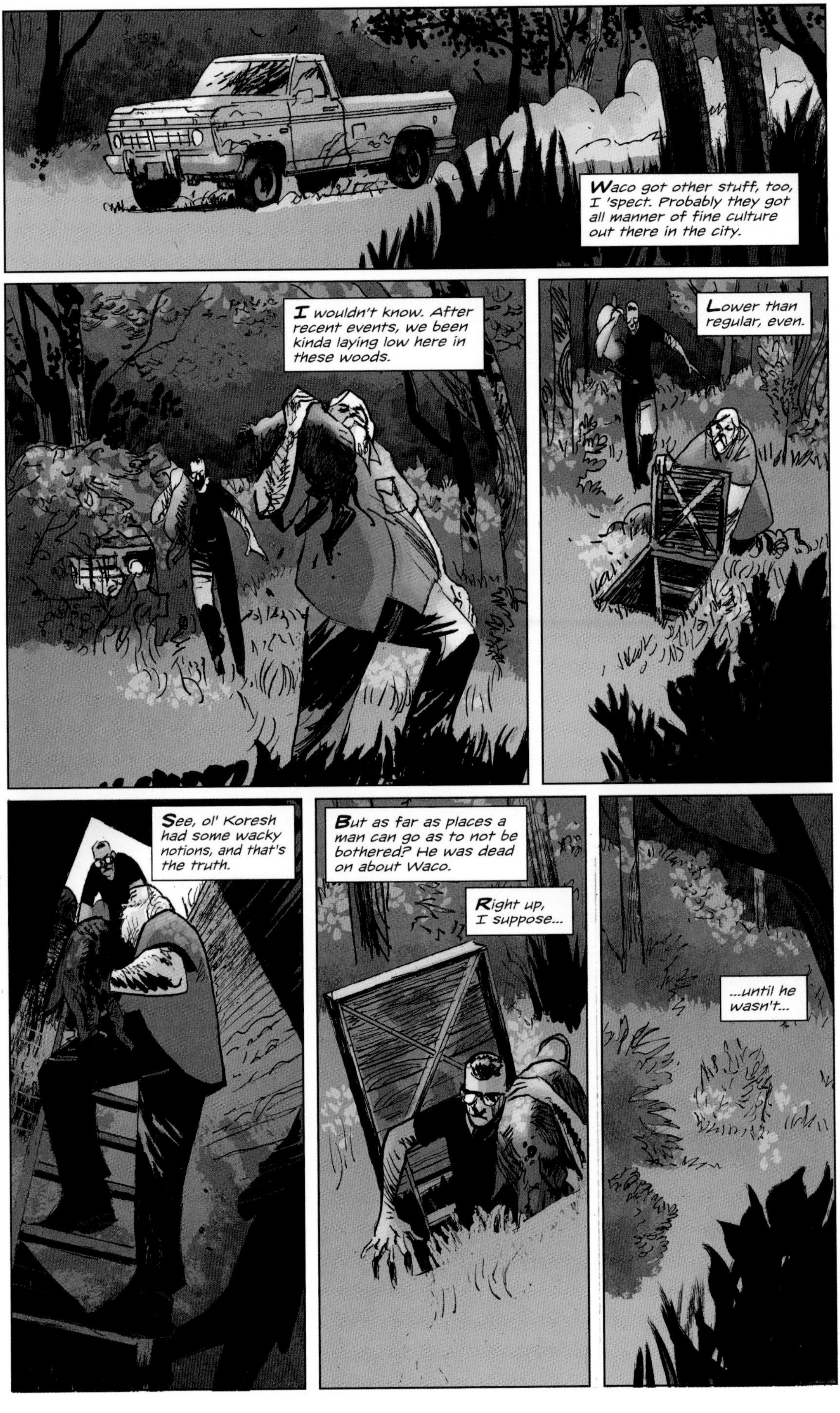
Waco got other stuff, too, I 'spect. Probably they got all manner of fine culture out there in the city.
I wouldn't know. After recent events, we been kinda laying low here in these woods.
Lower than regular, even.
See, ol' Koresh had some wacky notions, and that's the truth.
But as far as places a man can go as to not be bothered? He was dead on about Waco.
Right up, I suppose...
...until he wasn't...

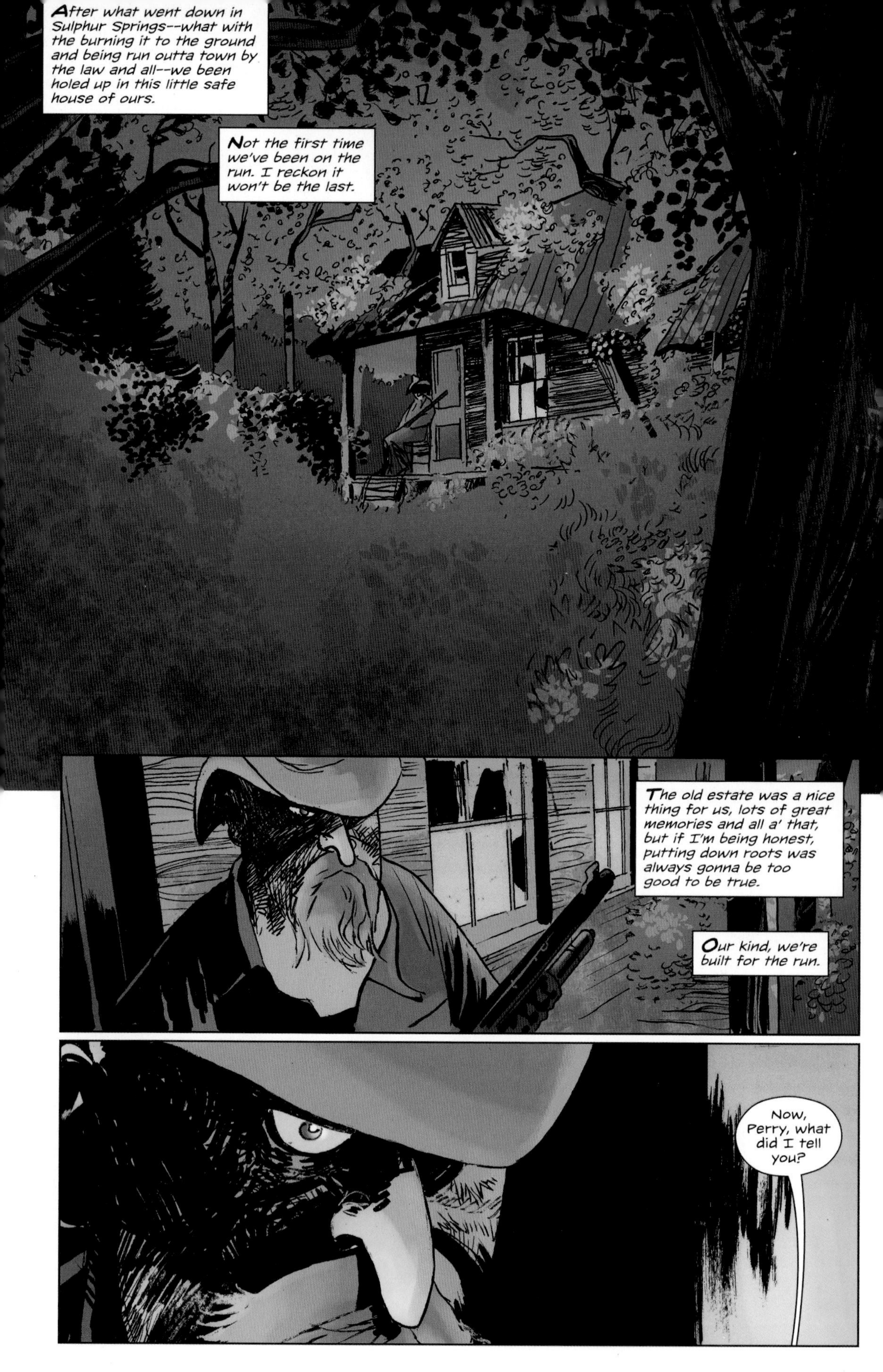
After what went down in Sulphur Springs--what with the burning it to the ground and being run outta town by the law and all--we been holed up in this little safe house of ours.
Not the first time we've been on the run. I reckon it won't be the last.
The old estate was a nice thing for us, lots of great memories and all a' that, but if I'm being honest, putting down roots was always gonna be too good to be true.
Our kind, we're built for the run.
Now, Perry, what did I tell you?

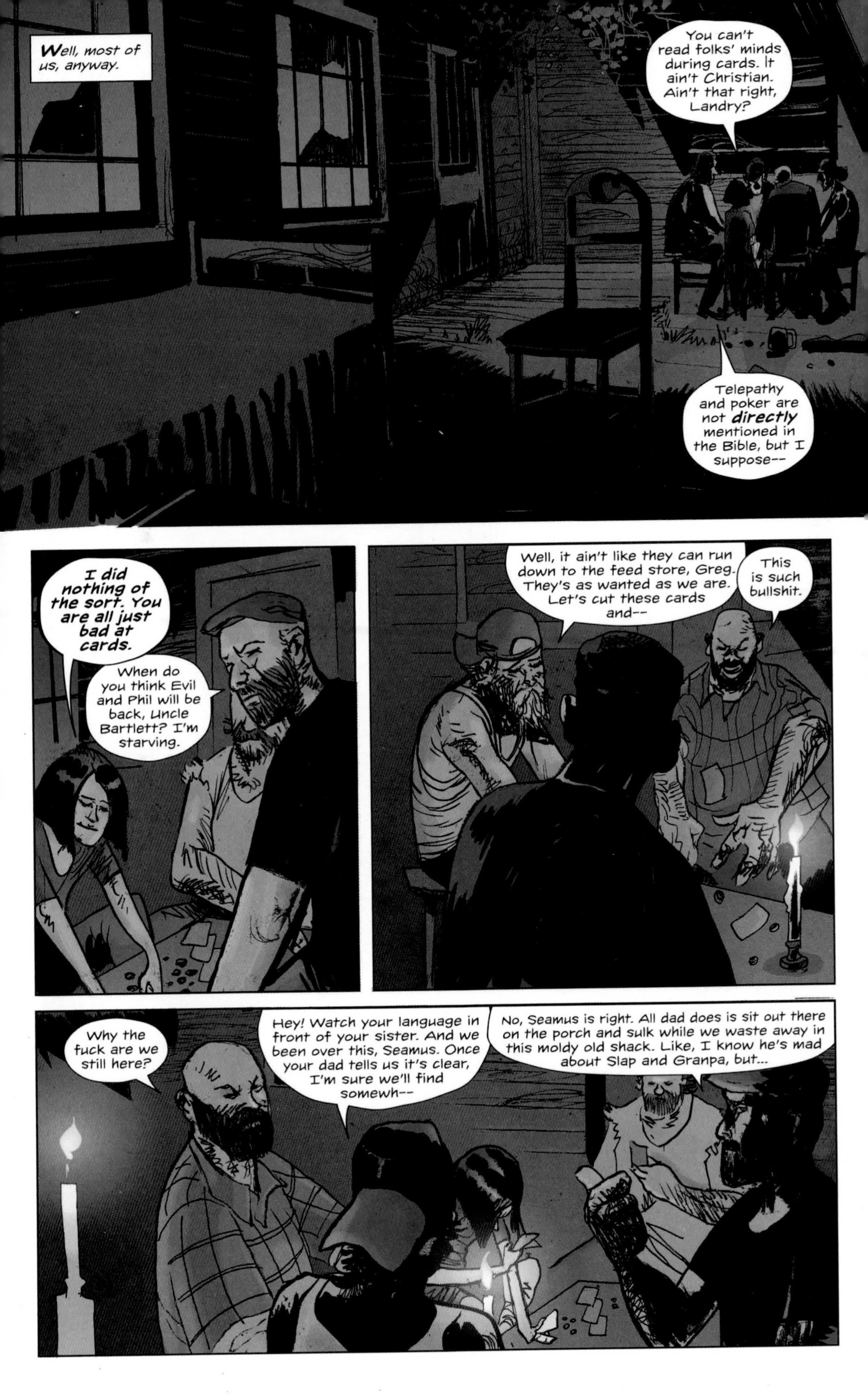
Well, most of us, anyway.
You can't read folks' minds during cards. It ain't Christian. Ain't that right, Landry?
Telepathy and poker are not directly mentioned in the Bible, but I suppose--
I did nothing of the sort. You are all just bad at cards.
When do you think Evil and Phil will be back, Uncle Bartlett? I'm starving.
Well, it ain't like they can run down to the feed store, Greg. They's as wanted as we are. Let's cut these cards and--
This is such bullshit.
Why the fuck are we still here?
Hey! Watch your language in front of your sister. And we been over this, Seamus. Once your dad tells us it's clear, I'm sure we'll find somewh--
No, Seamus is right. All dad does is sit out there on the porch and sulk while we waste away in this moldy old shack. Like, I know he's mad about Slap and Granpa, but...

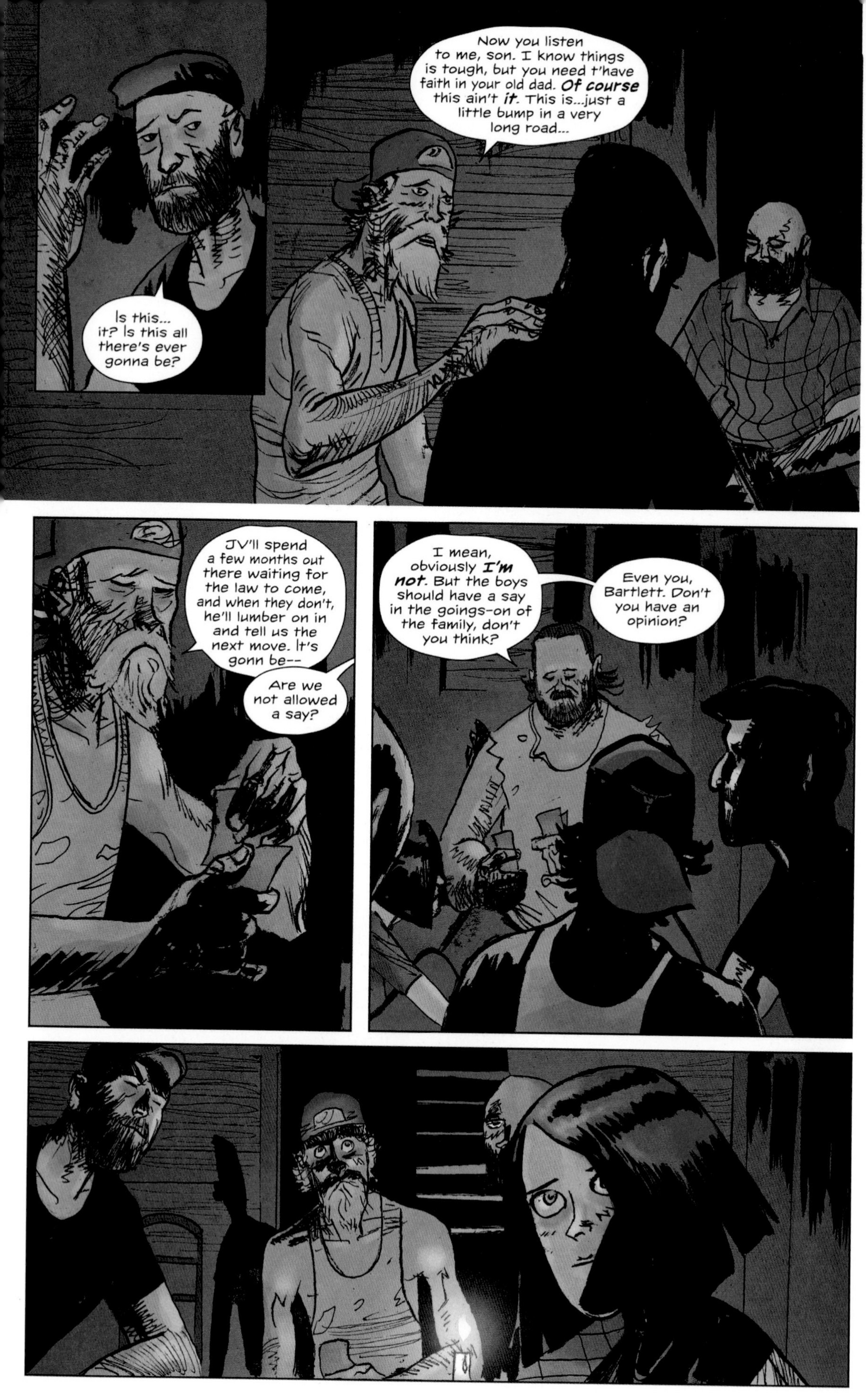
Is this... it? Is this all there's ever gonna be?
Now you listen to me, son. I know things is tough, but you need t'have faith in your old dad. **Of course** this ain't ***it***. This is...just a little bump in a very long road...
JV'll spend a few months out there waiting for the law to come, and when they don't, he'll lumber on in and tell us the next move. It's gonn be--
Are we not allowed a say?
I mean, obviously ***I'm not***. But the boys should have a say in the goings-on of the family, don't you think?
Even you, Bartlett. Don't you have an opinion?

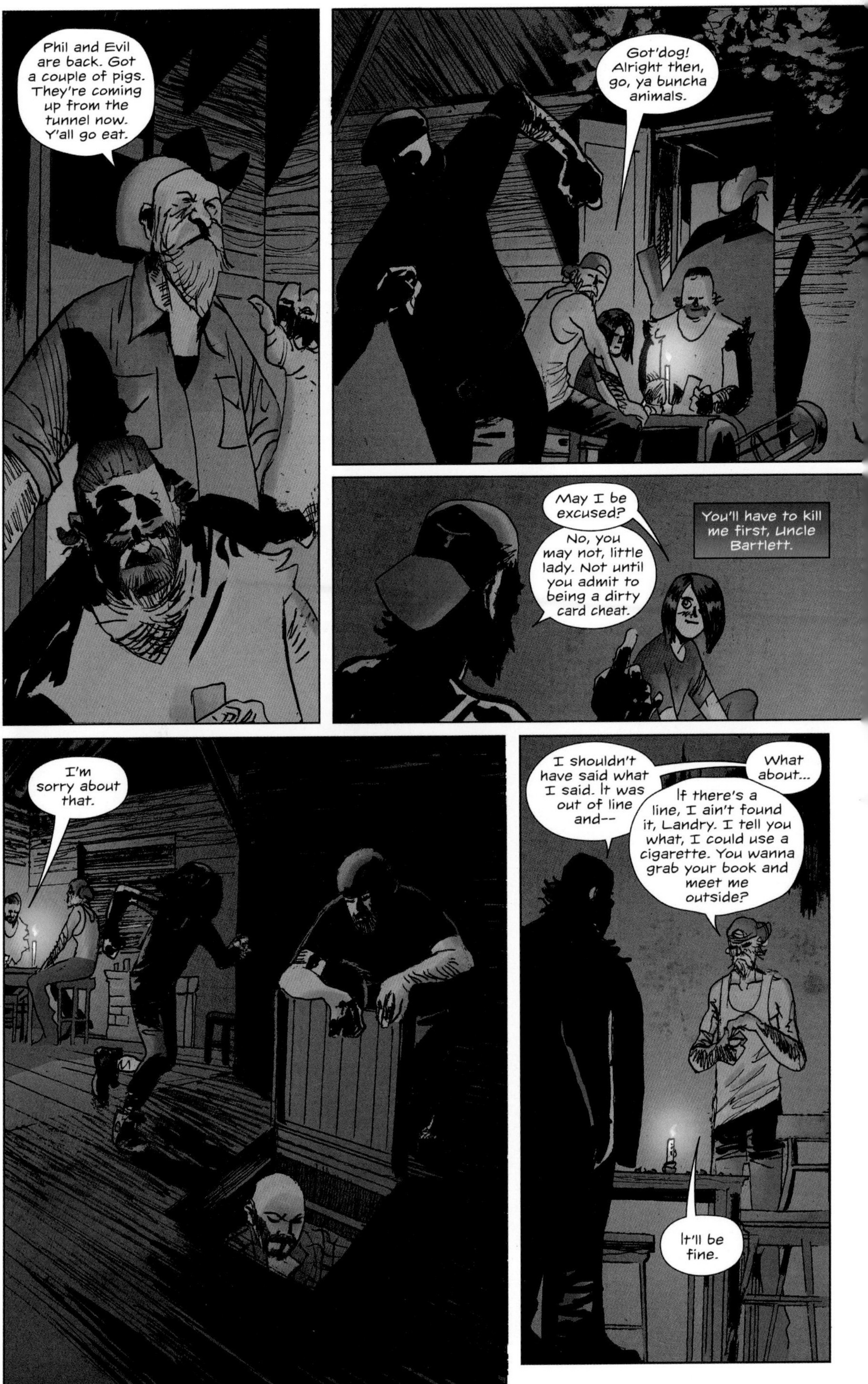
Phil and Evil are back. Got a couple of pigs. They're coming up from the tunnel now. Y'all go eat.
Got'dog! Alright then, go, ya buncha animals.
May I be excused?
No, you may not, little lady. Not until you admit to being a dirty card cheat.
You'll have to kill me first, Uncle Bartlett.
I'm sorry about that.
I shouldn't have said what I said. It was out of line and--
What about...
If there's a line, I ain't found it, Landry. I tell you what, I could use a cigarette. You wanna grab your book and meet me outside?
It'll be fine.

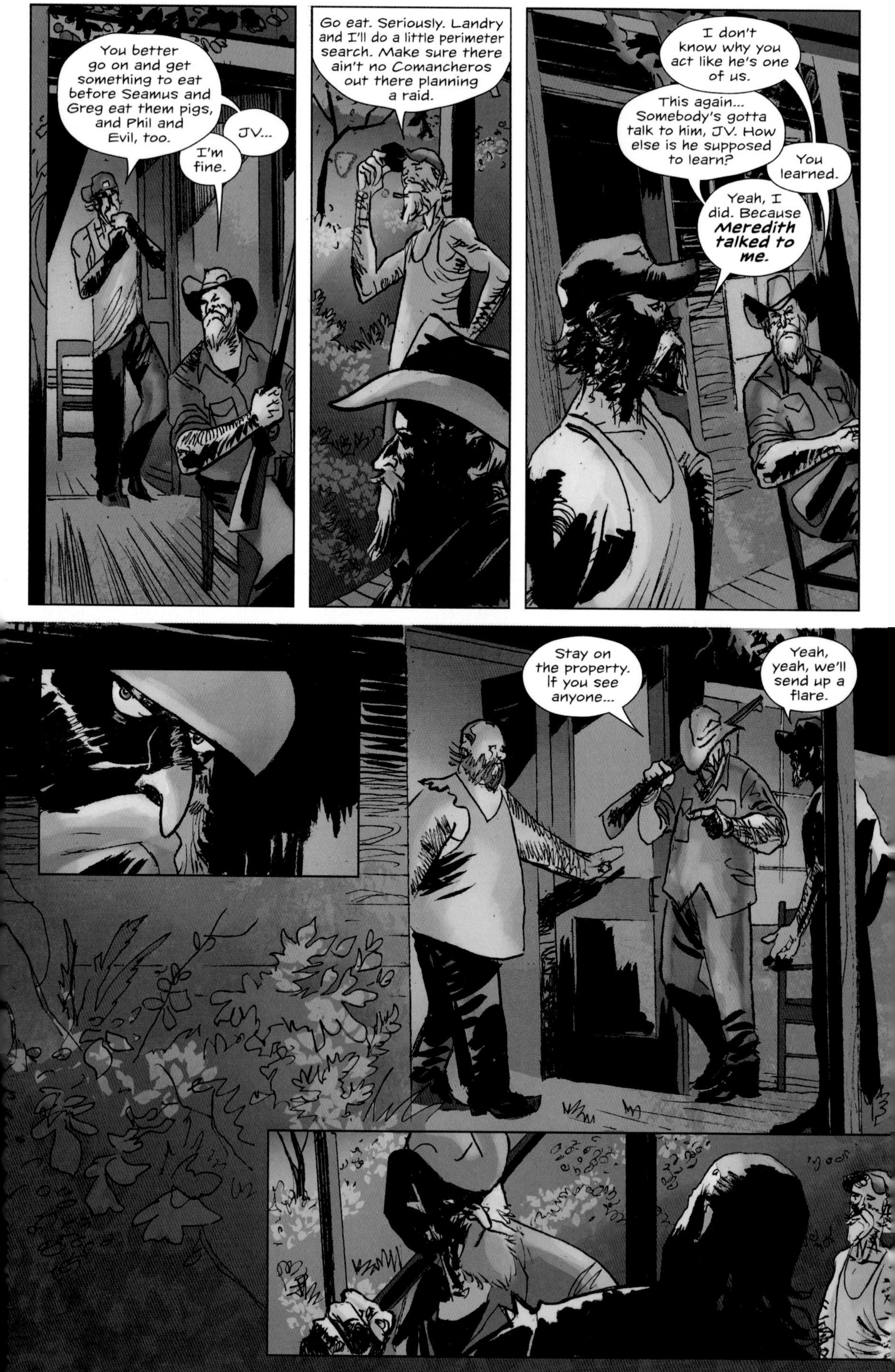

You better go on and get something to eat before Seamus and Greg eat them pigs, and Phil and Evil, too.
JV...
I'm fine.
Go eat. Seriously. Landry and I'll do a little perimeter search. Make sure there ain't no Comancheros out there planning a raid.
I don't know why you act like he's one of us.
This again... Somebody's gotta talk to him, JV. How else is he supposed to learn?
You learned.
Yeah, I did. Because Meredith talked to me.
Stay on the property. If you see anyone...
Yeah, yeah, we'll send up a flare.

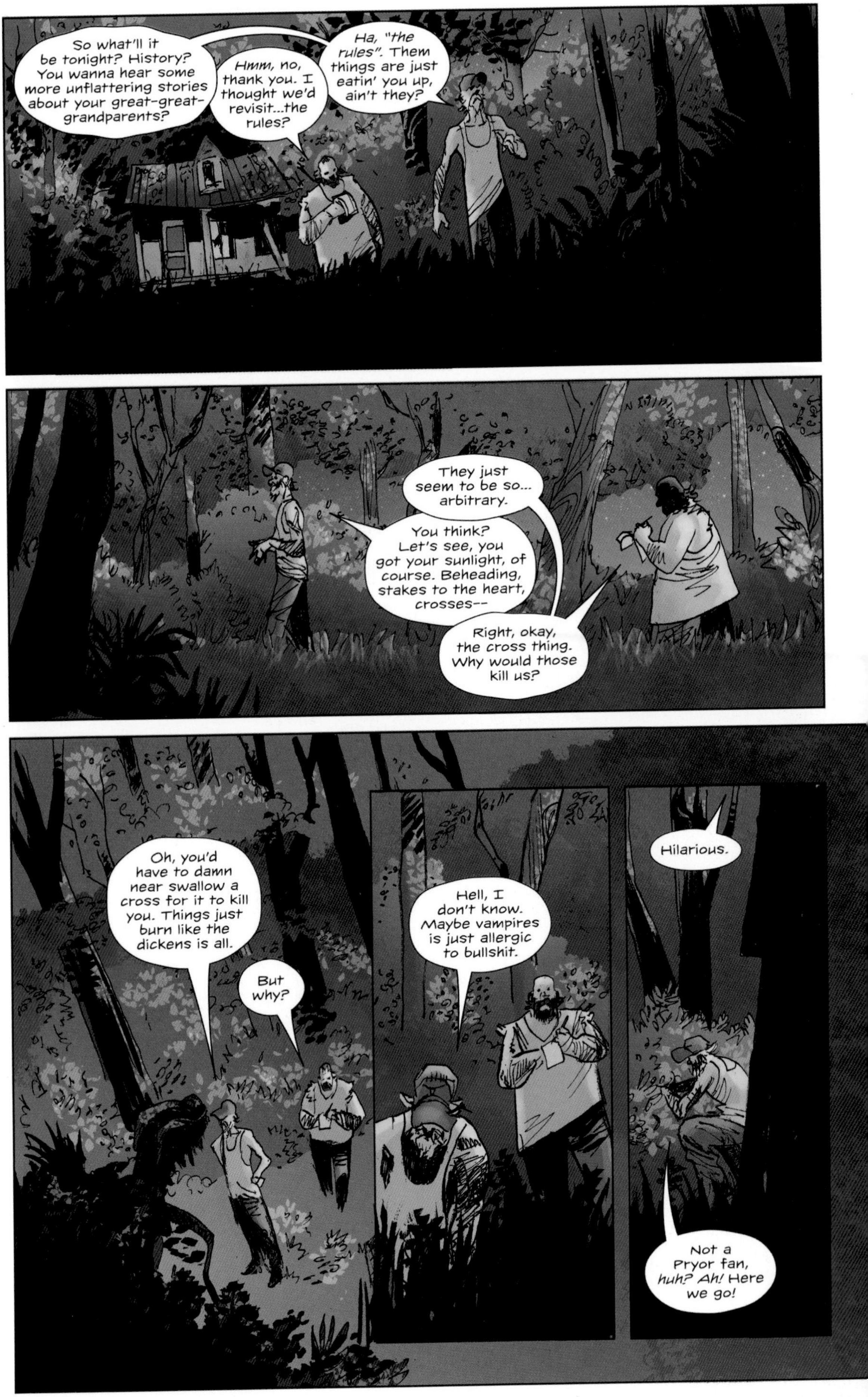
So what'll it be tonight? History? You wanna hear some more unflattering stories about your great-great-grandparents?
Hmm, no, thank you. I thought we'd revisit...the rules?
Ha, *"the rules"*. Them things are just eatin' you up, ain't they?
They just seem to be so... arbitrary.
You think? Let's see, you got your sunlight, of course. Beheading, stakes to the heart, crosses--
Right, okay, the cross thing. Why would those kill us?
Oh, you'd have to damn near swallow a cross for it to kill you. Things just burn like the dickens is all.
But why?
Hell, I don't know. Maybe vampires is just allergic to bullshit.
Hilarious.
Not a Pryor fan, *huh*? Ah! Here we go!

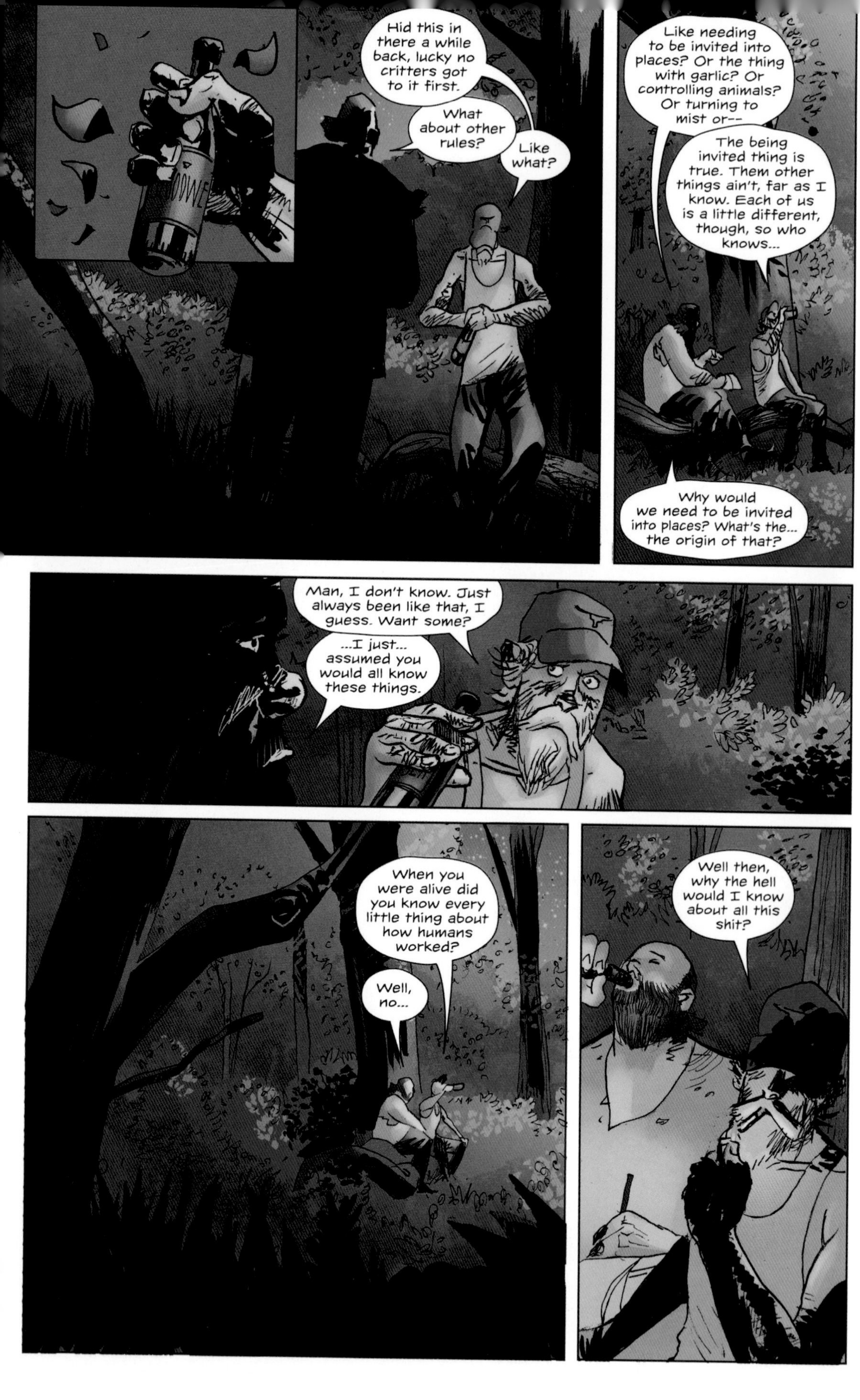
Hid this in there a while back, lucky no critters got to it first.
What about other rules?
Like what?
Like needing to be invited into places? Or the thing with garlic? Or controlling animals? Or turning to mist or--
The being invited thing is true. Them other things ain't, far as I know. Each of us is a little different, though, so who knows...
Why would we need to be invited into places? What's the... the origin of that?
Man, I don't know. Just always been like that, I guess. Want some?
...I just... assumed you would all know these things.
When you were alive did you know every little thing about how humans worked?
Well, no...
Well then, why the hell would I know about all this shit?

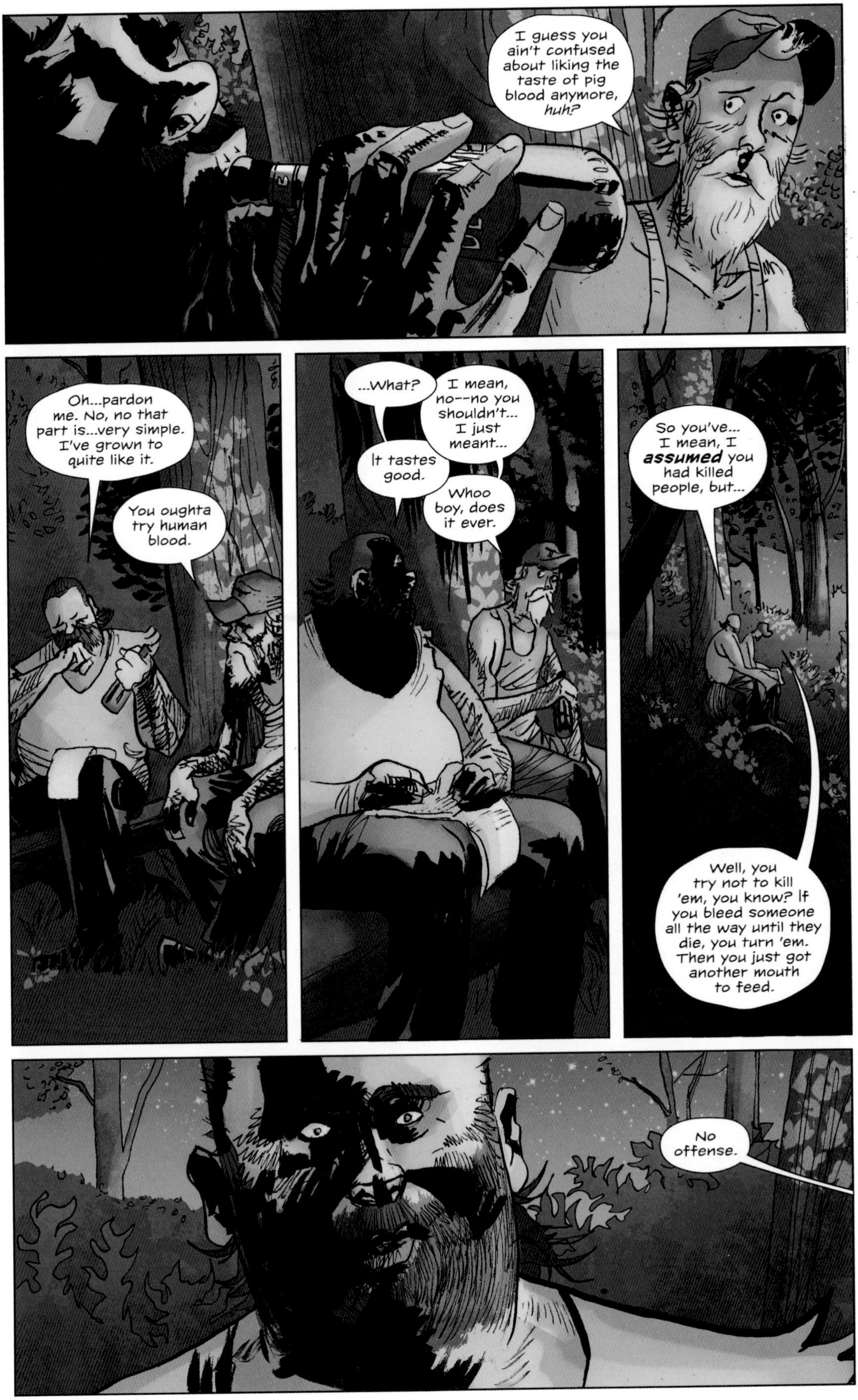
I guess you ain't confused about liking the taste of pig blood anymore, *huh?*
Oh...pardon me. No, no that part is...very simple. I've grown to quite like it.
You oughta try human blood.
...What?
I mean, no--no you shouldn't... I just meant...
It tastes good.
Whoo boy, does it ever.
So you've... I mean, I ***assumed*** you had killed people, but...
Well, you try not to kill 'em, you know? If you bleed someone all the way until they die, you turn 'em. Then you just got another mouth to feed.
No offense.

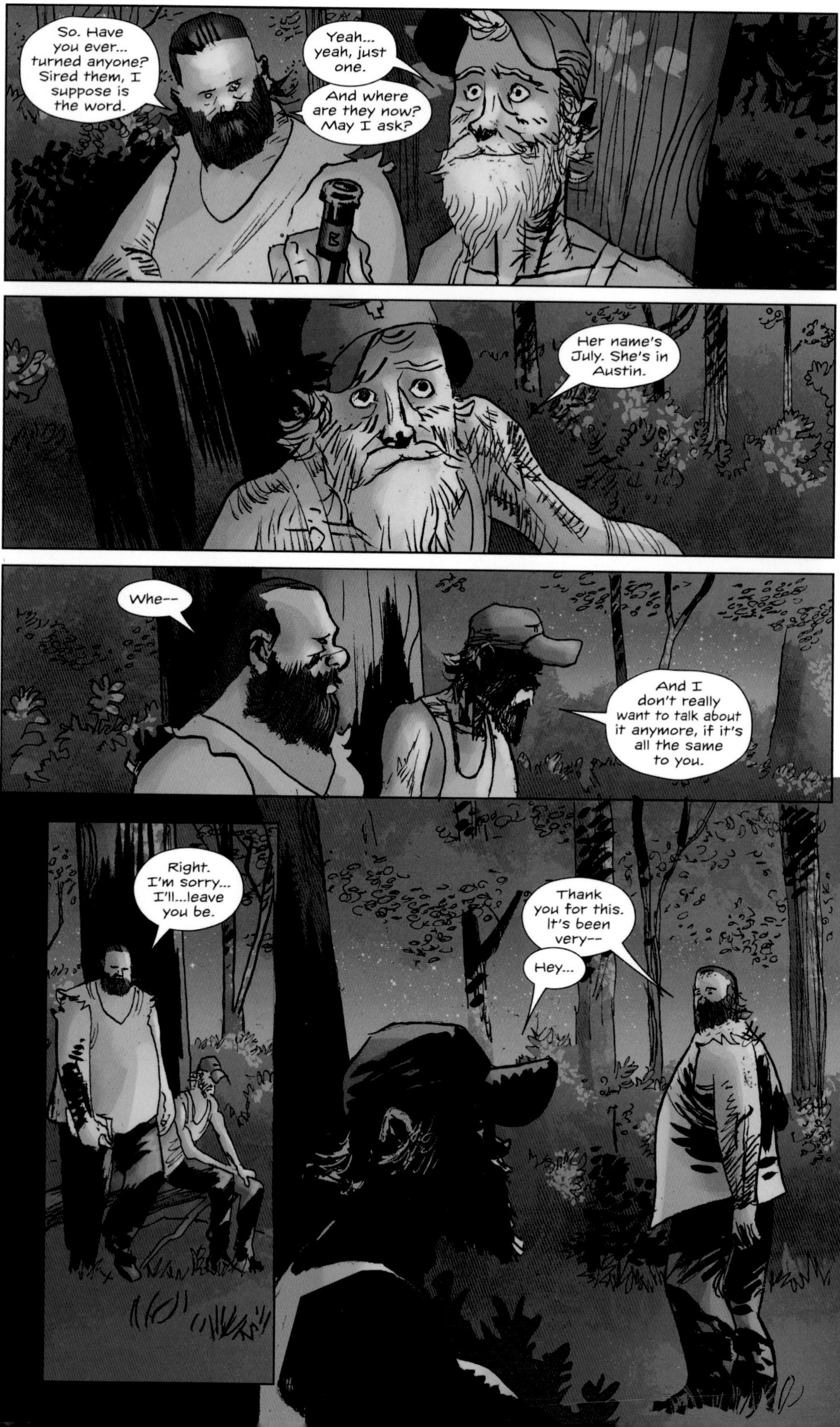
So. Have you ever... turned anyone? Sired them, I suppose is the word.
Yeah... yeah, just one.
And where are they now? May I ask?
Her name's July. She's in Austin.
Whe--
And I don't really want to talk about it anymore, if it's all the same to you.
Right. I'm sorry... I'll...leave you be.
Thank you for this. It's been very--
Hey...

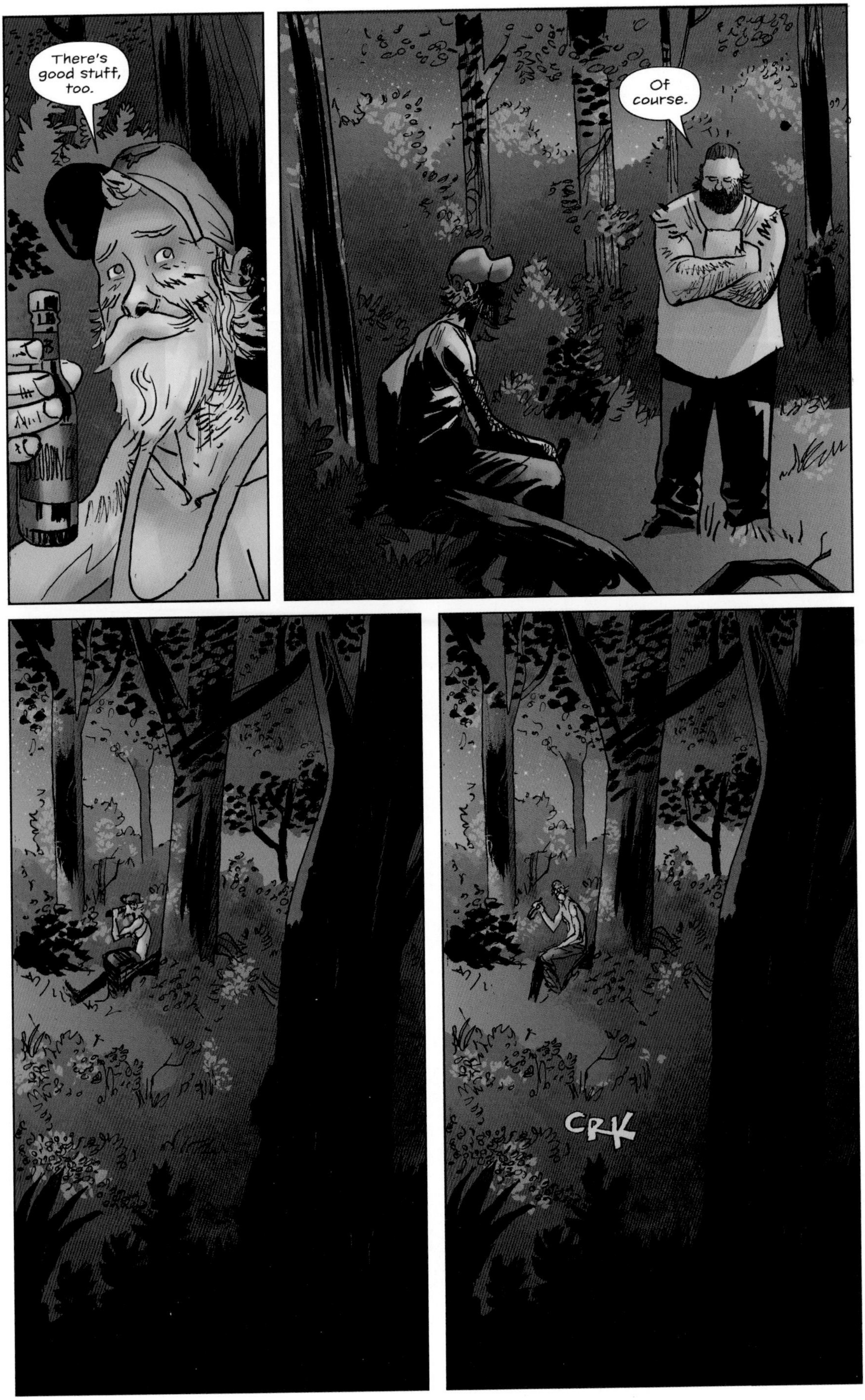
There's good stuff, too.
Of course.
CRK

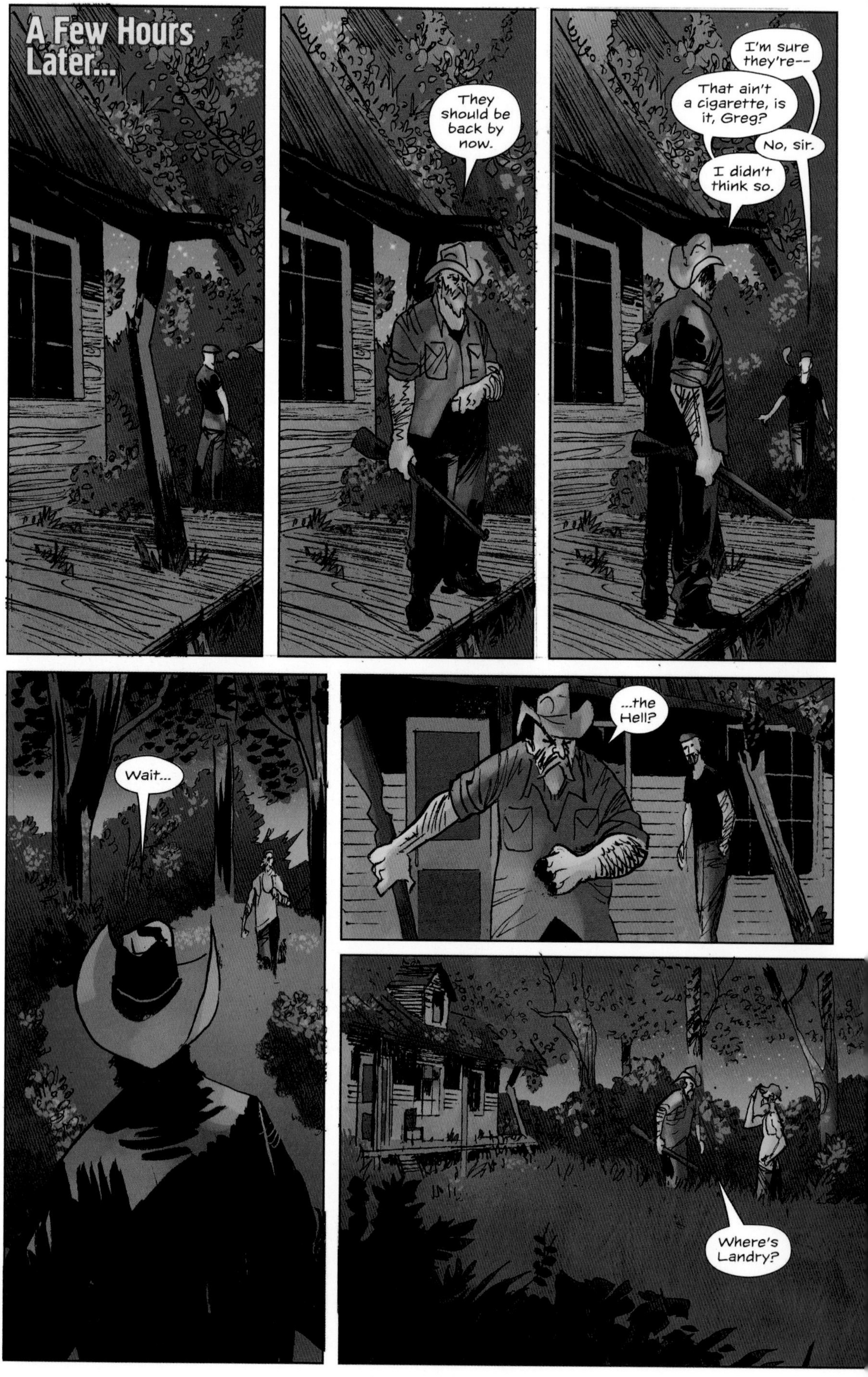
A Few Hours Later...
They should be back by now.
I'm sure they're--
That ain't a cigarette, is it, Greg?
No, sir.
I didn't think so.
Wait...
...the Hell?
Where's Landry?

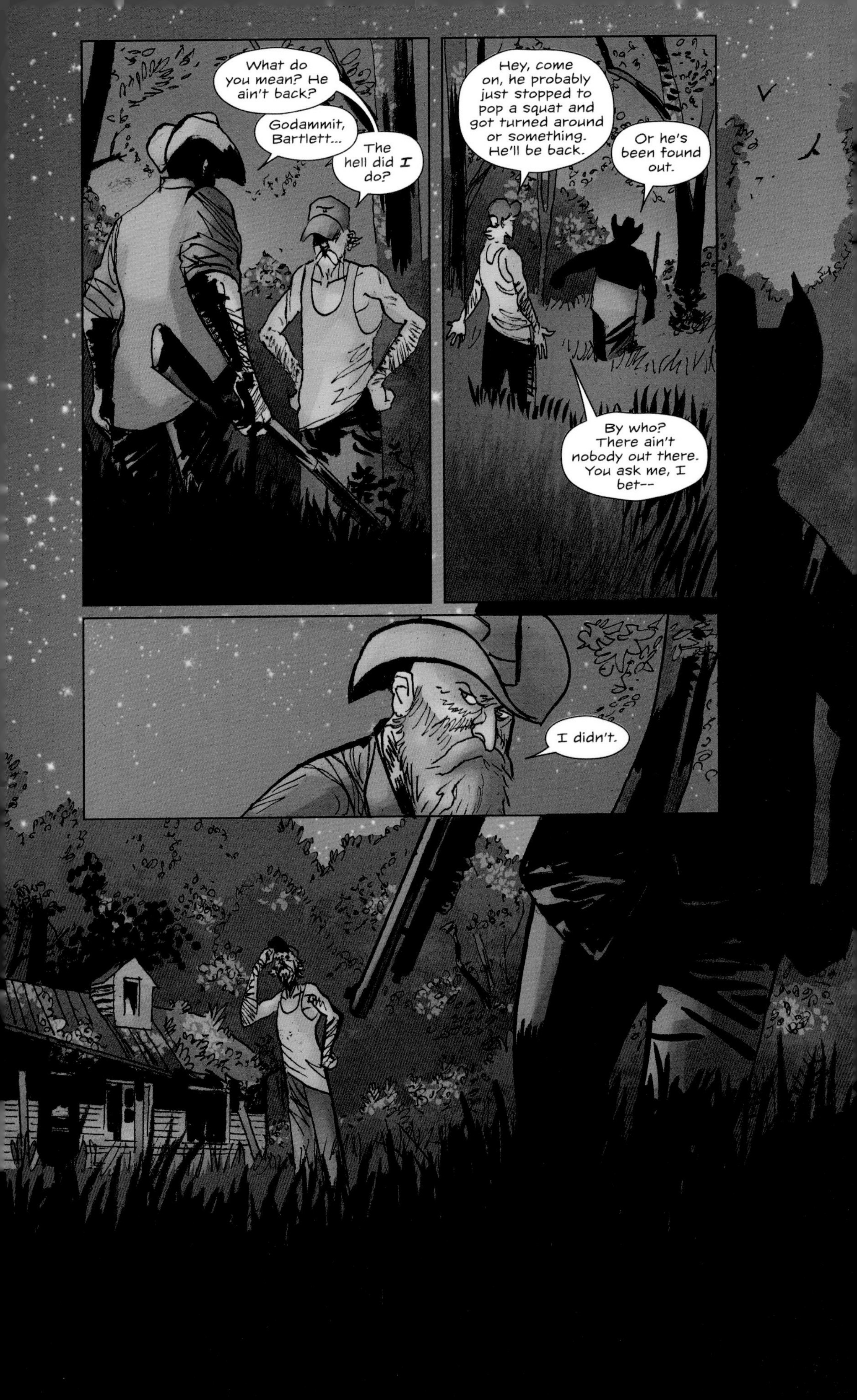
What do you mean? He ain't back?
Godammit, Bartlett...
The hell did I do?
Hey, come on, he probably just stopped to pop a squat and got turned around or something. He'll be back.
Or he's been found out.
By who? There ain't nobody out there. You ask me, I bet--
I didn't.

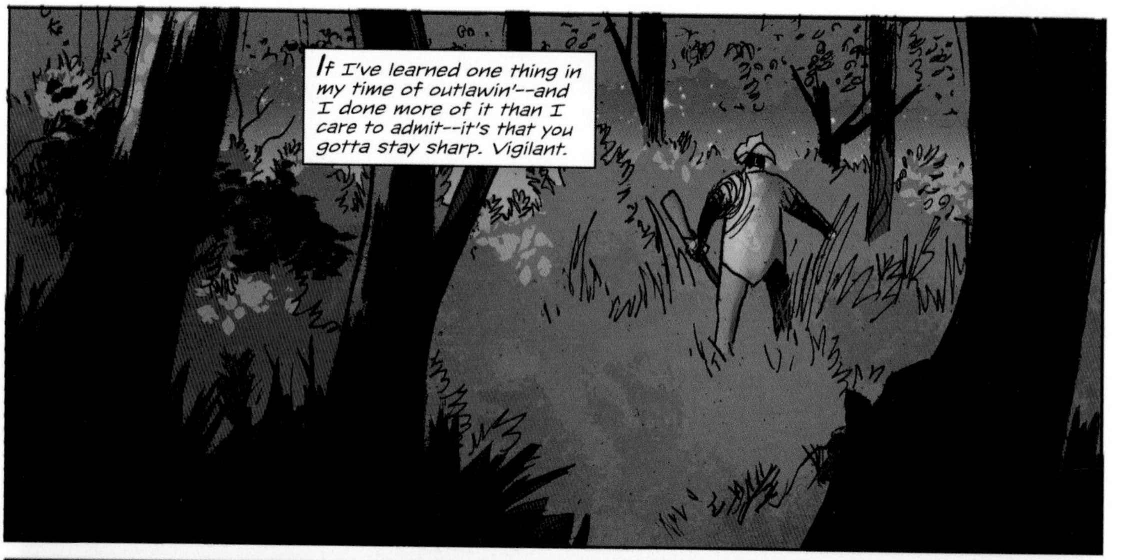
If I've learned one thing in my time of outlawin'--and I done more of it than I care to admit--it's that you gotta stay sharp. Vigilant.

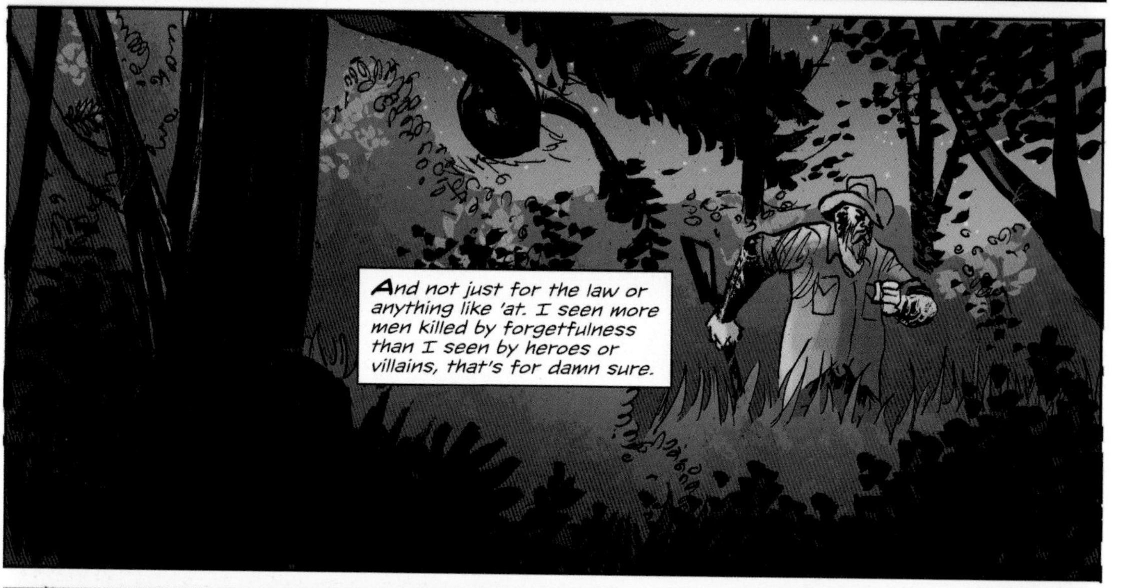
And not just for the law or anything like 'at. I seen more men killed by forgetfulness than I seen by heroes or villains, that's for damn sure.

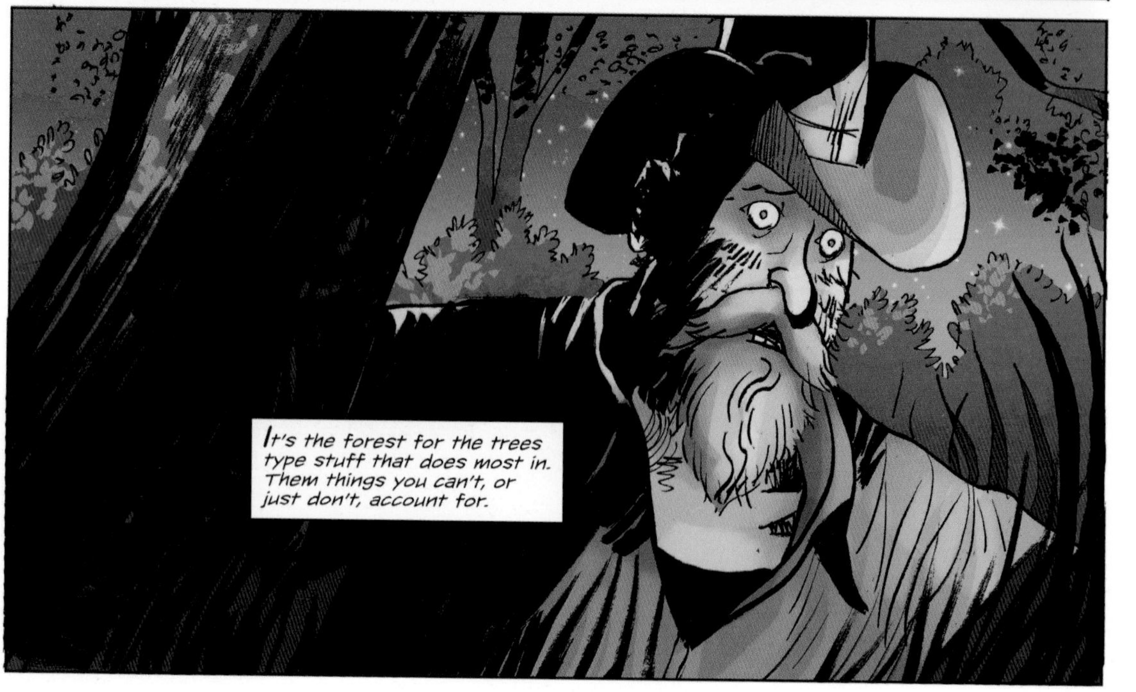
It's the forest for the trees type stuff that does most in. Them things you can't, or just don't, account for.

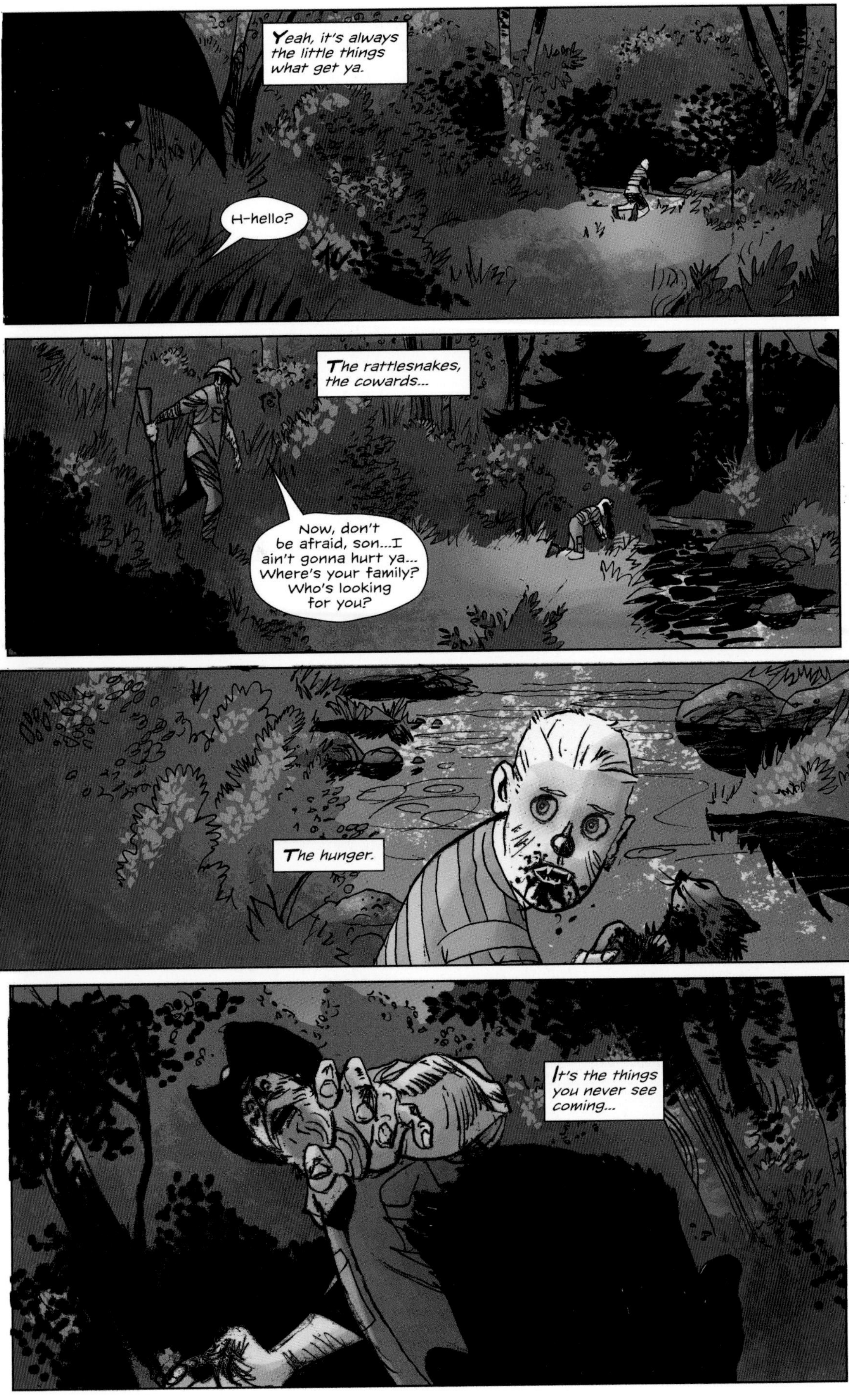

Yeah, it's always the little things what get ya.
H-hello?
The rattlesnakes, the cowards...
Now, don't be afraid, son...I ain't gonna hurt ya... Where's your family? Who's looking for you?
The hunger.
It's the things you never see coming...

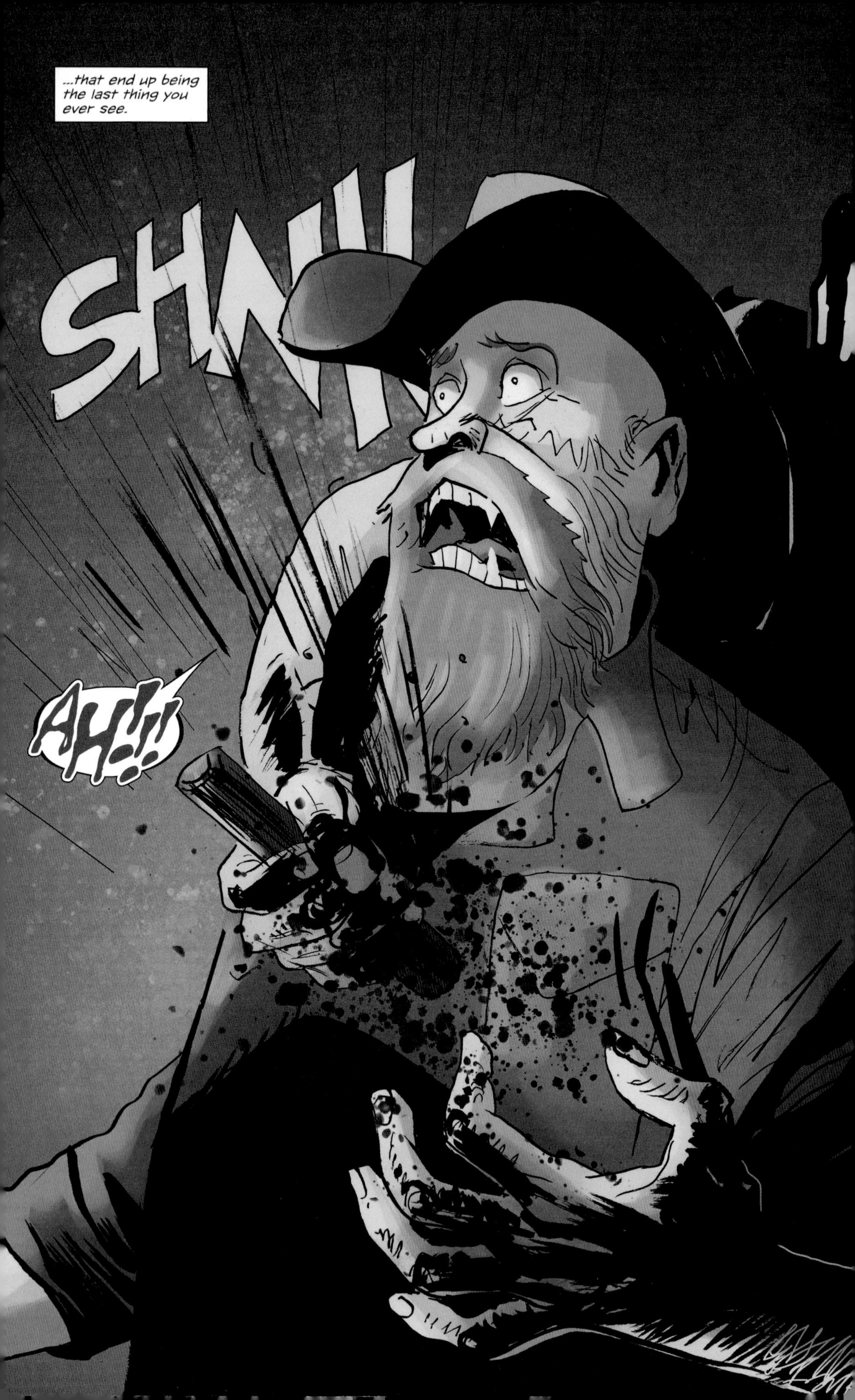
...that end up being the last thing you ever see.
SHNK
AH!!!

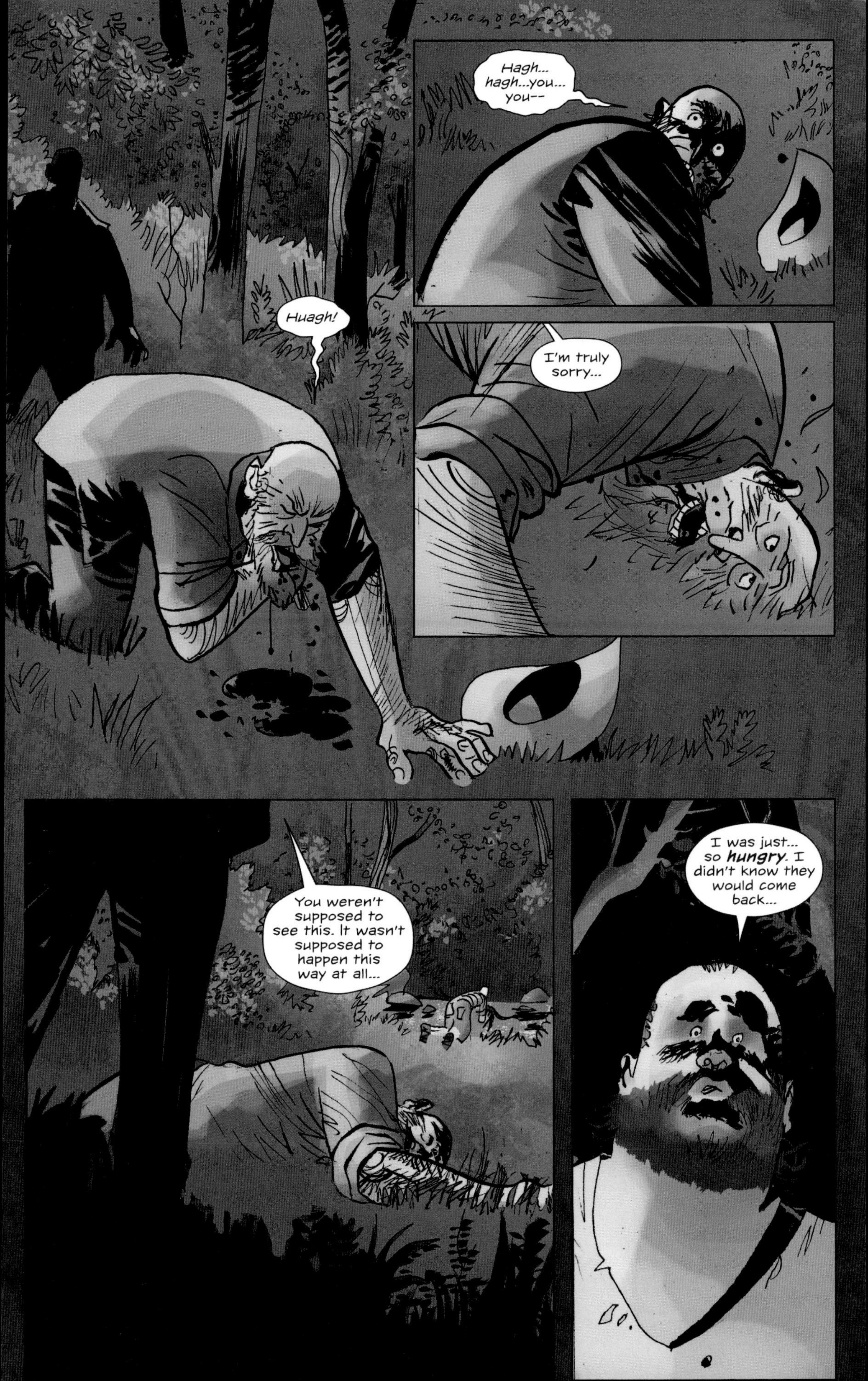
Hagh... hagh...you... you--
Huagh!
I'm truly sorry...
You weren't supposed to see this. It wasn't supposed to happen this way at all...
I was just... so **hungry**. I didn't know they would come back...

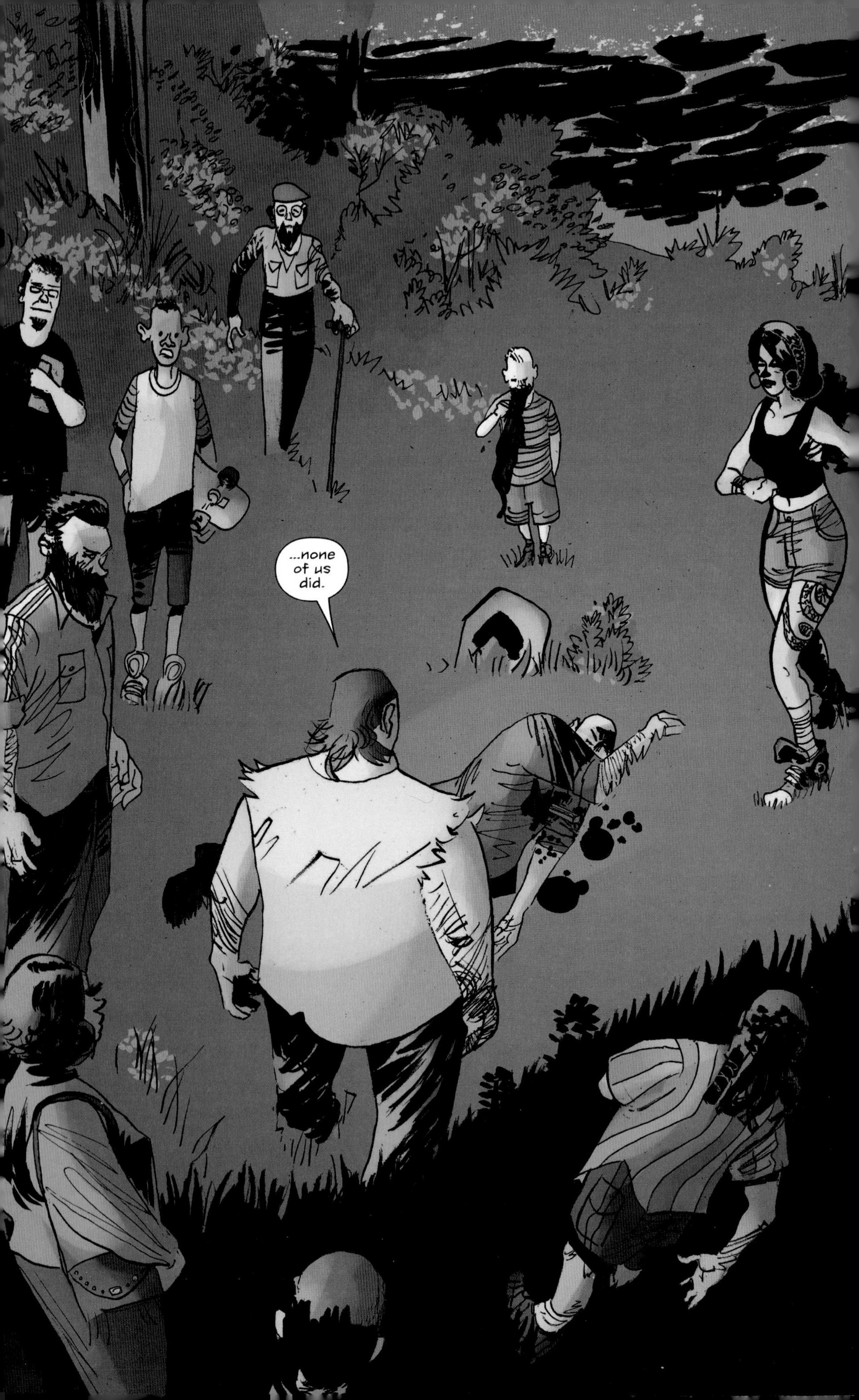
...none of us did.

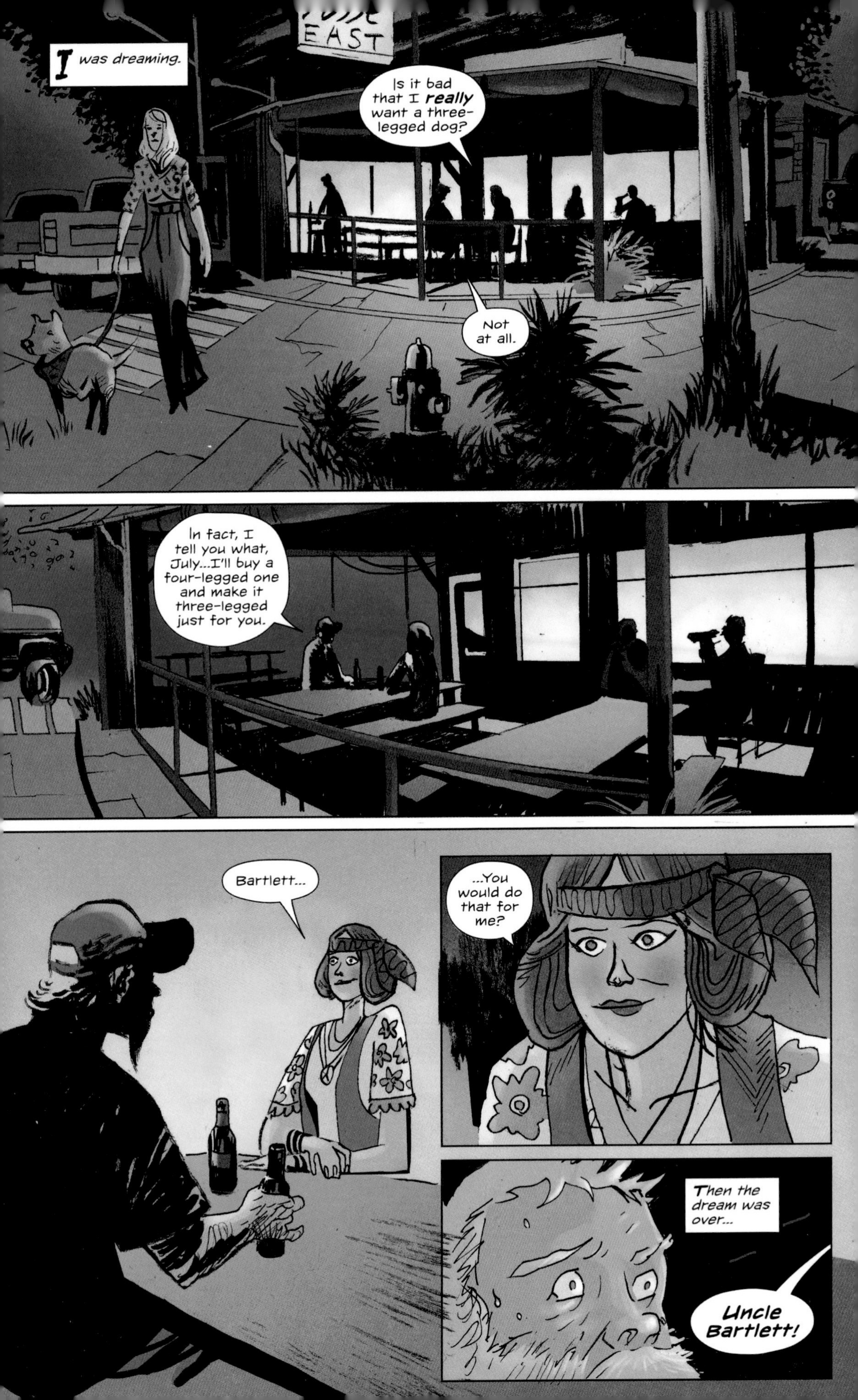
EAST
I was dreaming.
Is it bad that I really want a three-legged dog?
Not at all.
In fact, I tell you what, July...I'll buy a four-legged one and make it three-legged just for you.
Bartlett...
...You would do that for me?
Then the dream was over...
Uncle Bartlett!

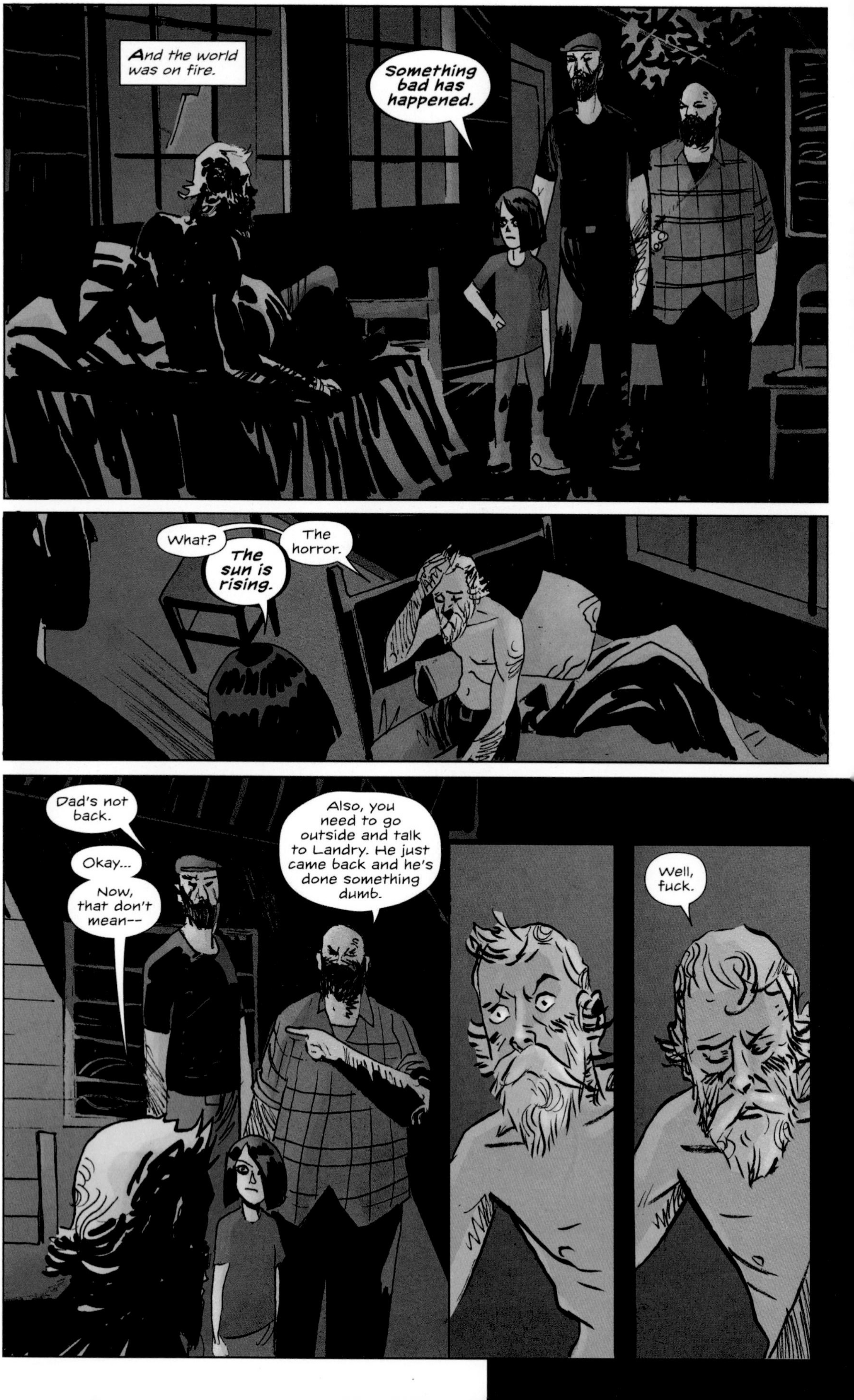
And the world was on fire.
Something bad has happened.
What?
The sun is rising.
The horror.
Dad's not back.
Okay...
Now, that don't mean--
Also, you need to go outside and talk to Landry. He just came back and he's done something dumb.
Well, fuck.

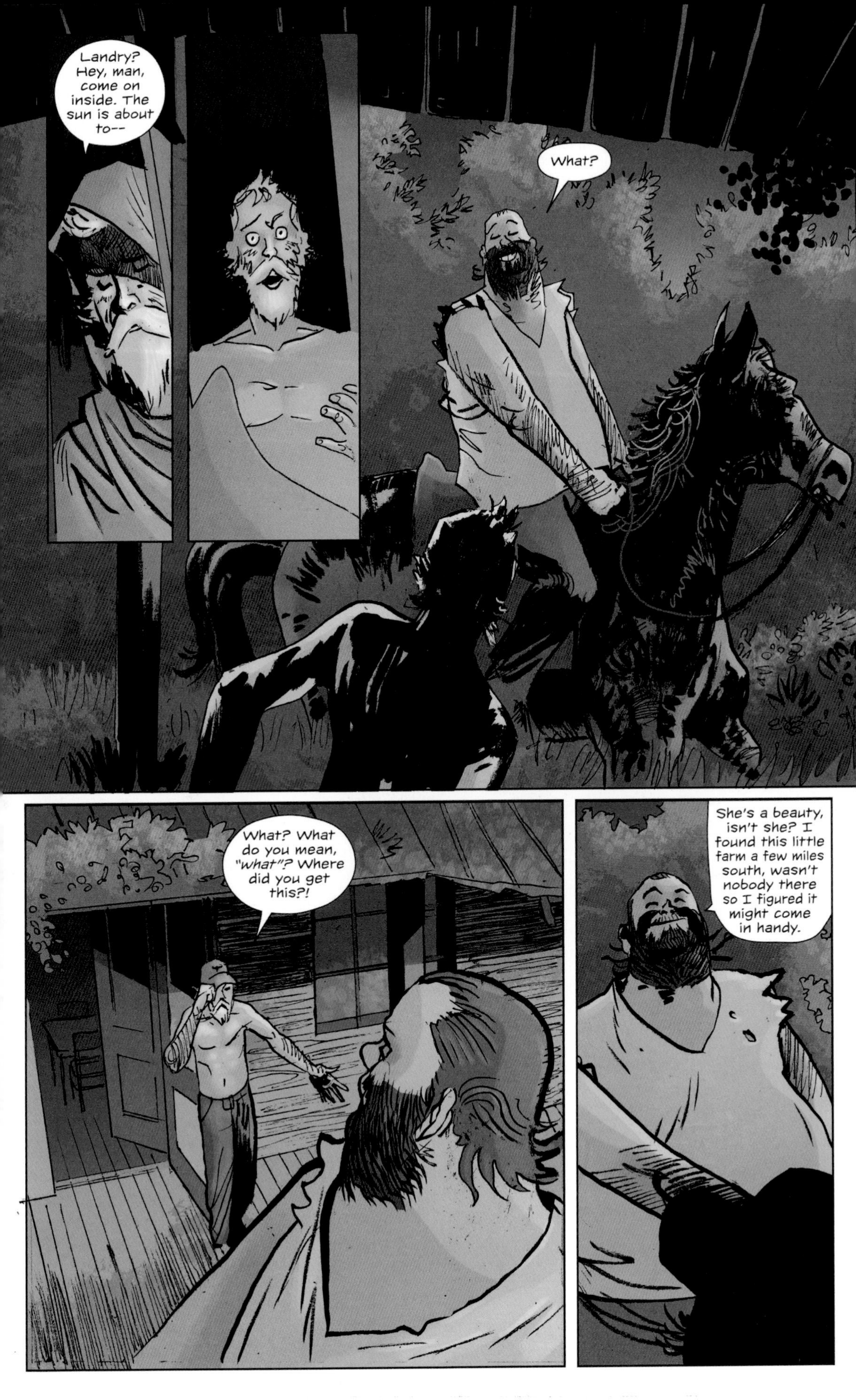

Landry? Hey, man, come on inside. The sun is about to--
What?
What? What do you mean, "what"? Where did you get this?!
She's a beauty, isn't she? I found this little farm a few miles south, wasn't nobody there so I figured it might come in handy.

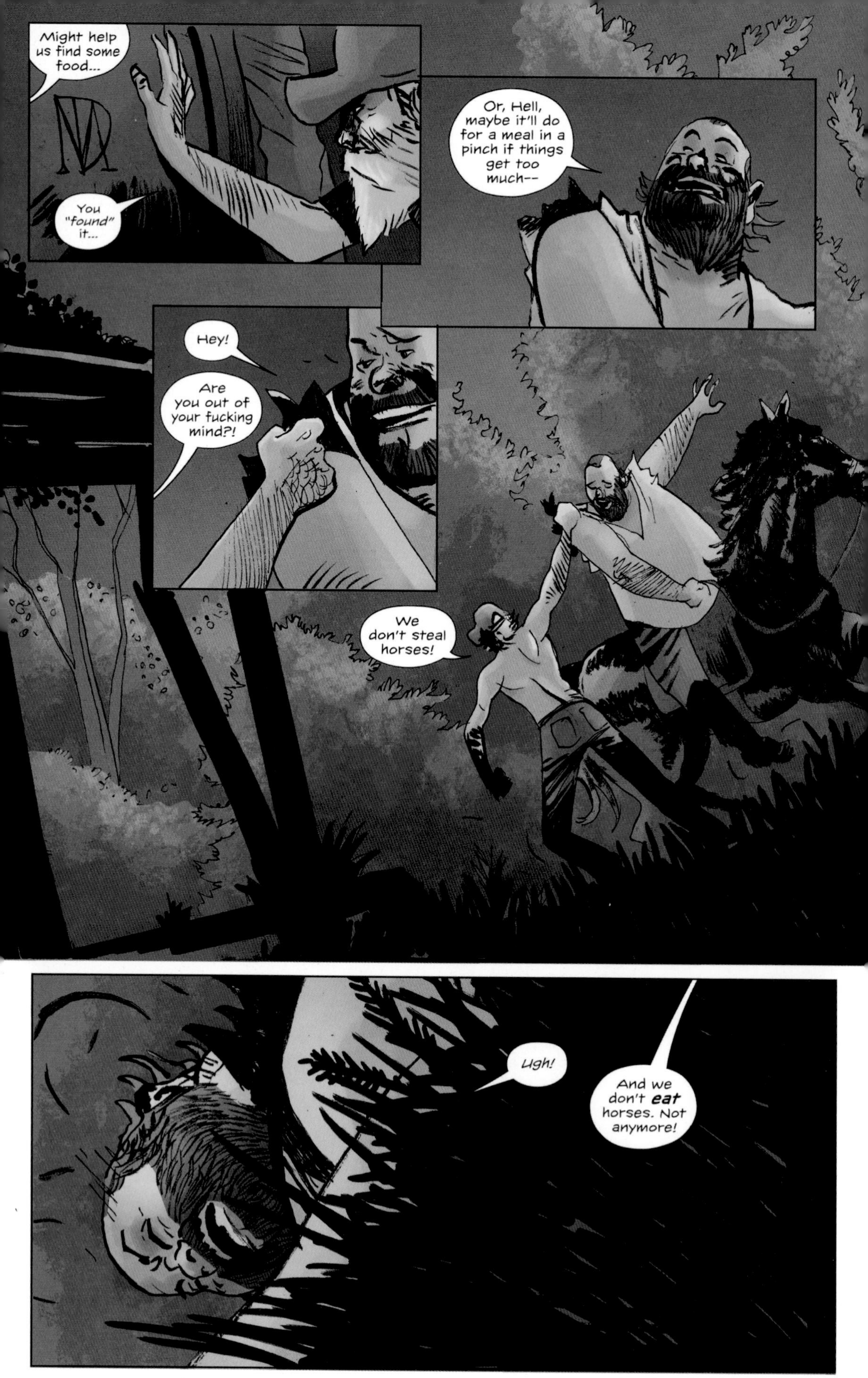

Might help us find some food...
You "found" it...
Or, Hell, maybe it'll do for a meal in a pinch if things get too much--
Hey!
Are you out of your fucking mind?!
We don't steal horses!
Ugh!
And we don't **eat** horses. Not anymore!

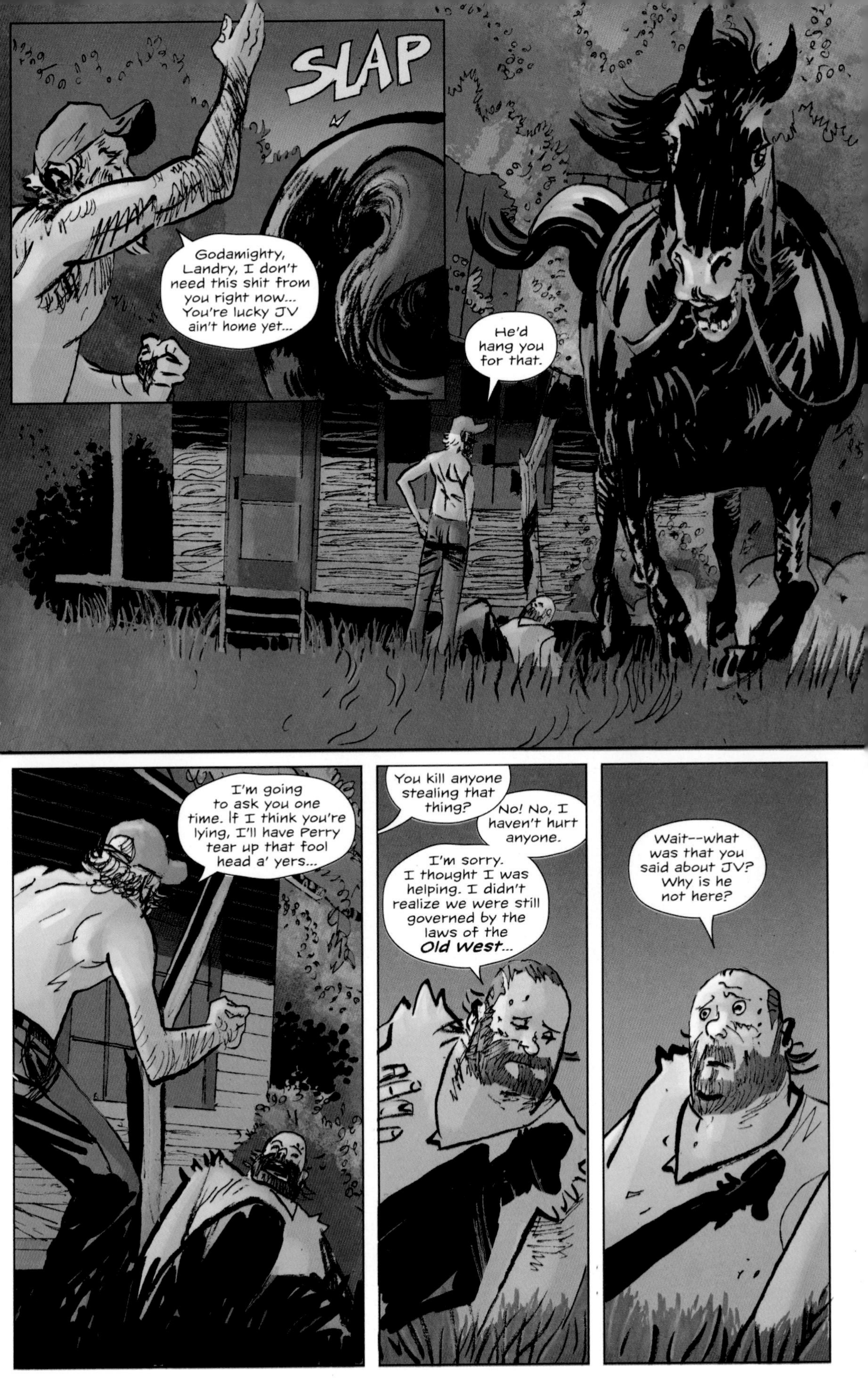
SLAP
Godamighty, Landry, I don't need this shit from you right now... You're lucky JV ain't home yet...
He'd hang you for that.
I'm going to ask you one time. If I think you're lying, I'll have Perry tear up that fool head a' yers...
You kill anyone stealing that thing?
No! No, I haven't hurt anyone.
I'm sorry. I thought I was helping. I didn't realize we were still governed by the laws of the Old West...
Wait--what was that you said about JV? Why is he not here?

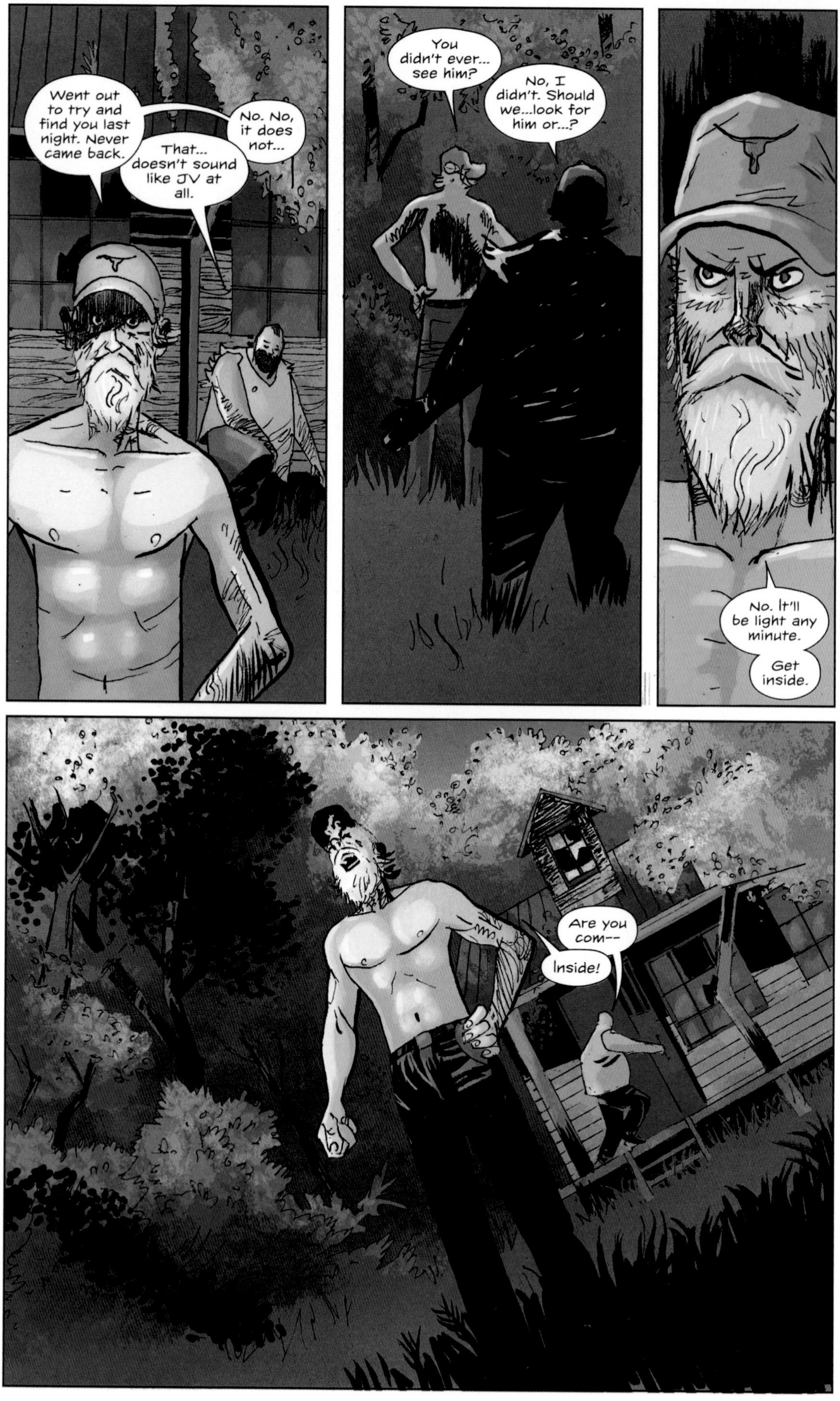
Went out to try and find you last night. Never came back.
That... doesn't sound like JV at all.
No. No, it does not...
You didn't ever... see him?
No, I didn't. Should we...look for him or...?
No. It'll be light any minute.
Get inside.
Are you com--
Inside!

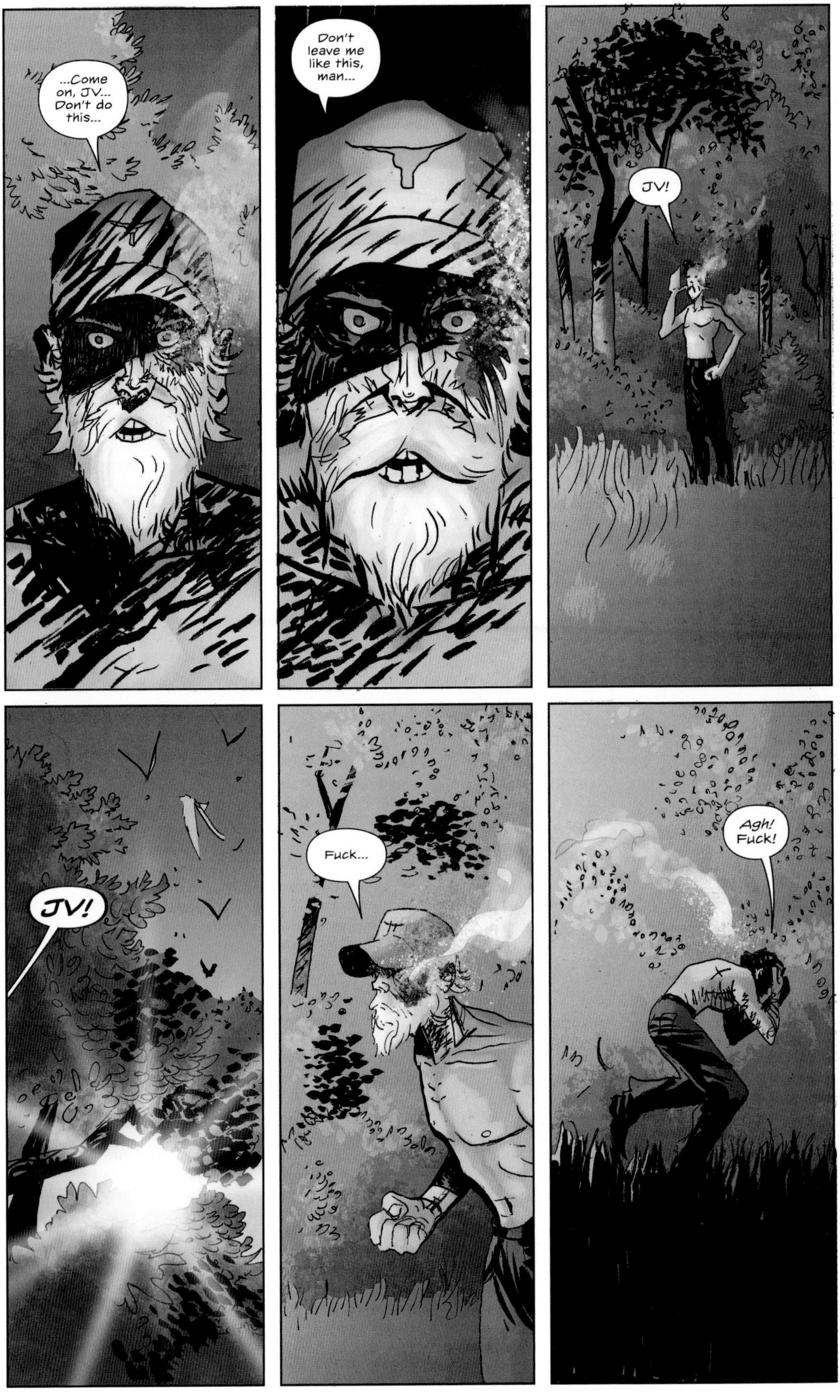
...Come on, JV... Don't do this...
Don't leave me like this, man...
JV!
JV!
Fuck...
Agh! Fuck!

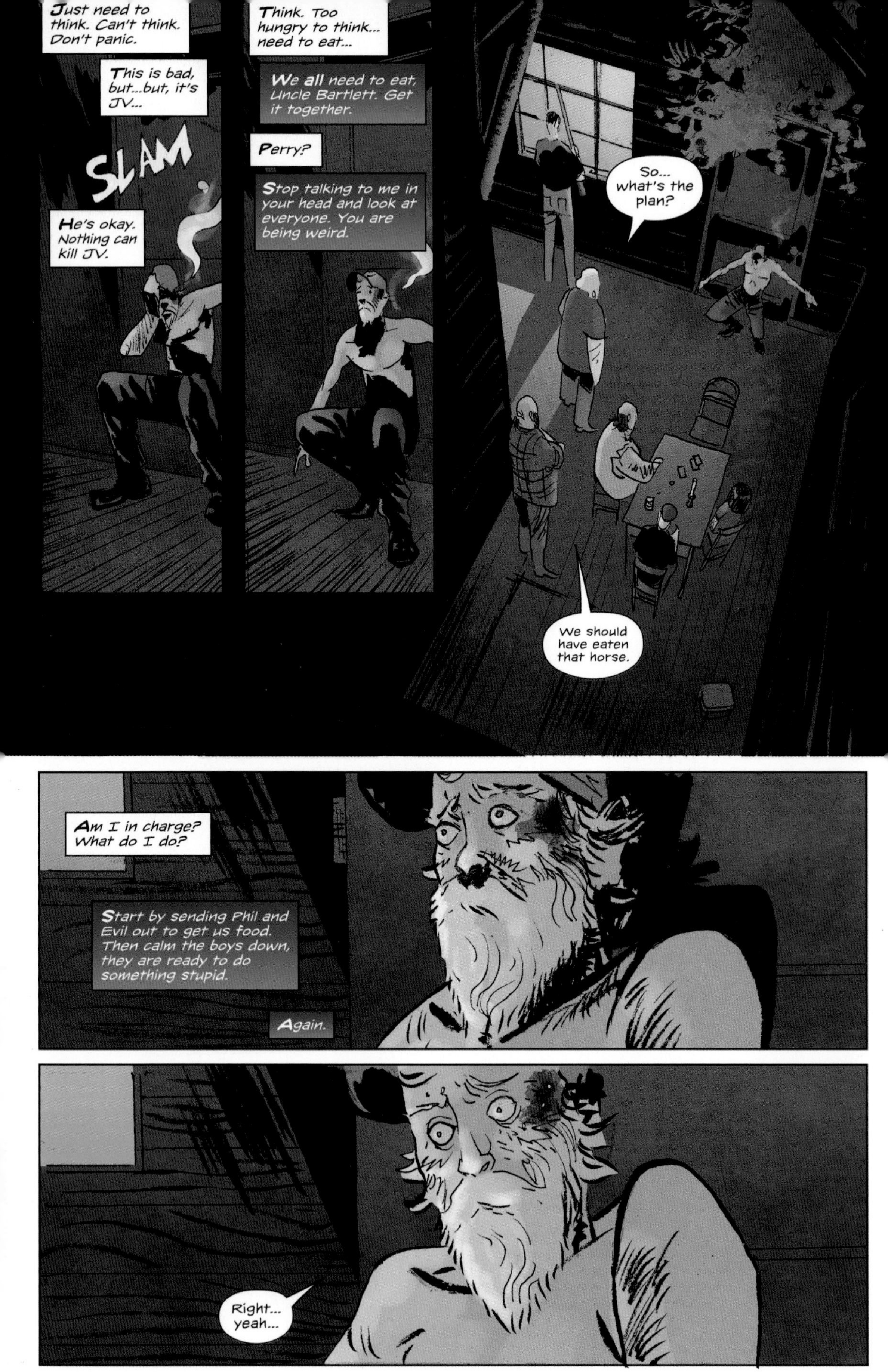
Just need to think. Can't think. Don't panic.
This is bad, but...but, it's JV...
SLAM
He's okay. Nothing can kill JV.
Think. Too hungry to think... need to eat...
We all need to eat, Uncle Bartlett. Get it together.
Perry?
Stop talking to me in your head and look at everyone. You are being weird.
So... what's the plan?
We should have eaten that horse.
Am I in charge? What do I do?
Start by sending Phil and Evil out to get us food. Then calm the boys down, they are ready to do something stupid.
Again.
Right... yeah...

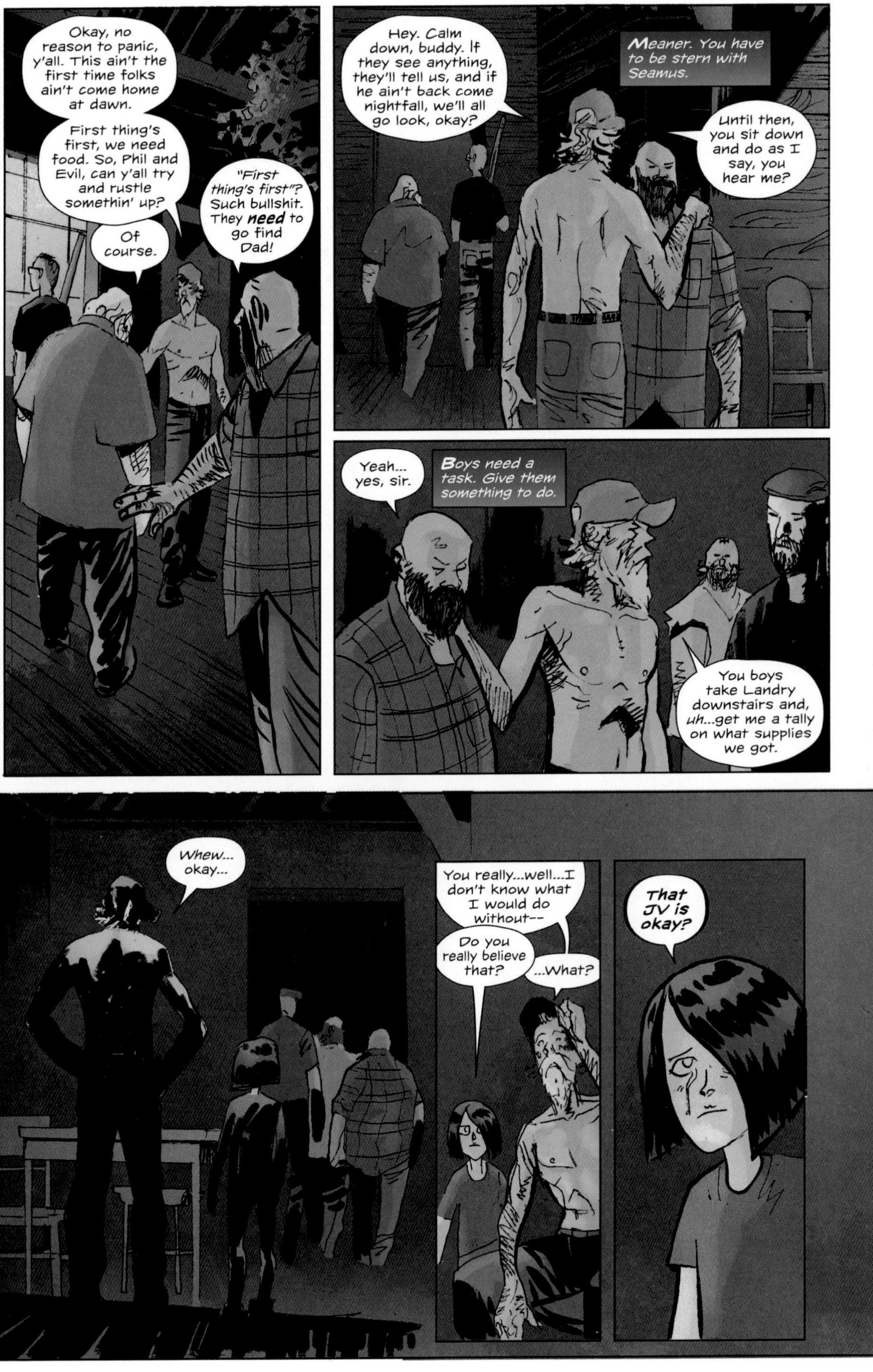
Okay, no reason to panic, y'all. This ain't the first time folks ain't come home at dawn.
First thing's first, we need food. So, Phil and Evil, can y'all try and rustle somethin' up?
Of course.
"First thing's first"? Such bullshit. They need to go find Dad!
Hey. Calm down, buddy. If they see anything, they'll tell us, and if he ain't back come nightfall, we'll all go look, okay?
Meaner. You have to be stern with Seamus.
Until then, you sit down and do as I say, you hear me?
Yeah... yes, sir.
Boys need a task. Give them something to do.
You boys take Landry downstairs and, uh...get me a tally on what supplies we got.
Whew... okay...
You really...well...I don't know what I would do without--
Do you really believe that?
...What?
That JV is okay?

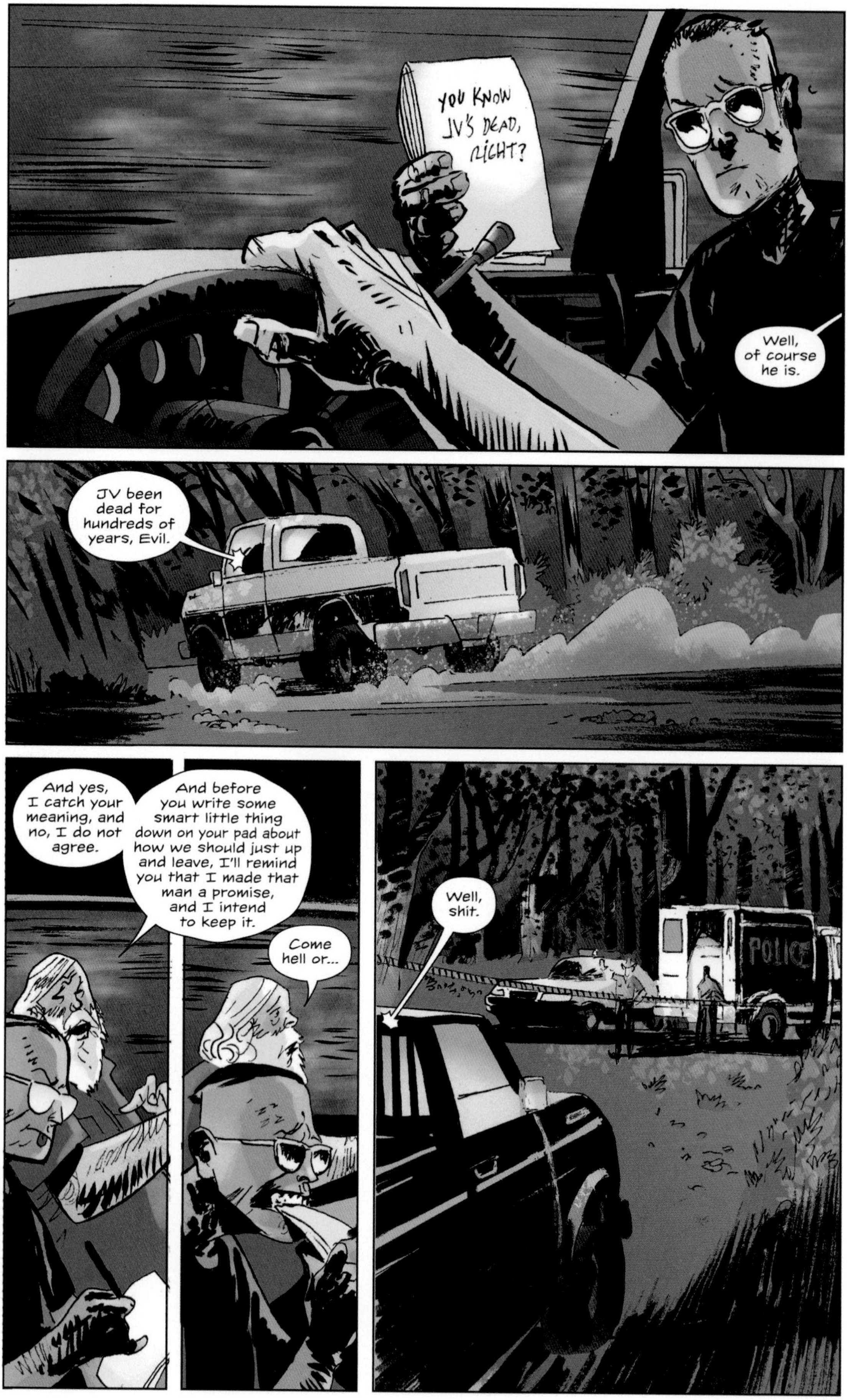
YOU KNOW JV'S DEAD, RIGHT?
Well, of course he is.
JV been dead for hundreds of years, Evil.
And yes, I catch your meaning, and no, I do not agree.
And before you write some smart little thing down on your pad about how we should just up and leave, I'll remind you that I made that man a promise, and I intend to keep it.
Come hell or...
Well, shit.
POLICE

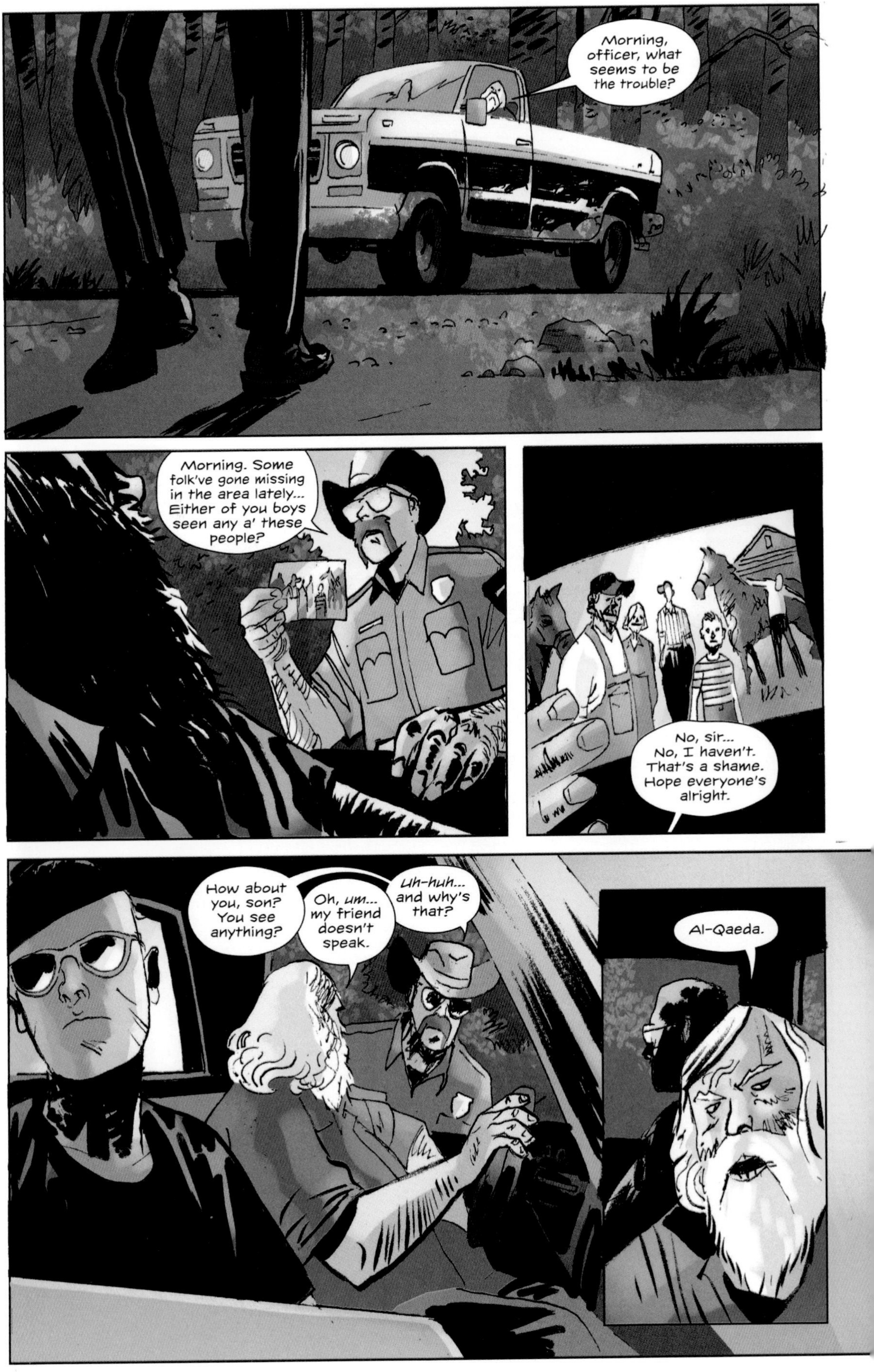

Morning, officer, what seems to be the trouble?
Morning. Some folk've gone missing in the area lately... Either of you boys seen any a' these people?
No, sir... No, I haven't. That's a shame. Hope everyone's alright.
How about you, son? You see anything?
Oh, um... my friend doesn't speak.
Uh-huh... and why's that?
Al-Qaeda.

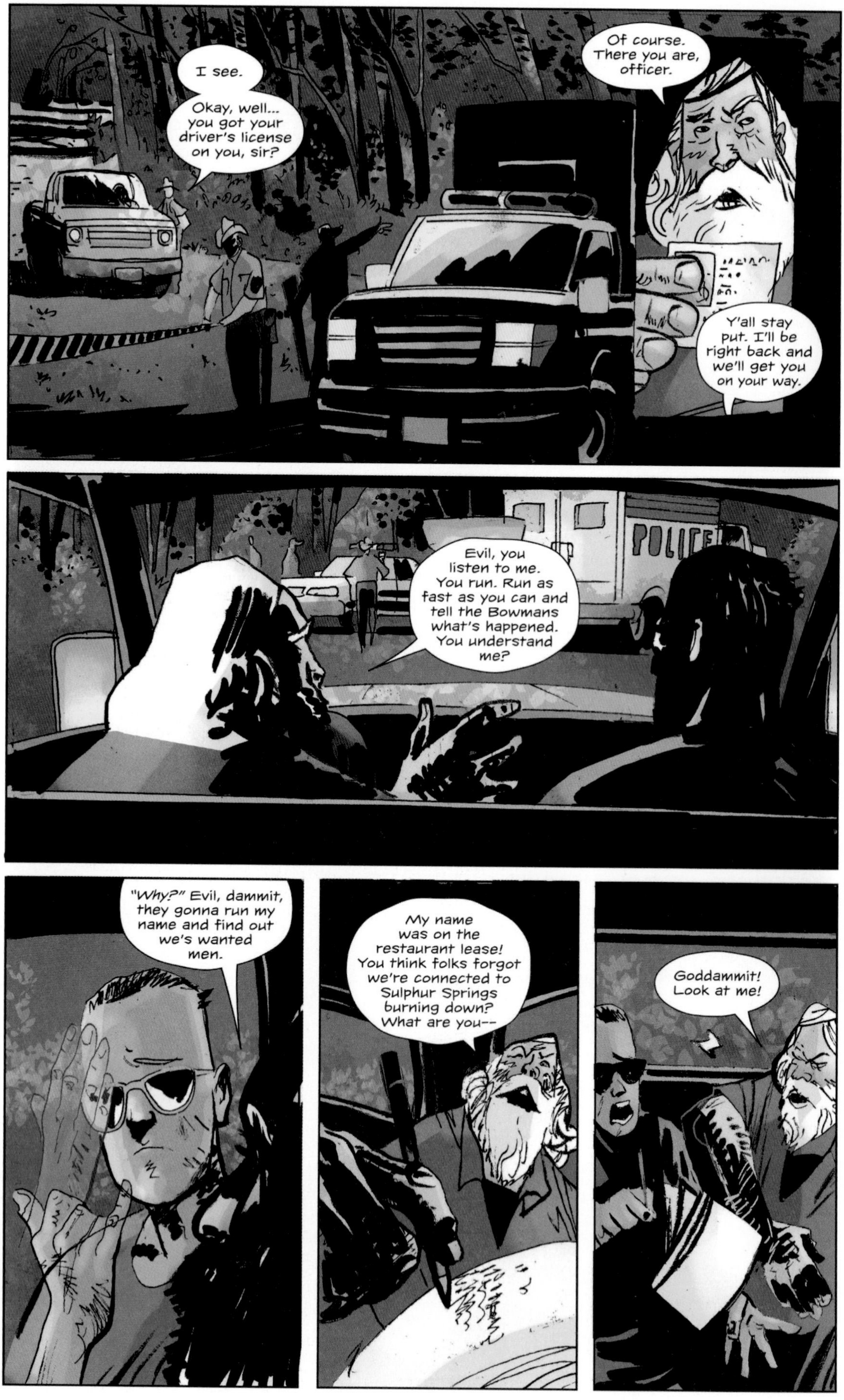
I see.
Okay, well... you got your driver's license on you, sir?
Of course. There you are, officer.
Y'all stay put. I'll be right back and we'll get you on your way.
POLICE
Evil, you listen to me. You run. Run as fast as you can and tell the Bowmans what's happened. You understand me?
"Why?" Evil, dammit, they gonna run my name and find out we's wanted men.
My name was on the restaurant lease! You think folks forgot we're connected to Sulphur Springs burning down? What are you--
Goddammit! Look at me!

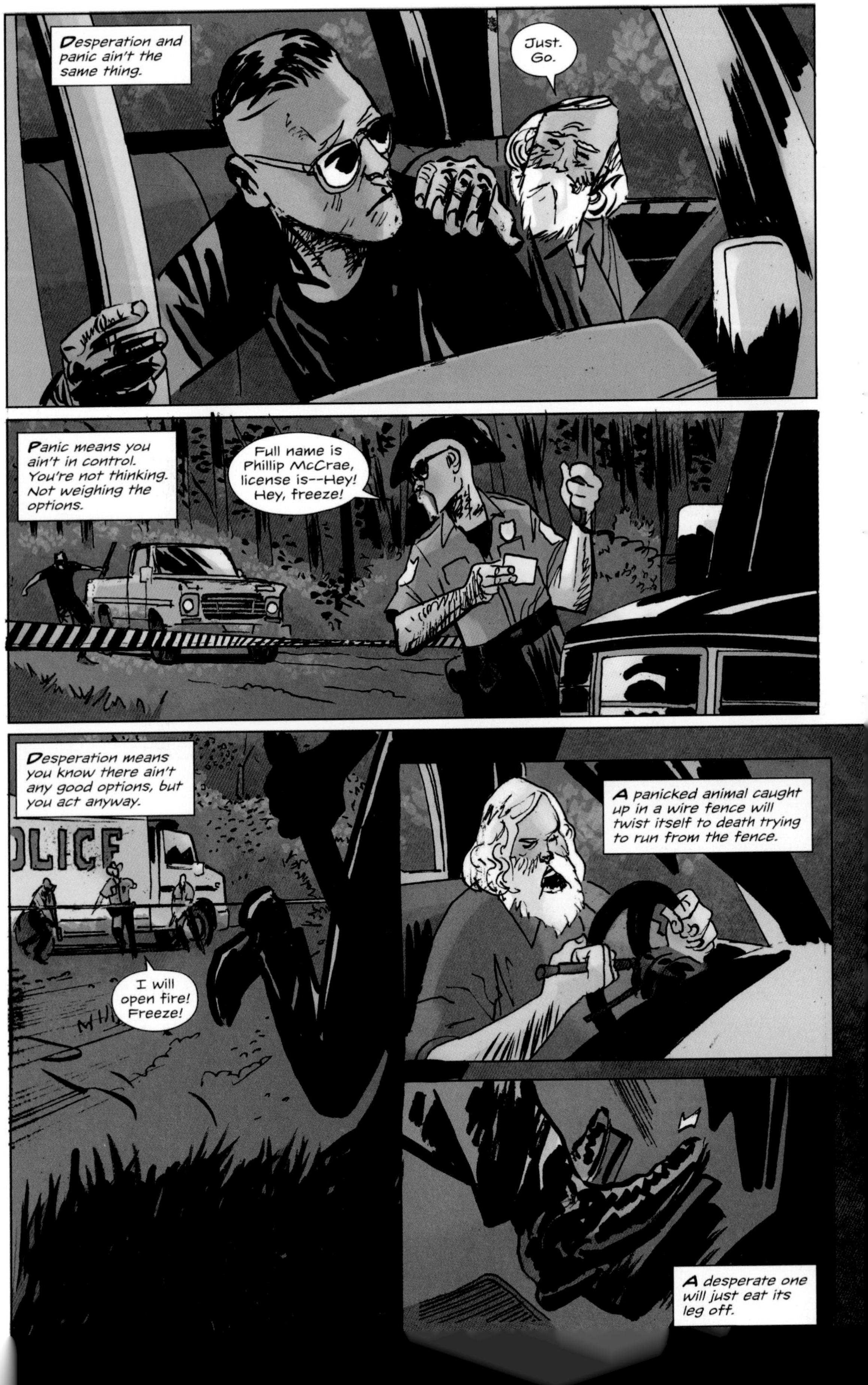
Desperation and panic ain't the same thing.
Just. Go.
Panic means you ain't in control. You're not thinking. Not weighing the options.
Full name is Phillip McCrae, license is--Hey! Hey, freeze!
Desperation means you know there ain't any good options, but you act anyway.
OLICE
I will open fire! Freeze!
A panicked animal caught up in a wire fence will twist itself to death trying to run from the fence.
A desperate one will just eat its leg off.

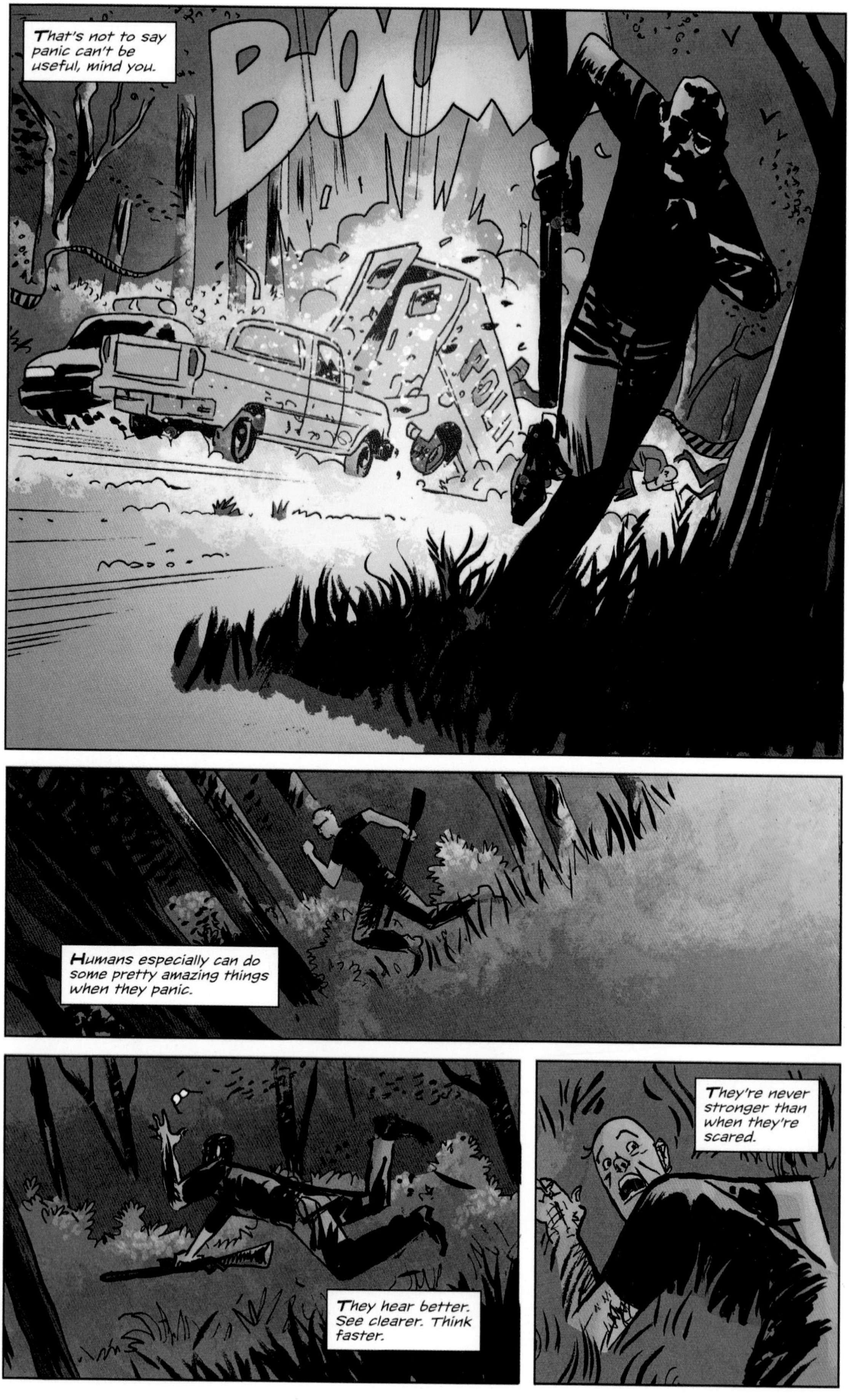
That's not to say panic can't be useful, mind you.
BOOM
Humans especially can do some pretty amazing things when they panic.
They hear better. See clearer. Think faster.
They're never stronger than when they're scared.

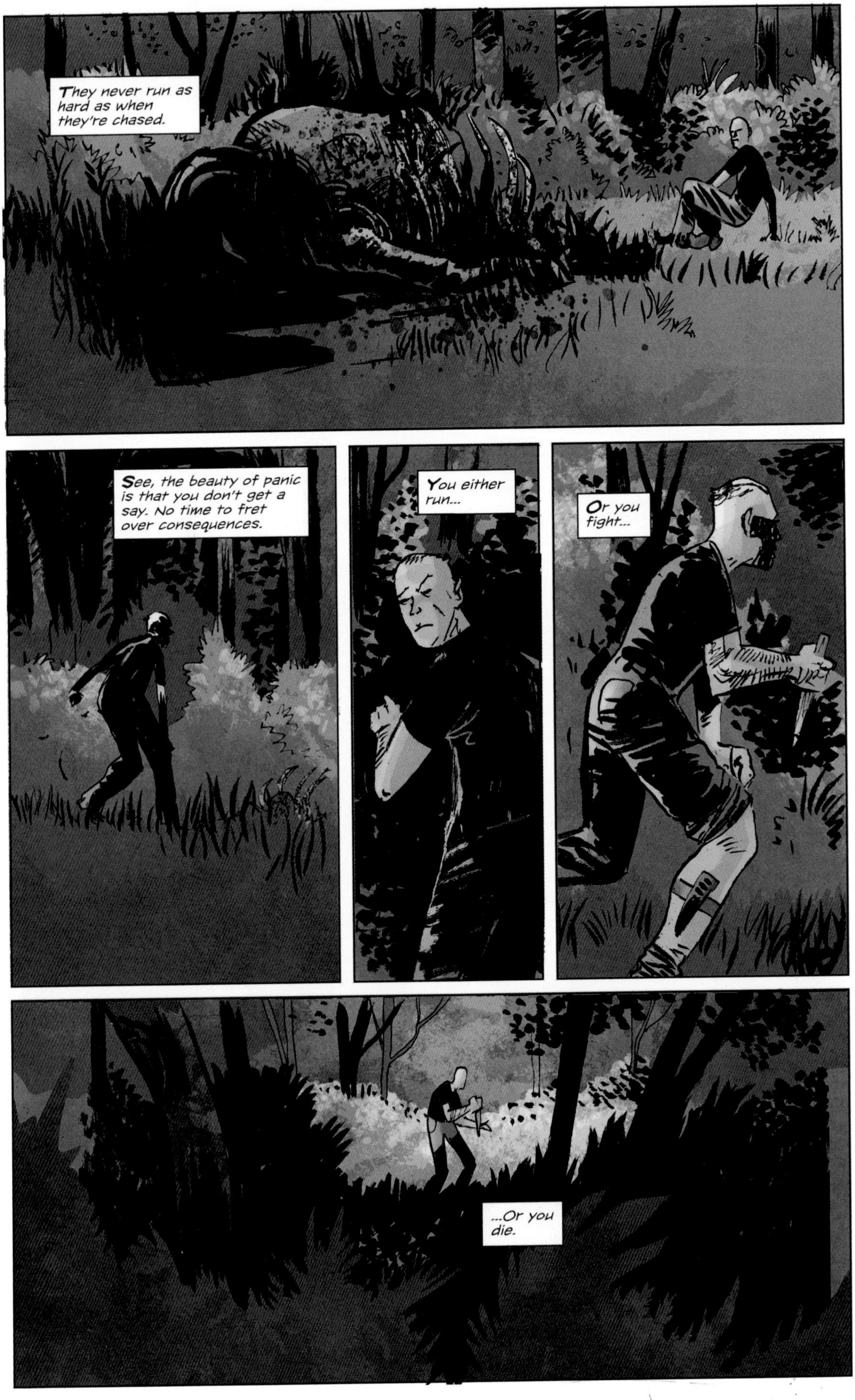
They never run as hard as when they're chased.
See, the beauty of panic is that you don't get a say. No time to fret over consequences.
You either run...
Or you fight...
...Or you die.

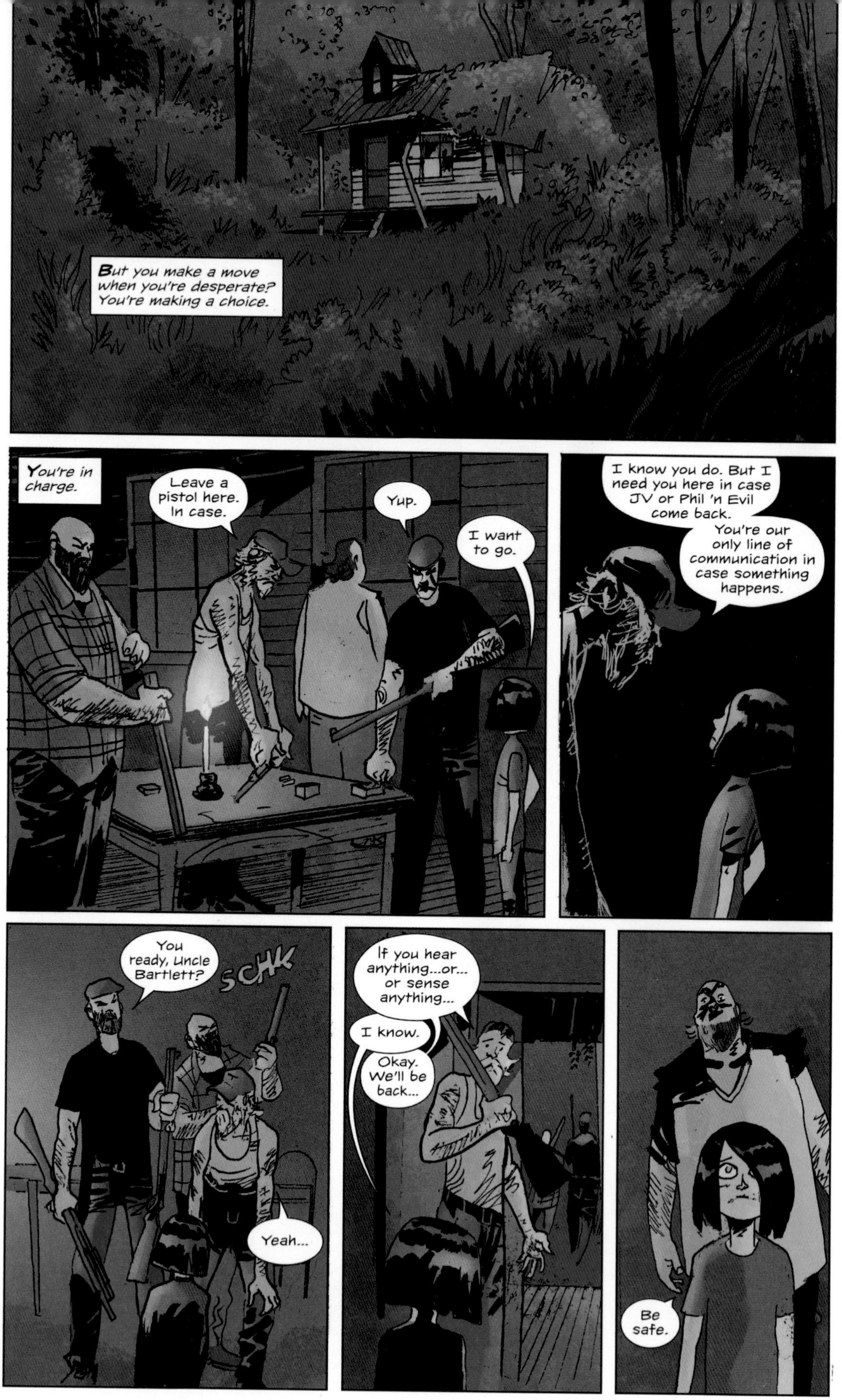
But you make a move when you're desperate? You're making a choice.
You're in charge.
Leave a pistol here. In case.
Yup.
I want to go.
I know you do. But I need you here in case JV or Phil 'n Evil come back.
You're our only line of communication in case something happens.
You ready, Uncle Bartlett?
SCHK
Yeah...
If you hear anything...or... or sense anything...
I know.
Okay. We'll be back...
Be safe.

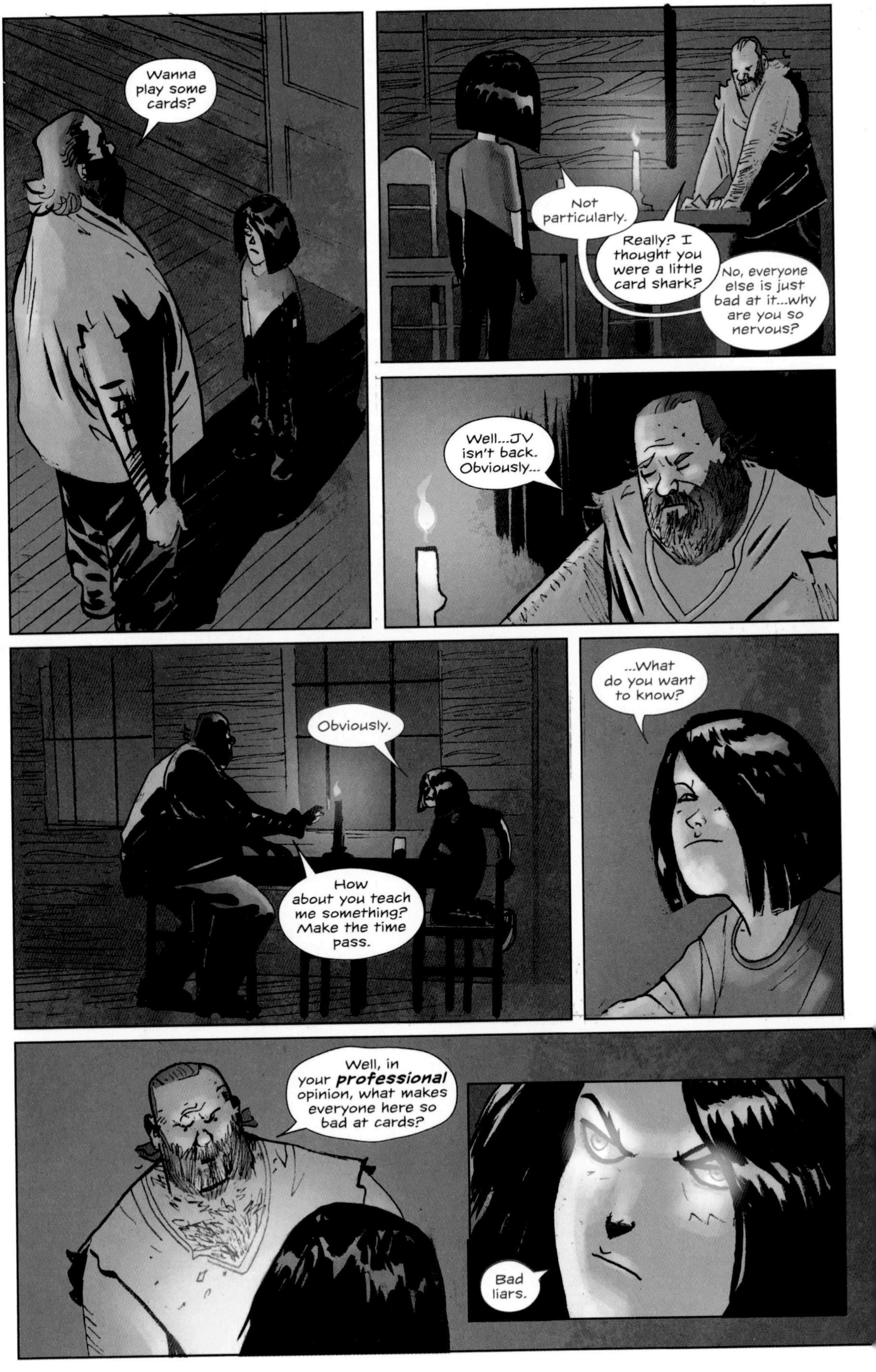
Wanna play some cards?
Not particularly.
Really? I thought you were a little card shark?
No, everyone else is just bad at it...why are you so nervous?
Well...JV isn't back. Obviously...
Obviously.
How about you teach me something? Make the time pass.
...What do you want to know?
Well, in your ***professional*** opinion, what makes everyone here so bad at cards?
Bad liars.

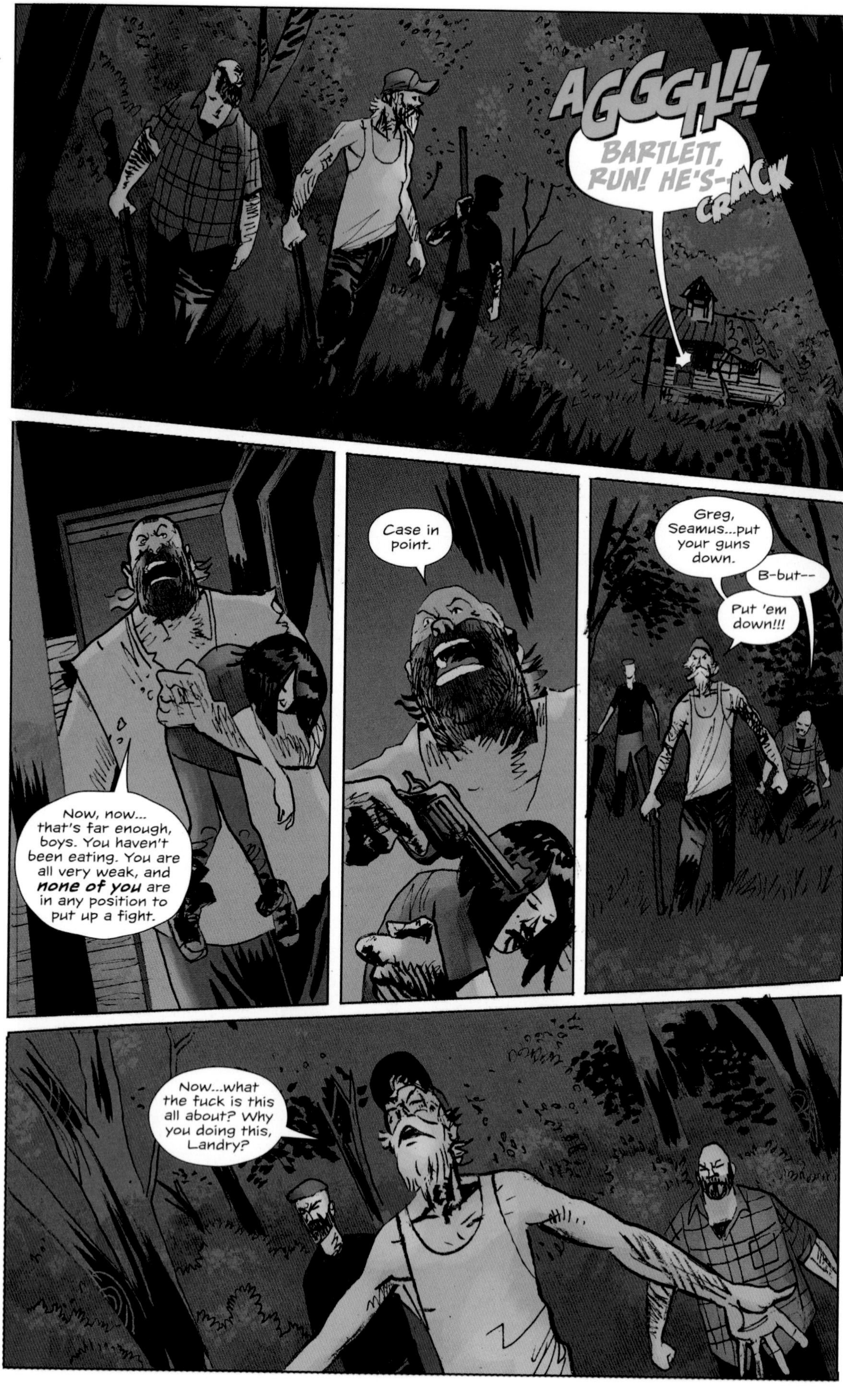
AGGGH!!!
BARTLETT, RUN! HE'S--
CRACK
Now, now... that's far enough, boys. You haven't been eating. You are all very weak, and ***none of you*** are in any position to put up a fight.
Case in point.
Greg, Seamus...put your guns down.
B-but--
Put 'em down!!!
Now...what the fuck is this all about? Why you doing this, Landry?

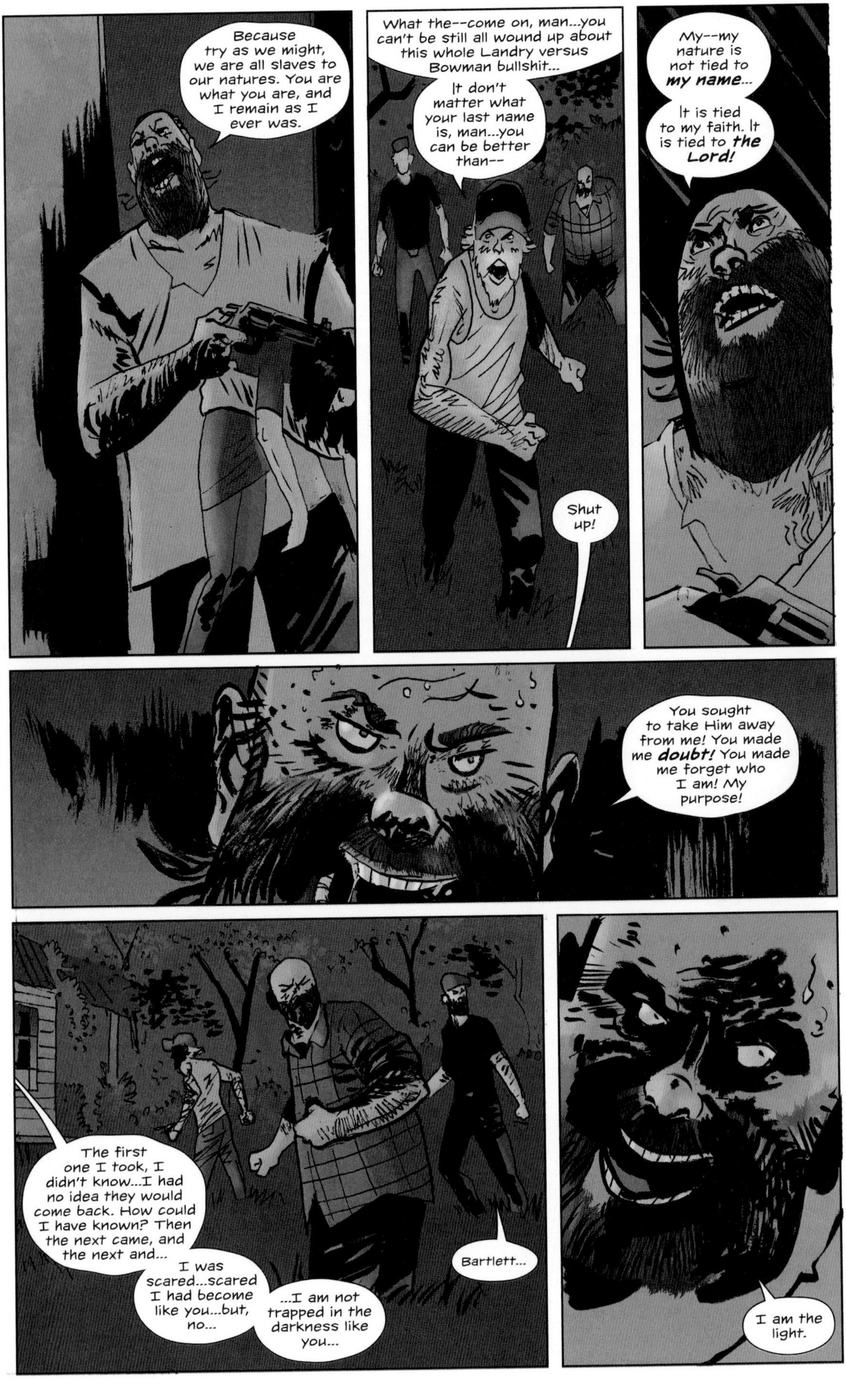
Because try as we might, we are all slaves to our natures. You are what you are, and I remain as I ever was.
What the--come on, man...you can't be still all wound up about this whole Landry versus Bowman bullshit...
It don't matter what your last name is, man...you can be better than--
Shut up!
My--my nature is not tied to **my name**...
It is tied to my faith. It is tied to **the Lord!**
You sought to take Him away from me! You made me **doubt!** You made me forget who I am! My purpose!
The first one I took, I didn't know...I had no idea they would come back. How could I have known? Then the next came, and the next and...
I was scared...scared I had become like you...but, no...
...I am not trapped in the darkness like you...
Bartlett...
I am the light.

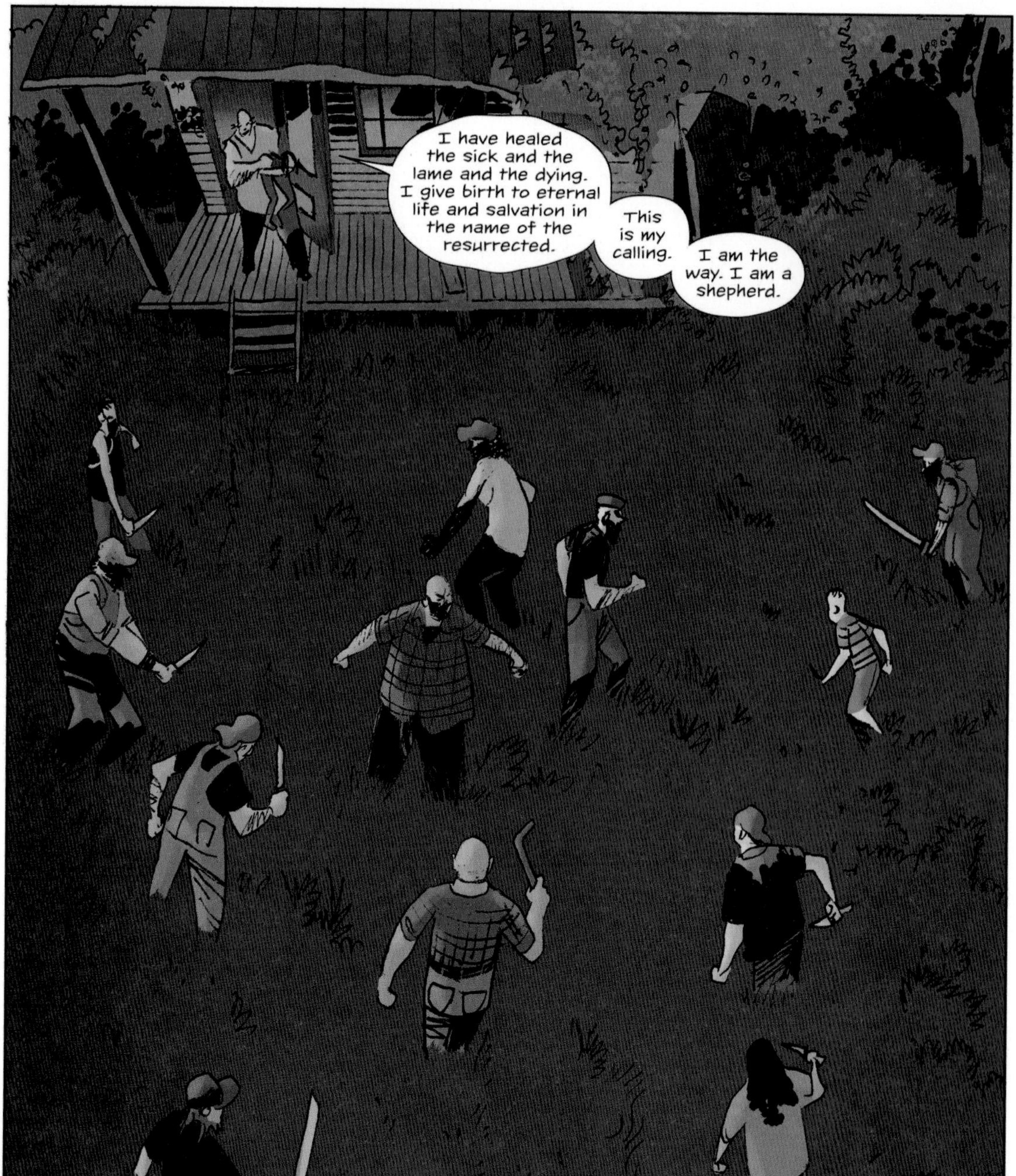
I have healed the sick and the lame and the dying. I give birth to eternal life and salvation in the name of the resurrected.
This is my calling.
I am the way. I am a shepherd.

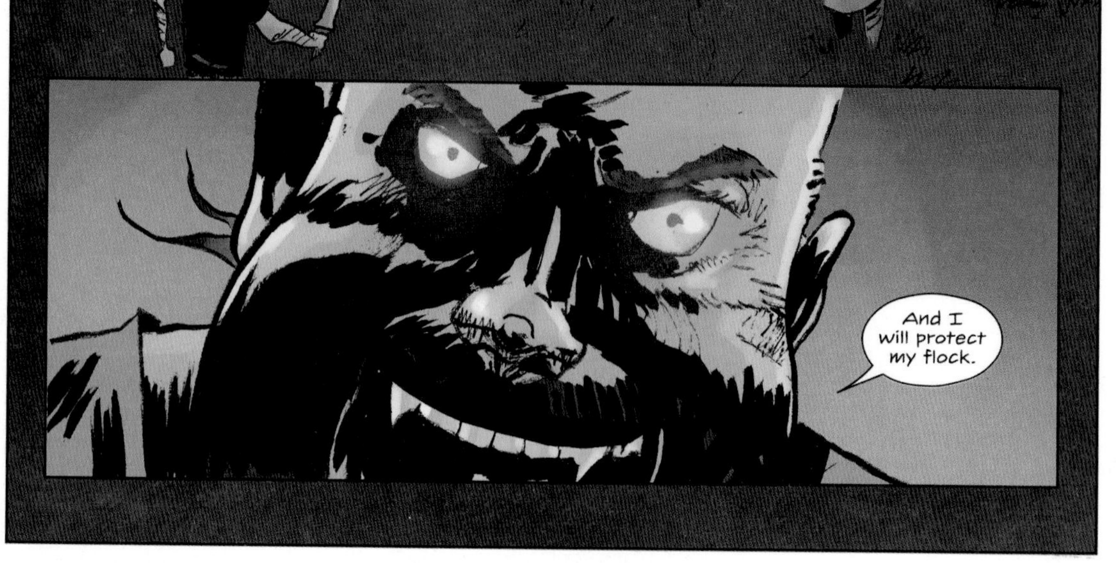
And I will protect my flock.

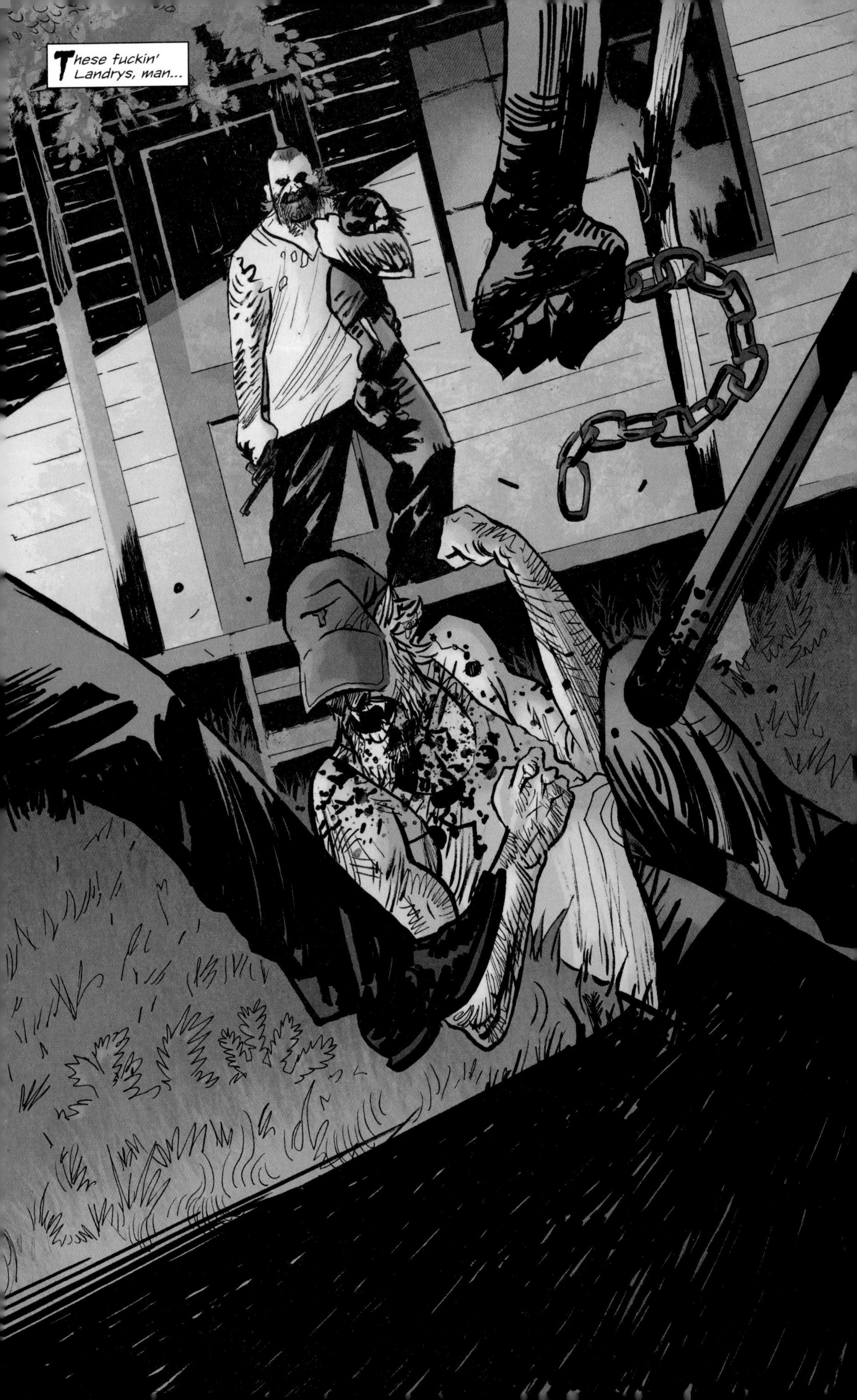
These fuckin' Landrys, man...

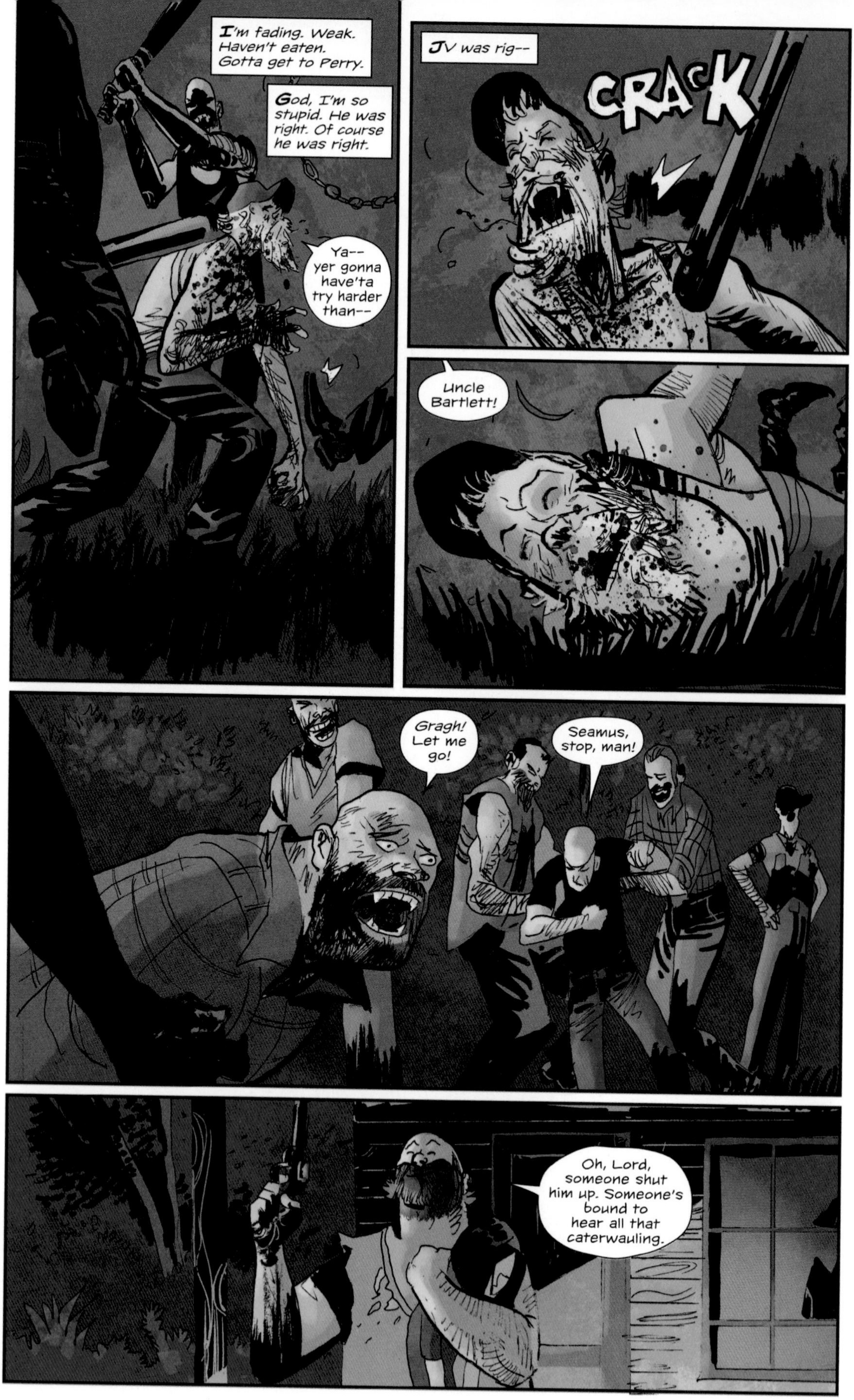
I'm fading. Weak. Haven't eaten. Gotta get to Perry.
God, I'm so stupid. He was right. Of course he was right.
Ya-- yer gonna have'ta try harder than--
JV was rig--
CRACK
Uncle Bartlett!
Gragh! Let me go!
Seamus, stop, man!
Oh, Lord, someone shut him up. Someone's bound to hear all that caterwauling.

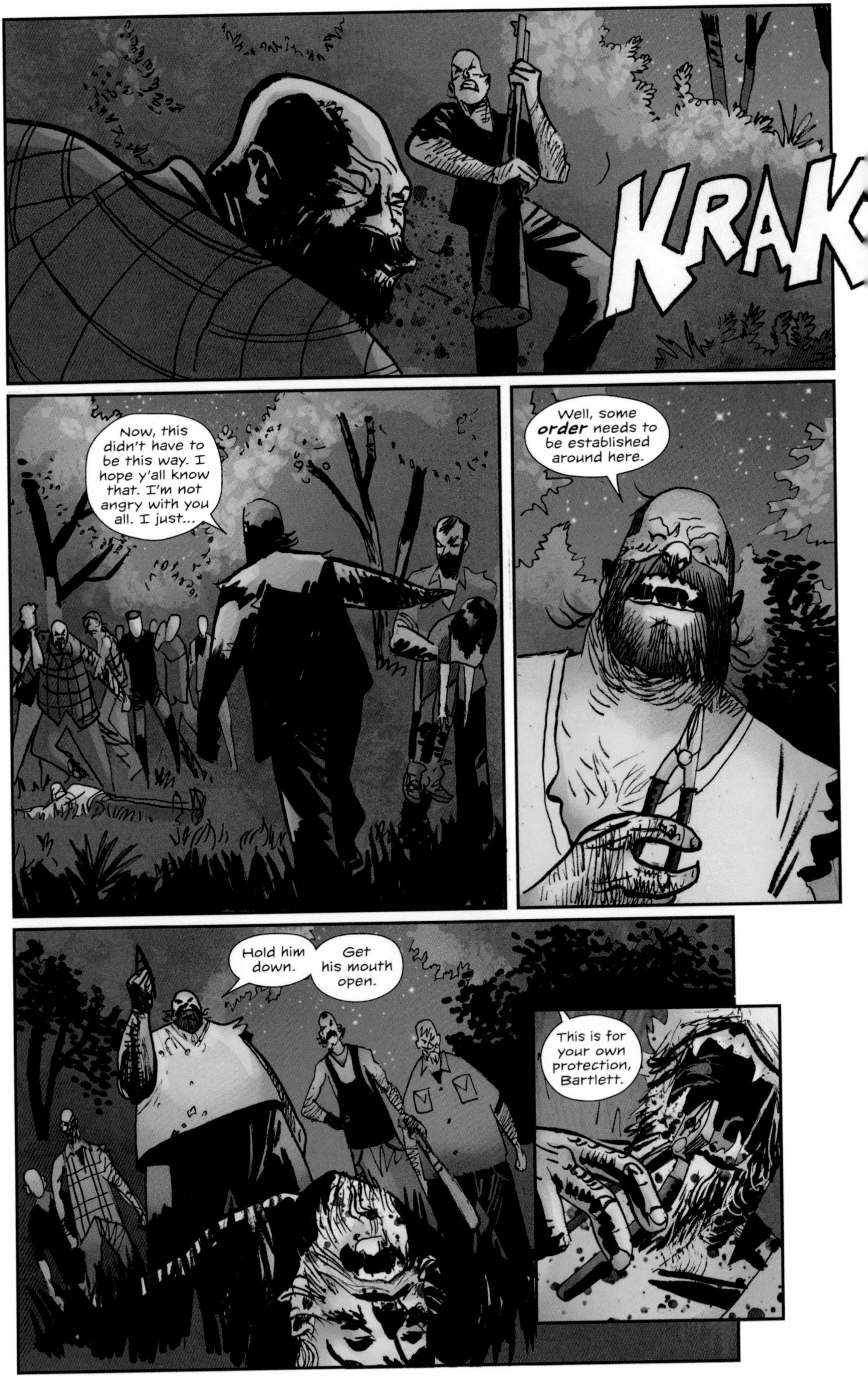
KRAK
Now, this didn't have to be this way. I hope y'all know that. I'm not angry with you all. I just...
Well, some order needs to be established around here.
Hold him down.
Get his mouth open.
This is for your own protection, Bartlett.

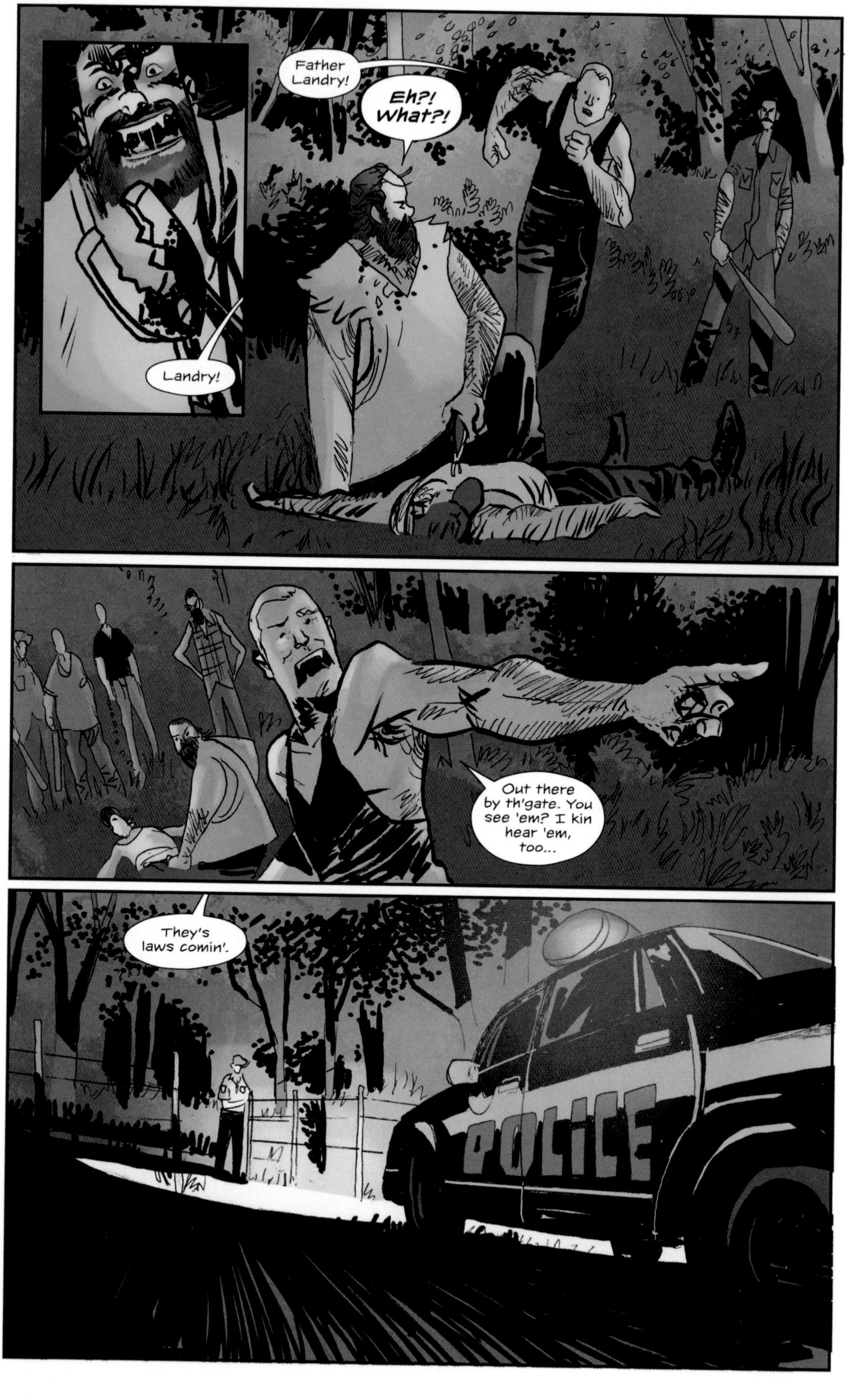
Father Landry!
Eh?! What?!
Landry!
Out there by th'gate. You see 'em? I kin hear 'em, too...
They's laws comin'.
POLICE

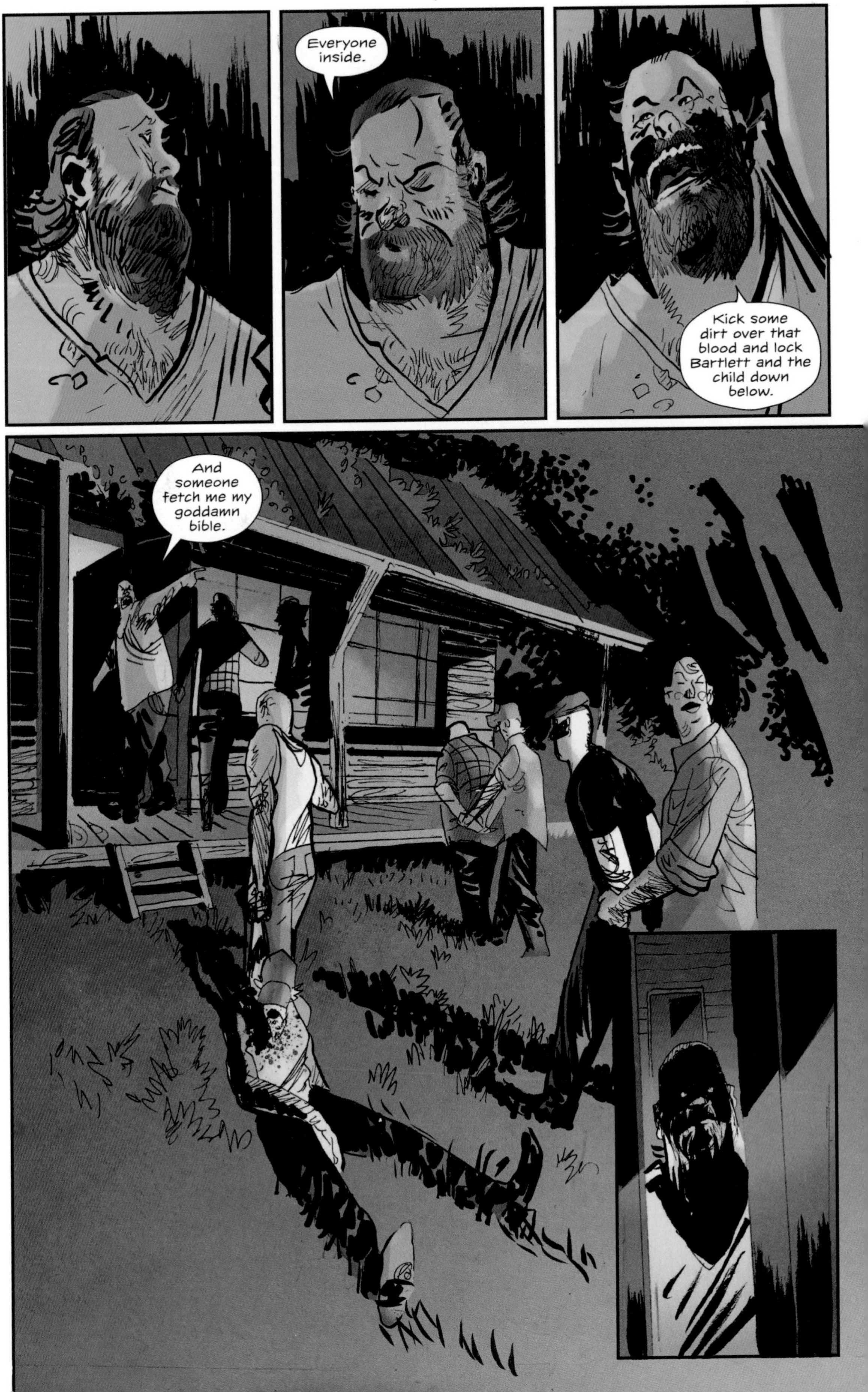
Everyone inside.
Kick some dirt over that blood and lock Bartlett and the child down below.
And someone fetch me my goddamn bible.

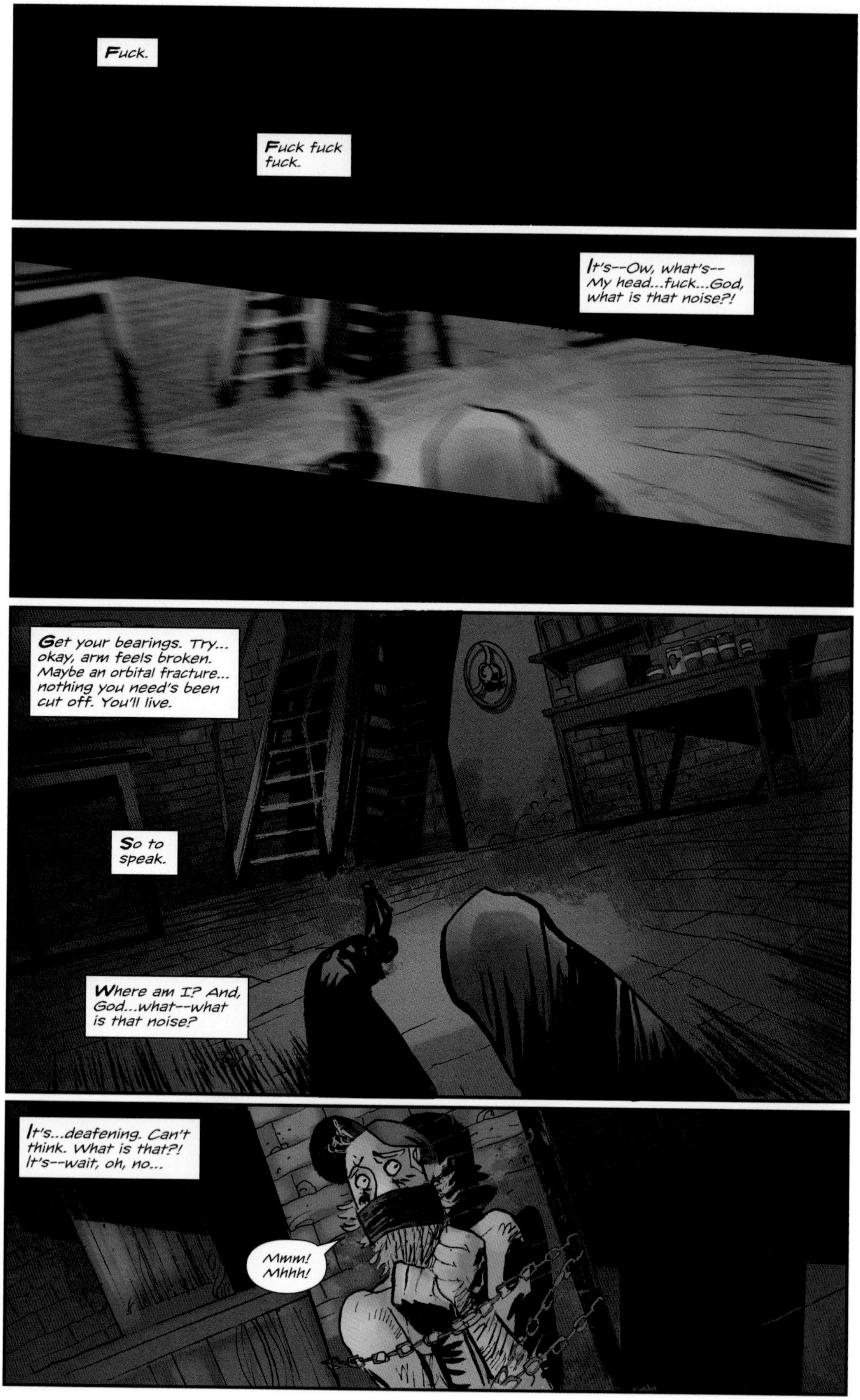
Fuck.
Fuck fuck fuck.
It's--Ow, what's-- My head...fuck...God, what is that noise?!
Get your bearings. Try... okay, arm feels broken. Maybe an orbital fracture... nothing you need's been cut off. You'll live.
So to speak.
Where am I? And, God...what--what is that noise?
It's...deafening. Can't think. What is that?! It's--wait, oh, no...
Mmm! Mhhh!

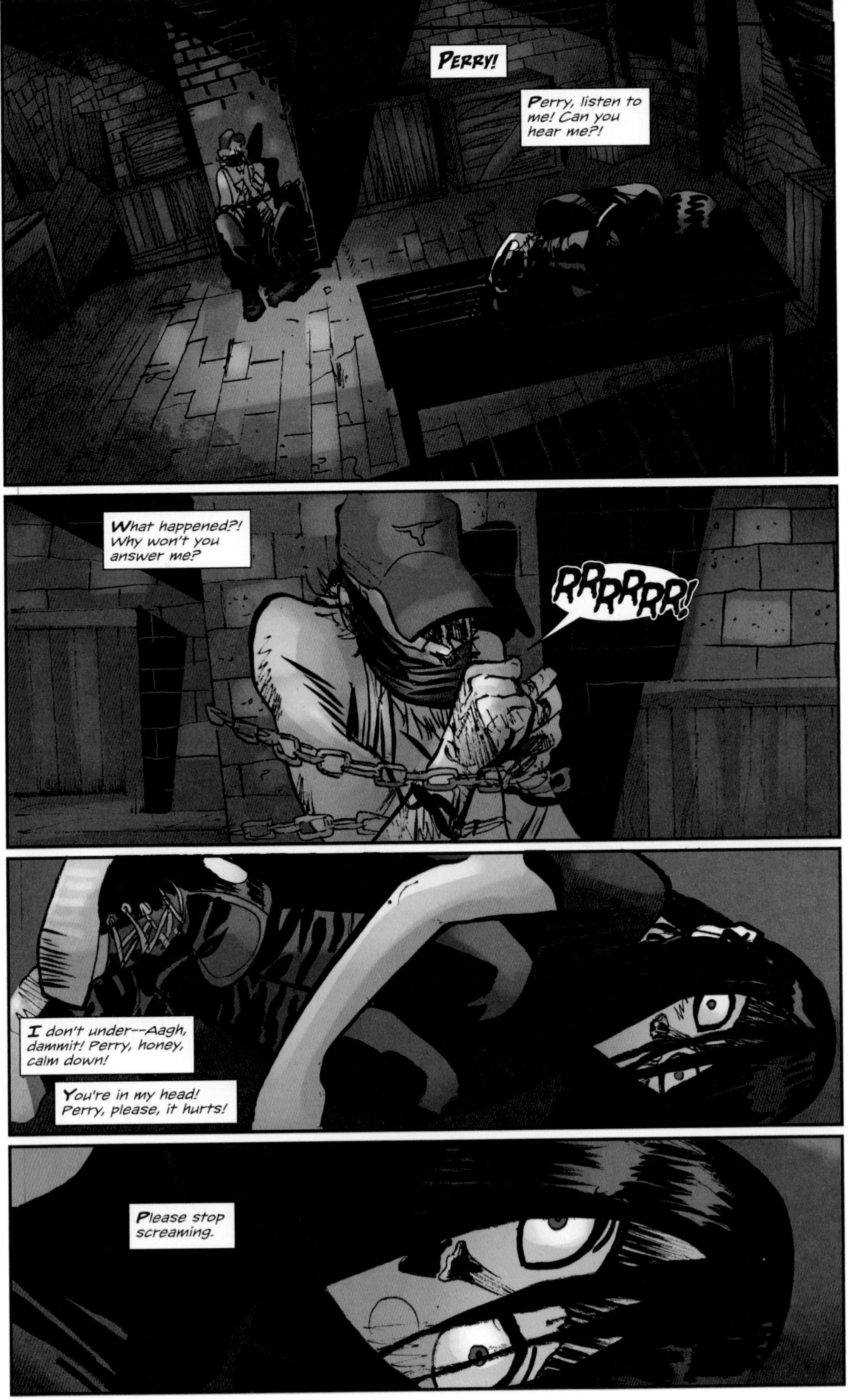
PERRY!
Perry, listen to me! Can you hear me?!
What happened?! Why won't you answer me?
RRRRRR!
I don't under--Aagh, dammit! Perry, honey, calm down!
You're in my head! Perry, please, it hurts!
Please stop screaming.

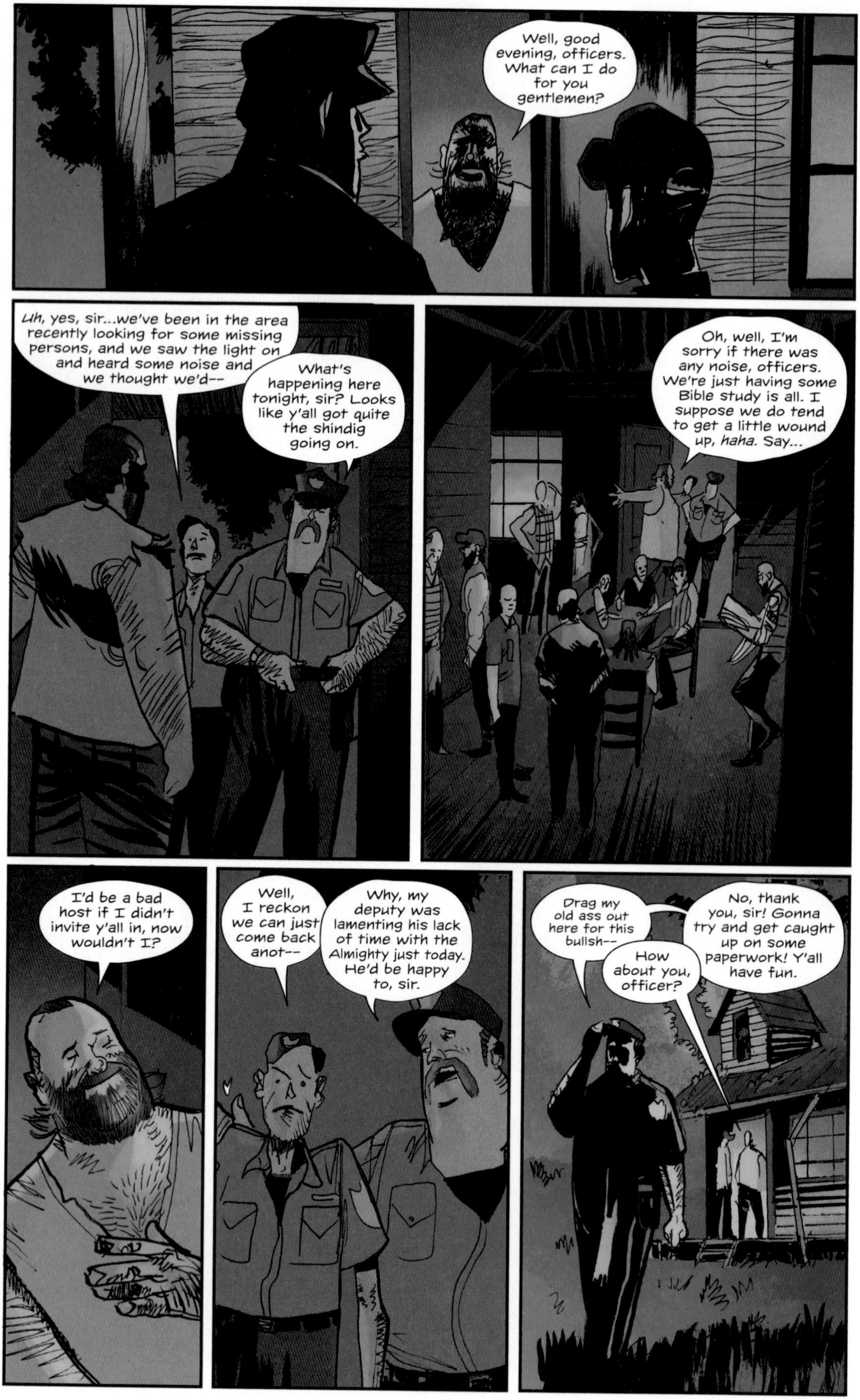
Well, good evening, officers. What can I do for you gentlemen?
Uh, yes, sir...we've been in the area recently looking for some missing persons, and we saw the light on and heard some noise and we thought we'd--
What's happening here tonight, sir? Looks like y'all got quite the shindig going on.
Oh, well, I'm sorry if there was any noise, officers. We're just having some Bible study is all. I suppose we do tend to get a little wound up, haha. Say...
I'd be a bad host if I didn't invite y'all in, now wouldn't I?
Well, I reckon we can just come back anot--
Why, my deputy was lamenting his lack of time with the Almighty just today. He'd be happy to, sir.
Drag my old ass out here for this bullsh--
How about you, officer?
No, thank you, sir! Gonna try and get caught up on some paperwork! Y'all have fun.

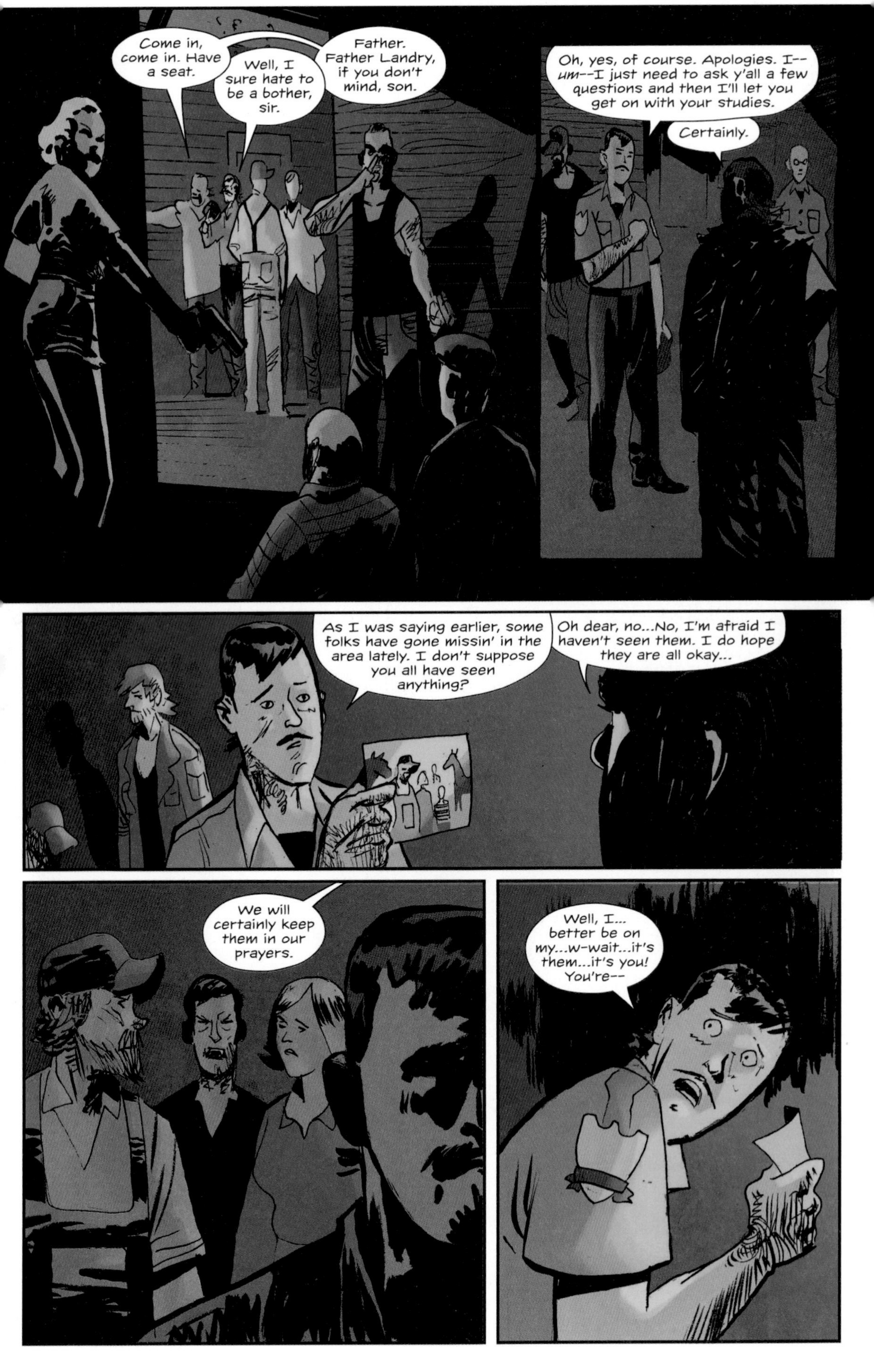
Come in, come in. Have a seat.
Well, I sure hate to be a bother, sir.
Father. Father Landry, if you don't mind, son.
Oh, yes, of course. Apologies. I-- um--I just need to ask y'all a few questions and then I'll let you get on with your studies.
Certainly.
As I was saying earlier, some folks have gone missin' in the area lately. I don't suppose you all have seen anything?
Oh dear, no...No, I'm afraid I haven't seen them. I do hope they are all okay...
We will certainly keep them in our prayers.
Well, I... better be on my...w-wait...it's them...it's you! You're--

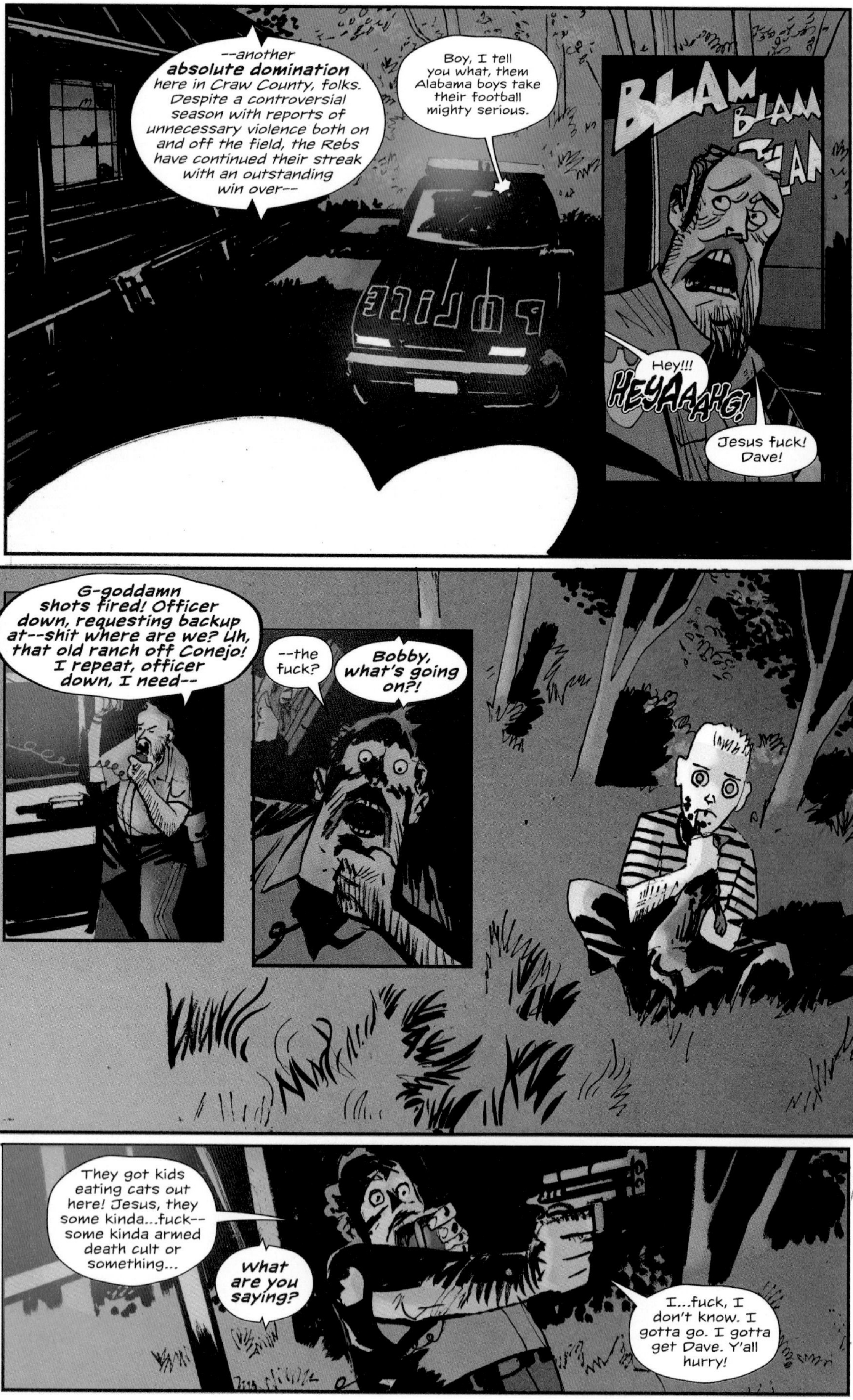
--another **absolute domination** here in Craw County, folks. Despite a controversial season with reports of unnecessary violence both on and off the field, the Rebs have continued their streak with an outstanding win over--
Boy, I tell you what, them Alabama boys take their football mighty serious.
POLICE
BLAM
BLAM
BLAM
Hey!!!
HEYAAAAHG!
Jesus fuck! Dave!
G-goddamn shots fired! Officer down, requesting backup at--shit where are we? Uh, that old ranch off Conejo! I repeat, officer down, I need--
--the fuck?
Bobby, what's going on?!
They got kids eating cats out here! Jesus, they some kinda...fuck-- some kinda armed death cult or something...
What are you saying?
I...fuck, I don't know. I gotta go. I gotta get Dave. Y'all hurry!

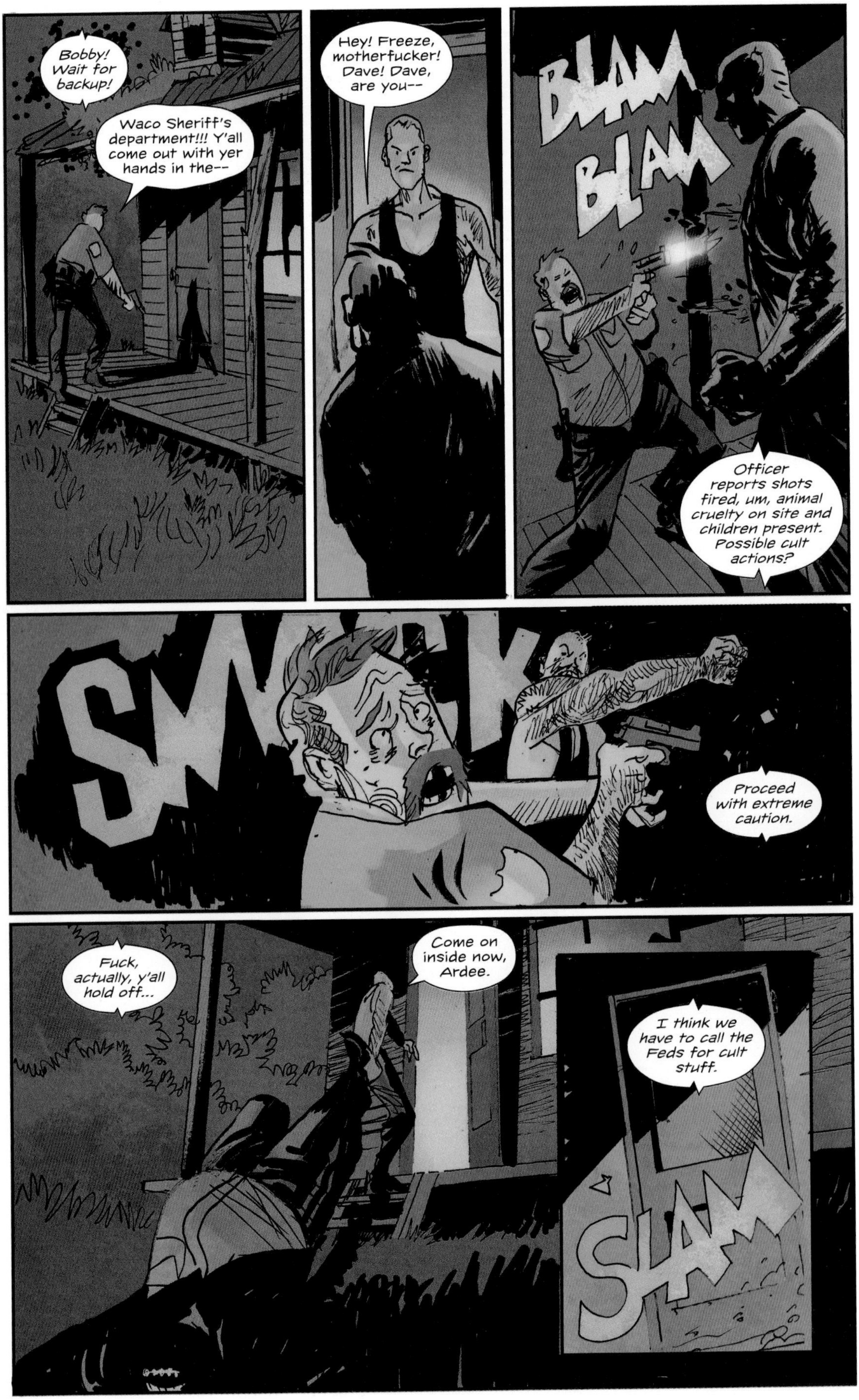

Bobby! Wait for backup!
Waco Sheriff's department!!! Y'all come out with yer hands in the--
Hey! Freeze, motherfucker! Dave! Dave, are you--
BLAM
BLAM
Officer reports shots fired, um, animal cruelty on site and children present. Possible cult actions?
Proceed with extreme caution.
Fuck, actually, y'all hold off...
Come on inside now, Ardee.
I think we have to call the Feds for cult stuff.
SLAM

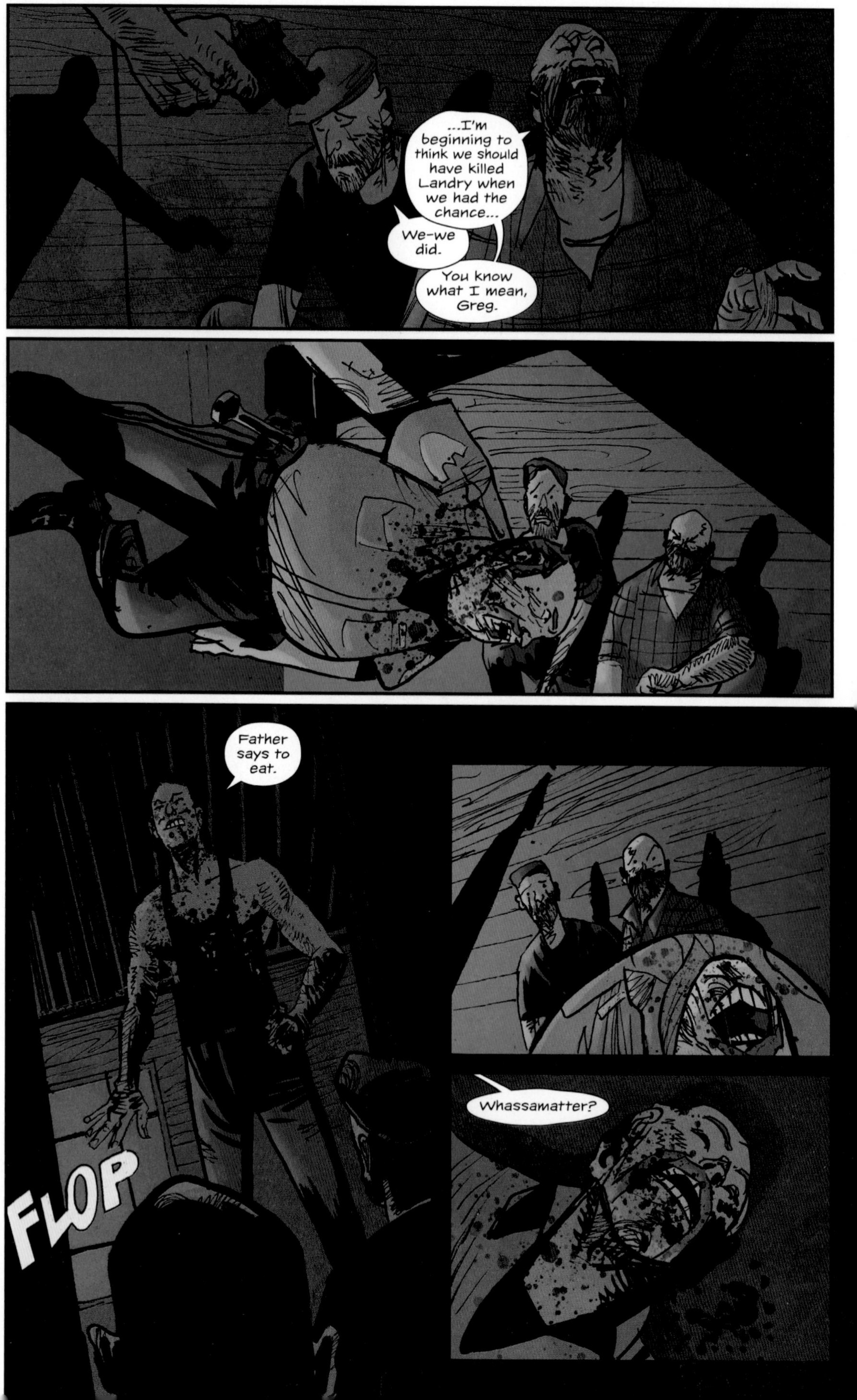
...I'm beginning to think we should have killed Landry when we had the chance...
We-we did.
You know what I mean, Greg.
Father says to eat.
FLOP
Whassamatter?

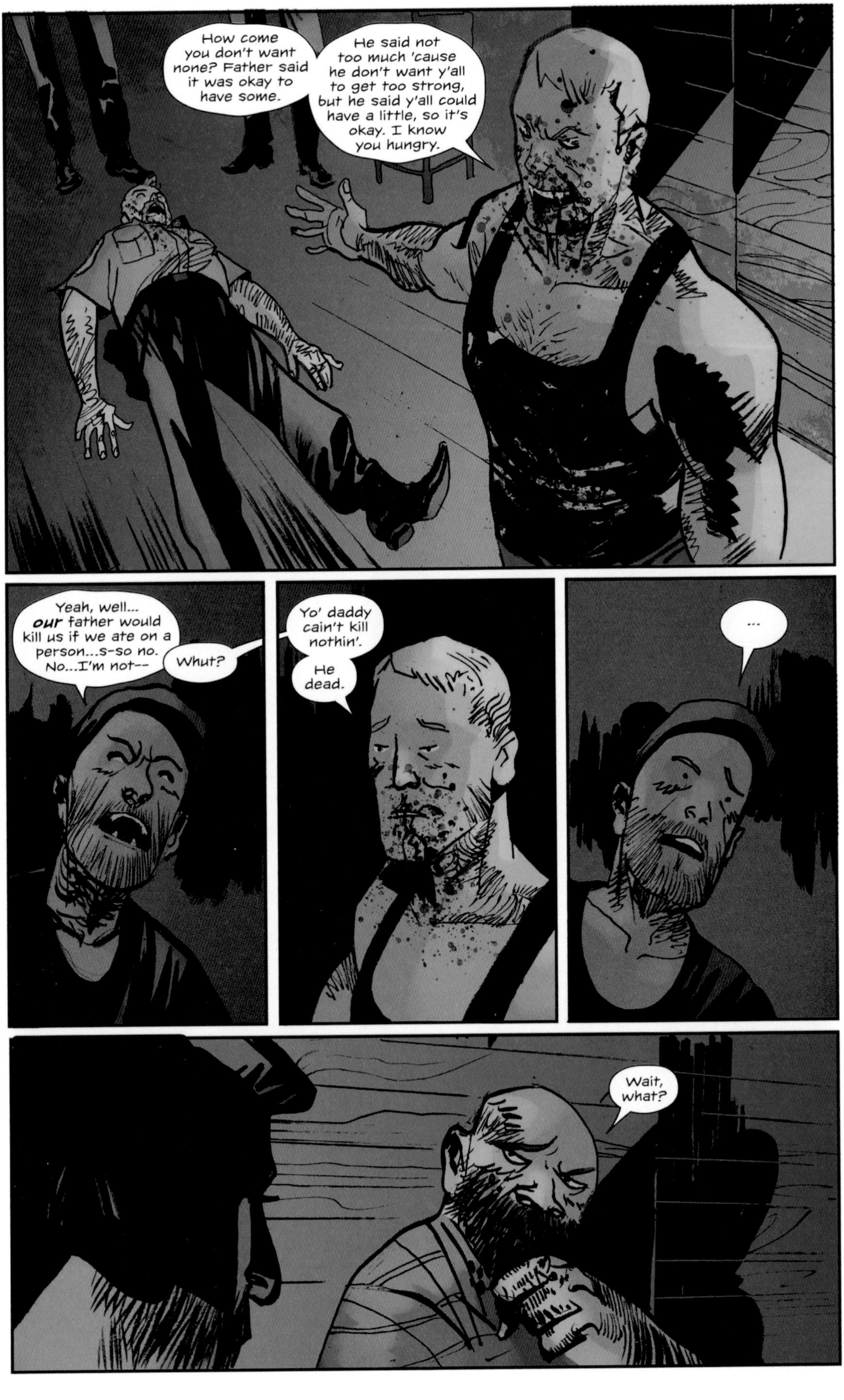
How come you don't want none? Father said it was okay to have some.
He said not too much 'cause he don't want y'all to get too strong, but he said y'all could have a little, so it's okay. I know you hungry.
Yeah, well... **our** father would kill us if we ate on a person...s-so no. No...I'm not--
Whut?
Yo' daddy cain't kill nothin'.
He dead.
...
Wait, what?

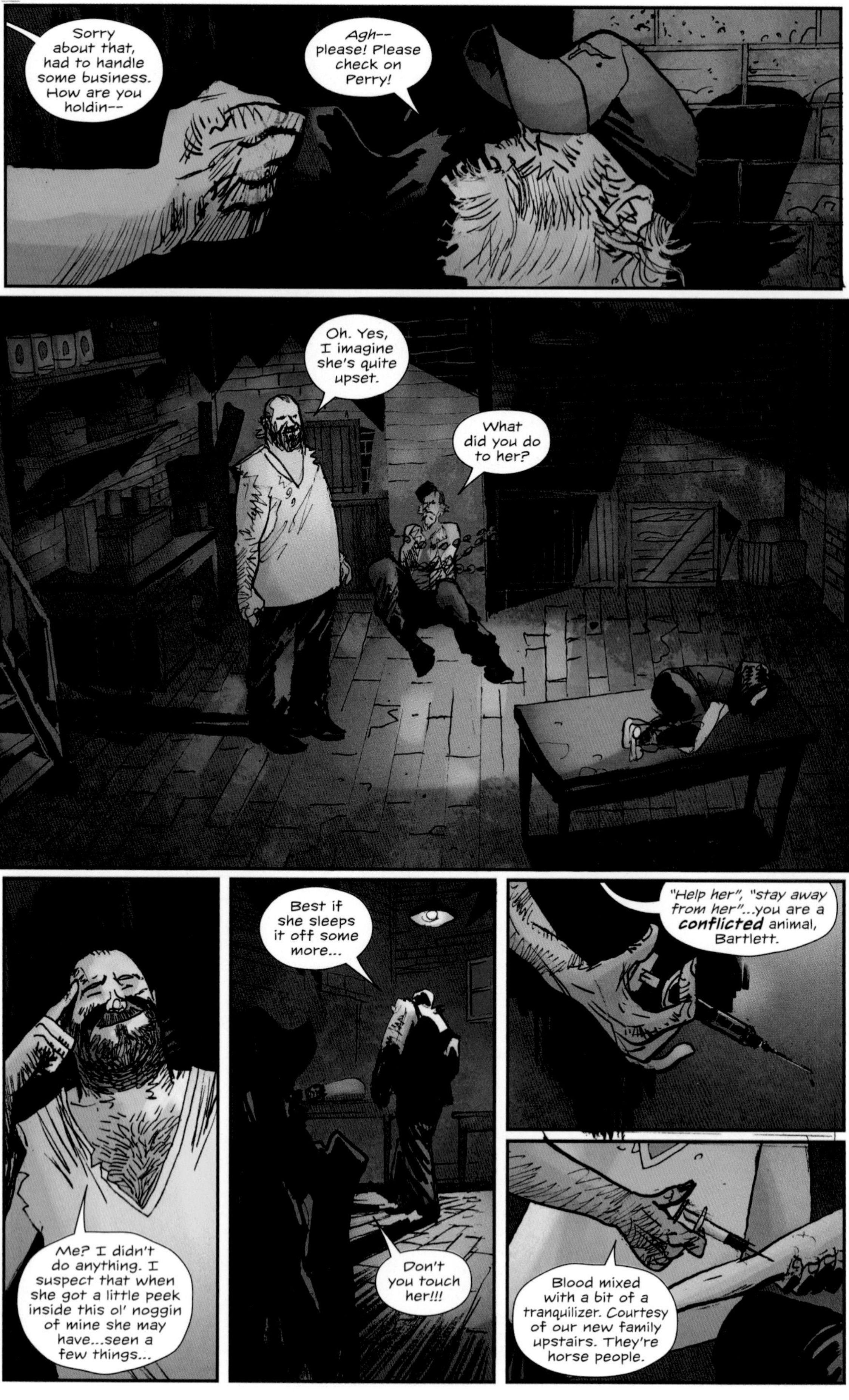
Sorry about that, had to handle some business. How are you holdin--
Agh-- please! Please check on Perry!
Oh. Yes, I imagine she's quite upset.
What did you do to her?
Me? I didn't do anything. I suspect that when she got a little peek inside this ol' noggin of mine she may have...seen a few things...
Best if she sleeps it off some more...
Don't you touch her!!!
"Help her", "stay away from her"...you are a **conflicted** animal, Bartlett.
Blood mixed with a bit of a tranquilizer. Courtesy of our new family upstairs. They're horse people.

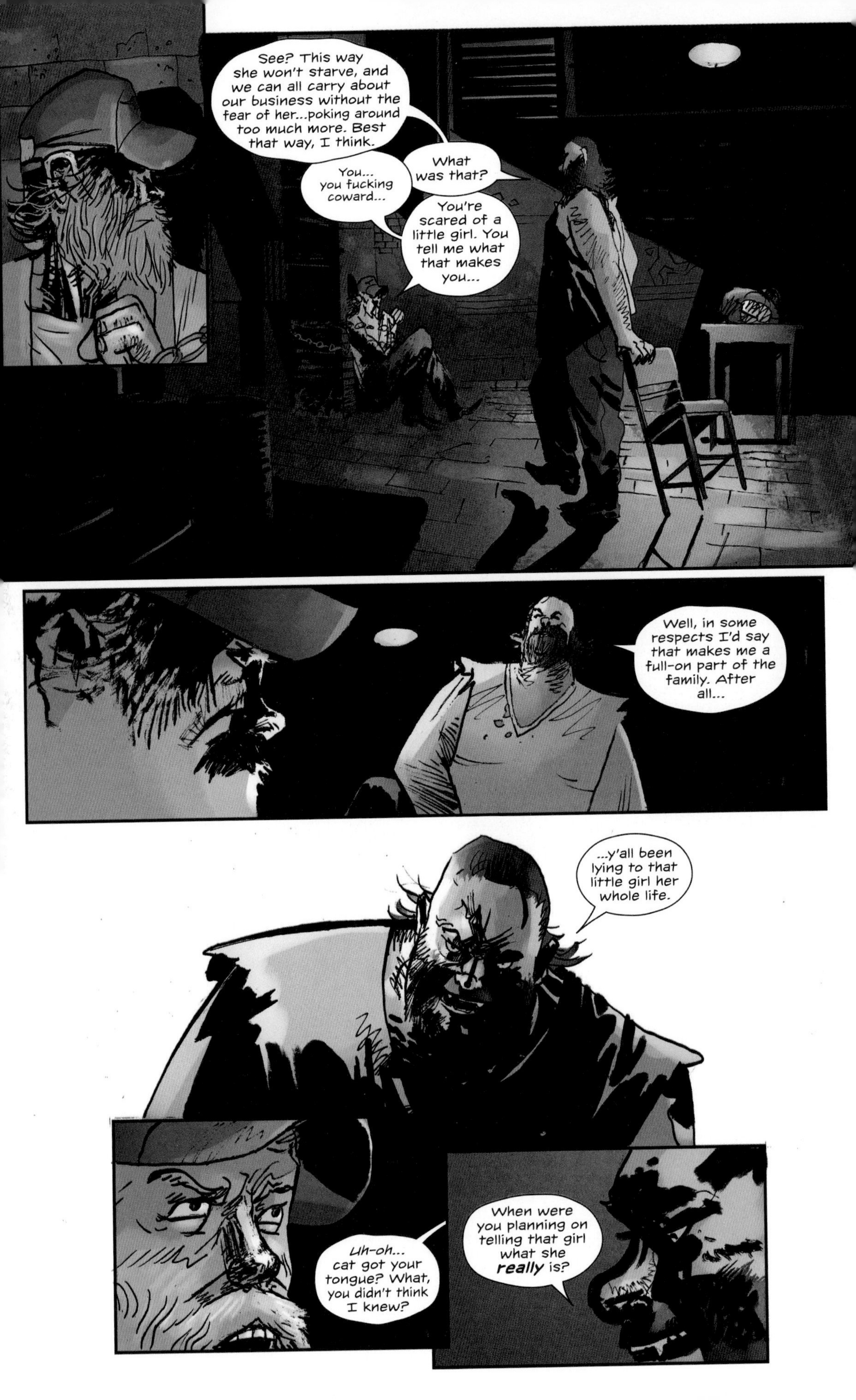

See? This way she won't starve, and we can all carry about our business without the fear of her...poking around too much more. Best that way, I think.
You... you fucking coward...
What was that?
You're scared of a little girl. You tell me what that makes you...
Well, in some respects I'd say that makes me a full-on part of the family. After all...
...y'all been lying to that little girl her whole life.
Uh-oh... cat got your tongue? What, you didn't think I knew?
When were you planning on telling that girl what she *really* is?

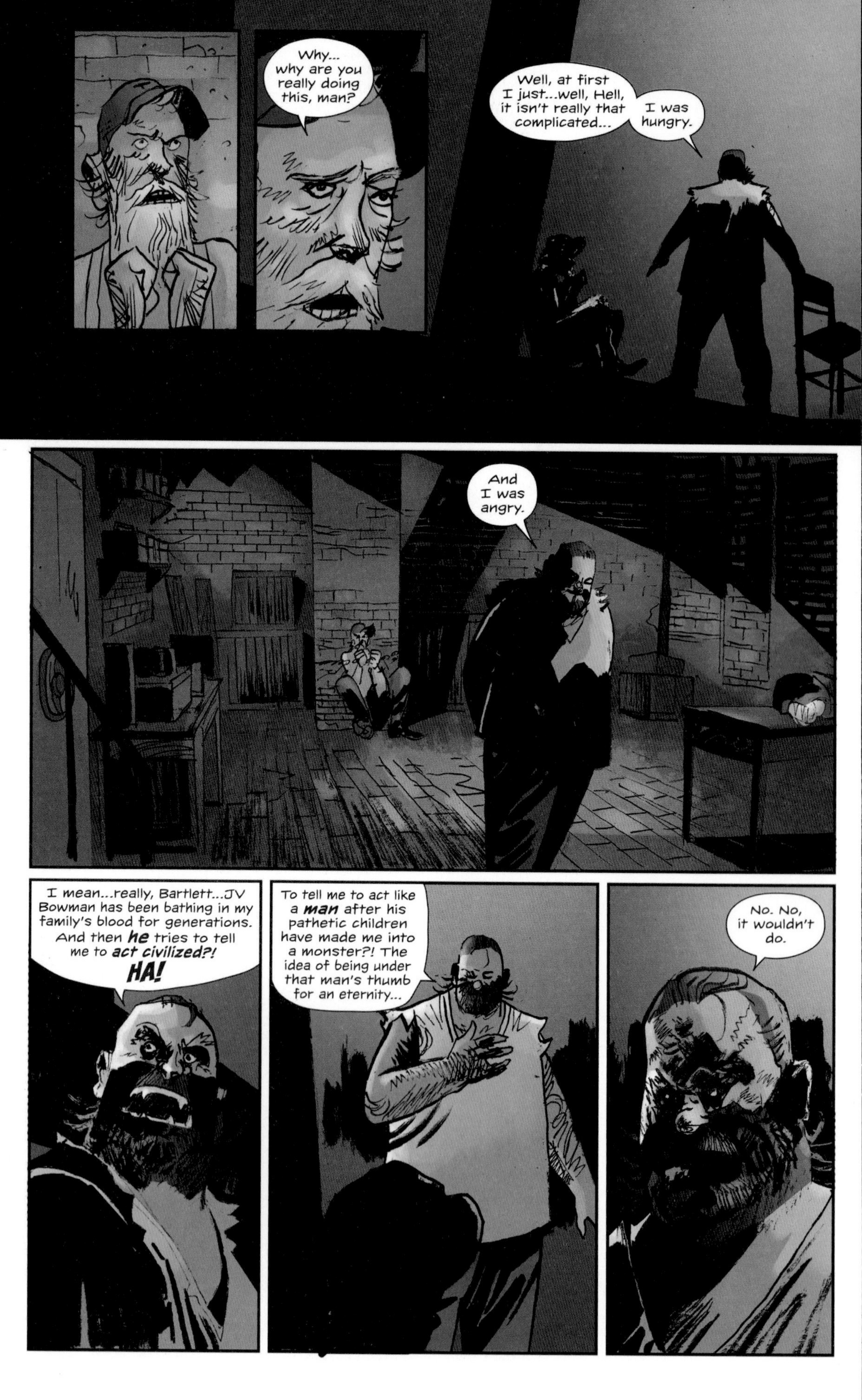
Why... why are you really doing this, man?
Well, at first I just...well, Hell, it isn't really that complicated...
I was hungry.
And I was angry.
I mean...really, Bartlett...JV Bowman has been bathing in my family's blood for generations. And then **he** tries to tell me to ***act civilized?!***
HA!
To tell me to act like a ***man*** after his pathetic children have made me into a monster?! The idea of being under that man's thumb for an eternity...
No. No, it wouldn't do.

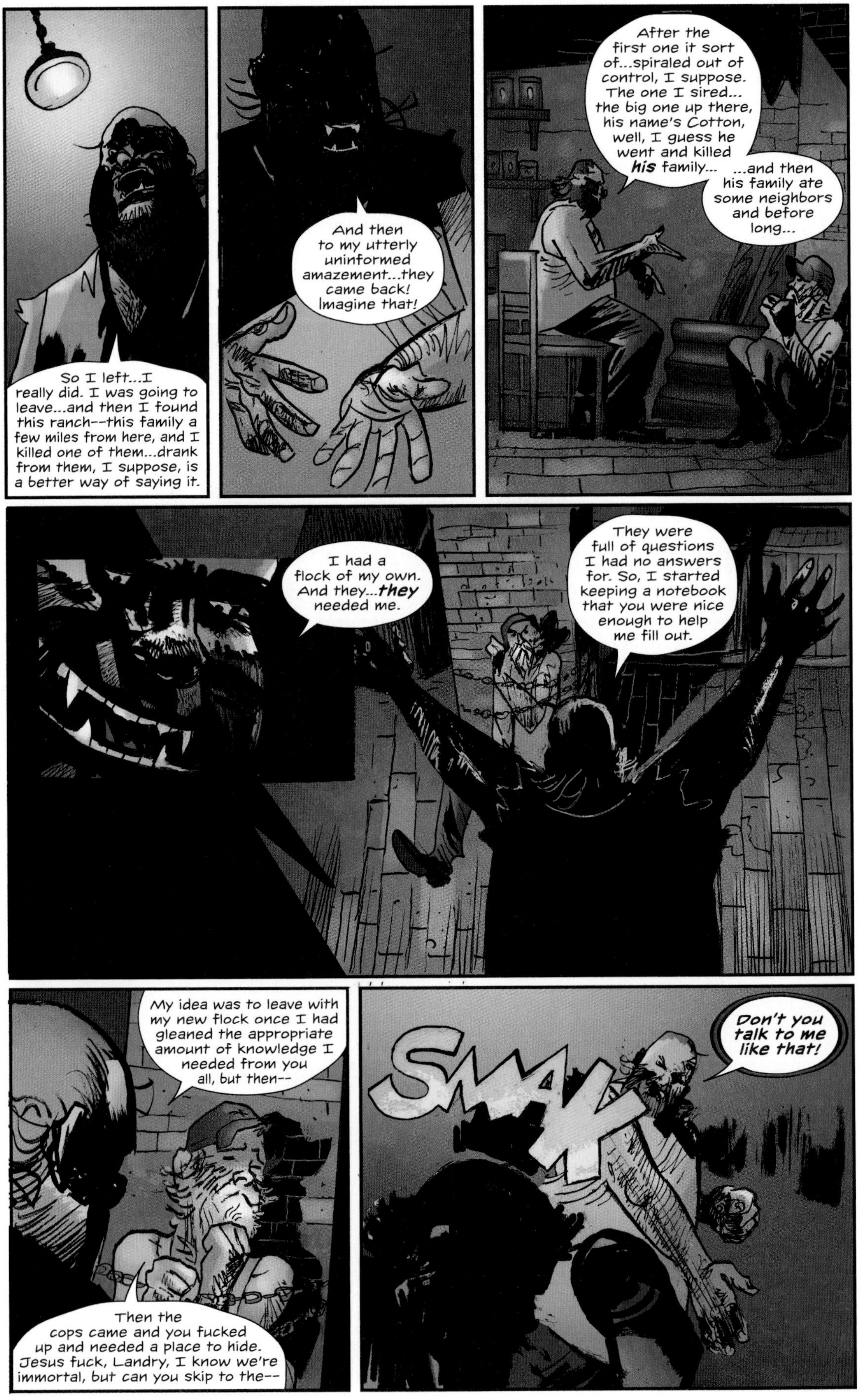
So I left...I really did. I was going to leave...and then I found this ranch--this family a few miles from here, and I killed one of them...drank from them, I suppose, is a better way of saying it.
And then to my utterly uninformed amazement...they came back! Imagine that!
After the first one it sort of...spiraled out of control, I suppose. The one I sired... the big one up there, his name's Cotton, well, I guess he went and killed *his* family...
...and then his family ate some neighbors and before long...
I had a flock of my own. And they...*they* needed me.
They were full of questions I had no answers for. So, I started keeping a notebook that you were nice enough to help me fill out.
My idea was to leave with my new flock once I had gleaned the appropriate amount of knowledge I needed from you all, but then--
Then the cops came and you fucked up and needed a place to hide. Jesus fuck, Landry, I know we're immortal, but can you skip to the--
SMAK
Don't you talk to me like that!

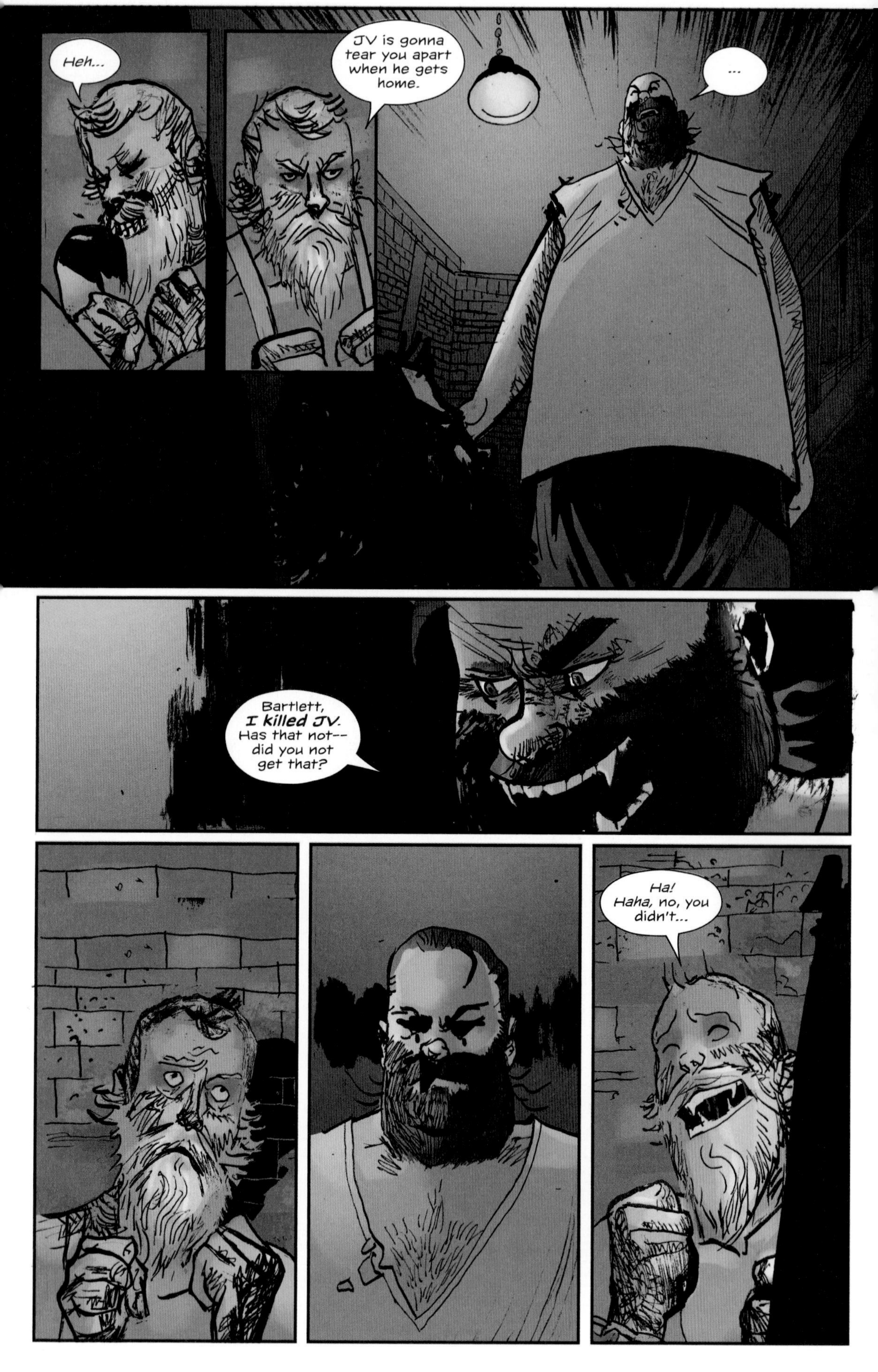
Heh...
JV is gonna tear you apart when he gets home.
...
Bartlett, I killed JV. Has that not-- did you not get that?
Ha! Haha, no, you didn't...

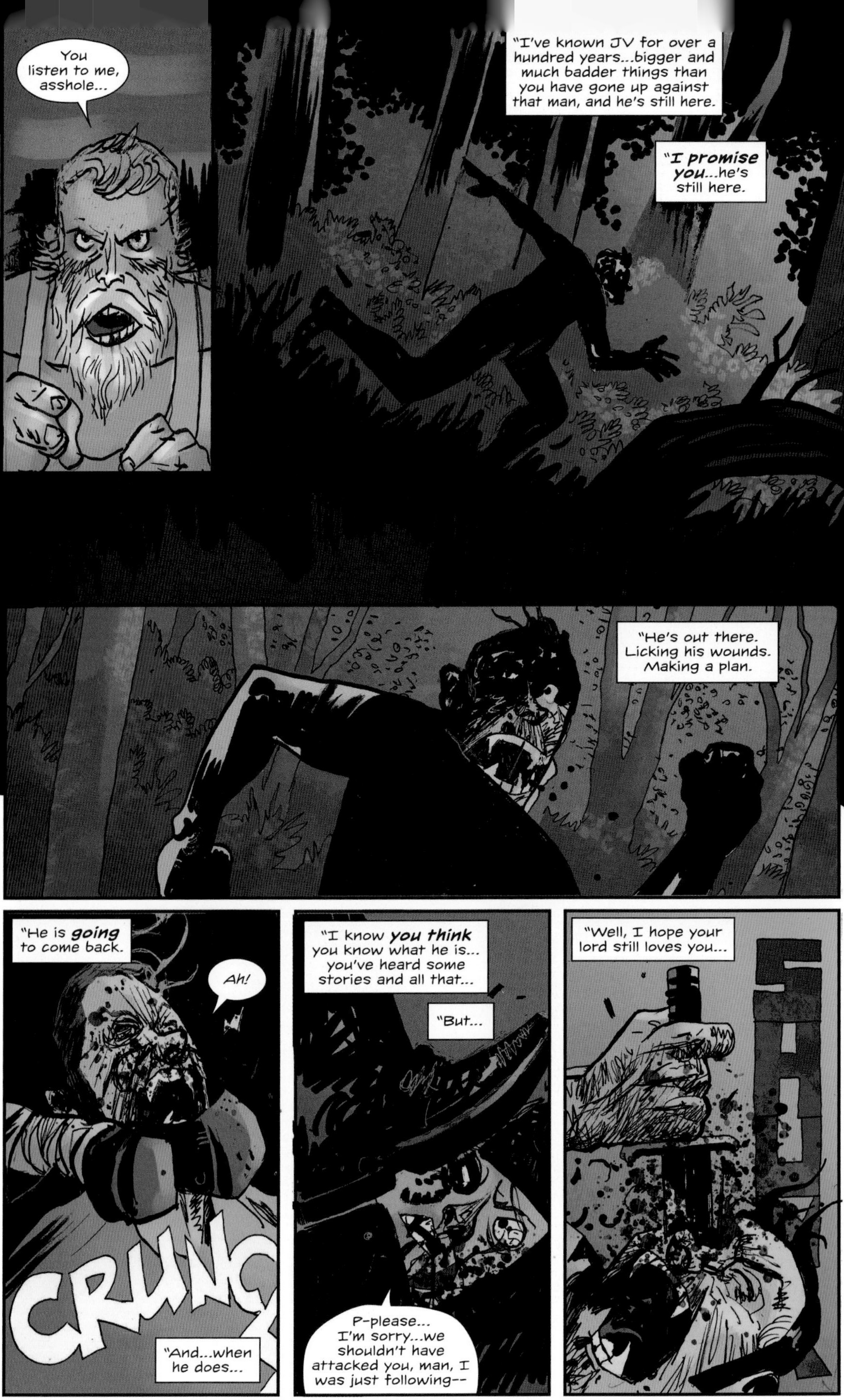
You listen to me, asshole...
"I've known JV for over a hundred years...bigger and much badder things than you have gone up against that man, and he's still here.
"I promise you...he's still here.
"He's out there. Licking his wounds. Making a plan.
"He is going to come back.
Ah!
CRUNC
"And...when he does...
"I know you think you know what he is... you've heard some stories and all that...
"But...
P-please... I'm sorry...we shouldn't have attacked you, man, I was just following--
"Well, I hope your lord still loves you...

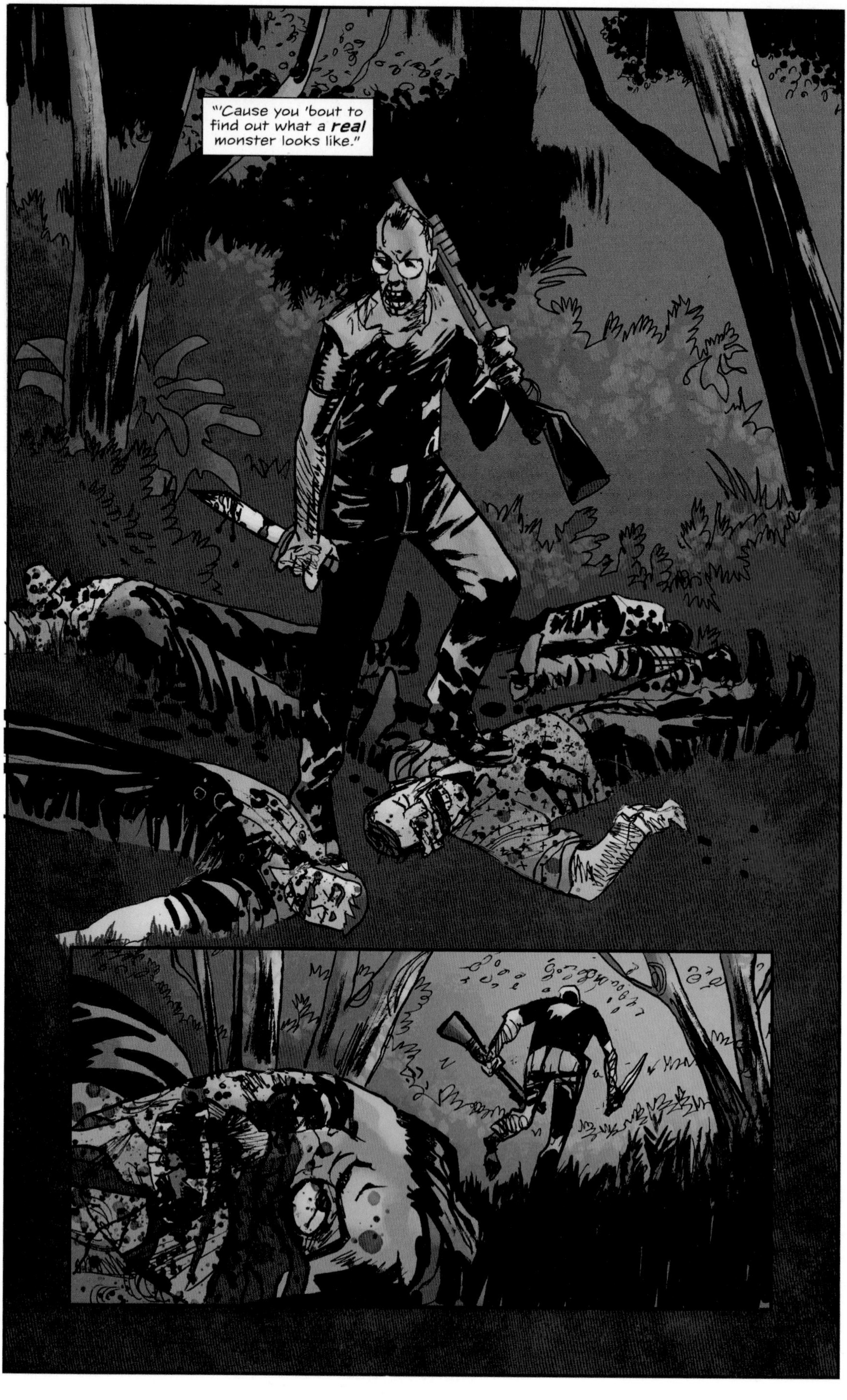
"'Cause you 'bout to find out what a ***real*** monster looks like."

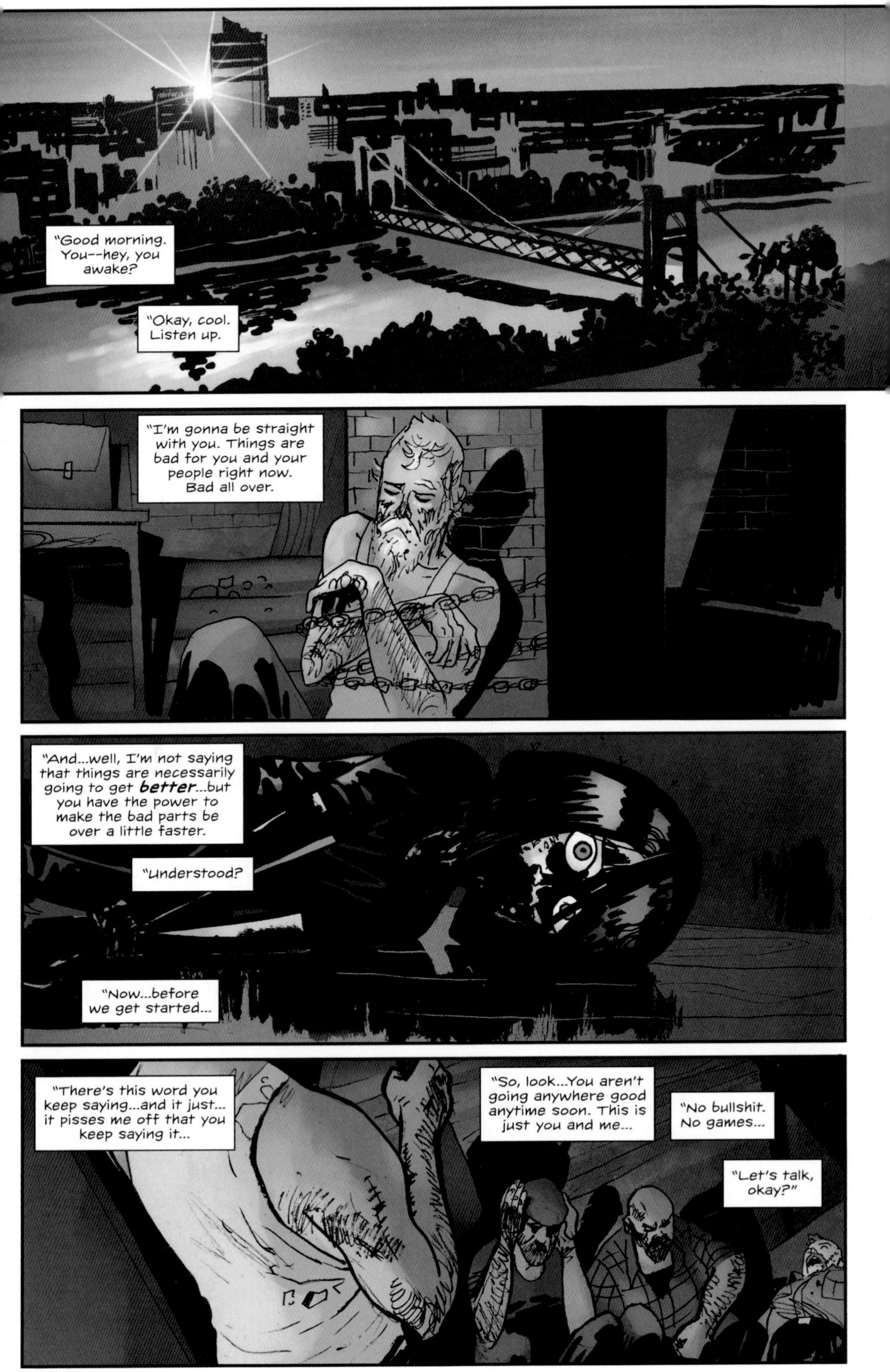
"Good morning. You--hey, you awake?
"Okay, cool. Listen up.
"I'm gonna be straight with you. Things are bad for you and your people right now. Bad all over.
"And...well, I'm not saying that things are necessarily going to get ***better***...but you have the power to make the bad parts be over a little faster.
"Understood?
"Now...before we get started...
"There's this word you keep saying...and it just... it pisses me off that you keep saying it...
"So, look...You aren't going anywhere good anytime soon. This is just you and me...
"No bullshit. No games...
"Let's talk, okay?"

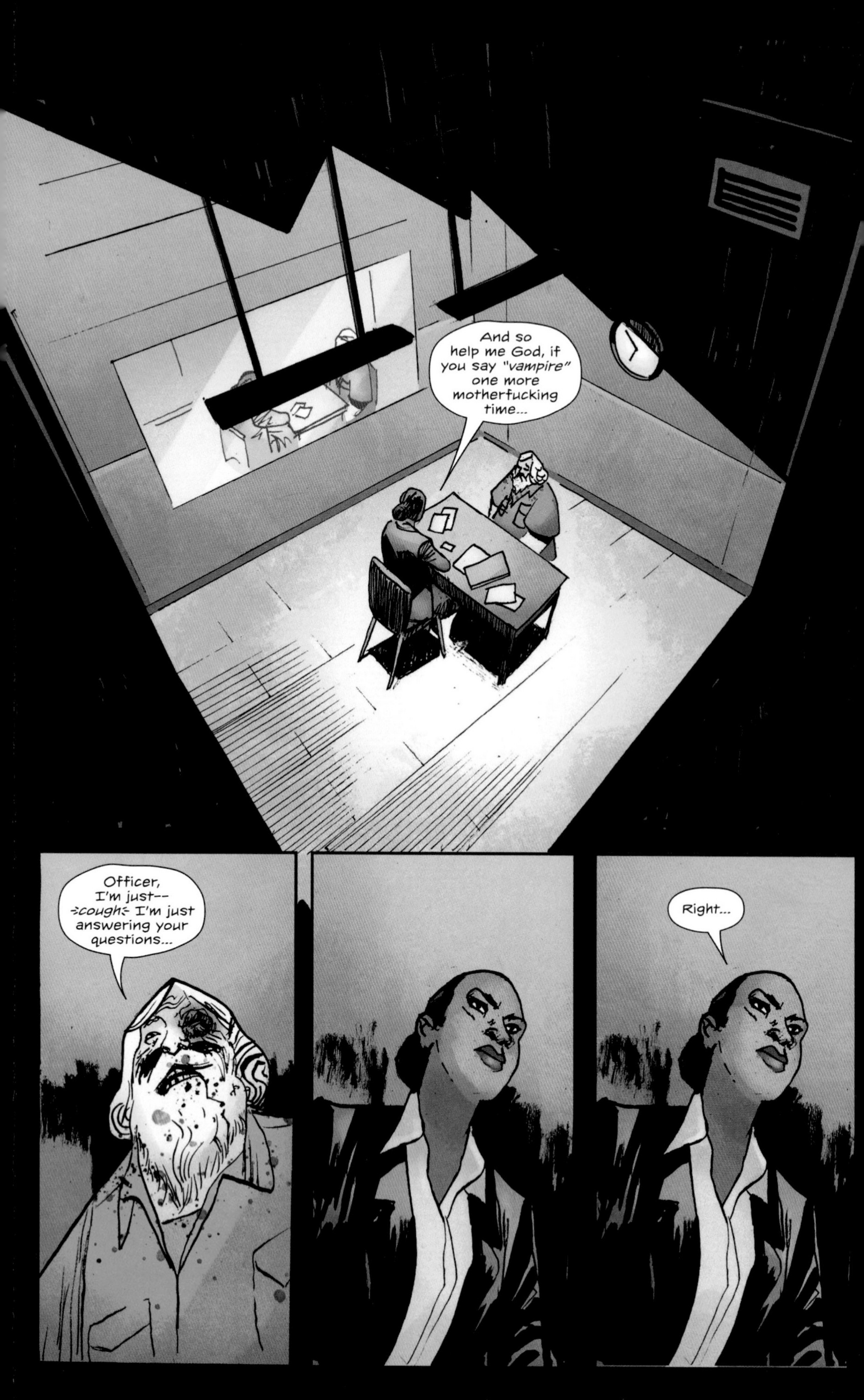
And so help me God, if you say "vampire" one more motherfucking time...
Officer, I'm just-- =cough= I'm just answering your questions...
Right...

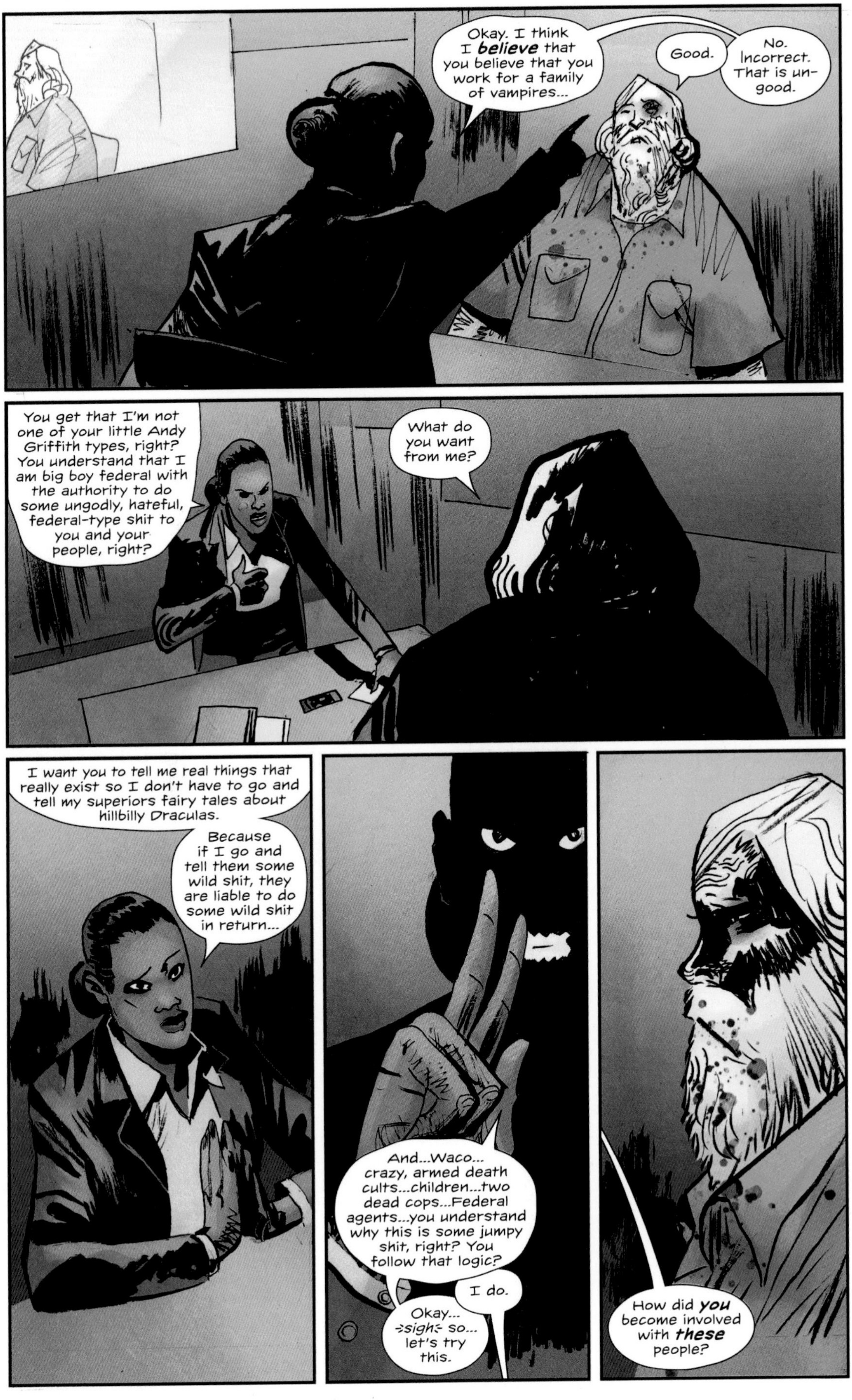
Okay. I think I *believe* that you believe that you work for a family of vampires...
Good.
No. Incorrect. That is un-good.
You get that I'm not one of your little Andy Griffith types, right? You understand that I am big boy federal with the authority to do some ungodly, hateful, federal-type shit to you and your people, right?
What do you want from me?
I want you to tell me real things that really exist so I don't have to go and tell my superiors fairy tales about hillbilly Draculas.
Because if I go and tell them some wild shit, they are liable to do some wild shit in return...
And...Waco... crazy, armed death cults...children...two dead cops...Federal agents...you understand why this is some jumpy shit, right? You follow that logic?
I do.
Okay... >sigh< so... let's try this.
How did *you* become involved with *these* people?

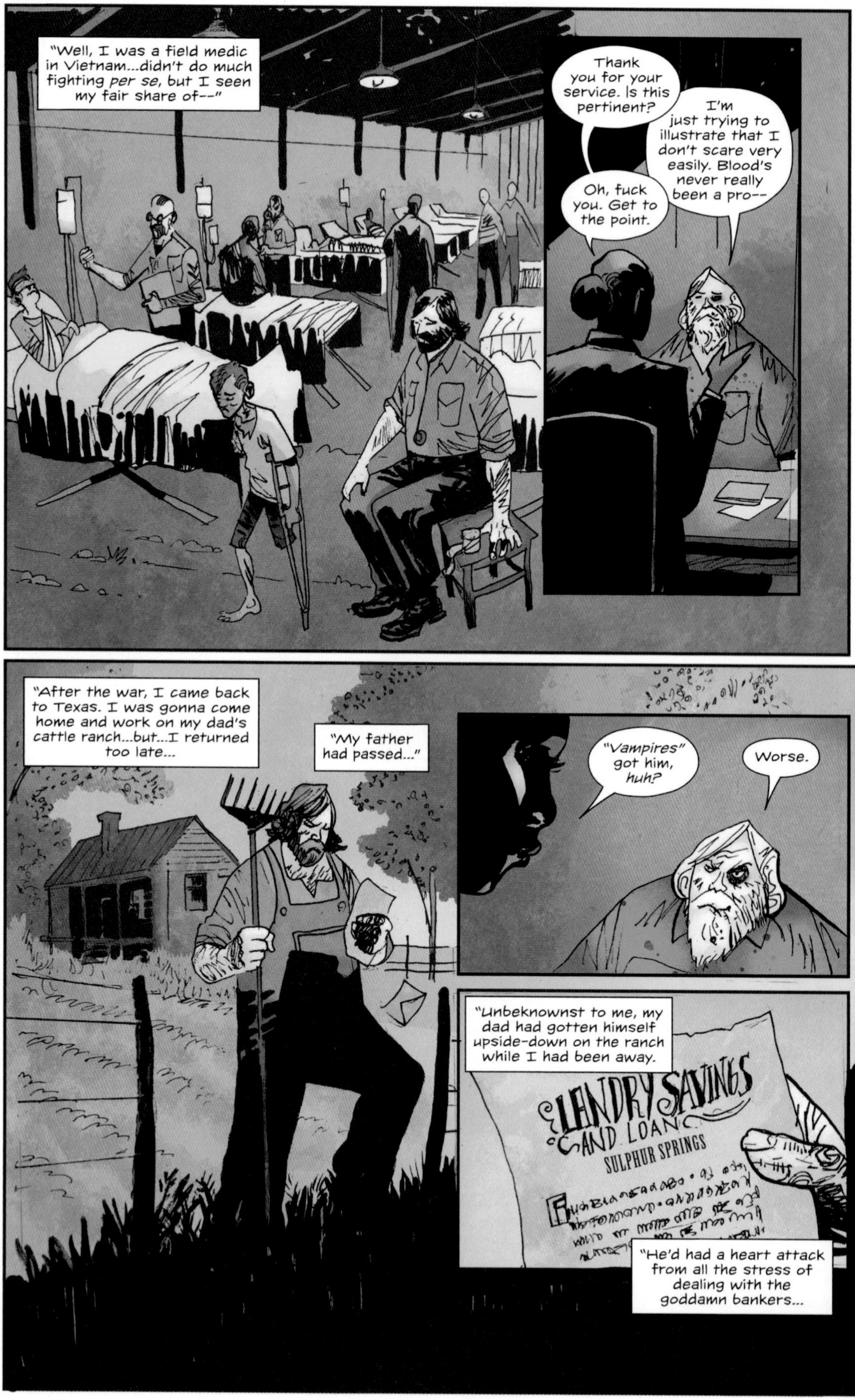
"Well, I was a field medic in Vietnam...didn't do much fighting *per se*, but I seen my fair share of--"
Thank you for your service. Is this pertinent?
I'm just trying to illustrate that I don't scare very easily. Blood's never really been a pro--
Oh, fuck you. Get to the point.
"After the war, I came back to Texas. I was gonna come home and work on my dad's cattle ranch...but...I returned too late...
"My father had passed..."
"*Vampires*" got him, *huh?*
Worse.
"Unbeknownst to me, my dad had gotten himself upside-down on the ranch while I had been away.
LANDRY SAVINGS AND LOAN
SULPHUR SPRINGS
"He'd had a heart attack from all the stress of dealing with the goddamn bankers...

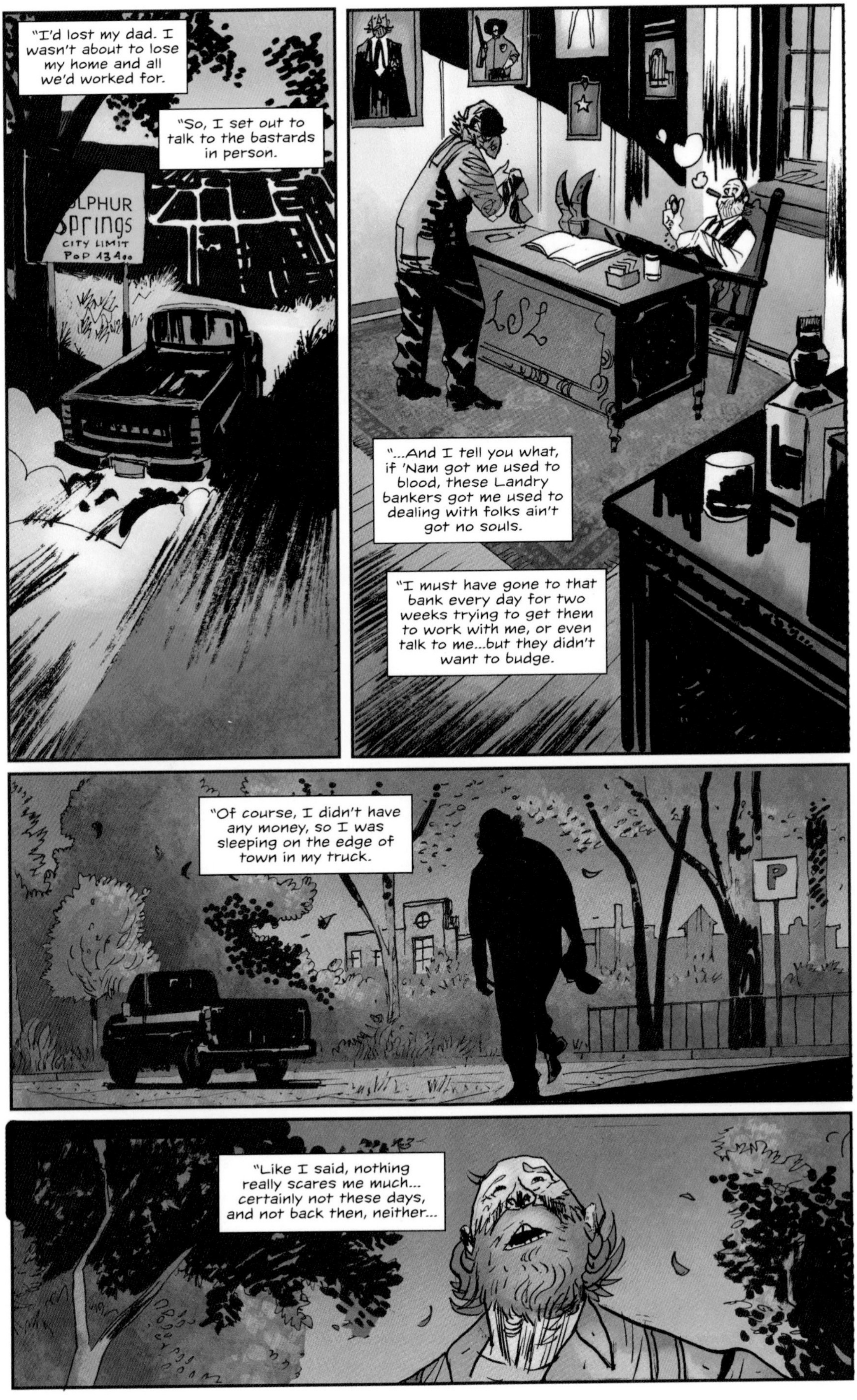
"I'd lost my dad. I wasn't about to lose my home and all we'd worked for.
"So, I set out to talk to the bastards in person.
OLPHUR Springs CITY LIMIT POP 13400
"...And I tell you what, if 'Nam got me used to blood, these Landry bankers got me used to dealing with folks ain't got no souls.
"I must have gone to that bank every day for two weeks trying to get them to work with me, or even talk to me...but they didn't want to budge.
"Of course, I didn't have any money, so I was sleeping on the edge of town in my truck.
P
"Like I said, nothing really scares me much... certainly not these days, and not back then, neither...

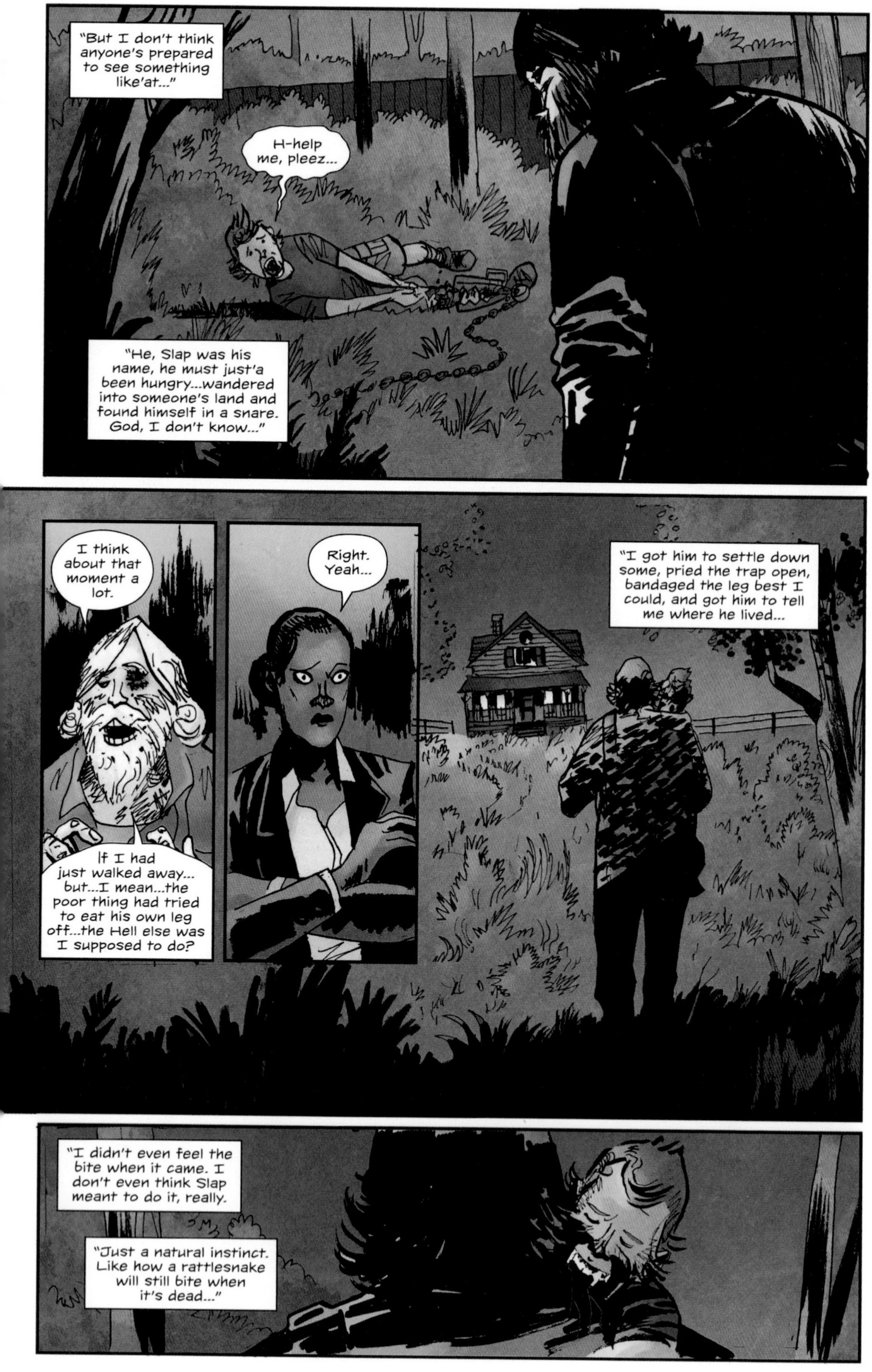
"But I don't think anyone's prepared to see something like'at..."
H-help me, pleez...
"He, Slap was his name, he must just'a been hungry...wandered into someone's land and found himself in a snare. God, I don't know..."
I think about that moment a lot.
If I had just walked away... but...I mean...the poor thing had tried to eat his own leg off...the Hell else was I supposed to do?
Right. Yeah...
"I got him to settle down some, pried the trap open, bandaged the leg best I could, and got him to tell me where he lived...
"I didn't even feel the bite when it came. I don't even think Slap meant to do it, really.
"Just a natural instinct. Like how a rattlesnake will still bite when it's dead..."

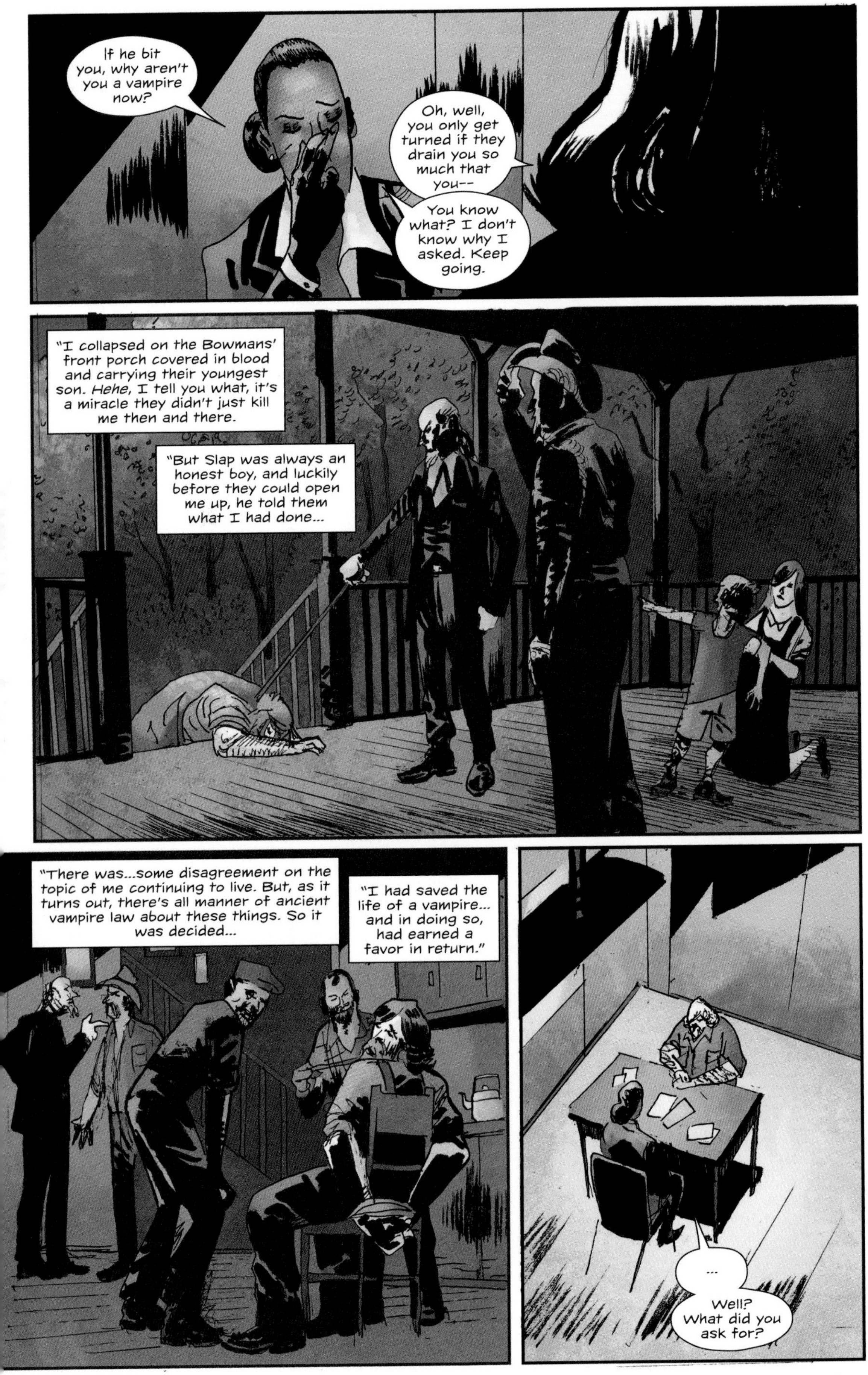
If he bit you, why aren't you a vampire now?
Oh, well, you only get turned if they drain you so much that you--
You know what? I don't know why I asked. Keep going.
"I collapsed on the Bowmans' front porch covered in blood and carrying their youngest son. *Hehe*, I tell you what, it's a miracle they didn't just kill me then and there.
"But Slap was always an honest boy, and luckily before they could open me up, he told them what I had done...
"There was...some disagreement on the topic of me continuing to live. But, as it turns out, there's all manner of ancient vampire law about these things. So it was decided...
"I had saved the life of a vampire... and in doing so, had earned a favor in return."
...
Well? What did you ask for?

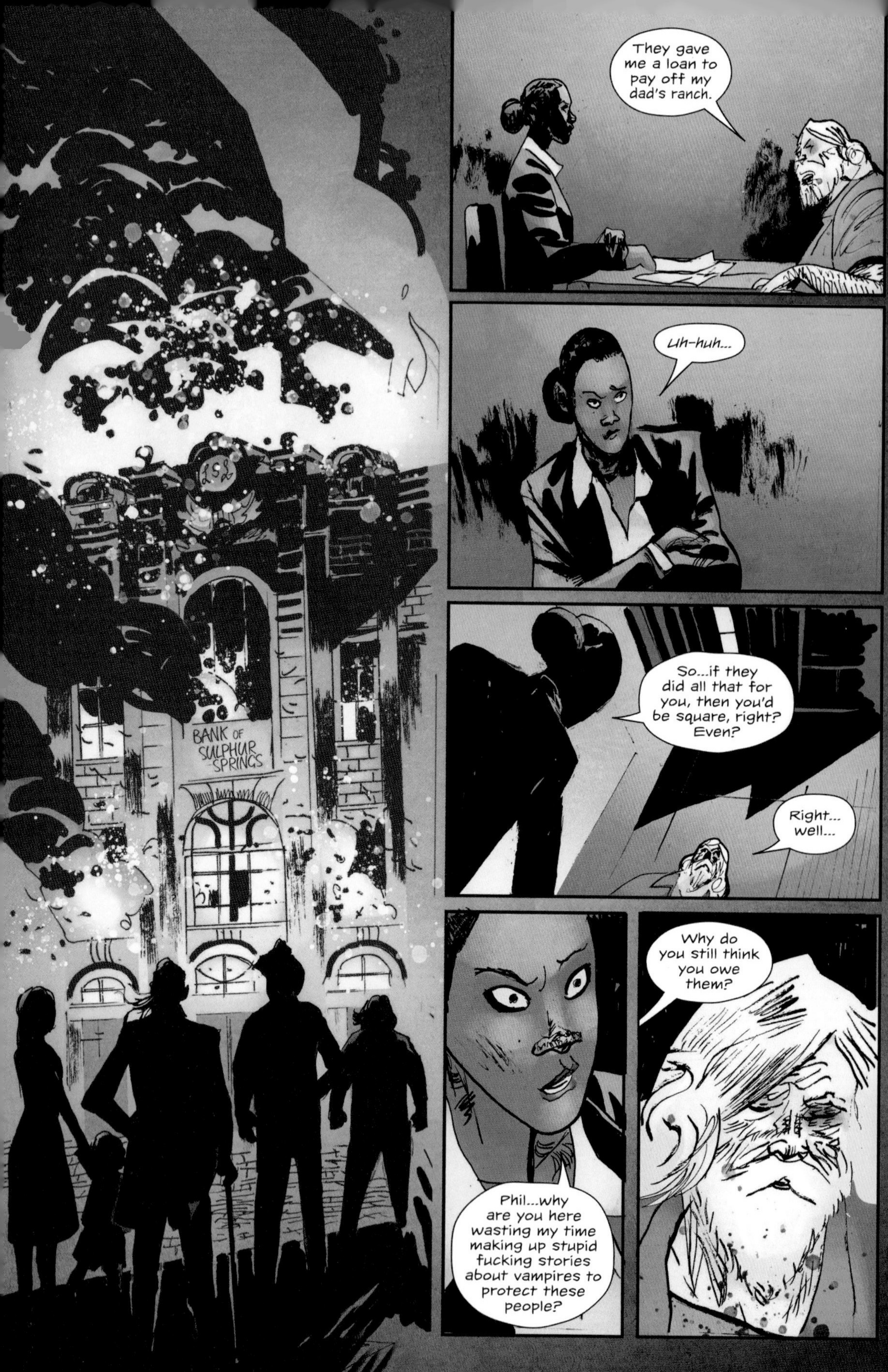
BANK OF SULPHUR SPRINGS
They gave me a loan to pay off my dad's ranch.
Uh-huh...
So...if they did all that for you, then you'd be square, right? Even?
Right... well...
Phil...why are you here wasting my time making up stupid fucking stories about vampires to protect these people?
Why do you still think you owe them?

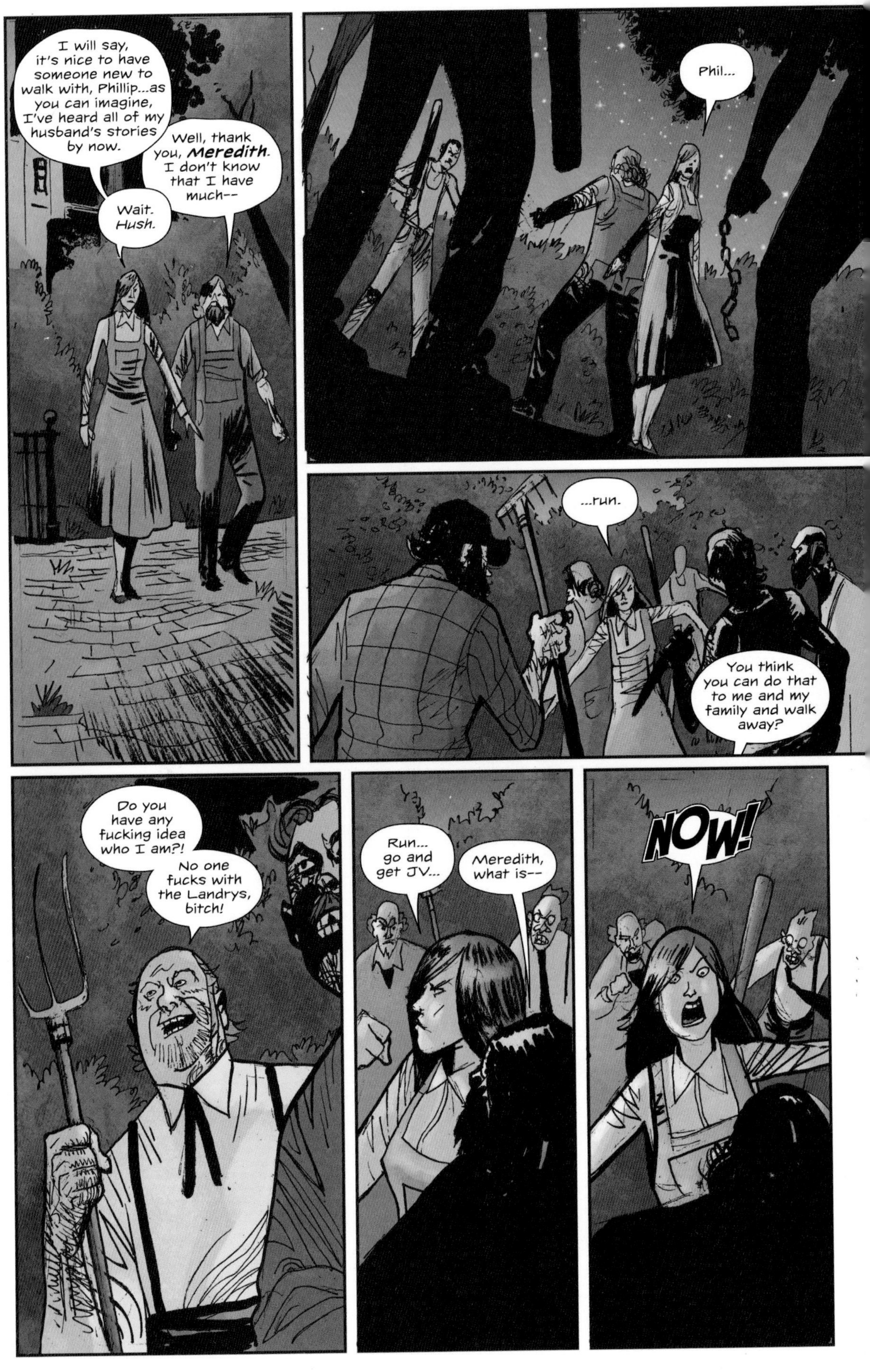
I will say, it's nice to have someone new to walk with, Phillip...as you can imagine, I've heard all of my husband's stories by now.
Well, thank you, **Meredith**. I don't know that I have much--
Wait. *Hush.*
Phil...
...run.
You think you can do that to me and my family and walk away?
Do you have any fucking idea who I am?!
No one fucks with the Landrys, bitch!
Run... go and get JV...
Meredith, what is--
NOW!

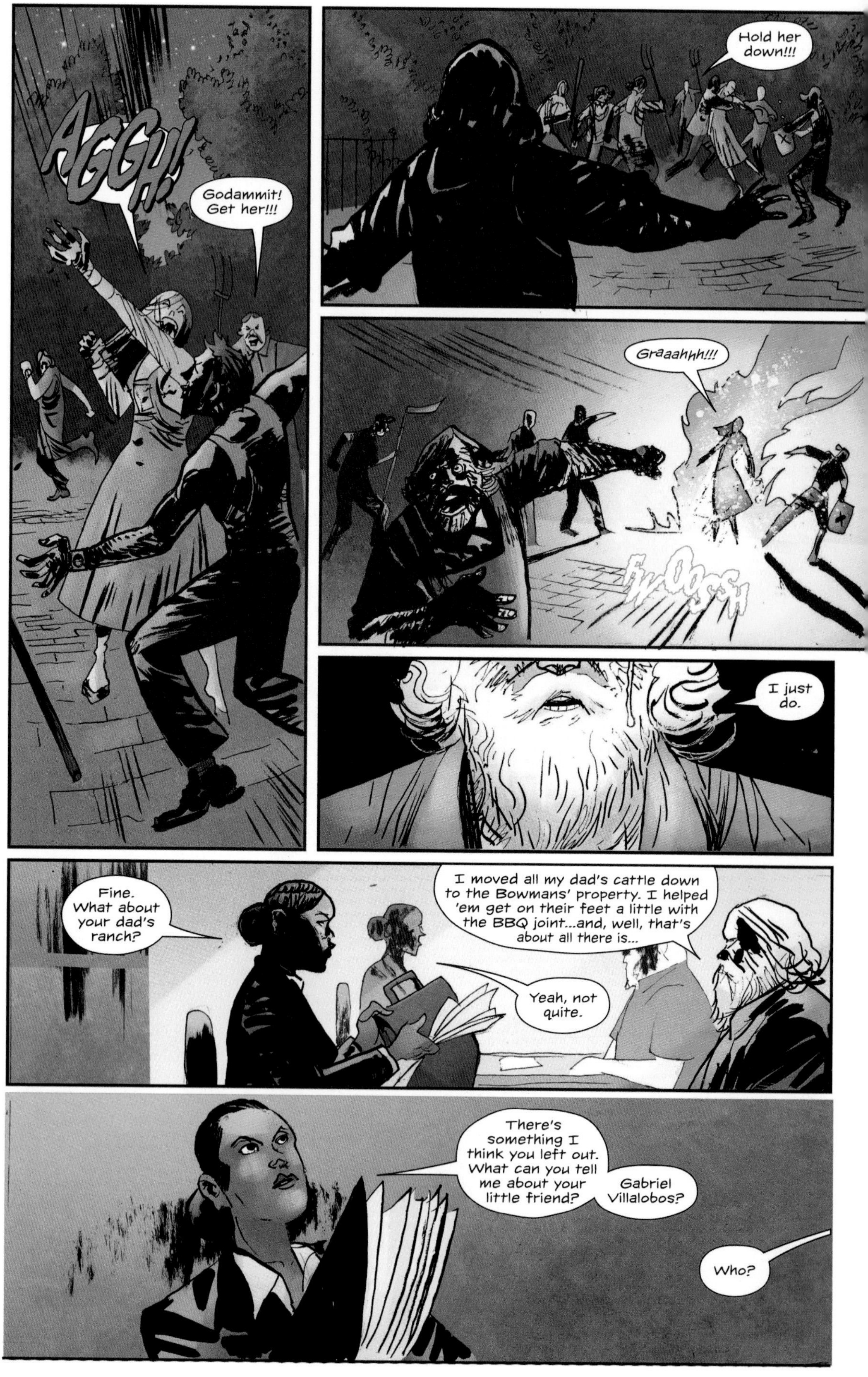
AGGH!
Godammit! Get her!!!
Hold her down!!!
Graaahhh!!!
FWOOSH
I just do.
Fine. What about your dad's ranch?
I moved all my dad's cattle down to the Bowmans' property. I helped 'em get on their feet a little with the BBQ joint...and, well, that's about all there is...
Yeah, not quite.
There's something I think you left out. What can you tell me about your little friend?
Gabriel Villalobos?
Who?

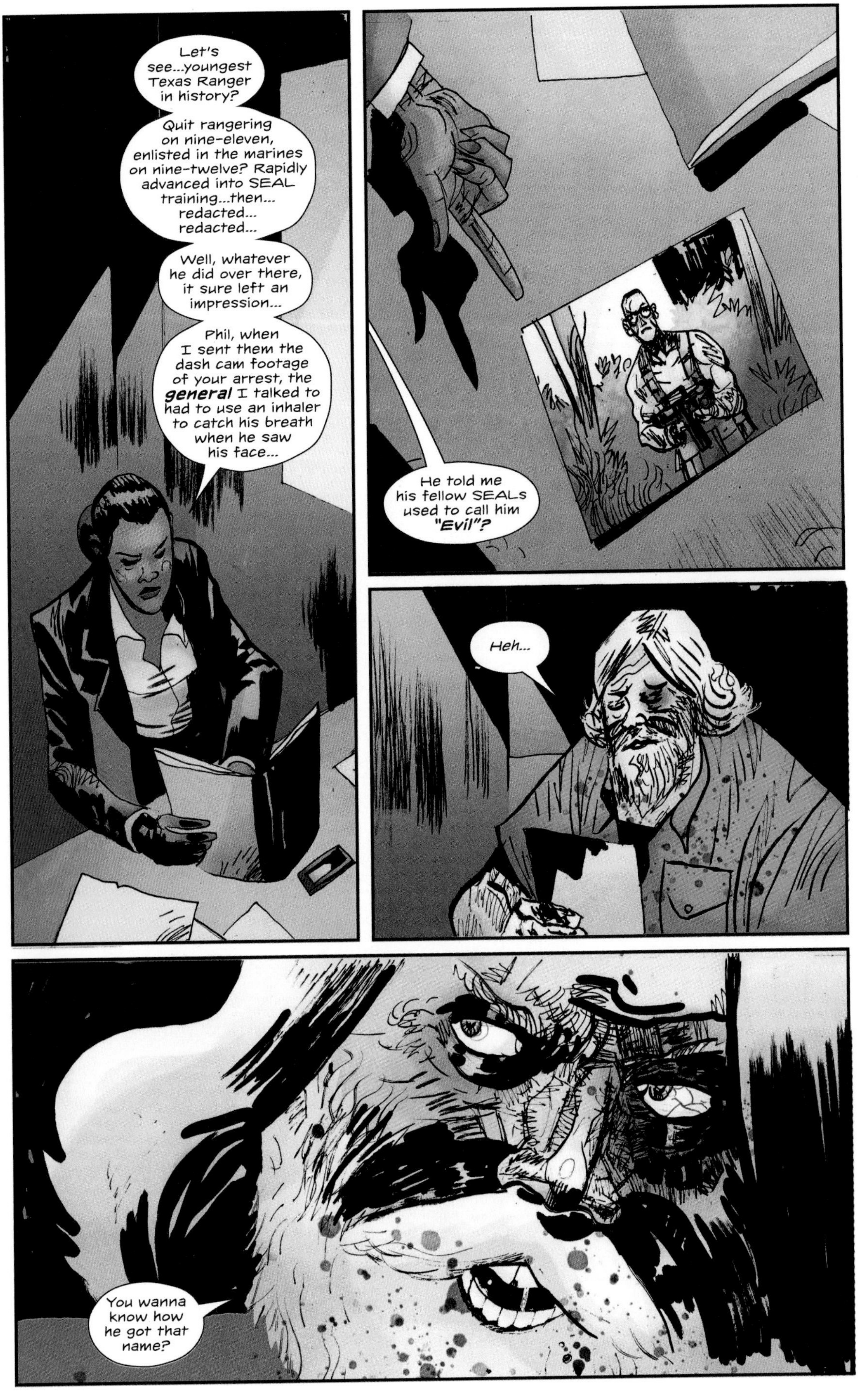
Let's see...youngest Texas Ranger in history?
Quit rangering on nine-eleven, enlisted in the marines on nine-twelve? Rapidly advanced into SEAL training...then... redacted... redacted...
Well, whatever he did over there, it sure left an impression...
Phil, when I sent them the dash cam footage of your arrest, the **general** I talked to had to use an inhaler to catch his breath when he saw his face...
He told me his fellow SEALs used to call him ***"Evil"?***
Heh...
You wanna know how he got that name?

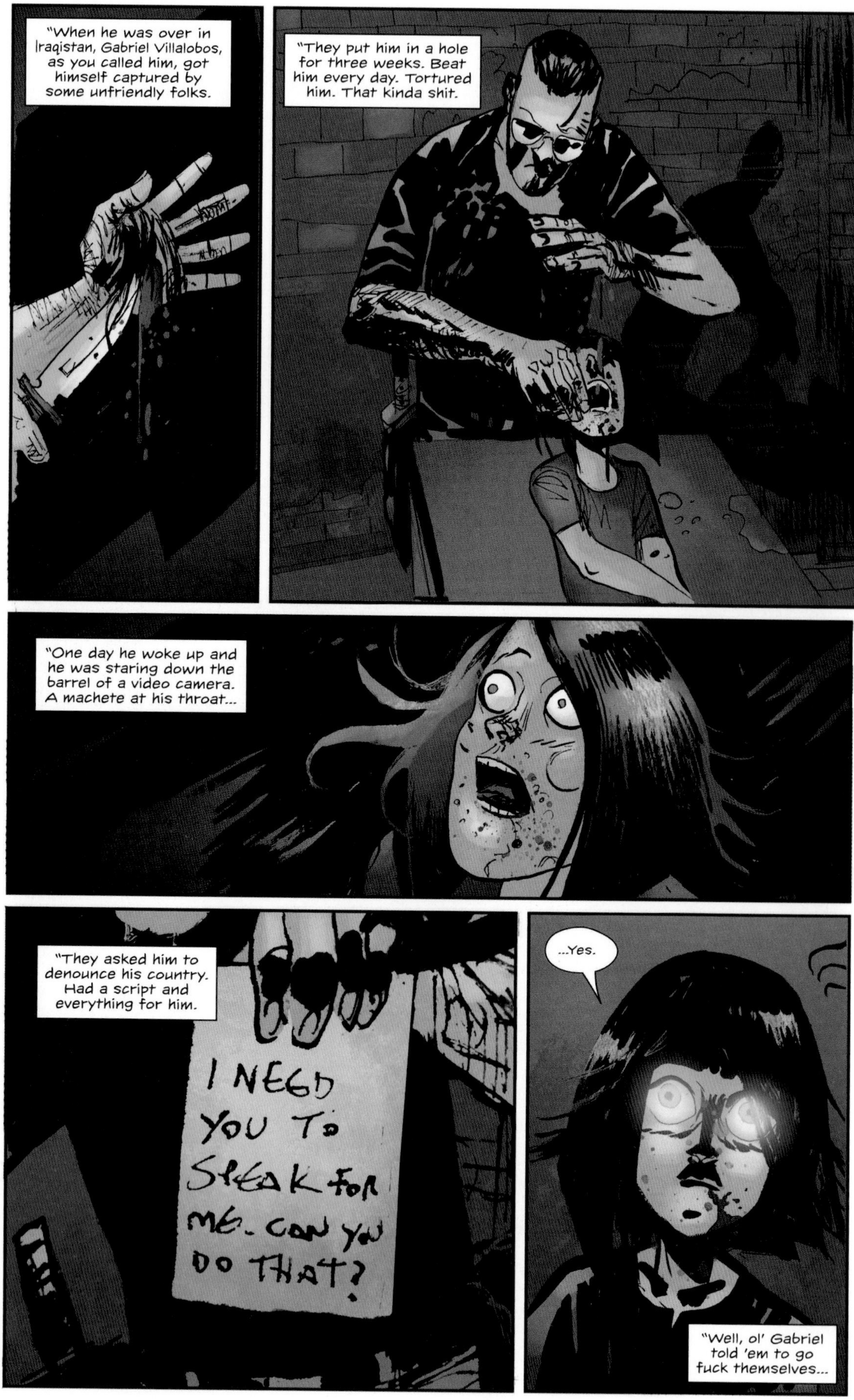
"When he was over in Iraqistan, Gabriel Villalobos, as you called him, got himself captured by some unfriendly folks.
"They put him in a hole for three weeks. Beat him every day. Tortured him. That kinda shit.
"One day he woke up and he was staring down the barrel of a video camera. A machete at his throat...
"They asked him to denounce his country. Had a script and everything for him.
I NEED YOU TO SPEAK FOR ME. CAN YOU DO THAT?
...Yes.
"Well, ol' Gabriel told 'em to go fuck themselves...

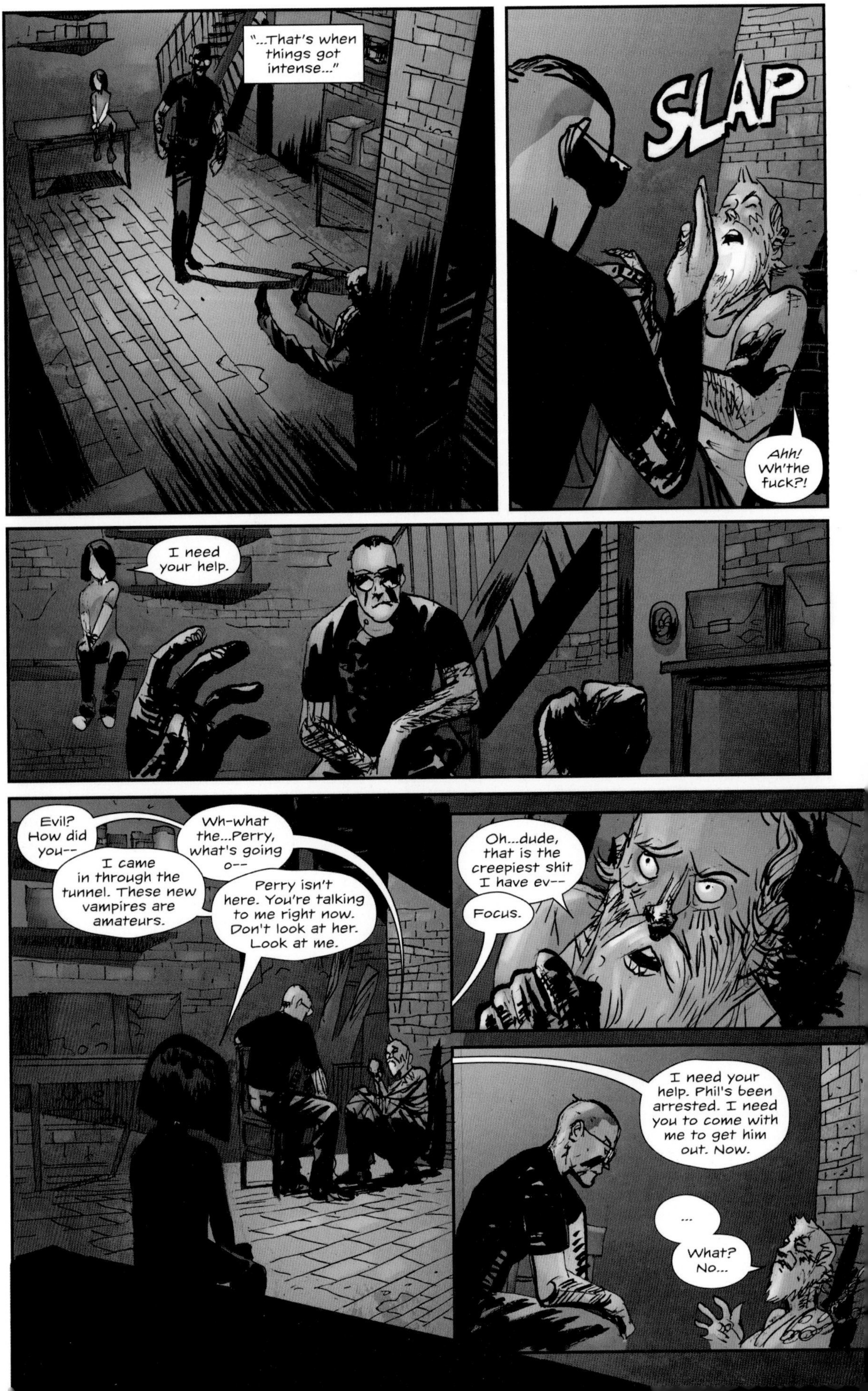
"...That's when things got intense..."
SLAP
Ahh! Wh'the fuck?!
I need your help.
Evil? How did you--
Wh-what the...Perry, what's going o--
I came in through the tunnel. These new vampires are amateurs.
Perry isn't here. You're talking to me right now. Don't look at her. Look at me.
Oh...dude, that is the creepiest shit I have ev--
Focus.
I need your help. Phil's been arrested. I need you to come with me to get him out. Now.
...
What? No...

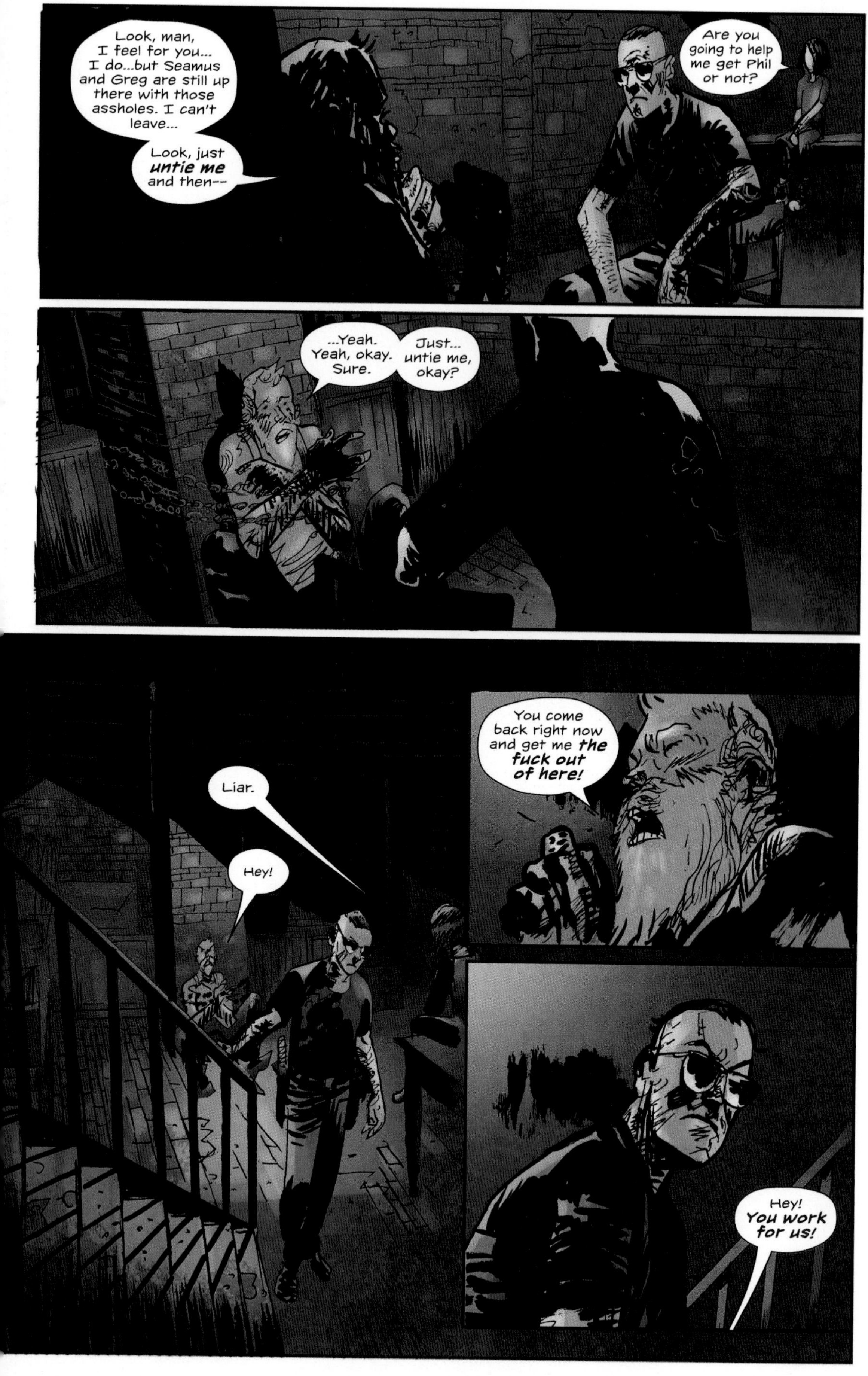
Look, man, I feel for you... I do...but Seamus and Greg are still up there with those assholes. I can't leave...
Look, just *untie me* and then--
Are you going to help me get Phil or not?
...Yeah. Yeah, okay. Sure.
Just... untie me, okay?
Liar.
Hey!
You come back right now and get me ***the fuck out of here!***
Hey! ***You work for us!***

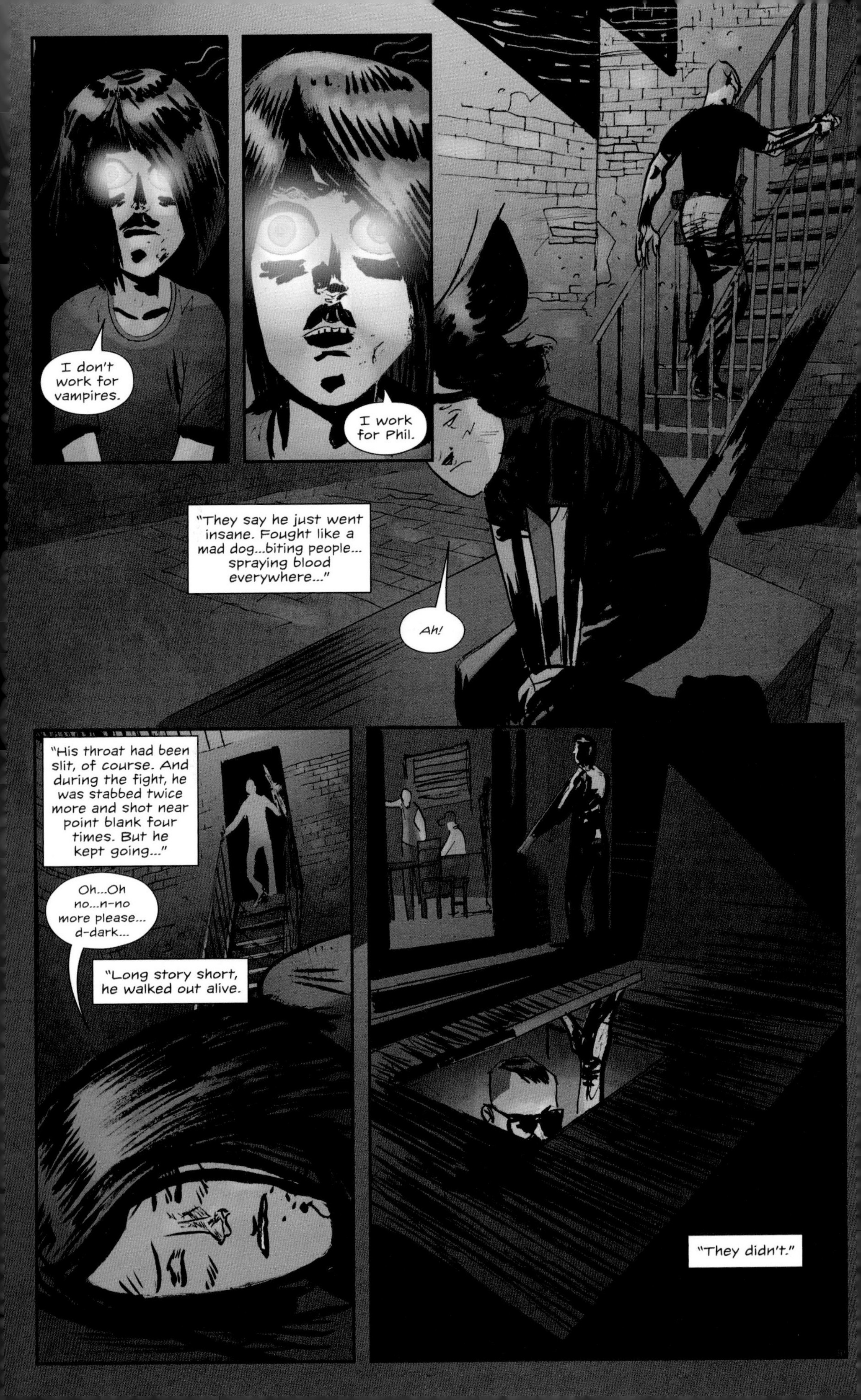
I don't work for vampires.
I work for Phil.
"They say he just went insane. Fought like a mad dog...biting people... spraying blood everywhere..."
Ah!
"His throat had been slit, of course. And during the fight, he was stabbed twice more and shot near point blank four times. But he kept going..."
Oh...Oh no...n-no more please... d-dark...
"Long story short, he walked out alive.
"They didn't."

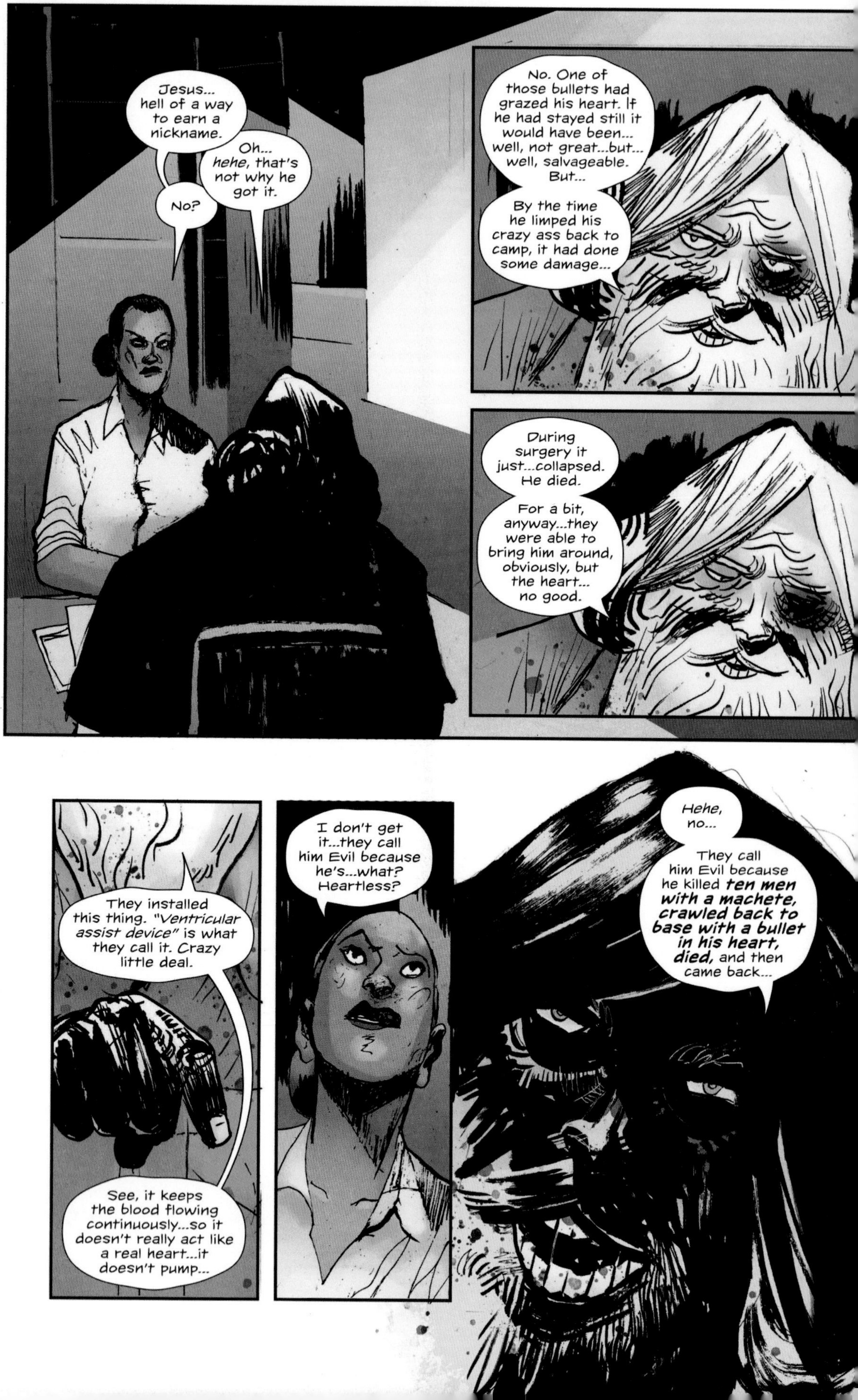
Jesus... hell of a way to earn a nickname.
Oh... *hehe,* that's not why he got it.
No?
No. One of those bullets had grazed his heart. If he had stayed still it would have been... well, not great...but... well, salvageable. But...
By the time he limped his crazy ass back to camp, it had done some damage...
During surgery it just...collapsed. He died.
For a bit, anyway...they were able to bring him around, obviously, but the heart... no good.
They installed this thing. "*Ventricular assist device*" is what they call it. Crazy little deal.
See, it keeps the blood flowing continuously...so it doesn't really act like a real heart...it doesn't pump...
I don't get it...they call him Evil because he's...what? Heartless?
Hehe, no...
They call him Evil because he killed ***ten men with a machete, crawled back to base with a bullet in his heart, died,*** and then came back...

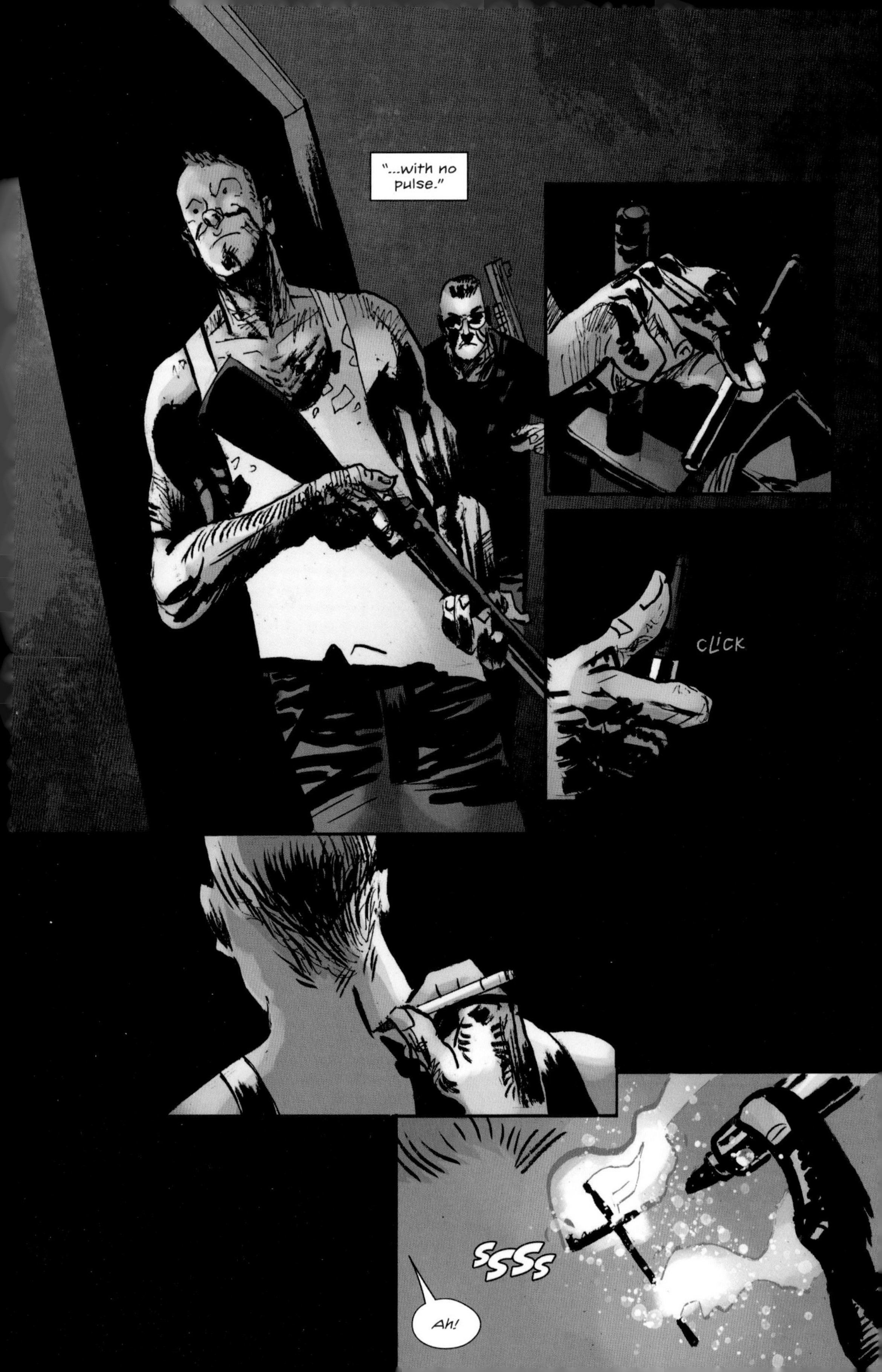
"...with no
pulse."
CLICK
SSSS
Ah!

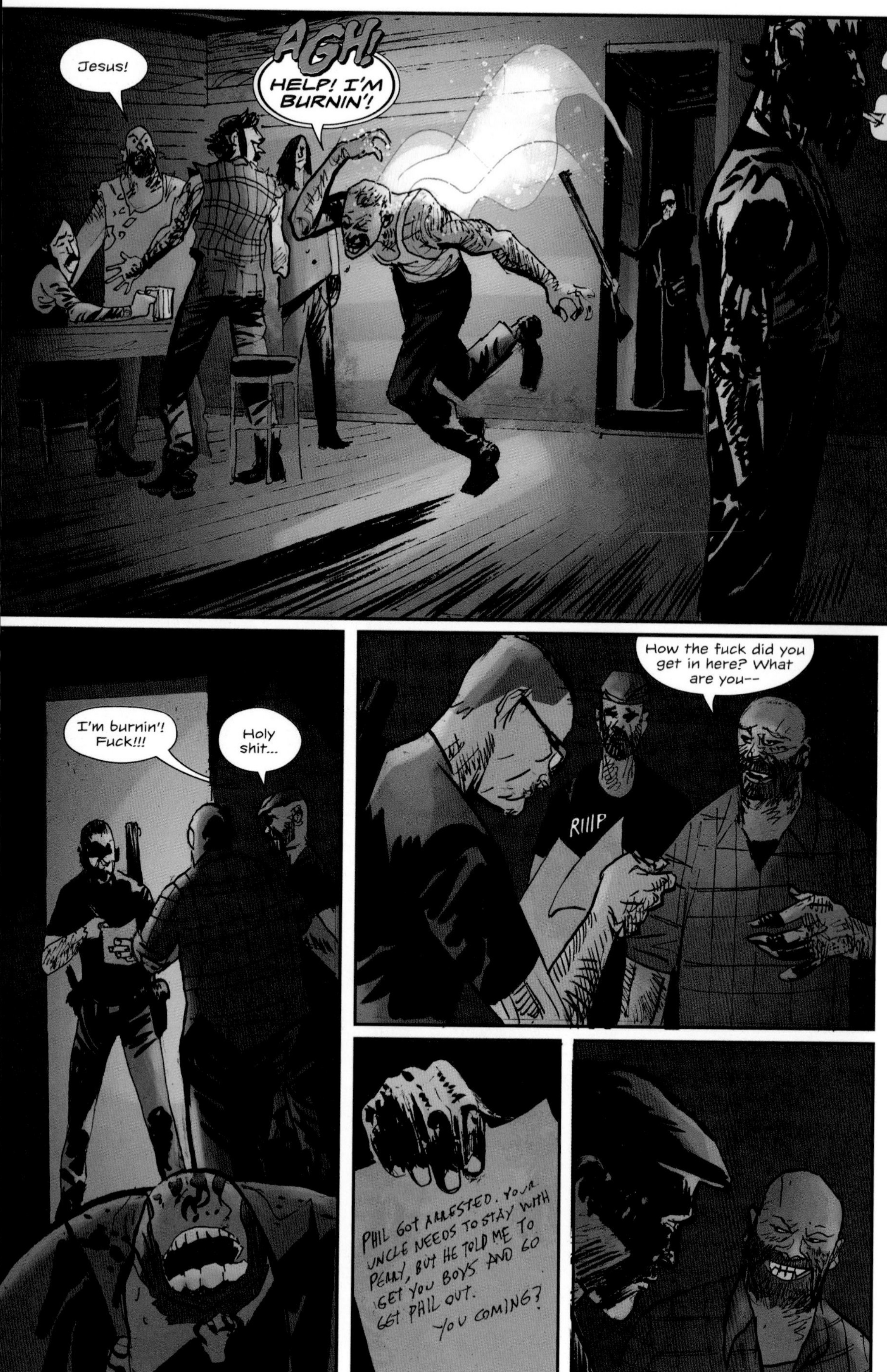
Jesus!
AGH!
HELP! I'M BURNIN'!
I'm burnin'! Fuck!!!
Holy shit...
How the fuck did you get in here? What are you--
RIIP
PHIL GOT ARRESTED. YOUR UNCLE NEEDS TO STAY WITH PERRY, BUT HE TOLD ME TO GET YOU BOYS AND GO GET PHIL OUT.
YOU COMING?

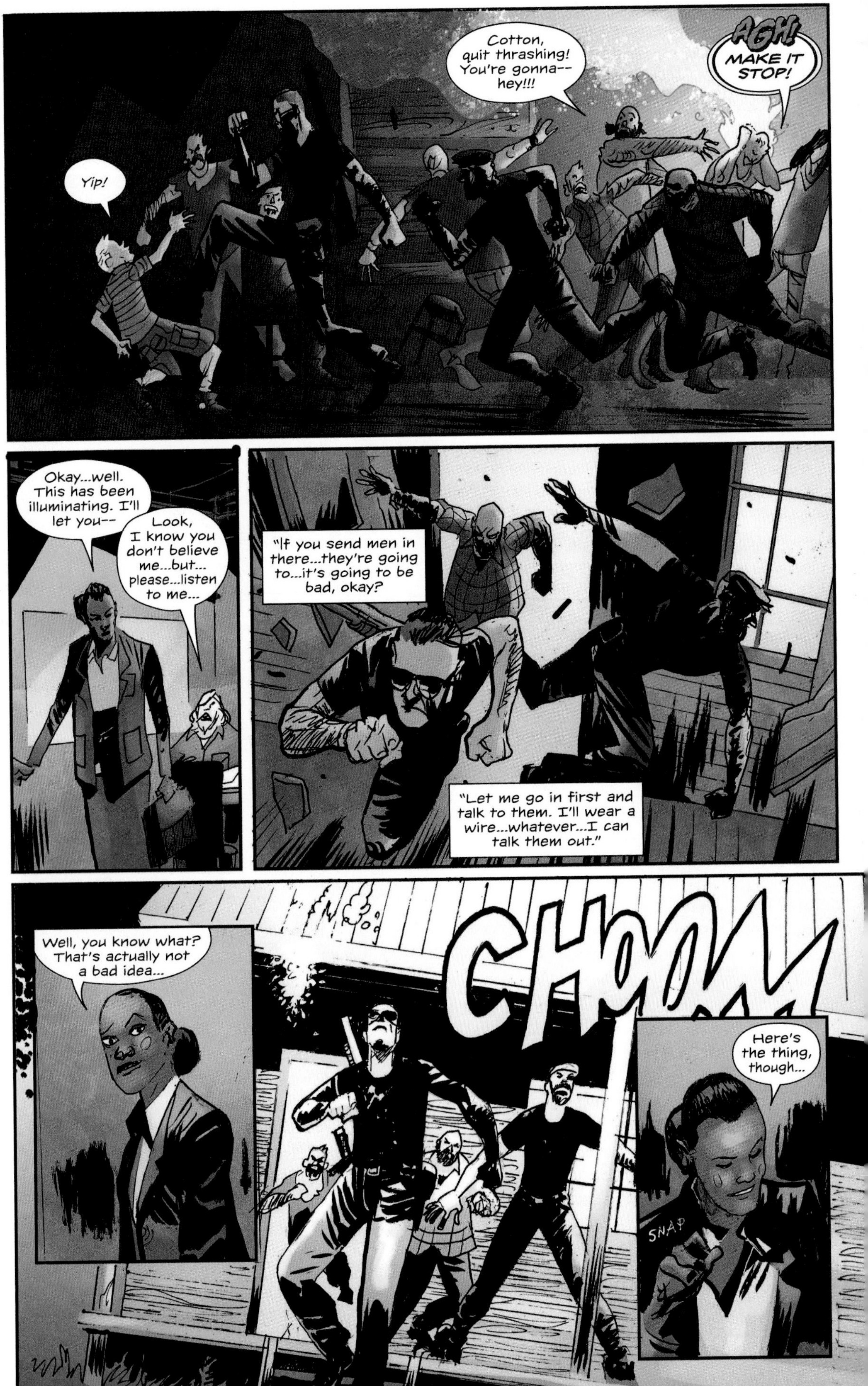
Yip!
Cotton, quit thrashing! You're gonna-- hey!!!
AGH! MAKE IT STOP!
Okay...well. This has been illuminating. I'll let you--
Look, I know you don't believe me...but... please...listen to me...
"If you send men in there...they're going to...it's going to be bad, okay?
"Let me go in first and talk to them. I'll wear a wire...whatever...I can talk them out."
Well, you know what? That's actually not a bad idea...
CHOOM
Here's the thing, though...
SNAP

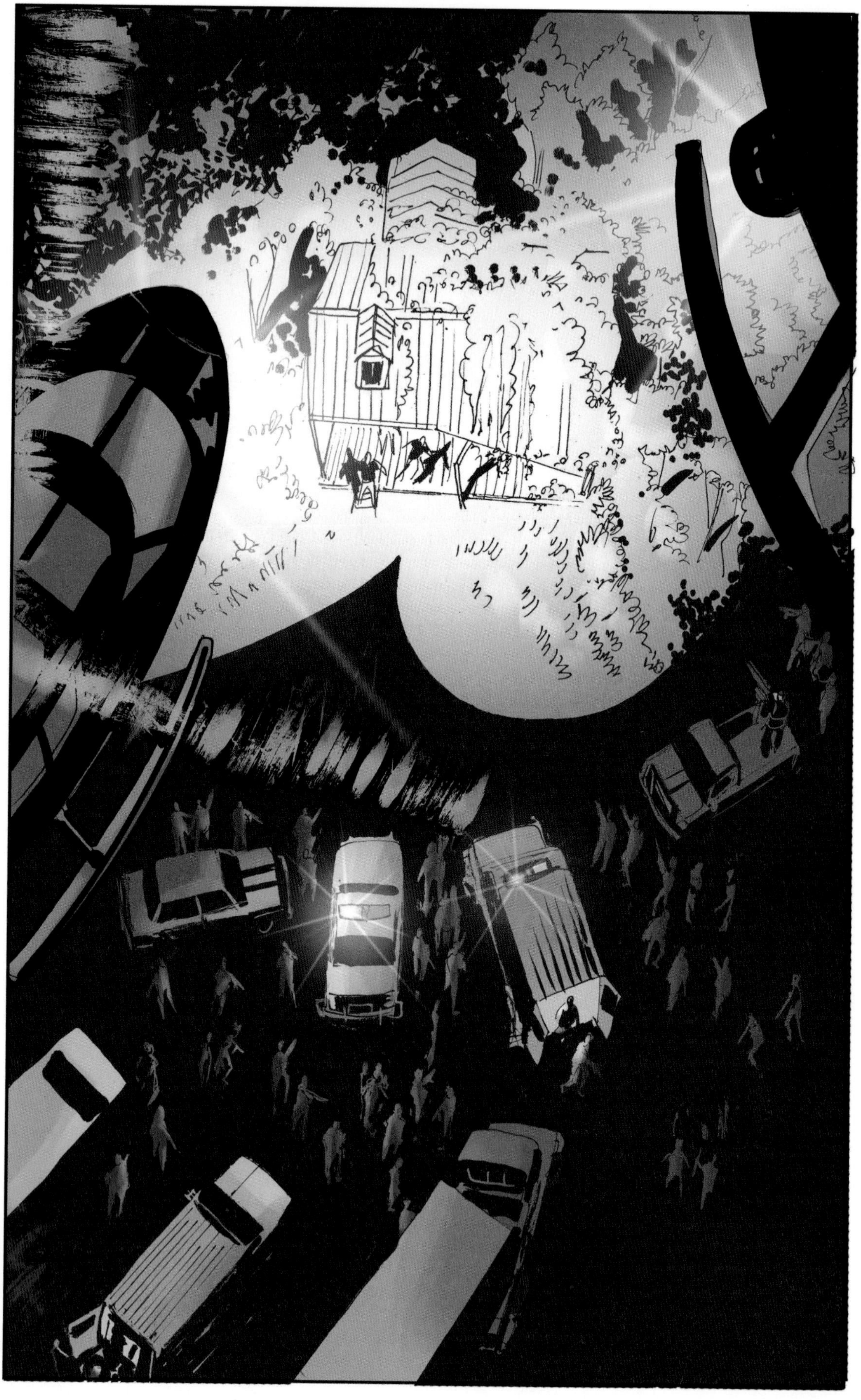

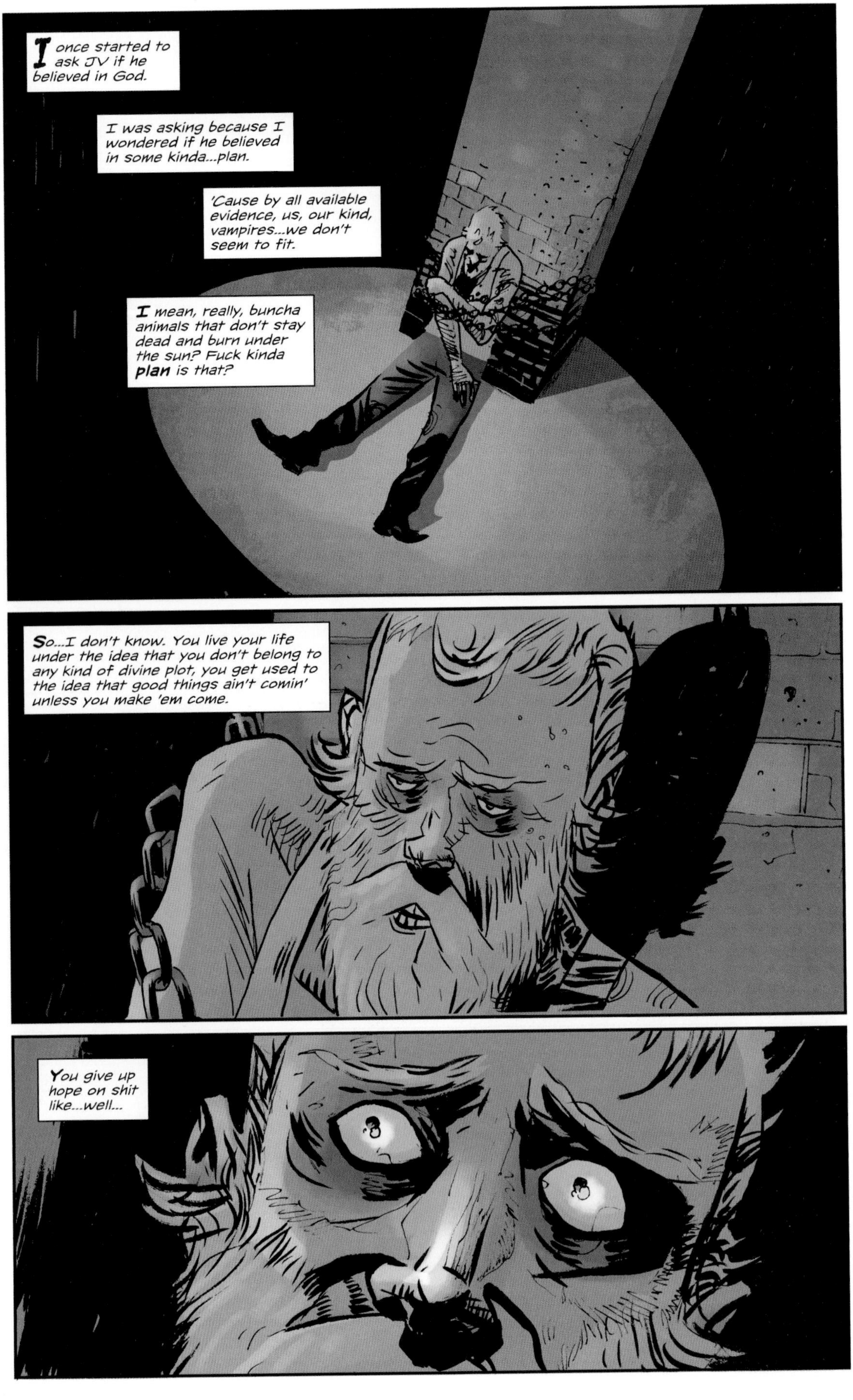
I once started to ask JV if he believed in God.
I was asking because I wondered if he believed in some kinda...plan.
'Cause by all available evidence, us, our kind, vampires...we don't seem to fit.
I mean, really, buncha animals that don't stay dead and burn under the sun? Fuck kinda plan is that?
So...I don't know. You live your life under the idea that you don't belong to any kind of divine plot, you get used to the idea that good things ain't comin' unless you make 'em come.
You give up hope on shit like...well...

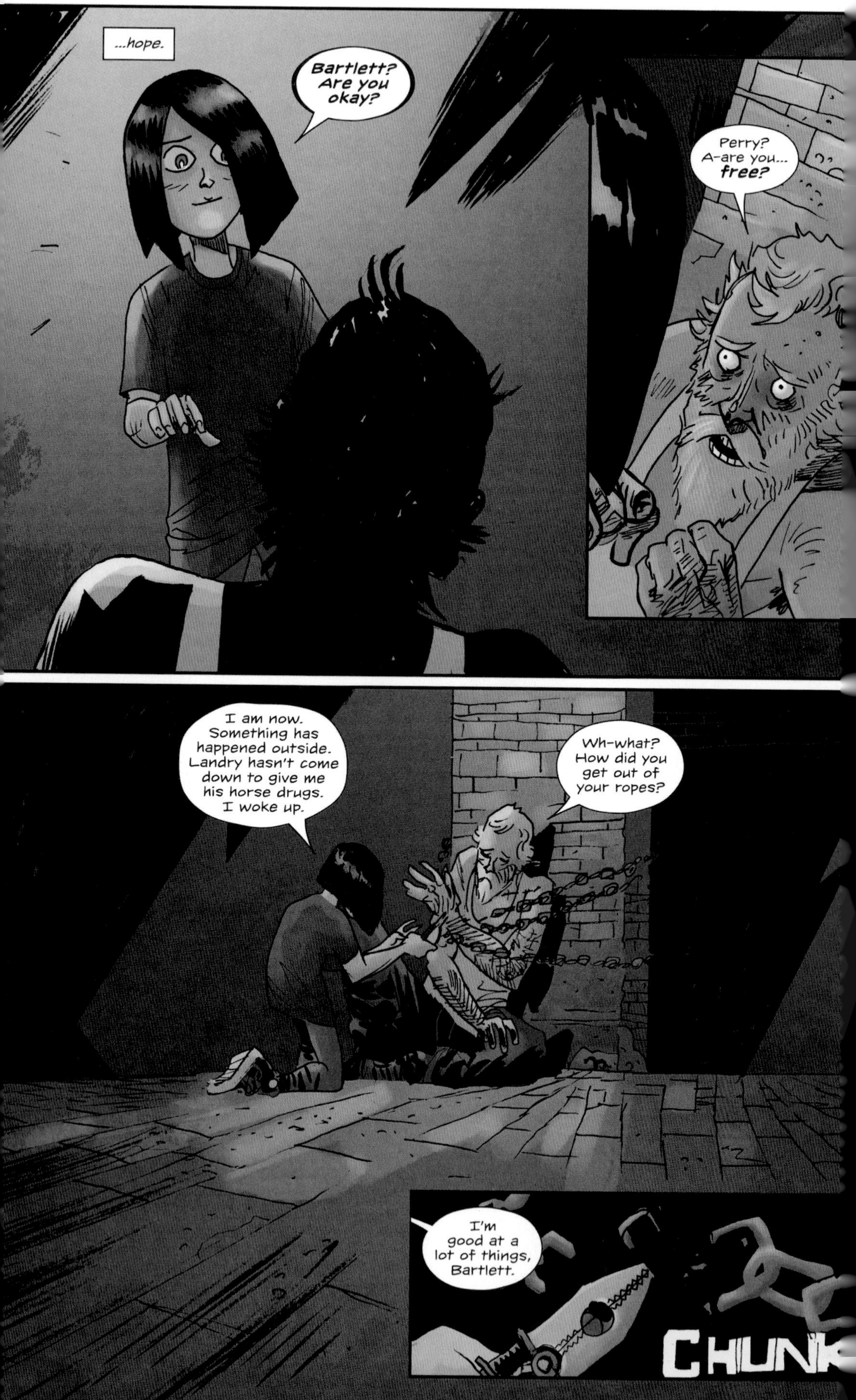
...hope.
Bartlett? Are you okay?
Perry? A-are you... free?
I am now. Something has happened outside. Landry hasn't come down to give me his horse drugs. I woke up.
Wh-what? How did you get out of your ropes?
I'm good at a lot of things, Bartlett.
CHUNK

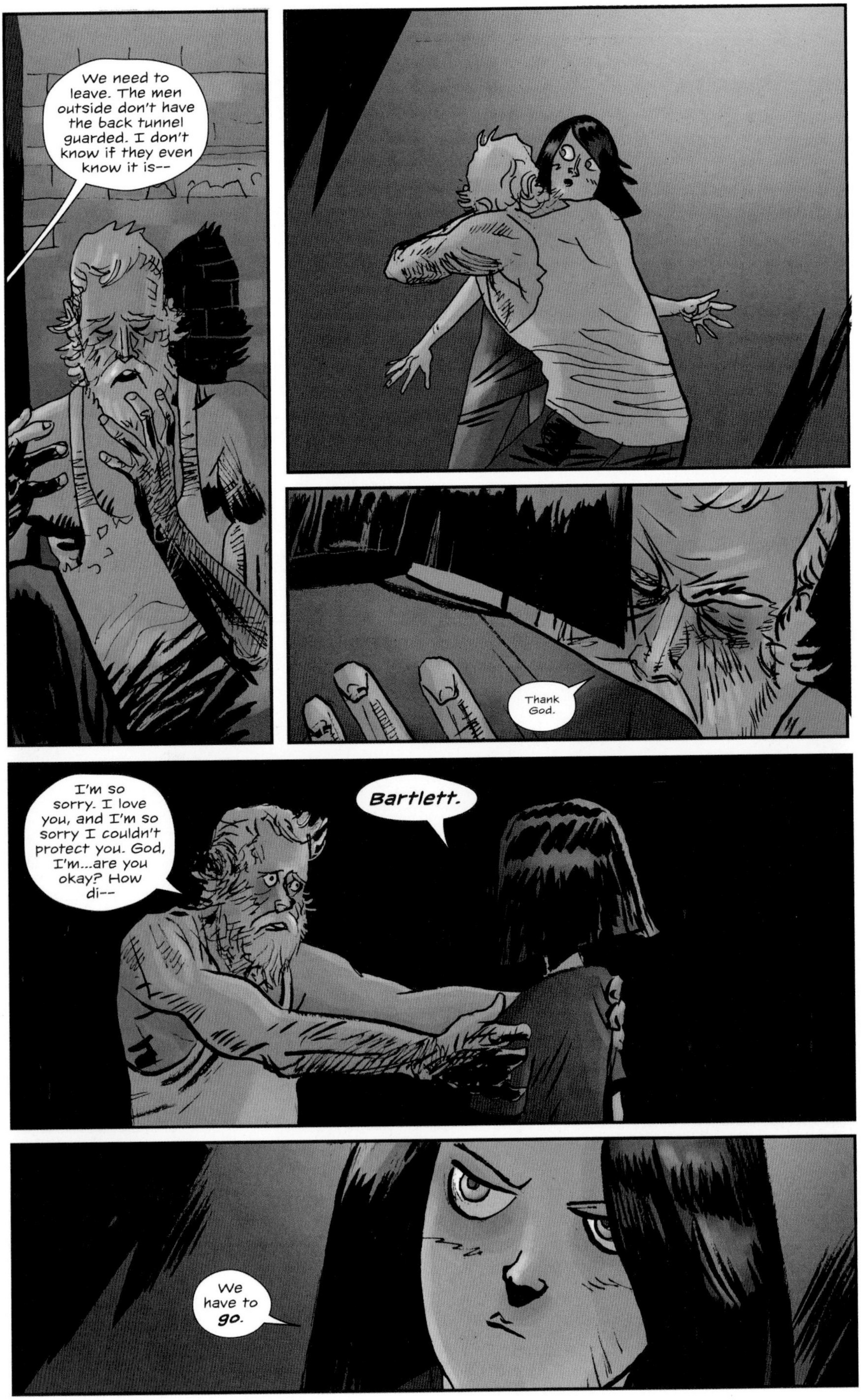
We need to leave. The men outside don't have the back tunnel guarded. I don't know if they even know it is--
Thank God.
I'm so sorry. I love you, and I'm so sorry I couldn't protect you. God, I'm...are you okay? How di--
Bartlett.
We have to go.

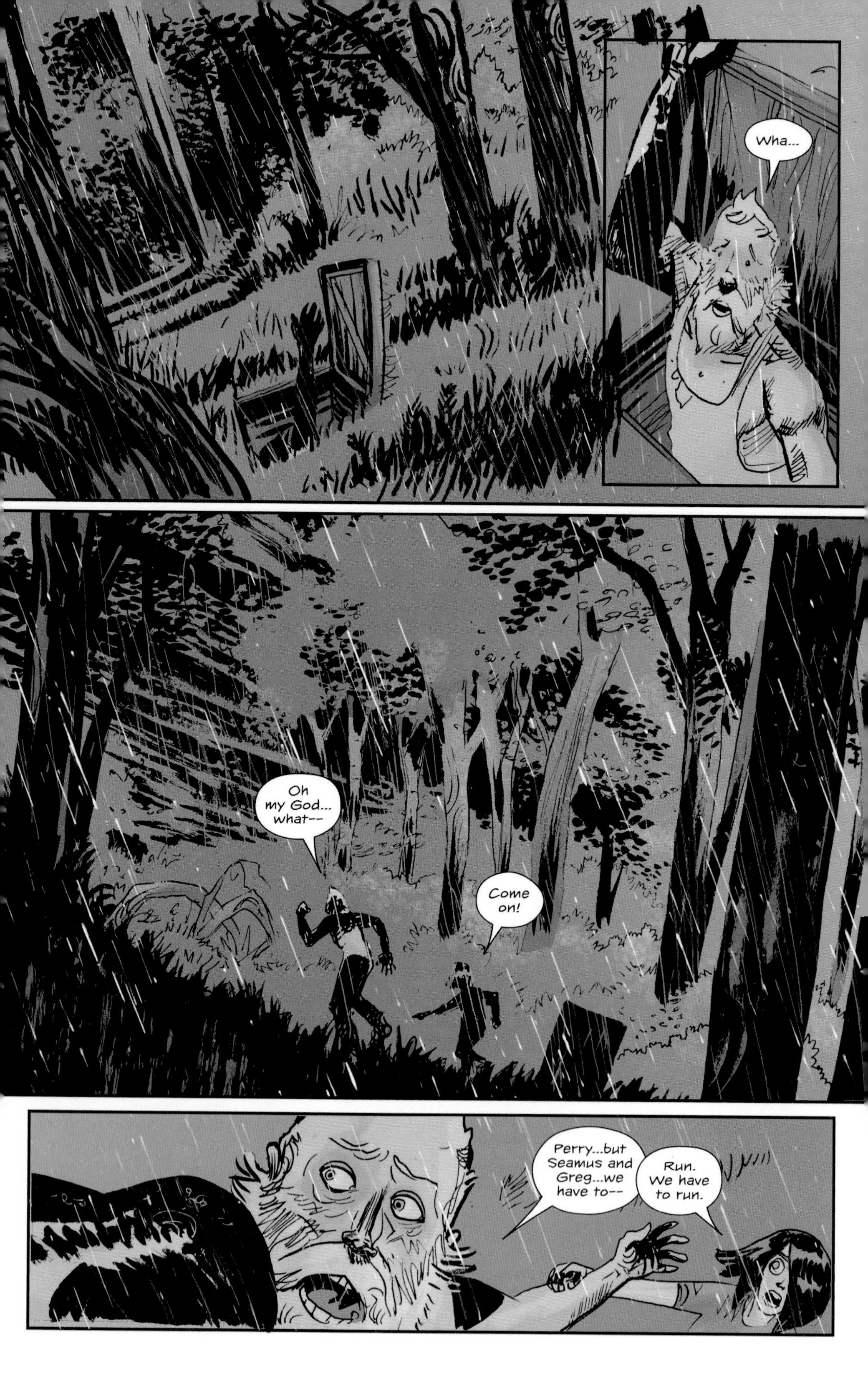
Wha...
Oh my God... what--
Come on!
Perry...but Seamus and Greg...we have to--
Run. We have to run.

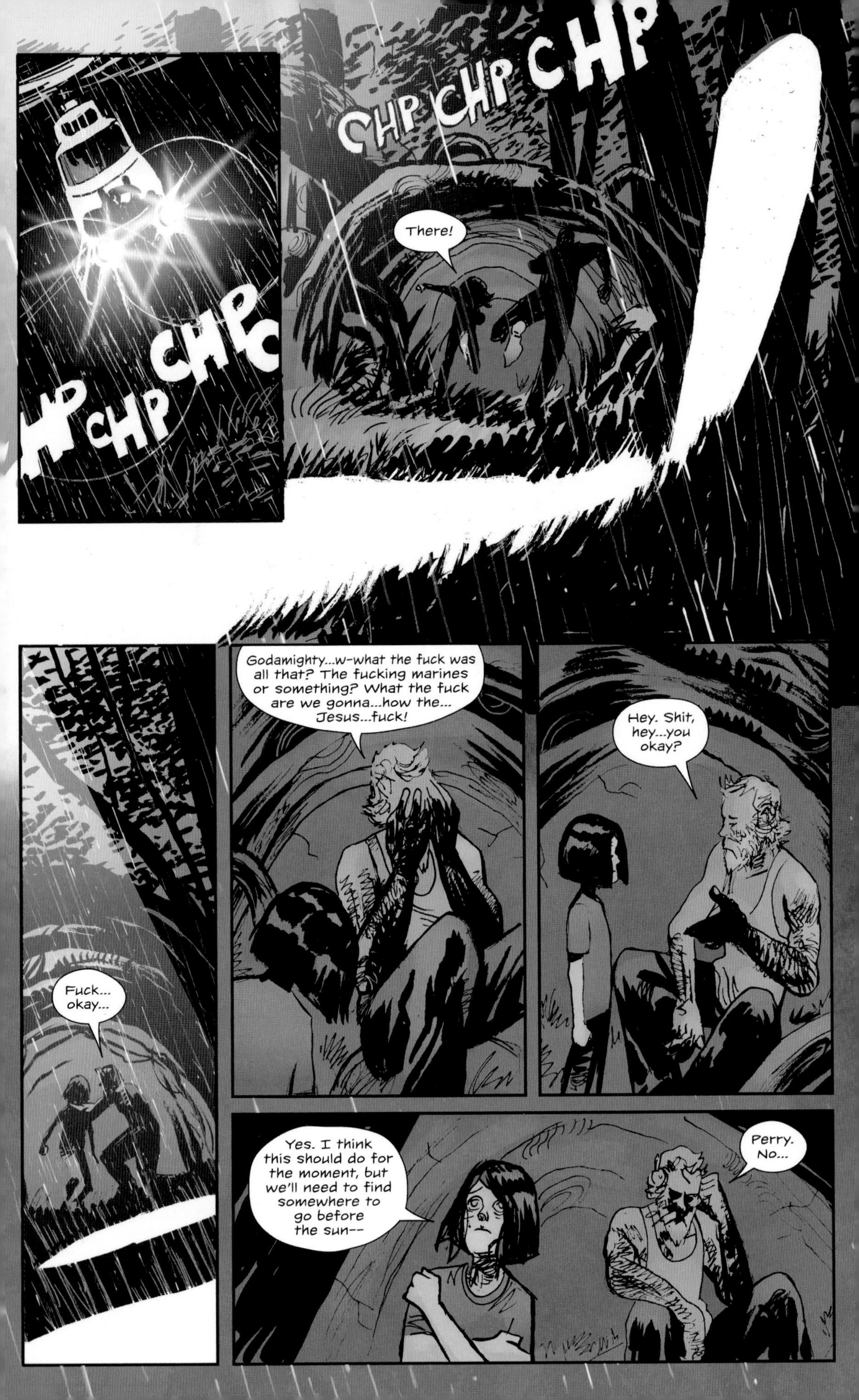
HP CHP CHP
CHP CHP CHP
There!
Fuck... okay...
Godamighty...w-what the fuck was all that? The fucking marines or something? What the fuck are we gonna...how the... Jesus...fuck!
Hey. Shit, hey...you okay?
Yes. I think this should do for the moment, but we'll need to find somewhere to go before the sun--
Perry. No...

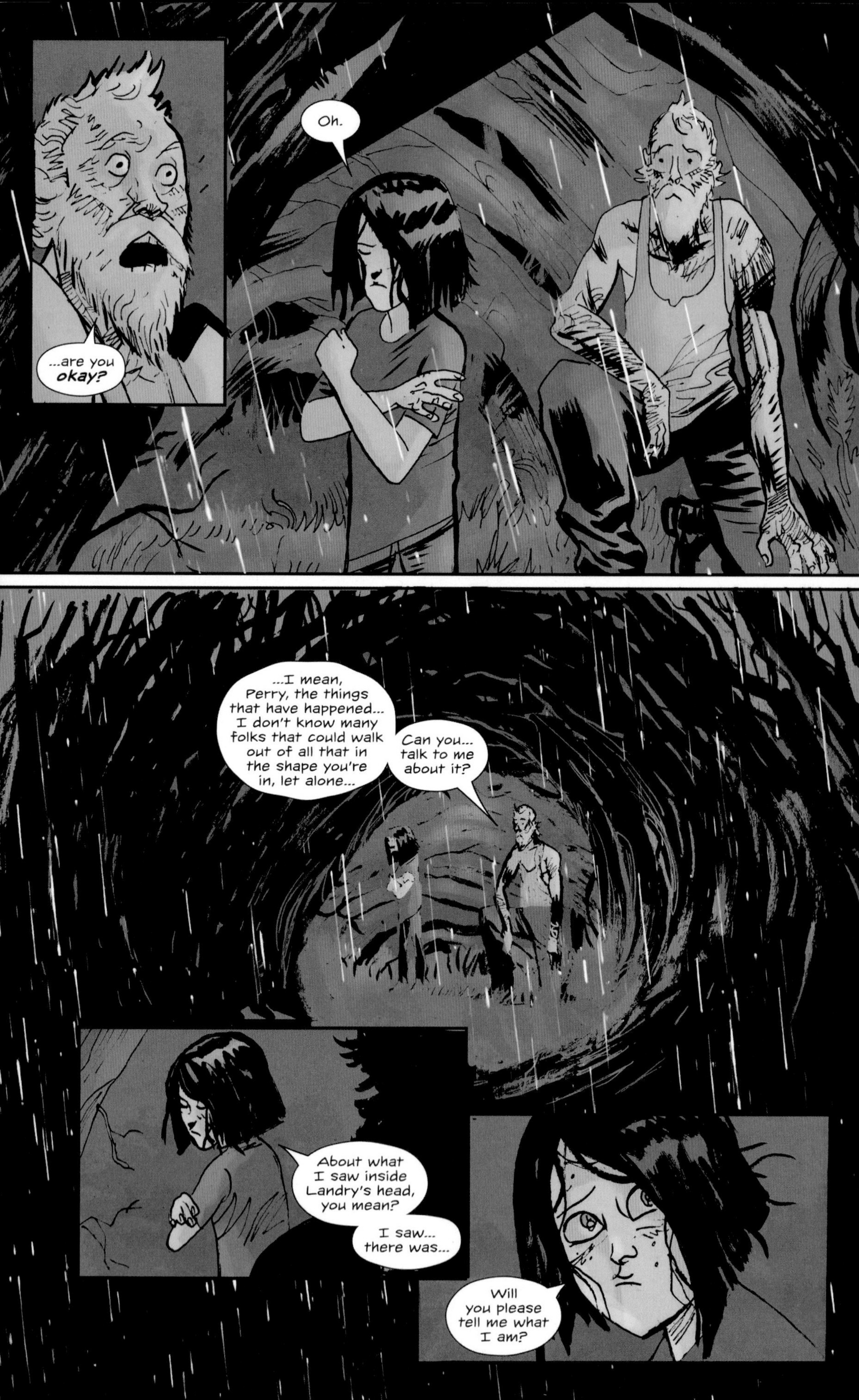

...are you okay?
Oh.
...I mean, Perry, the things that have happened... I don't know many folks that could walk out of all that in the shape you're in, let alone...
Can you... talk to me about it?
About what I saw inside Landry's head, you mean?
I saw... there was...
Will you please tell me what I am?

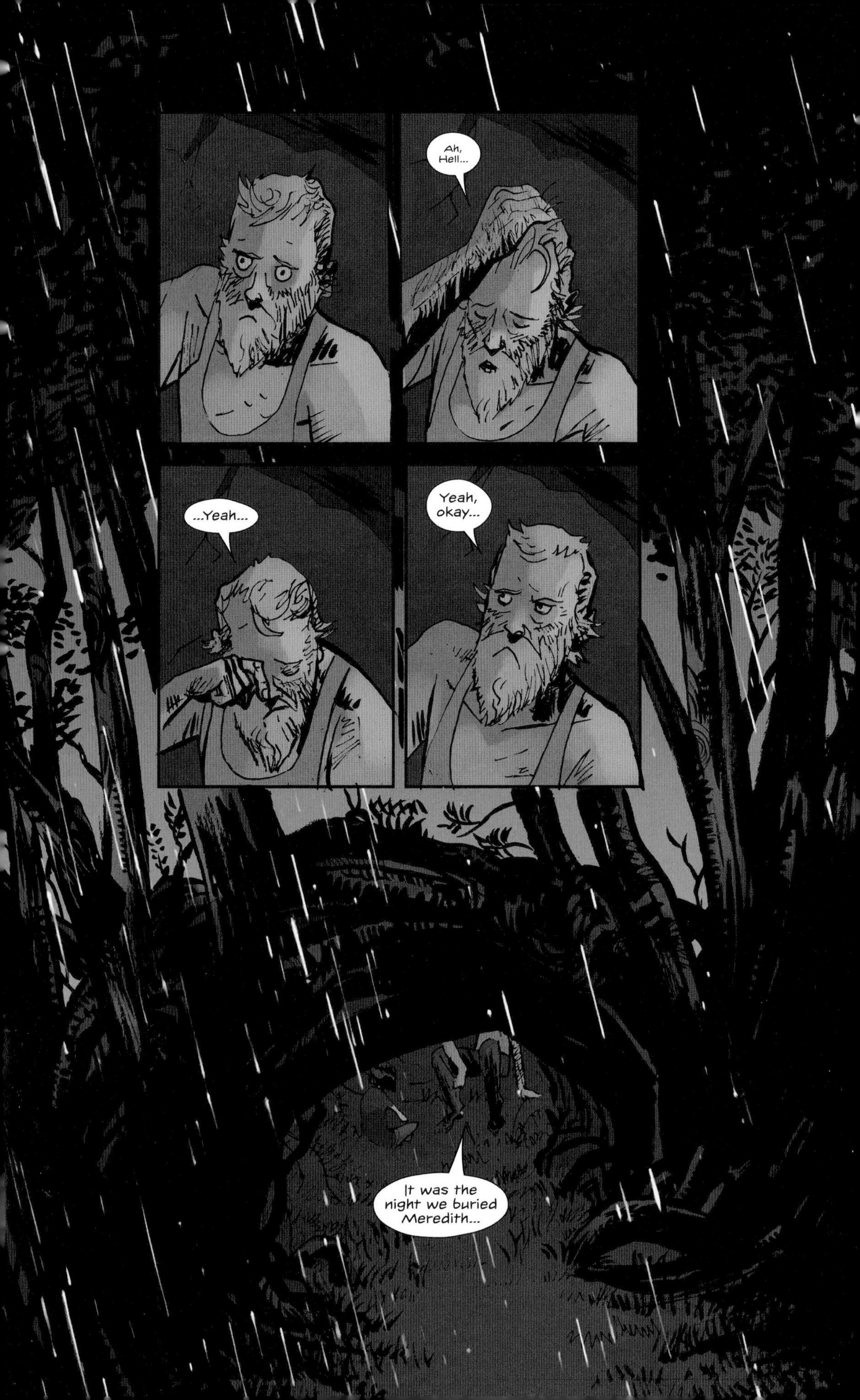
Ah, Hell...
...Yeah...
Yeah, okay...
It was the night we buried Meredith...

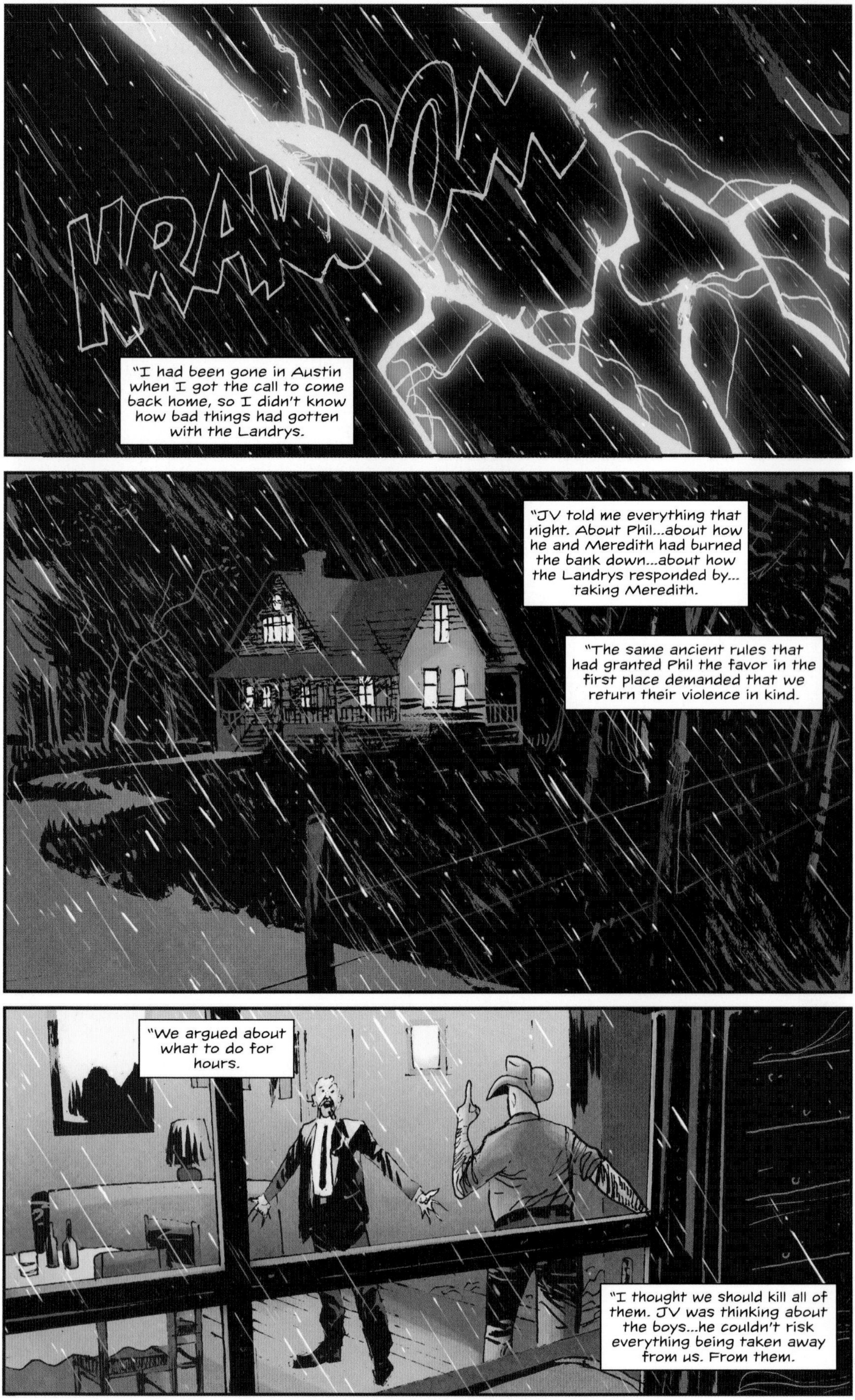
KRAWOOOM
"I had been gone in Austin when I got the call to come back home, so I didn't know how bad things had gotten with the Landrys.
"JV told me everything that night. About Phil...about how he and Meredith had burned the bank down...about how the Landrys responded by... taking Meredith.
"The same ancient rules that had granted Phil the favor in the first place demanded that we return their violence in kind.
"We argued about what to do for hours.
"I thought we should kill all of them. JV was thinking about the boys...he couldn't risk everything being taken away from us. From them.

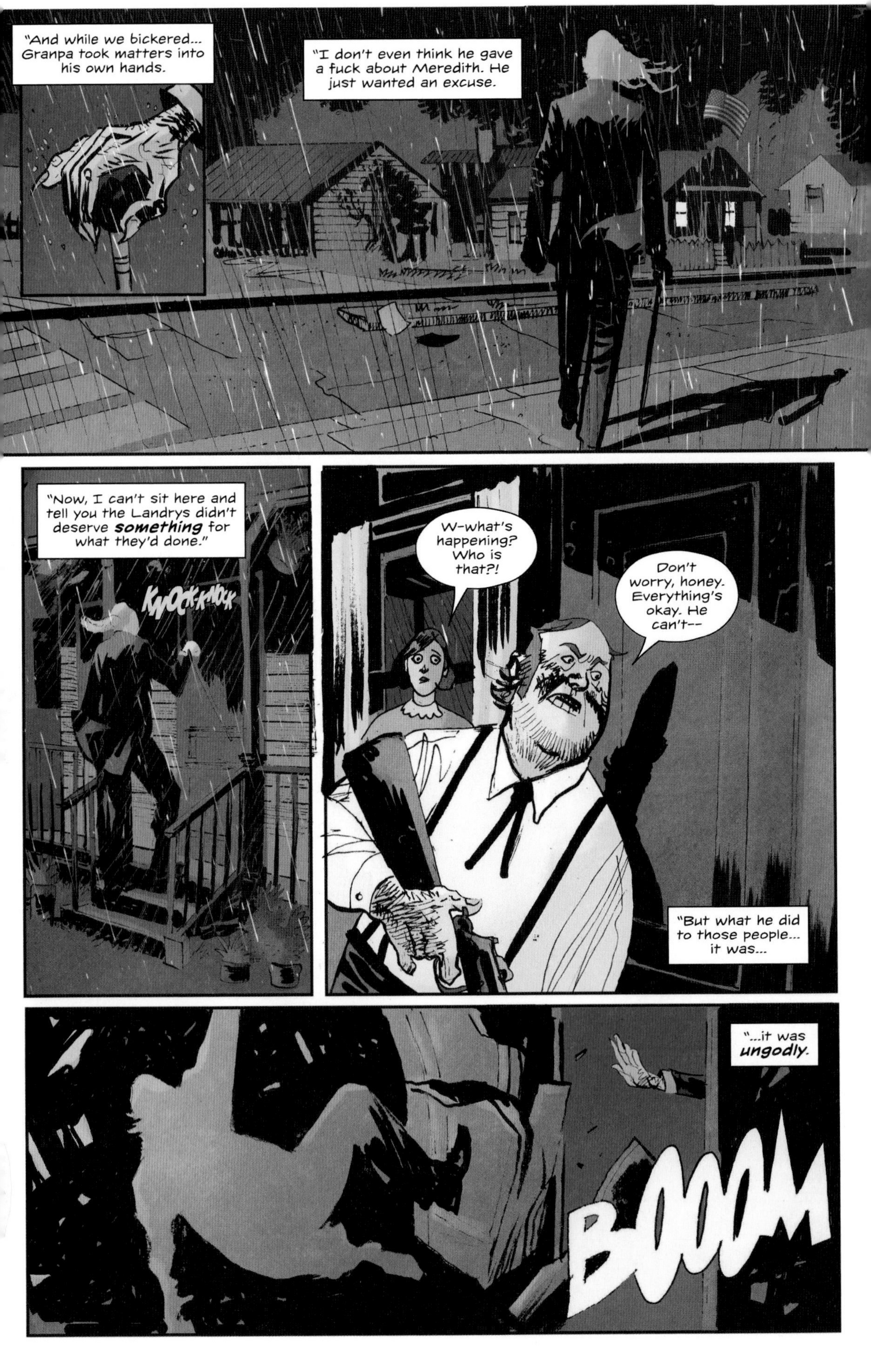
"And while we bickered... Granpa took matters into his own hands.
"I don't even think he gave a fuck about Meredith. He just wanted an excuse.
"Now, I can't sit here and tell you the Landrys didn't deserve **something** for what they'd done."
KNOCK-KNOCK
W-what's happening? Who is that?!
Don't worry, honey. Everything's okay. He can't--
"But what he did to those people... it was...
"...it was **ungodly**.
BOOOM

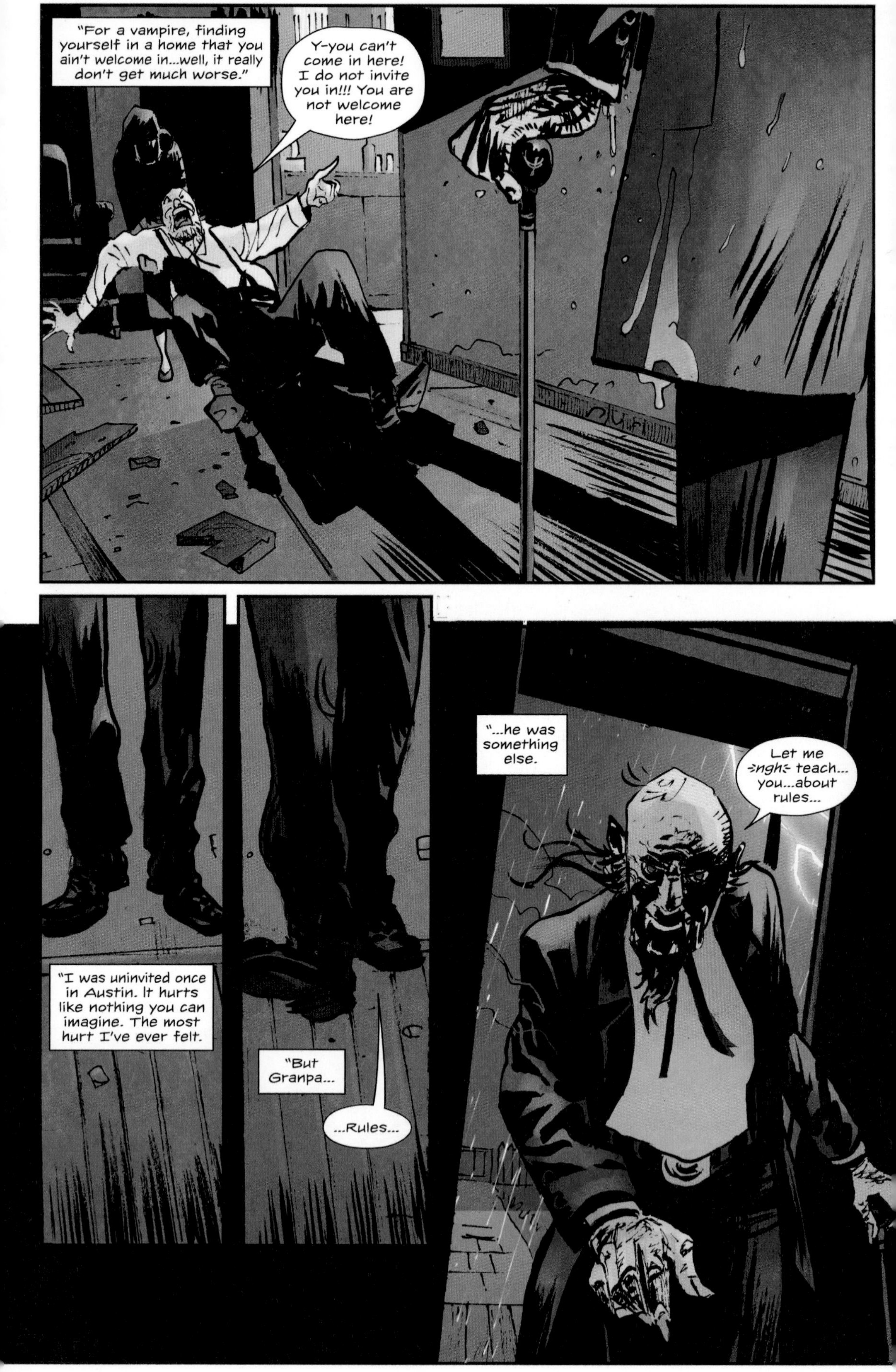
"For a vampire, finding yourself in a home that you ain't welcome in...well, it really don't get much worse."
Y-you can't come in here! I do not invite you in!!! You are not welcome here!
"I was uninvited once in Austin. It hurts like nothing you can imagine. The most hurt I've ever felt.
"But Granpa...
...Rules...
"...he was something else.
Let me -ngh- teach... you...about rules...

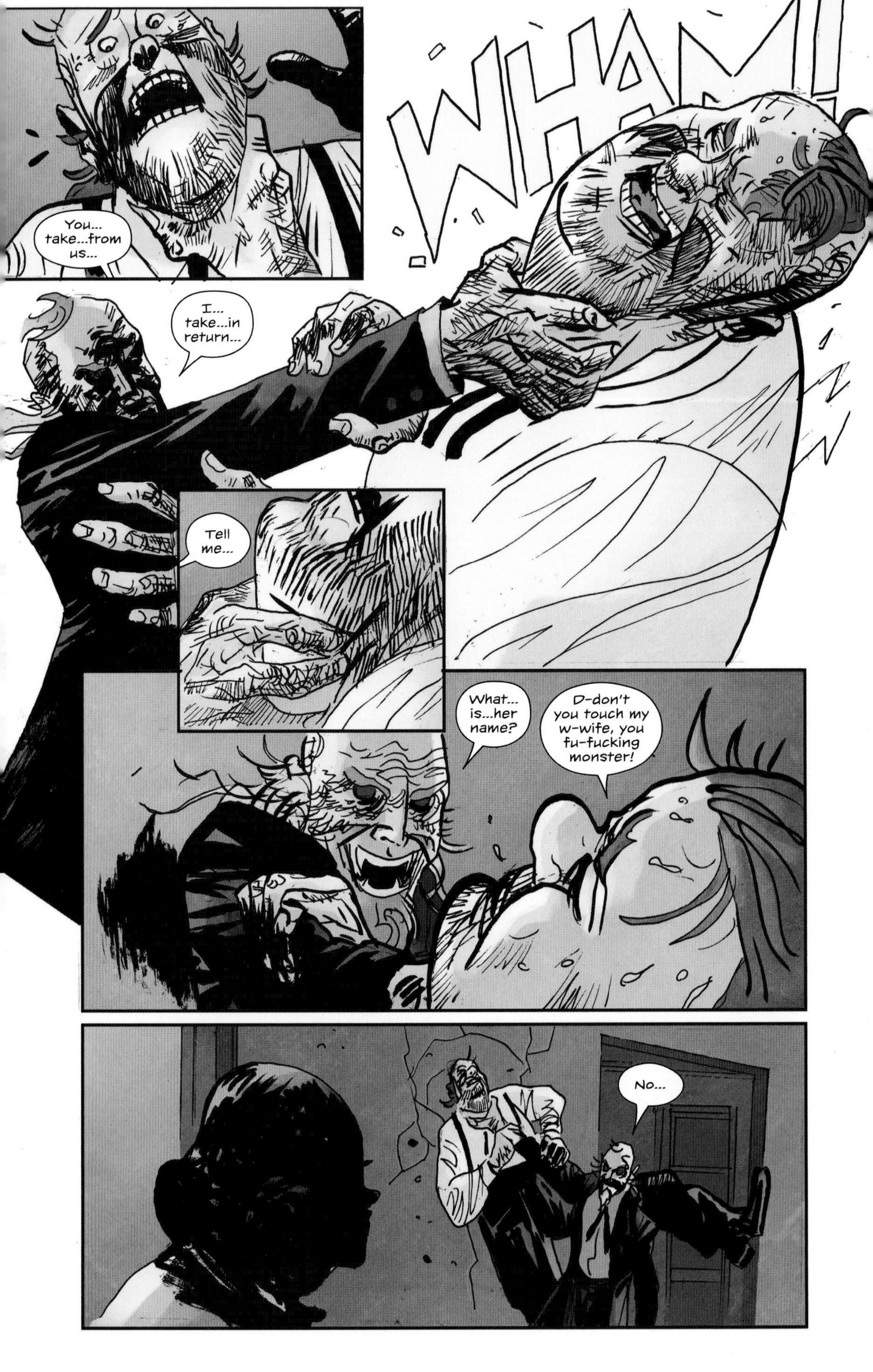
You... take...from us...
WHAM!
I... take...in return...
Tell me...
What... is...her name?
D-don't you touch my w-wife, you fu-fucking monster!
No...

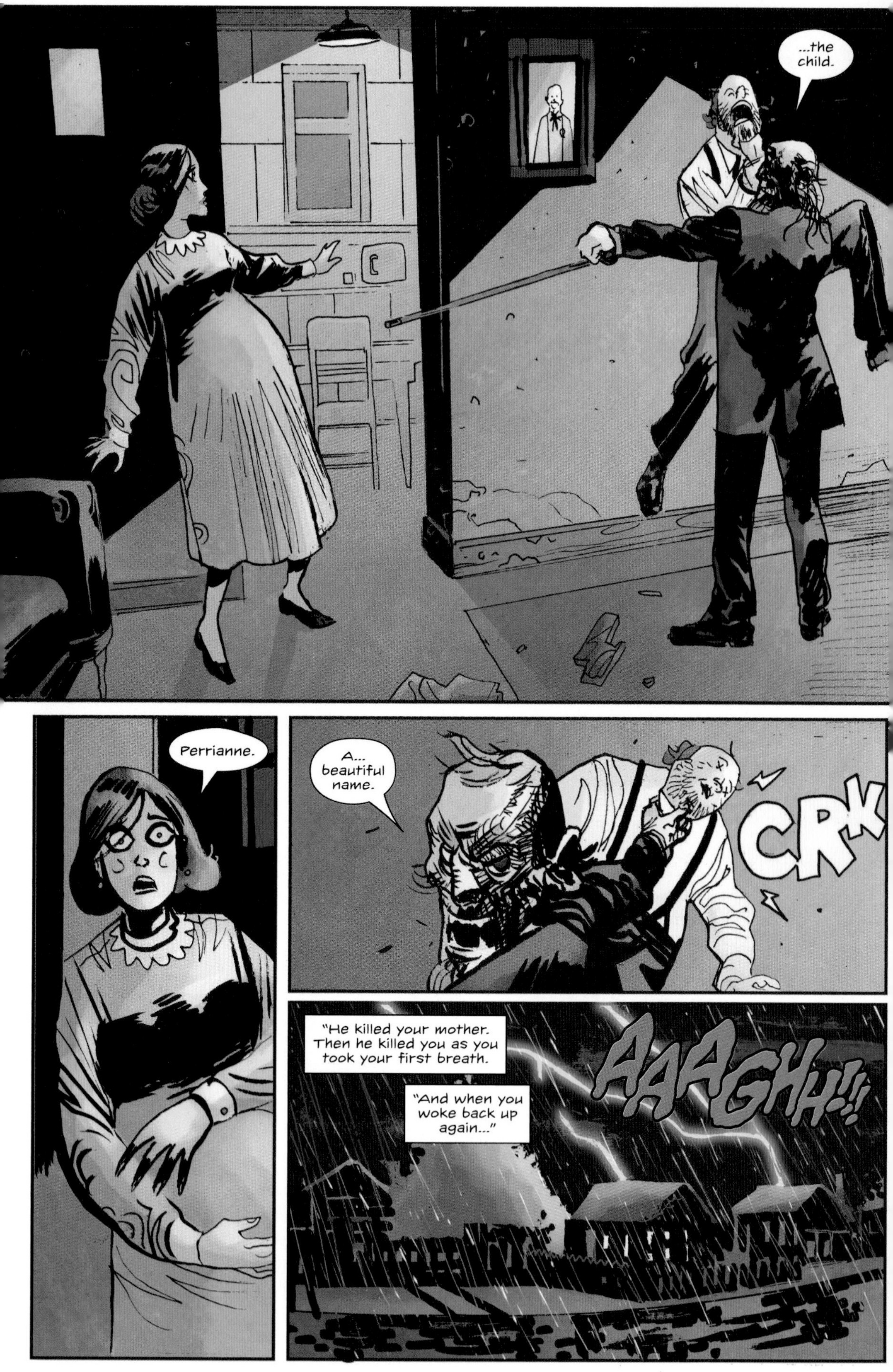
...the child.
Perrianne.
A... beautiful name.
CRK
"He killed your mother. Then he killed you as you took your first breath.
"And when you woke back up again..."
AAAGHH!!!

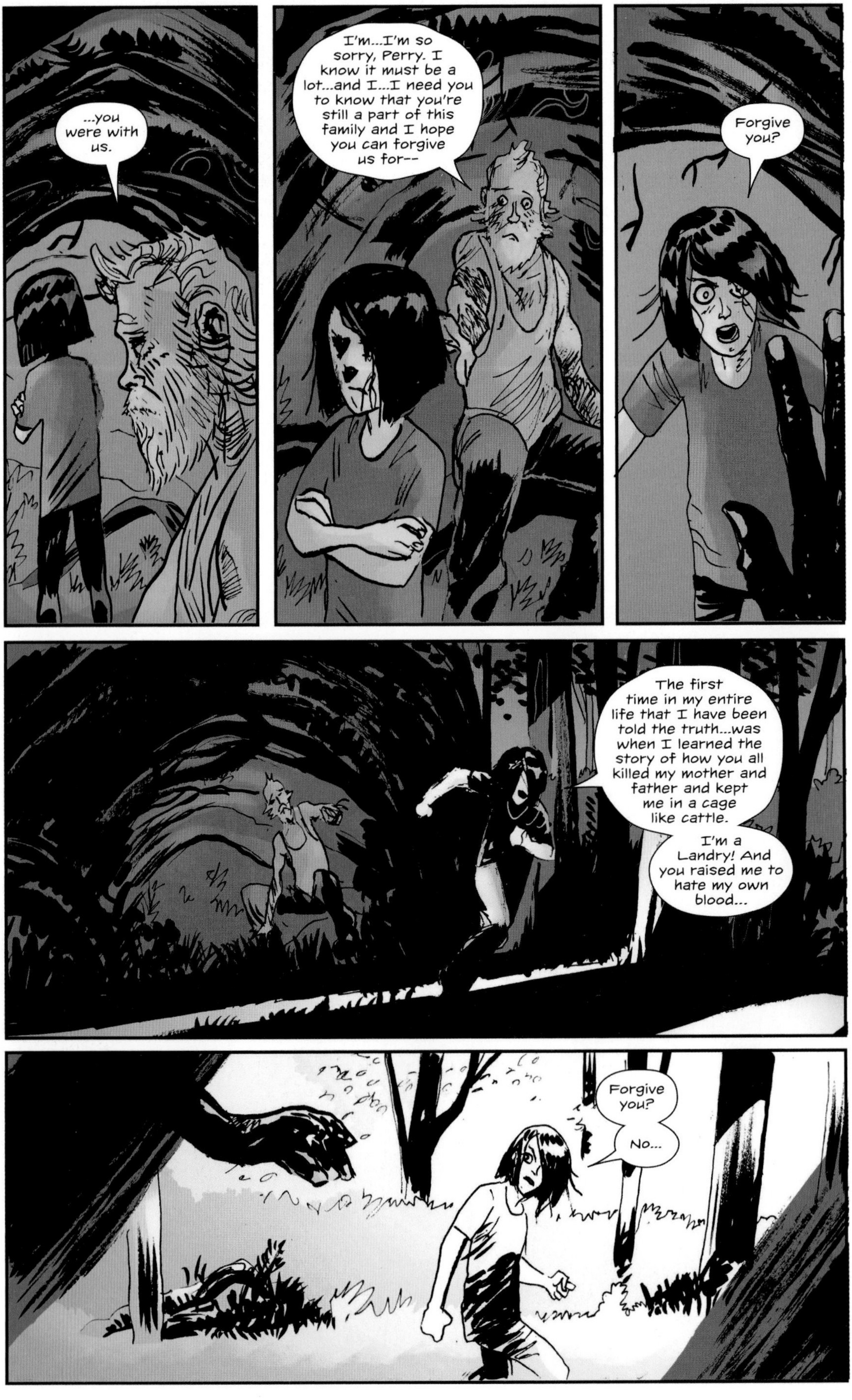
...you were with us.
I'm...I'm so sorry, Perry. I know it must be a lot...and I...I need you to know that you're still a part of this family and I hope you can forgive us for--
Forgive you?
The first time in my entire life that I have been told the truth...was when I learned the story of how you all killed my mother and father and kept me in a cage like cattle.
I'm a Landry! And you raised me to hate my own blood...
Forgive you?
No...

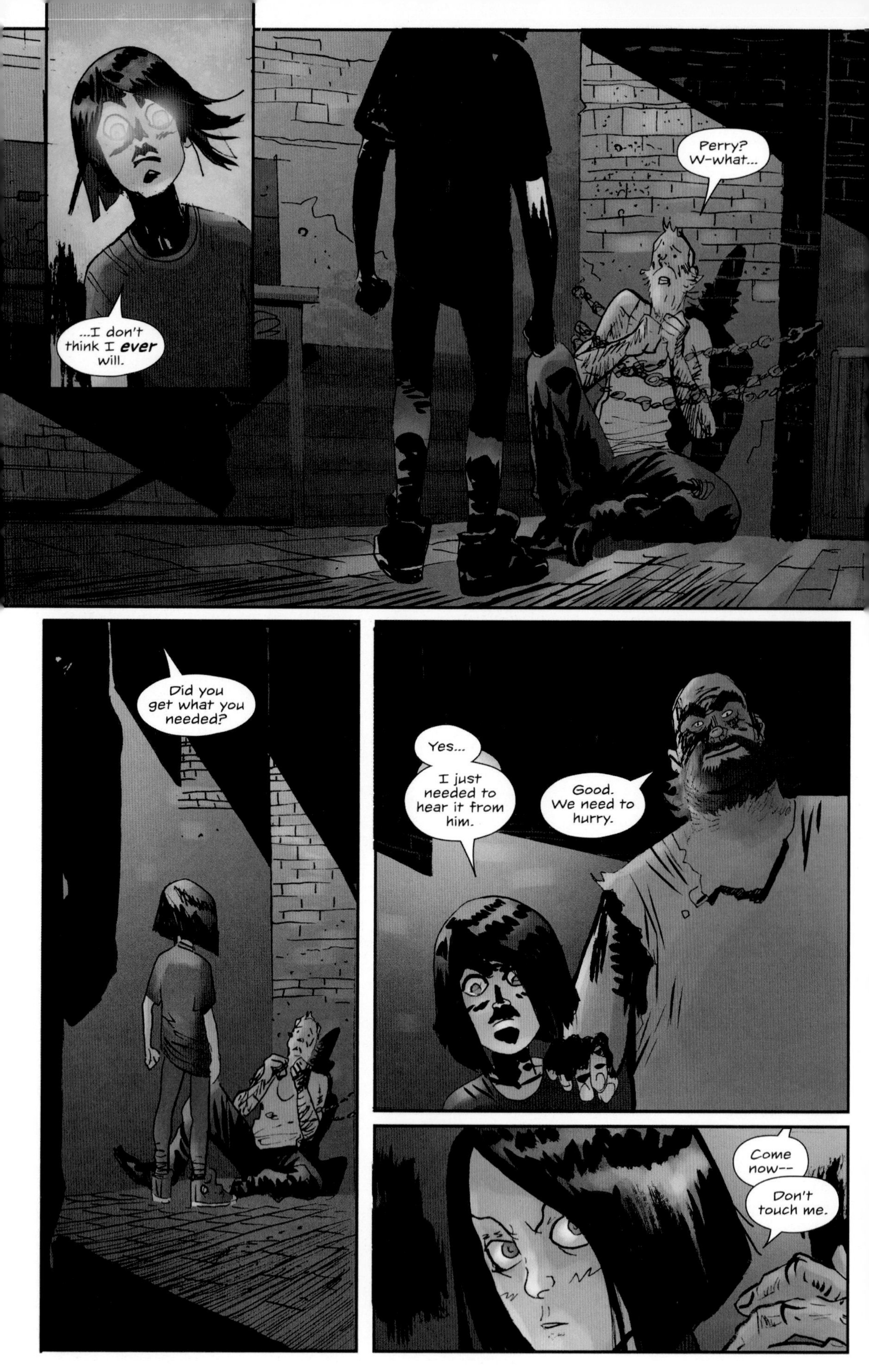
...I don't think I **ever** will.
Perry? W-what...
Did you get what you needed?
Yes...
I just needed to hear it from him.
Good. We need to hurry.
Come now--
Don't touch me.

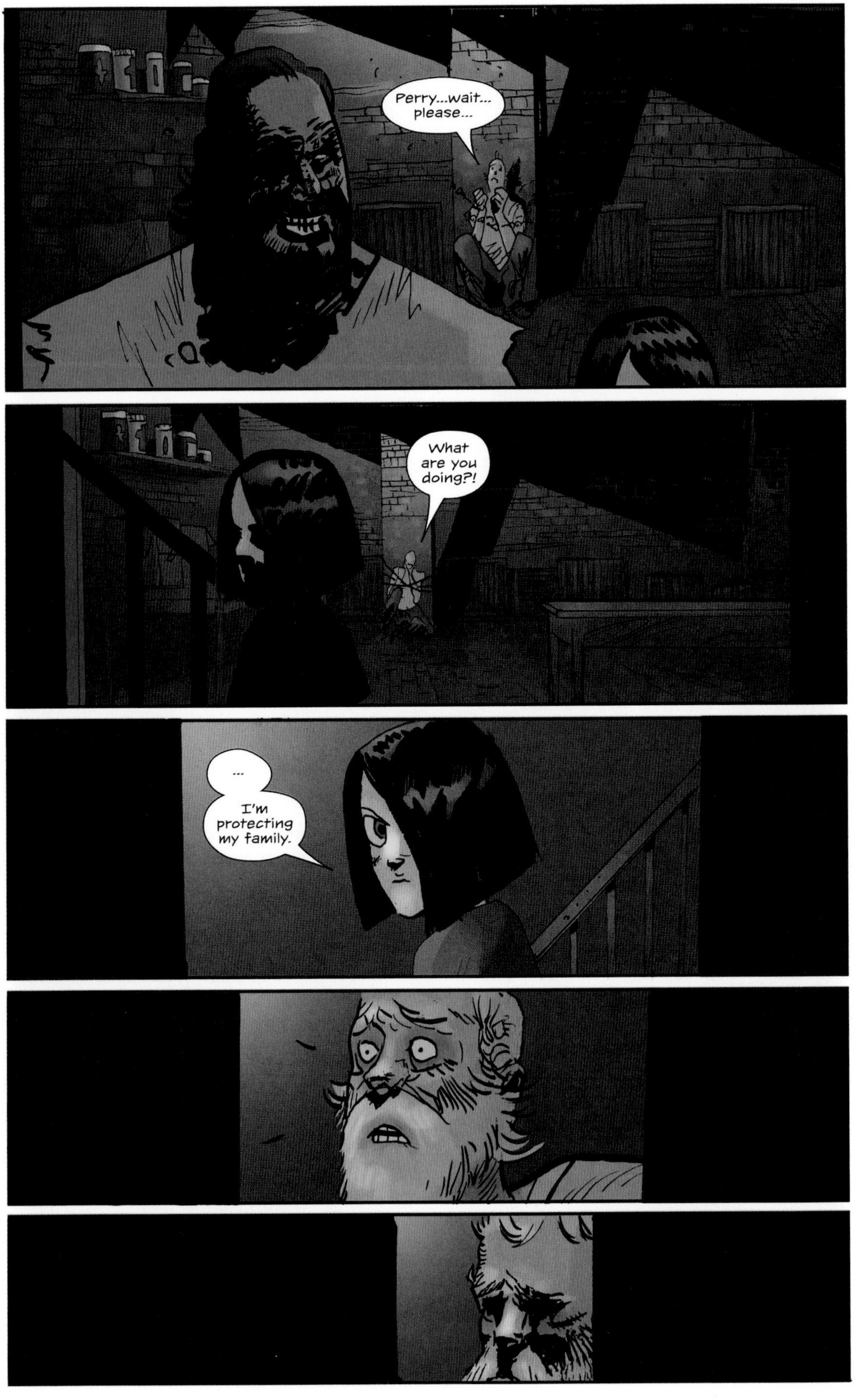

Perry...wait... please...
What are you doing?!
...
I'm protecting my family.

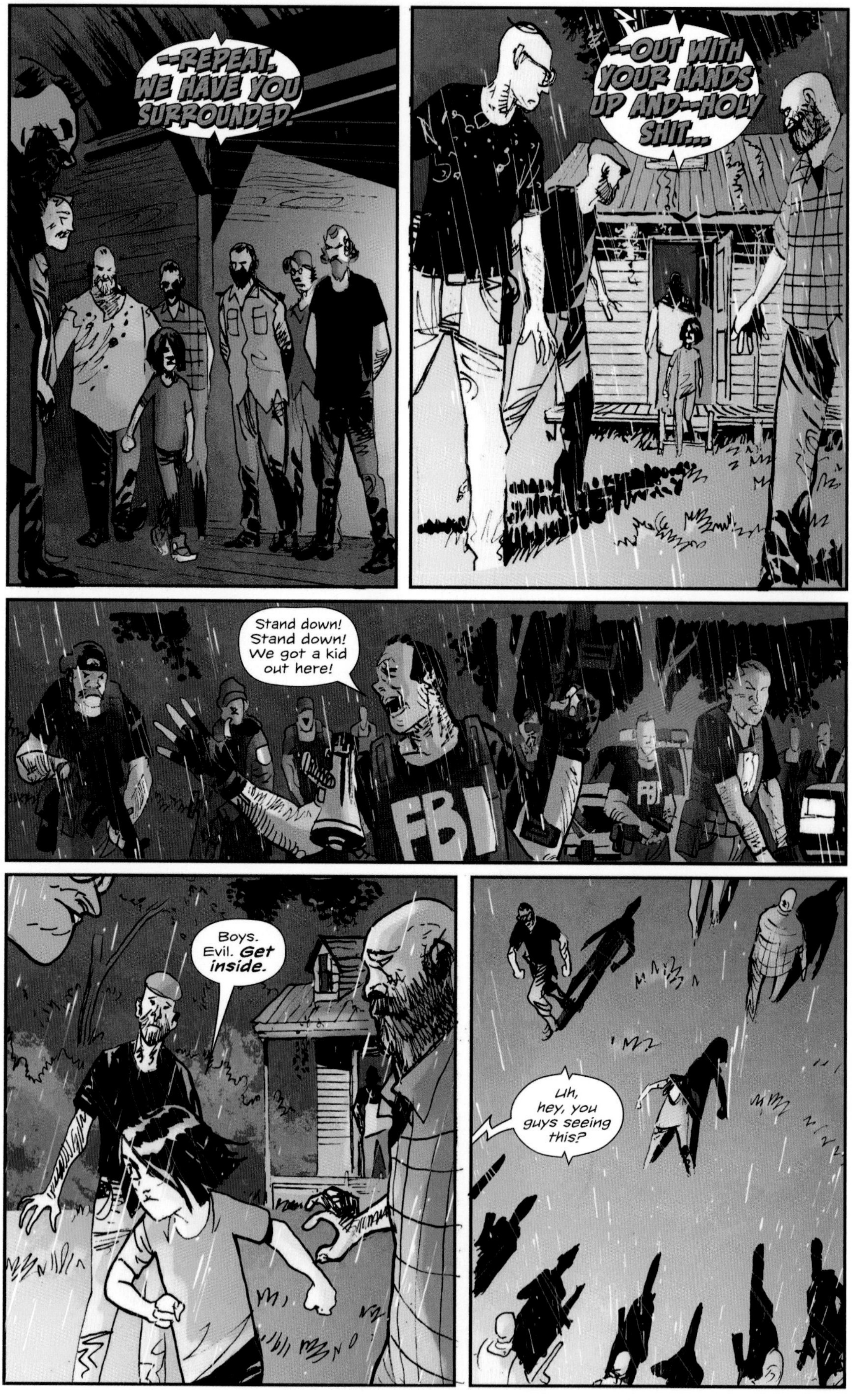
--REPEAT. WE HAVE YOU SURROUNDED.
--OUT WITH YOUR HANDS UP AND--HOLY SHIT...
Stand down! Stand down! We got a kid out here!
Boys. Evil. **Get inside.**
Uh, hey, you guys seeing this?

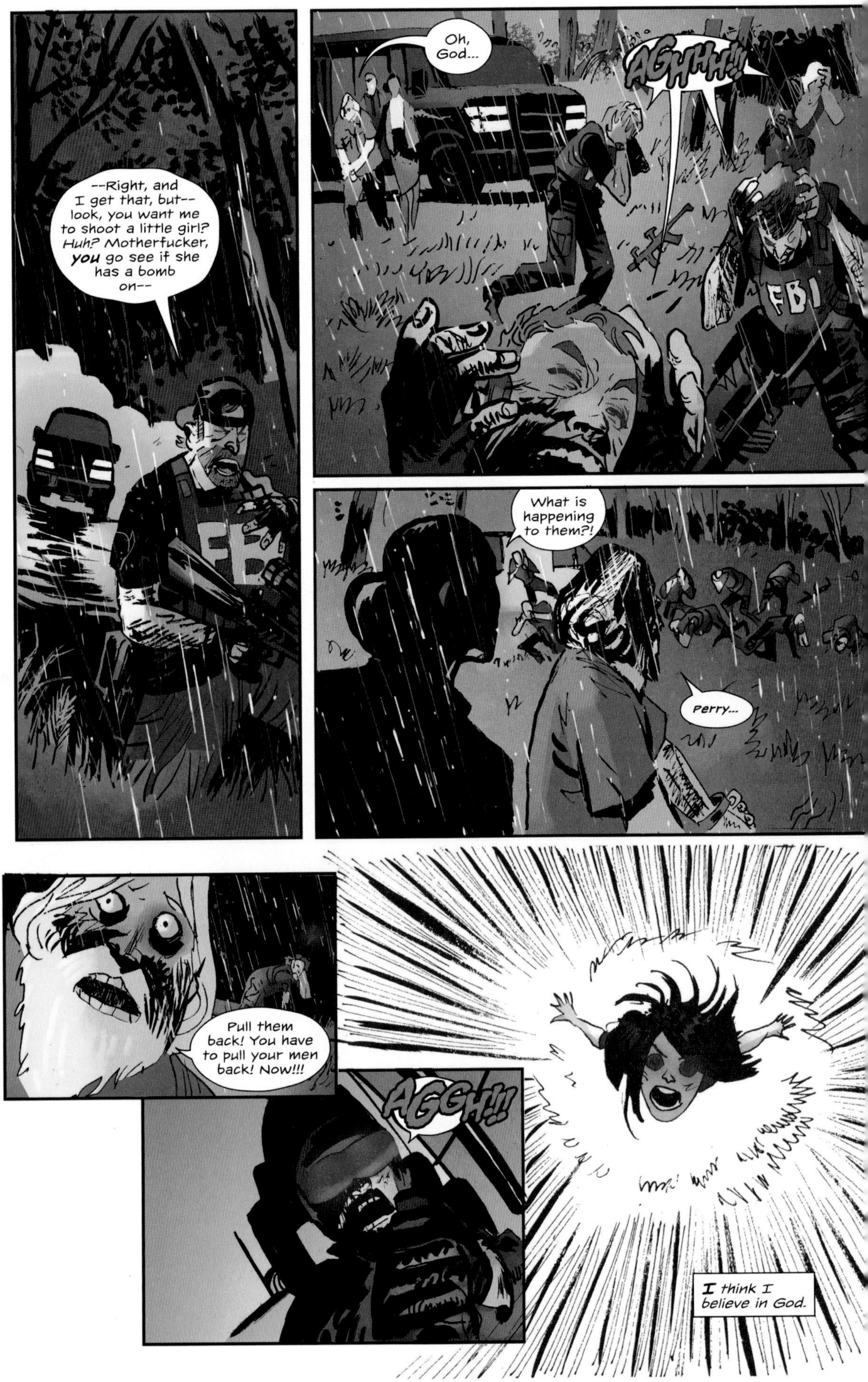
--Right, and I get that, but-- look, you want me to shoot a little girl? Huh? Motherfucker, you go see if she has a bomb on--
Oh, God...
AGHHH!!
FBI
FBI
FBI
What is happening to them?!
Perry...
Pull them back! You have to pull your men back! Now!!!
AGGH!!
I think I believe in God.

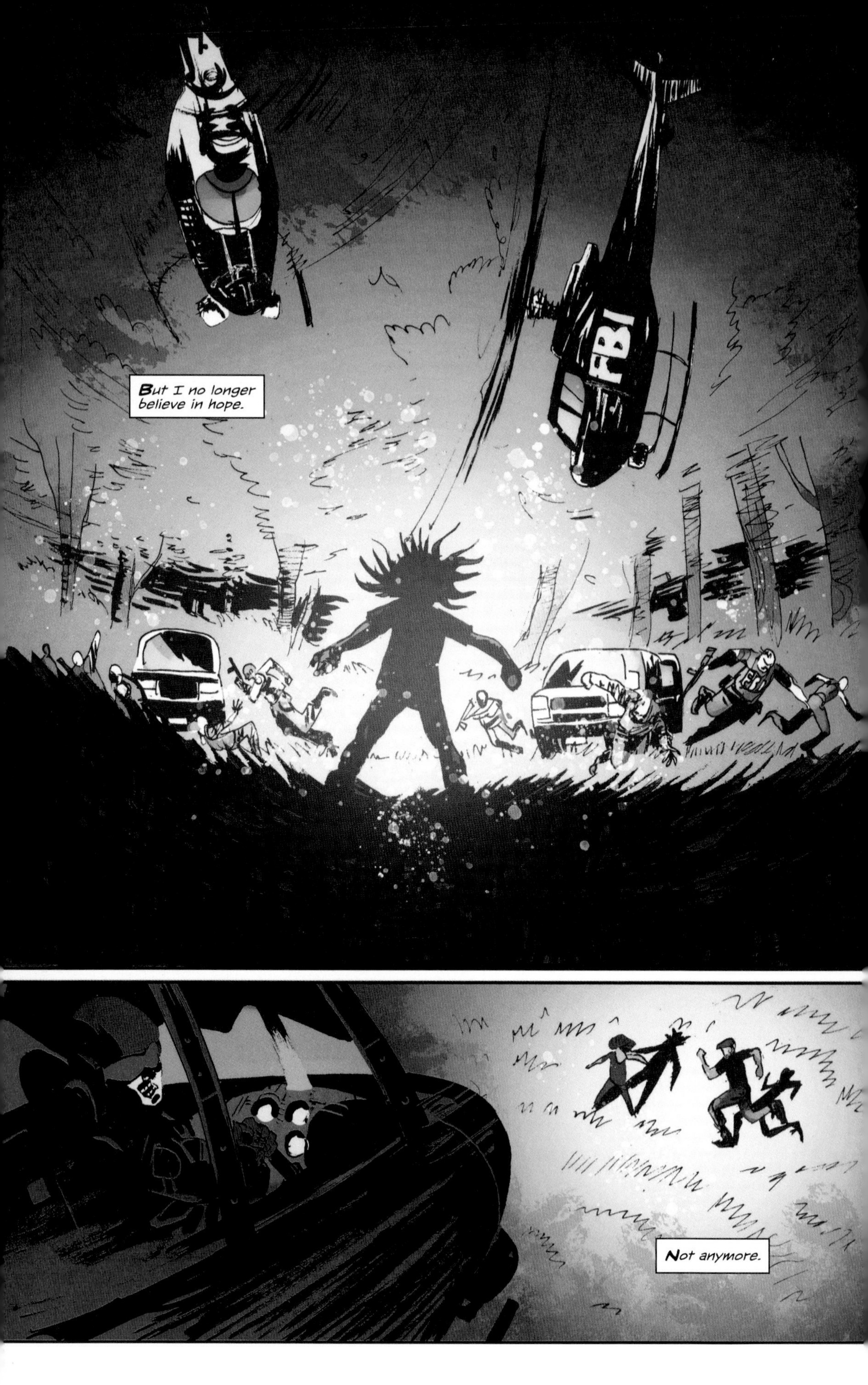
But I no longer believe in hope.
FBI
Not anymore.

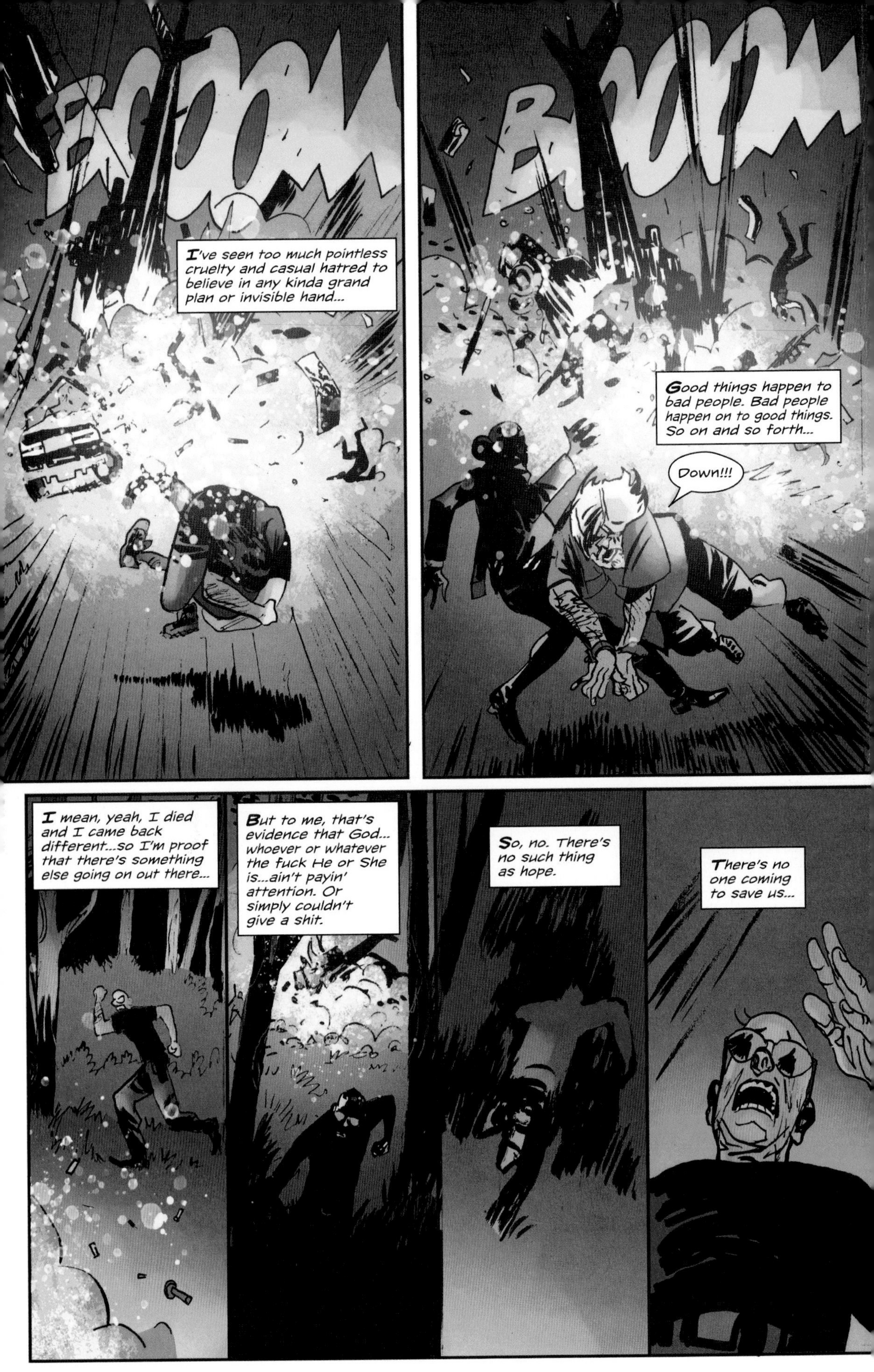
BOOOM
I've seen too much pointless cruelty and casual hatred to believe in any kinda grand plan or invisible hand...
BOOOM
Good things happen to bad people. Bad people happen on to good things. So on and so forth...
Down!!!
I mean, yeah, I died and I came back different...so I'm proof that there's something else going on out there...
But to me, that's evidence that God... whoever or whatever the fuck He or She is...ain't payin' attention. Or simply couldn't give a shit.
So, no. There's no such thing as hope.
There's no one coming to save us...

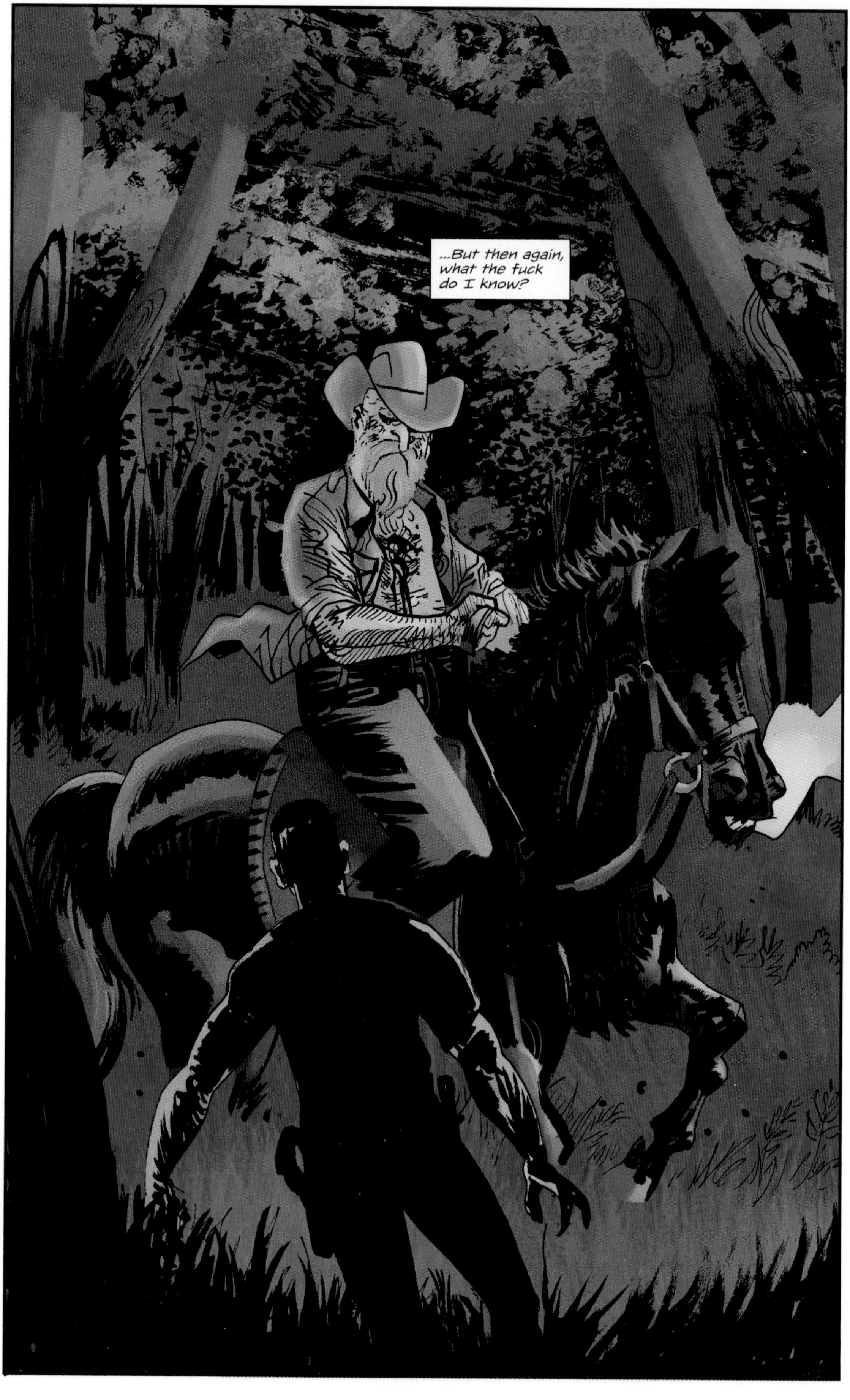
...But then again, what the fuck do I know?

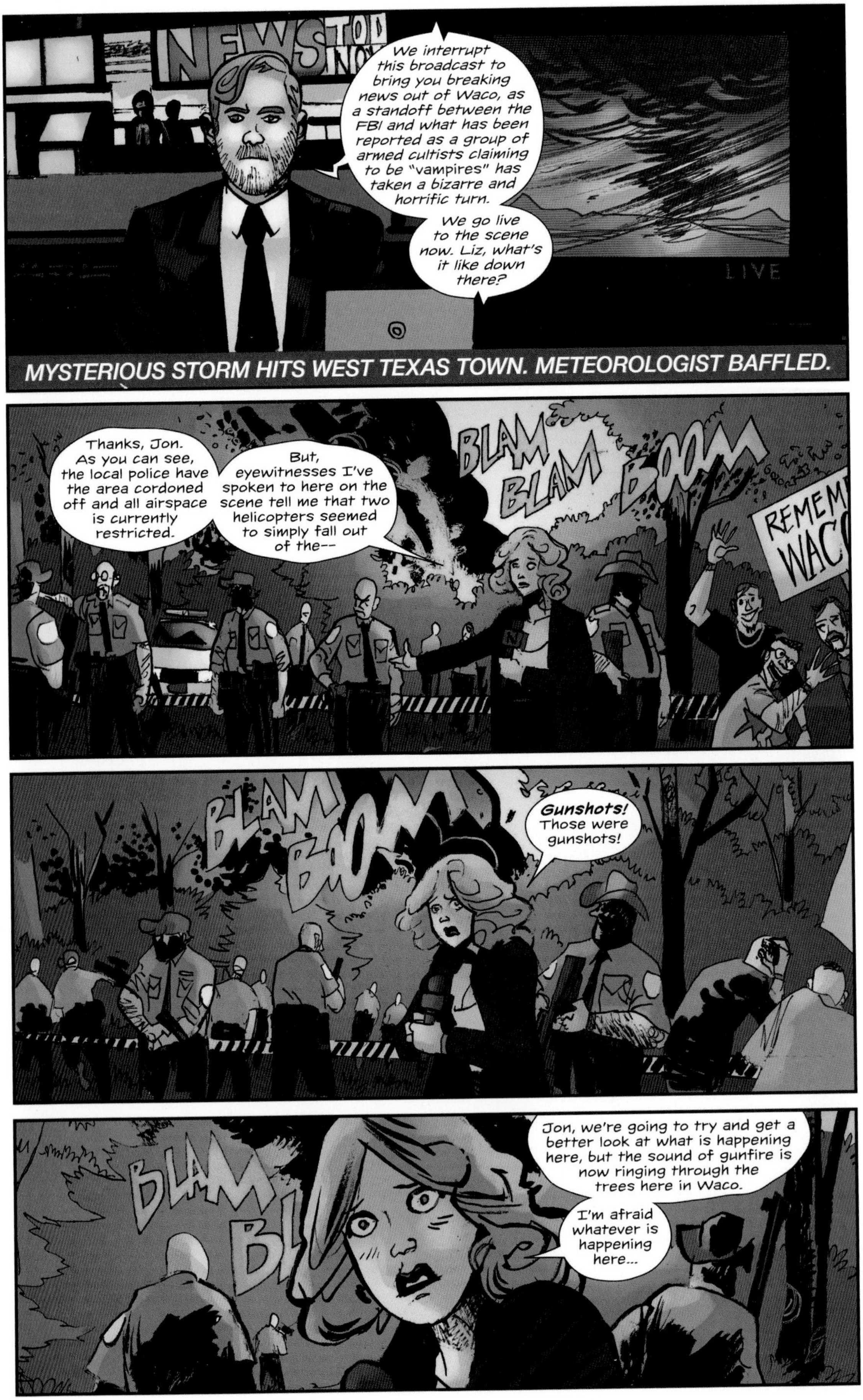
We interrupt this broadcast to bring you breaking news out of Waco, as a standoff between the FBI and what has been reported as a group of armed cultists claiming to be "vampires" has taken a bizarre and horrific turn.
We go live to the scene now. Liz, what's it like down there?
LIVE
MYSTERIOUS STORM HITS WEST TEXAS TOWN. METEOROLOGIST BAFFLED.
Thanks, Jon. As you can see, the local police have the area cordoned off and all airspace is currently restricted.
But, eyewitnesses I've spoken to here on the scene tell me that two helicopters seemed to simply fall out of the--
BLAM BLAM BOOM
BLAM BOOM
Gunshots! Those were gunshots!
BLAM
Jon, we're going to try and get a better look at what is happening here, but the sound of gunfire is now ringing through the trees here in Waco.
I'm afraid whatever is happening here...

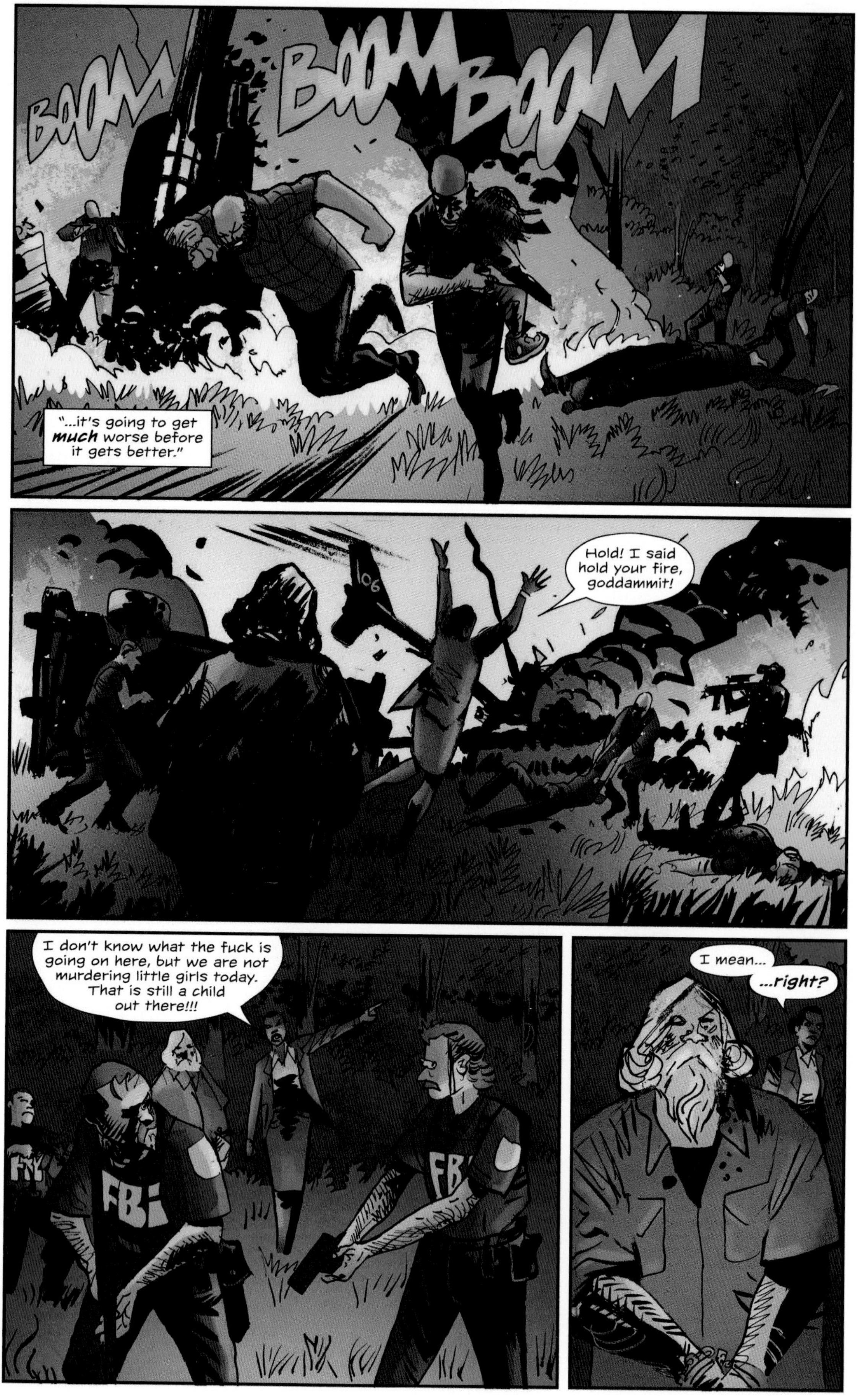
BOOM BOOM BOOM
"...it's going to get **much** worse before it gets better."
106
Hold! I said hold your fire, goddammit!
FBI
I don't know what the fuck is going on here, but we are not murdering little girls today. That is still a child out there!!!
I mean...
...right?

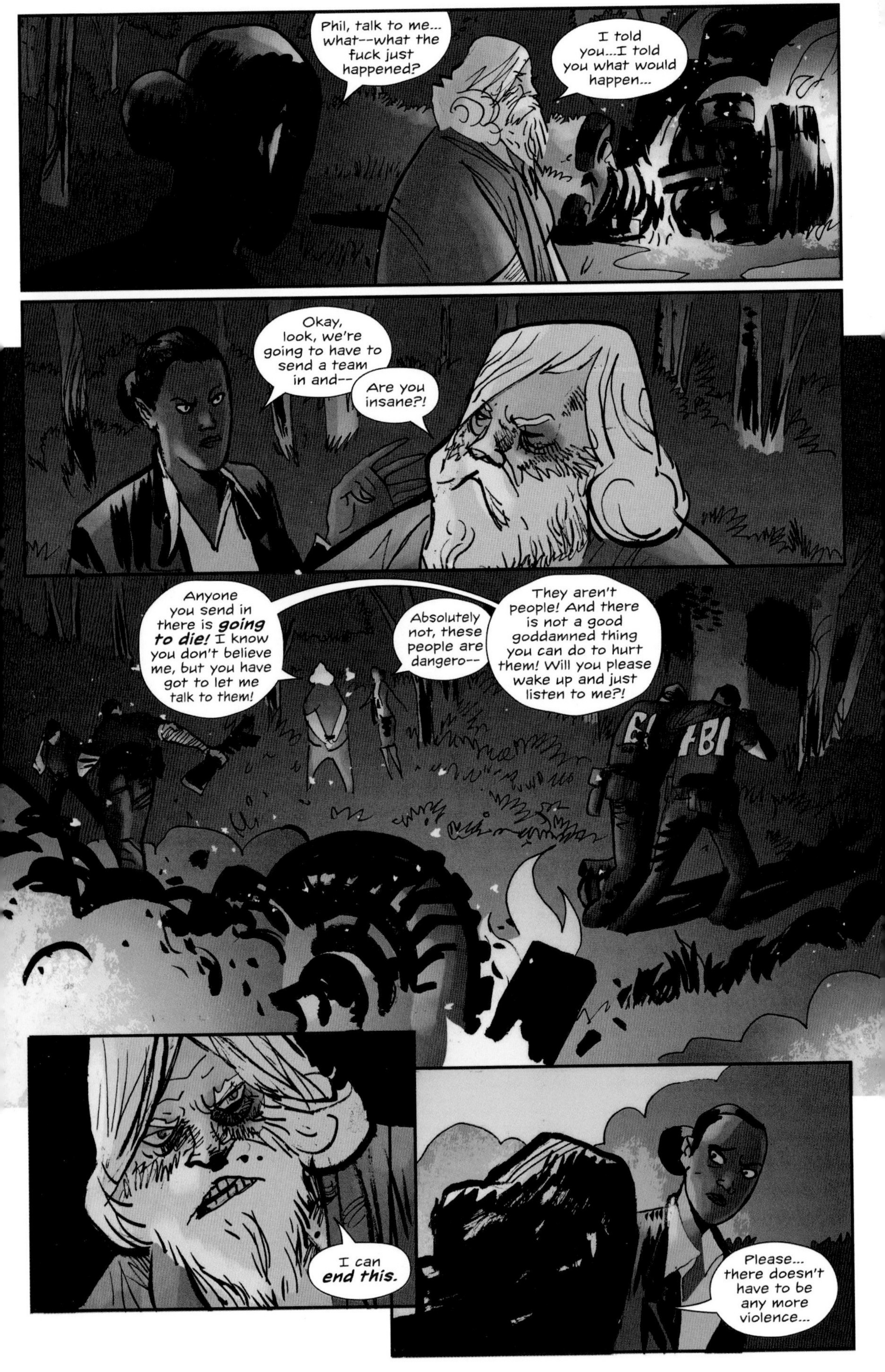
Phil, talk to me... what--what the fuck just happened?
I told you...I told you what would happen...
Okay, look, we're going to have to send a team in and--
Are you insane?!
Anyone you send in there is **going to die!** I know you don't believe me, but you have got to let me talk to them!
Absolutely not, these people are dangero--
They aren't people! And there is not a good goddamned thing you can do to hurt them! Will you please wake up and just listen to me?!
FBI
I can **end this.**
Please... there doesn't have to be any more violence...

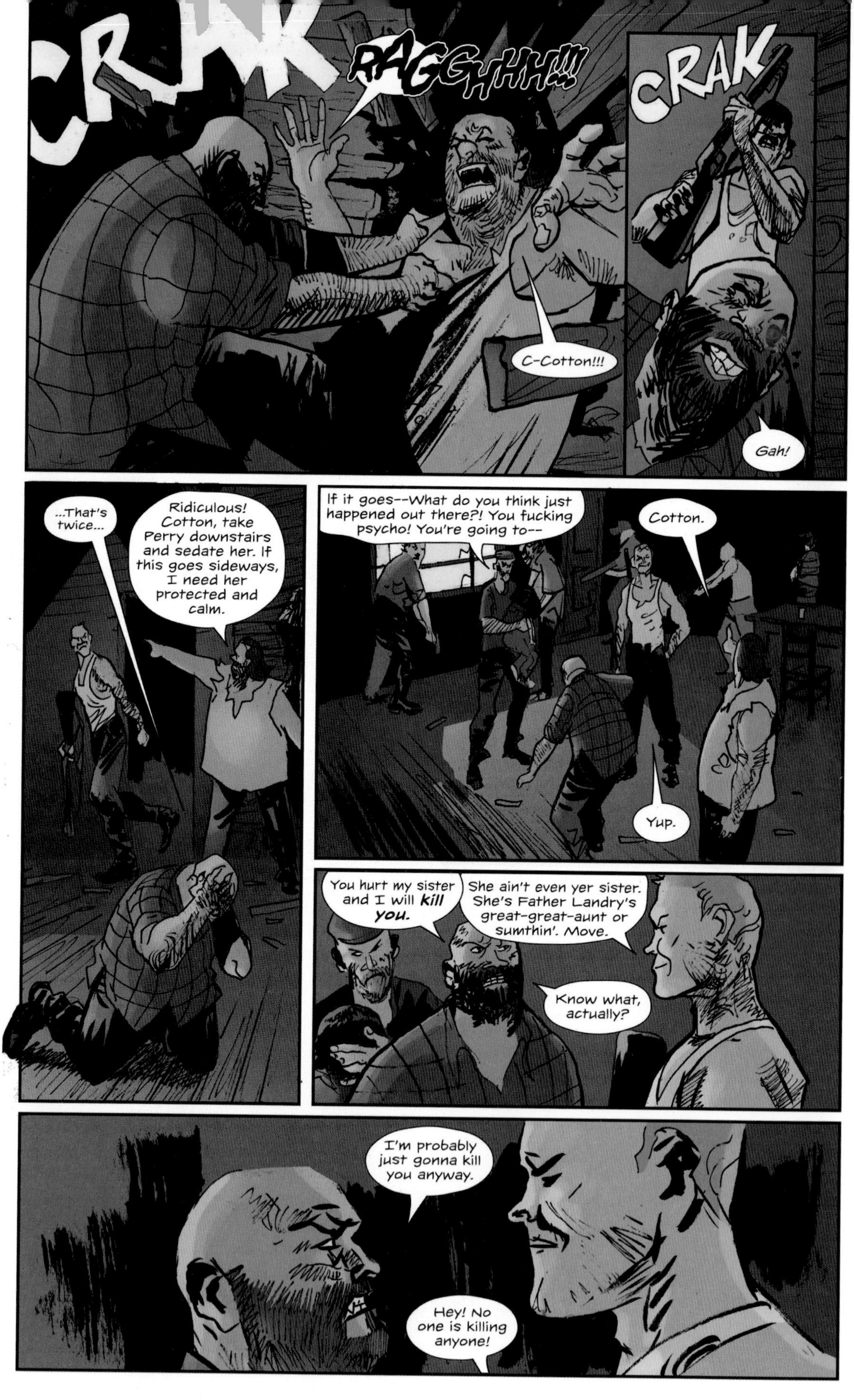
CRAK
RAGGHHH!!!
CRAK
C-Cotton!!!
Gah!
...That's twice...
Ridiculous! Cotton, take Perry downstairs and sedate her. If this goes sideways, I need her protected and calm.
If it goes--What do you think just happened out there?! You fucking psycho! You're going to--
Cotton.
Yup.
You hurt my sister and I will *kill you.*
She ain't even yer sister. She's Father Landry's great-great-aunt or sumthin'. Move.
Know what, actually?
I'm probably just gonna kill you anyway.
Hey! No one is killing anyone!

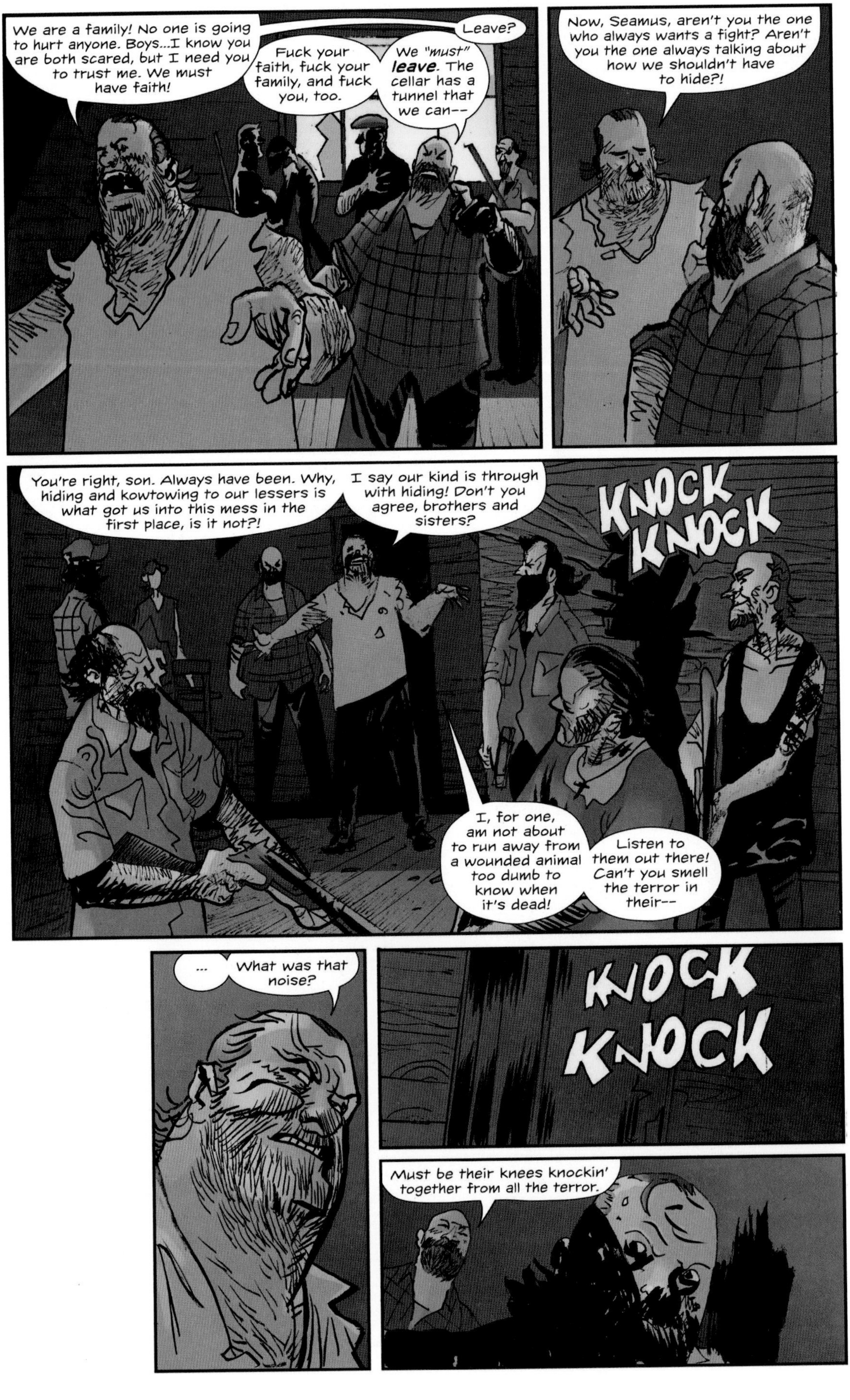
We are a family! No one is going to hurt anyone. Boys...I know you are both scared, but I need you to trust me. We must have faith!
Leave?
Fuck your faith, fuck your family, and fuck you, too.
We "must" leave. The cellar has a tunnel that we can--
Now, Seamus, aren't you the one who always wants a fight? Aren't you the one always talking about how we shouldn't have to hide?!
You're right, son. Always have been. Why, hiding and kowtowing to our lessers is what got us into this mess in the first place, is it not?!
I say our kind is through with hiding! Don't you agree, brothers and sisters?
KNOCK KNOCK
I, for one, am not about to run away from a wounded animal too dumb to know when it's dead!
Listen to them out there! Can't you smell the terror in their--
...
What was that noise?
KNOCK KNOCK
Must be their knees knockin' together from all the terror.

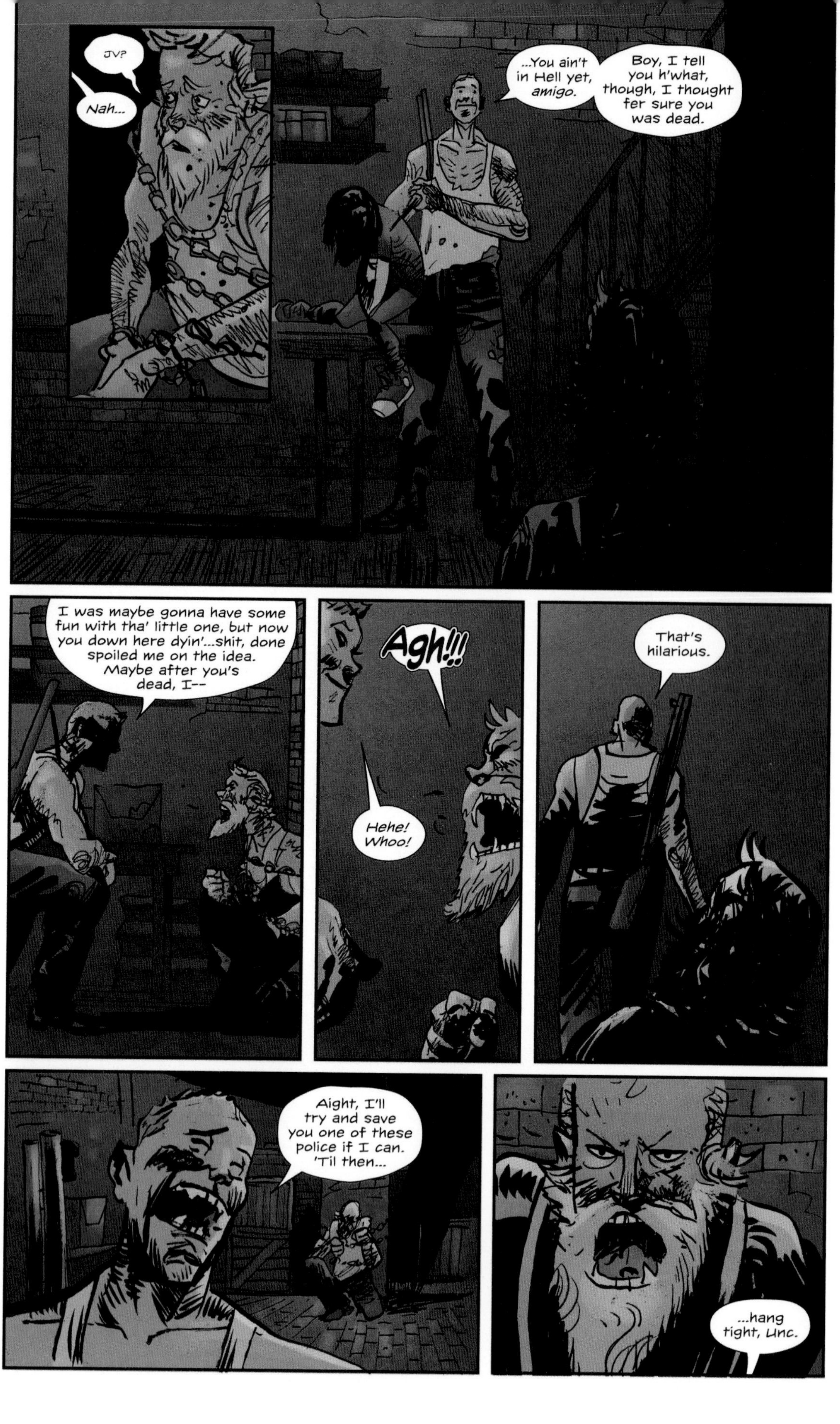
JV?
Nah...
...You ain't in Hell yet, *amigo.*
Boy, I tell you h'what, though, I thought fer sure you was dead.
I was maybe gonna have some fun with tha' little one, but now you down here dyin'...shit, done spoiled me on the idea. Maybe after you's dead, I--
Agh!!!
Hehe! Whoo!
That's hilarious.
Aight, I'll try and save you one of these police if I can. 'Til then...
...hang tight, Unc.

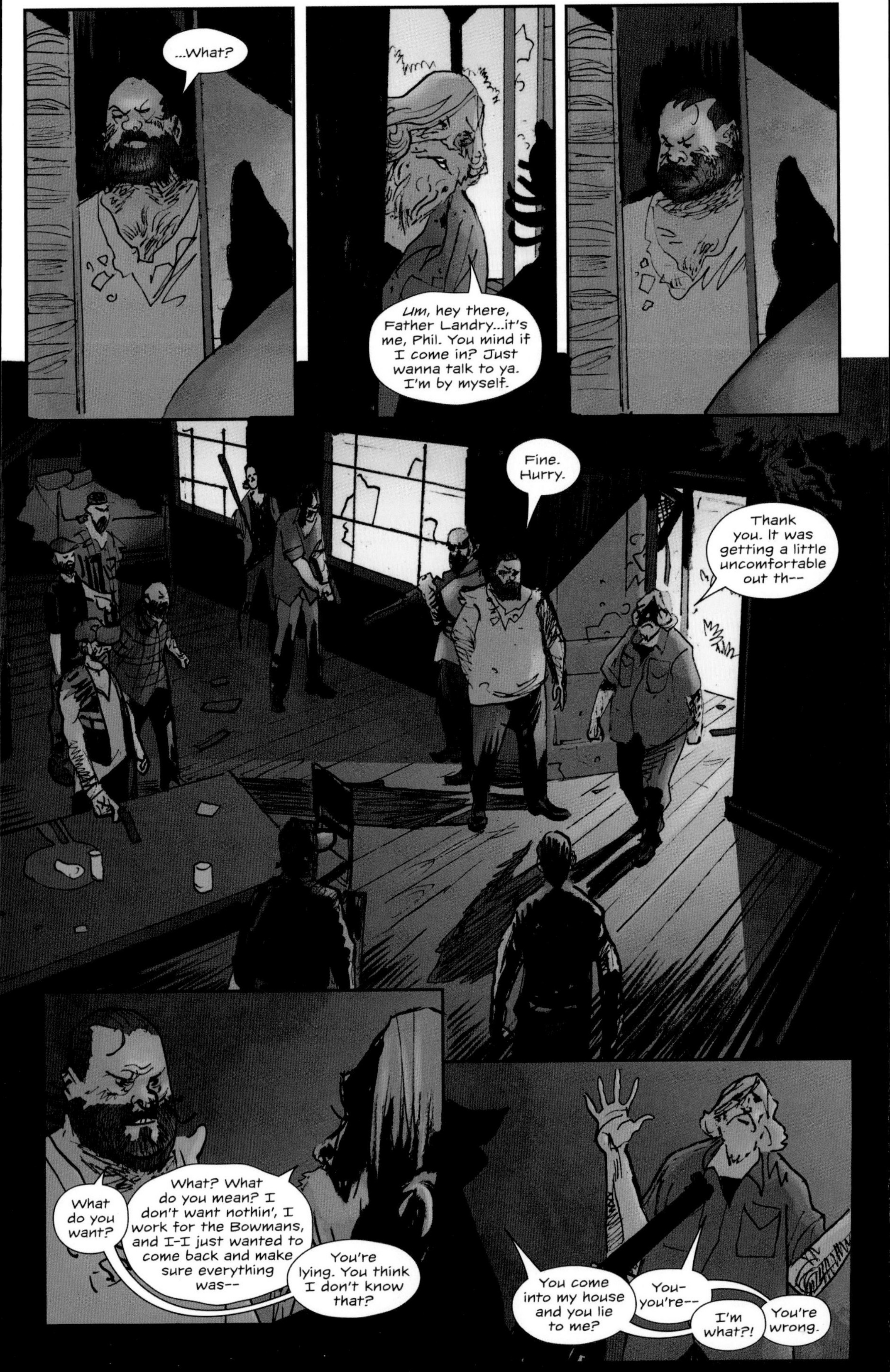

...What?
Um, hey there, Father Landry...it's me, Phil. You mind if I come in? Just wanna talk to ya. I'm by myself.
Fine. Hurry.
Thank you. It was getting a little uncomfortable out th--
What do you want?
What? What do you mean? I don't want nothin', I work for the Bowmans, and I-I just wanted to come back and make sure everything was--
You're lying. You think I don't know that?
You come into my house and you lie to me?
You- you're--
I'm what?!
You're wrong.

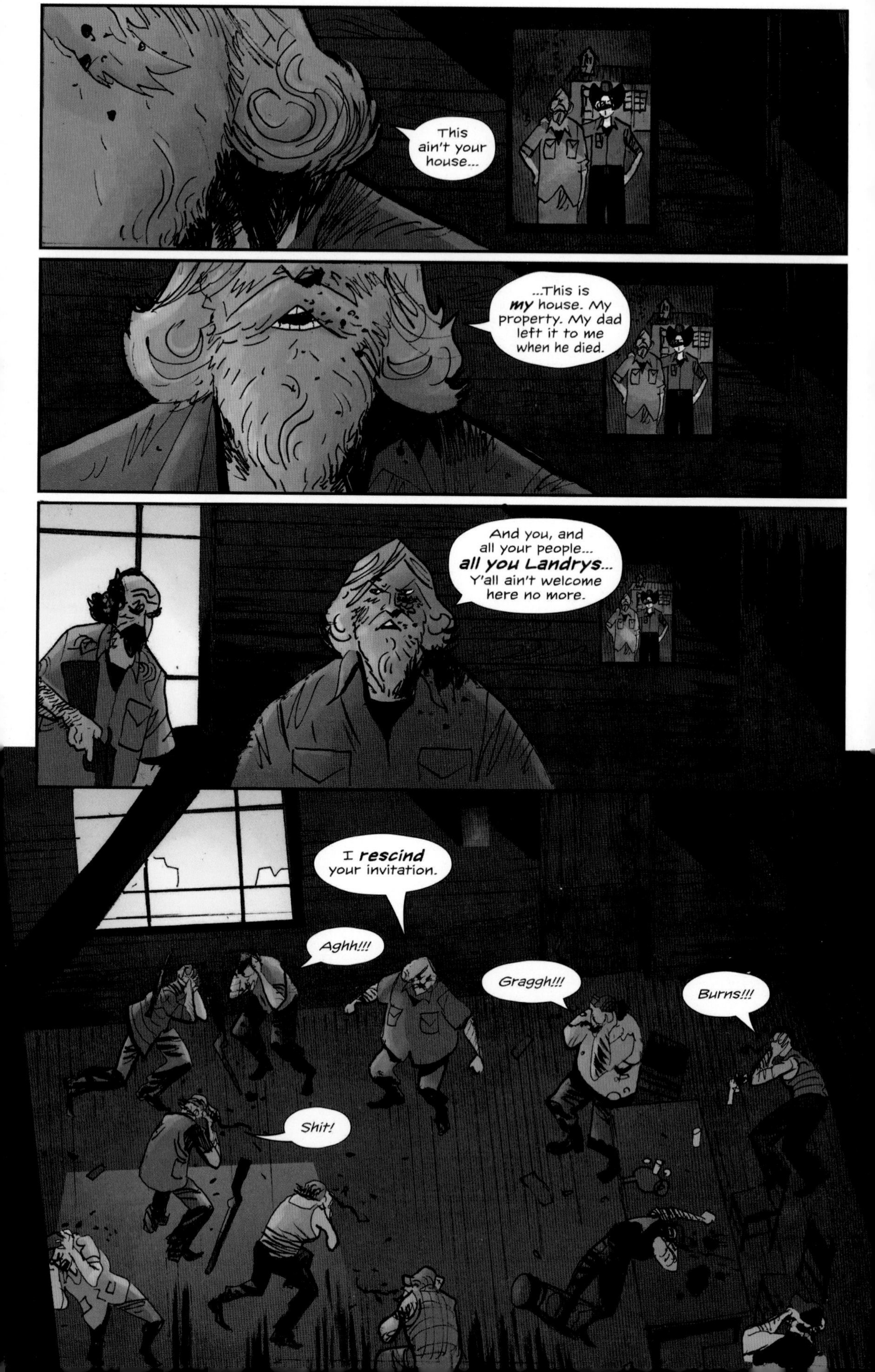
This ain't your house...
...This is **my** house. My property. My dad left it to me when he died.
And you, and all your people... **all you Landrys**... Y'all ain't welcome here no more.
I **rescind** your invitation.
Aghh!!!
Gragggh!!!
Burns!!!
Shit!

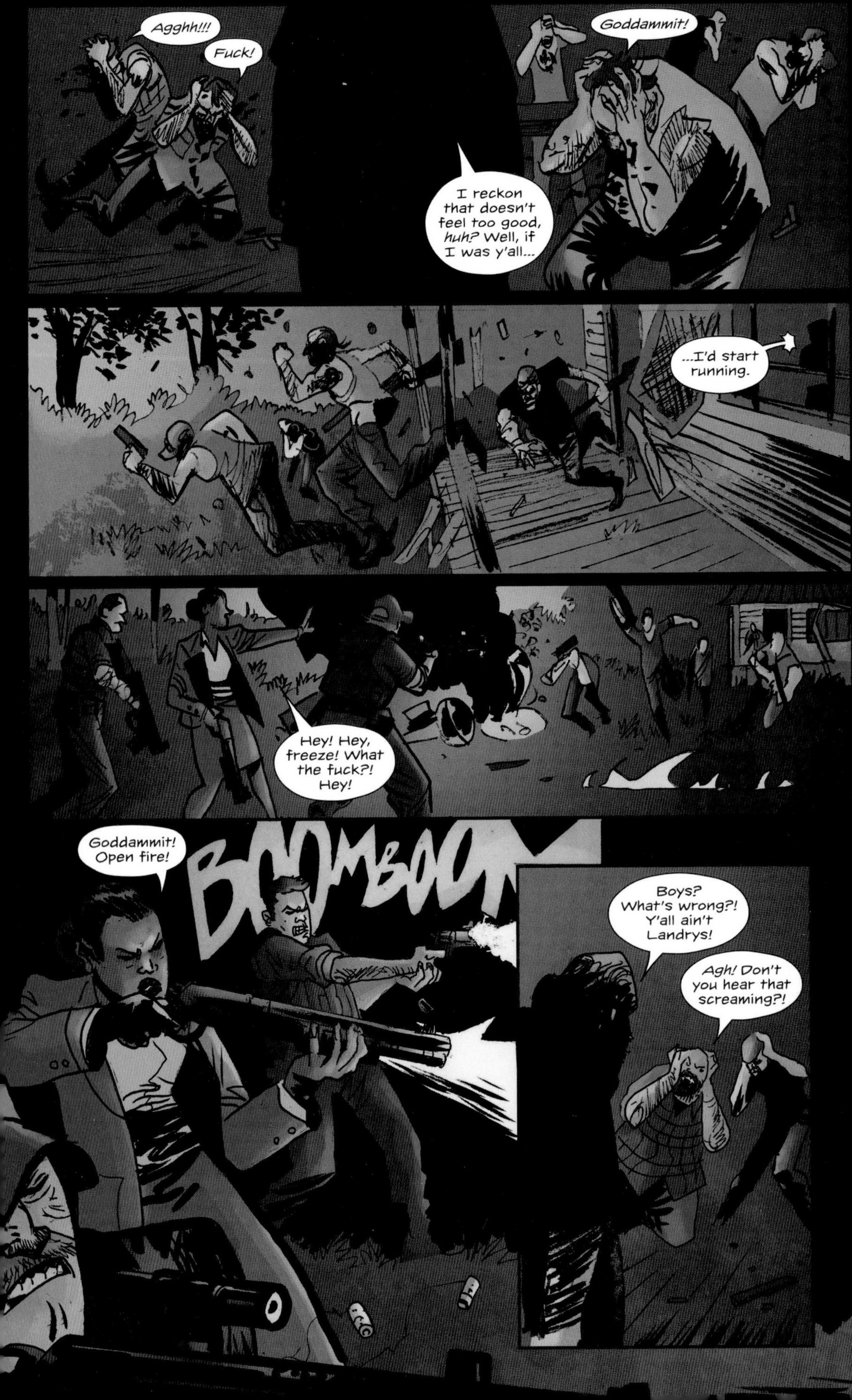
Agghh!!!
Fuck!
Goddammit!
I reckon that doesn't feel too good, *huh?* Well, if I was y'all...
...I'd start running.
Hey! Hey, freeze! What the fuck?! Hey!
Goddammit! Open fire!
BOOMBOOM
Boys? What's wrong?! Y'all ain't Landrys!
Agh! Don't you hear that screaming?!

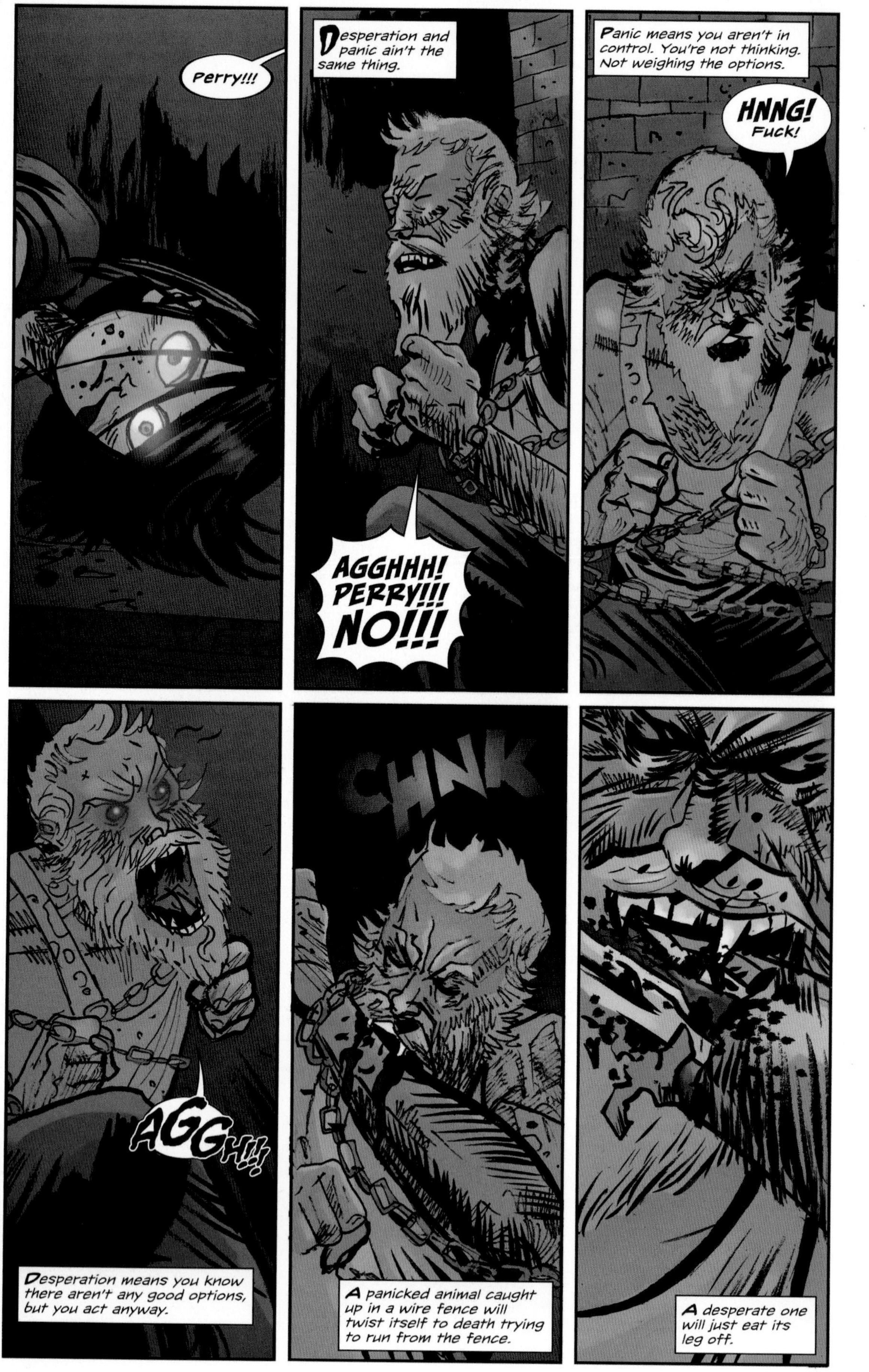
Perry!!!
Desperation and panic ain't the same thing.
AGGHHH! PERRY!!! NO!!!
Panic means you aren't in control. You're not thinking. Not weighing the options.
HNNG! Fuck!
AGGH!!!
Desperation means you know there aren't any good options, but you act anyway.
CHNK
A panicked animal caught up in a wire fence will twist itself to death trying to run from the fence.
A desperate one will just eat its leg off.

That's not to say panic can't be useful, mind you.

The human body especially can do some pretty amazing things when it panics.

They hear better. See clearer. Think faster.

BUUM BOOM

CL-CLK

They're never stronger than when they're scared.

AGHHH!!!

See, the beauty of panic is that you don't get a say. No time to fret over consequences.

Aghh--

GRAGH!!!

You either run...

...or you fight...

GRAAAGHH!!!

Where you think you're going, bi--

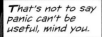

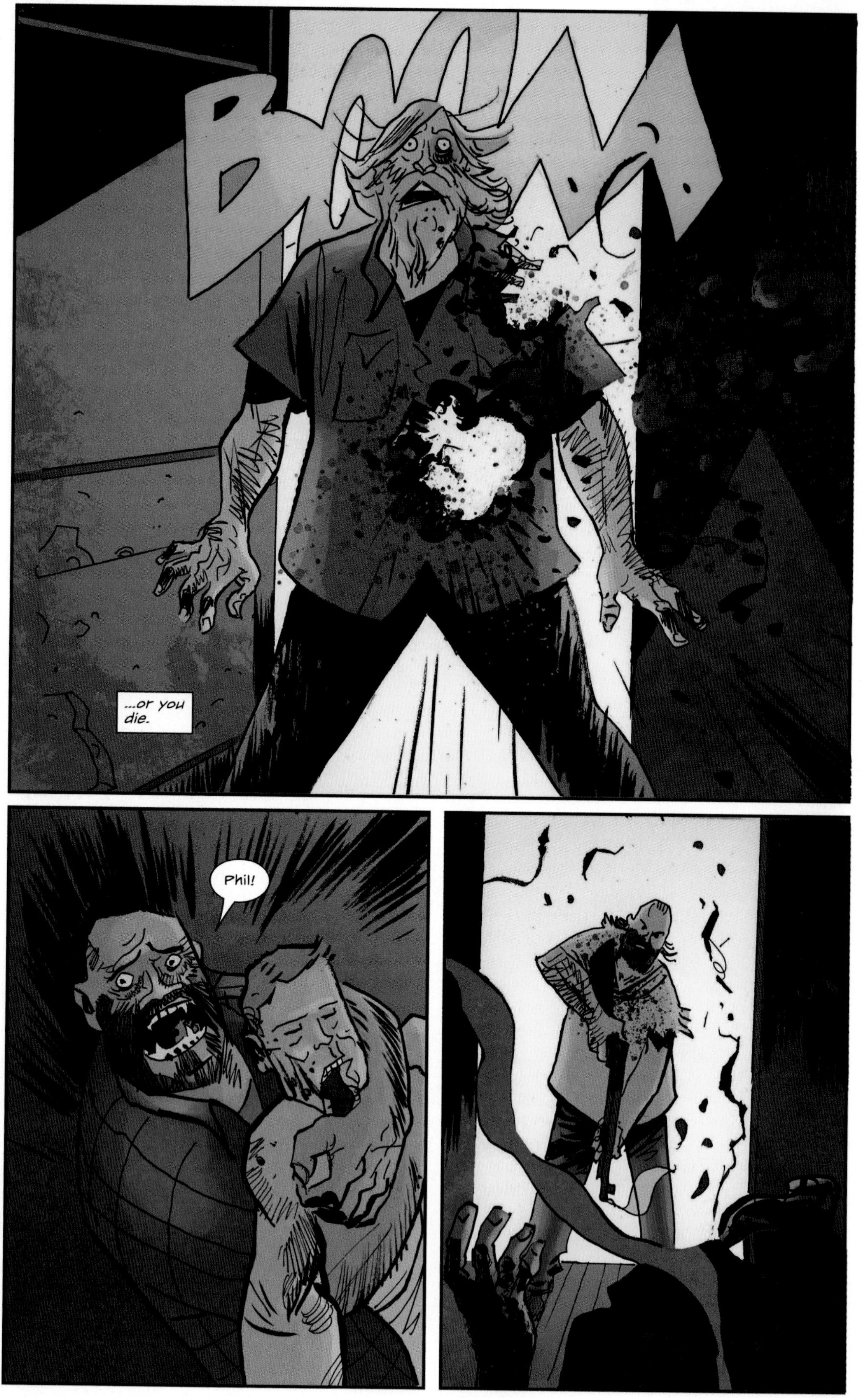
...or you die.
Phil!

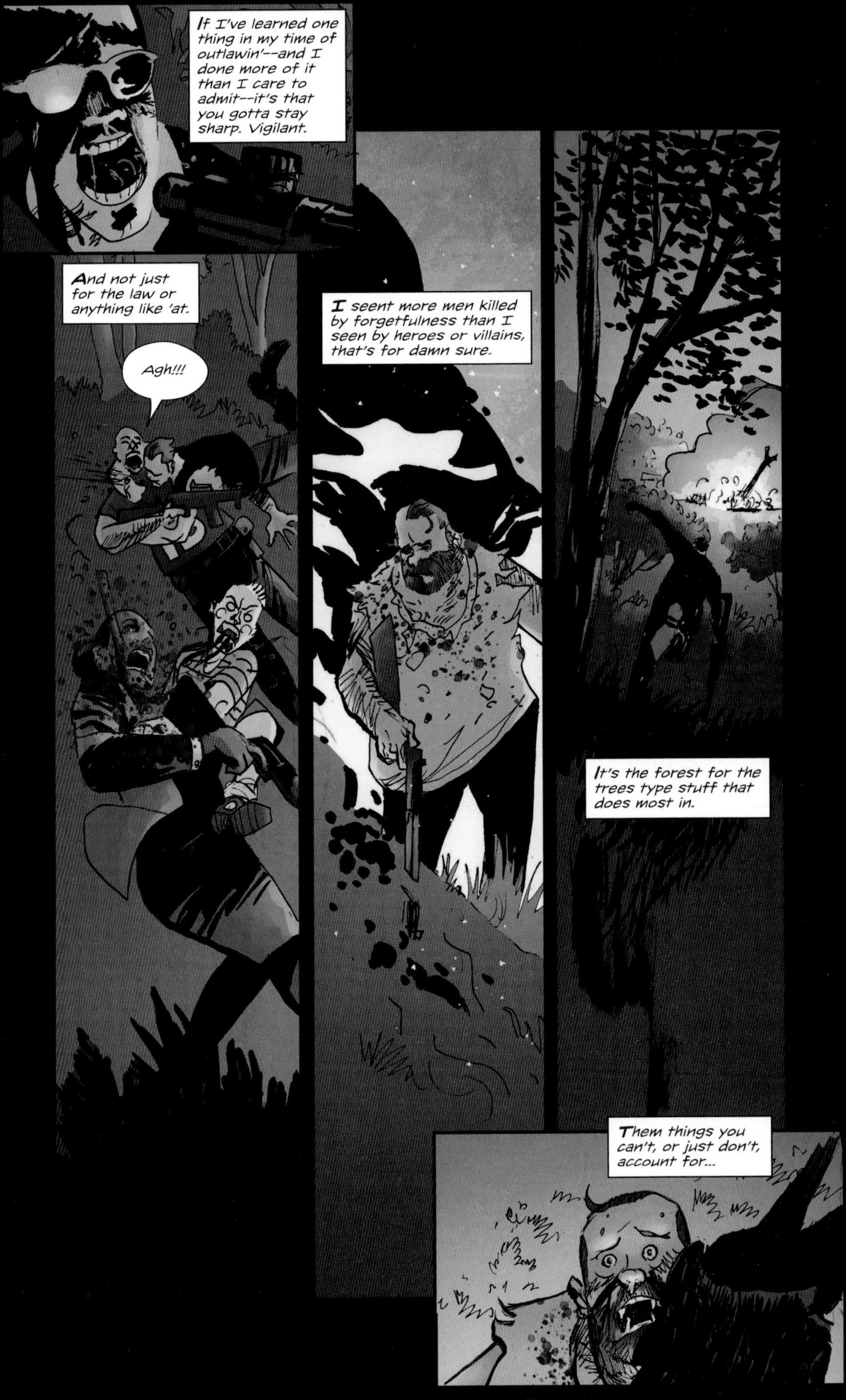
If I've learned one thing in my time of outlawin'--and I done more of it than I care to admit--it's that you gotta stay sharp. Vigilant.
And not just for the law or anything like 'at.
Agh!!!
I seent more men killed by forgetfulness than I seen by heroes or villains, that's for damn sure.
It's the forest for the trees type stuff that does most in.
Them things you can't, or just don't, account for...

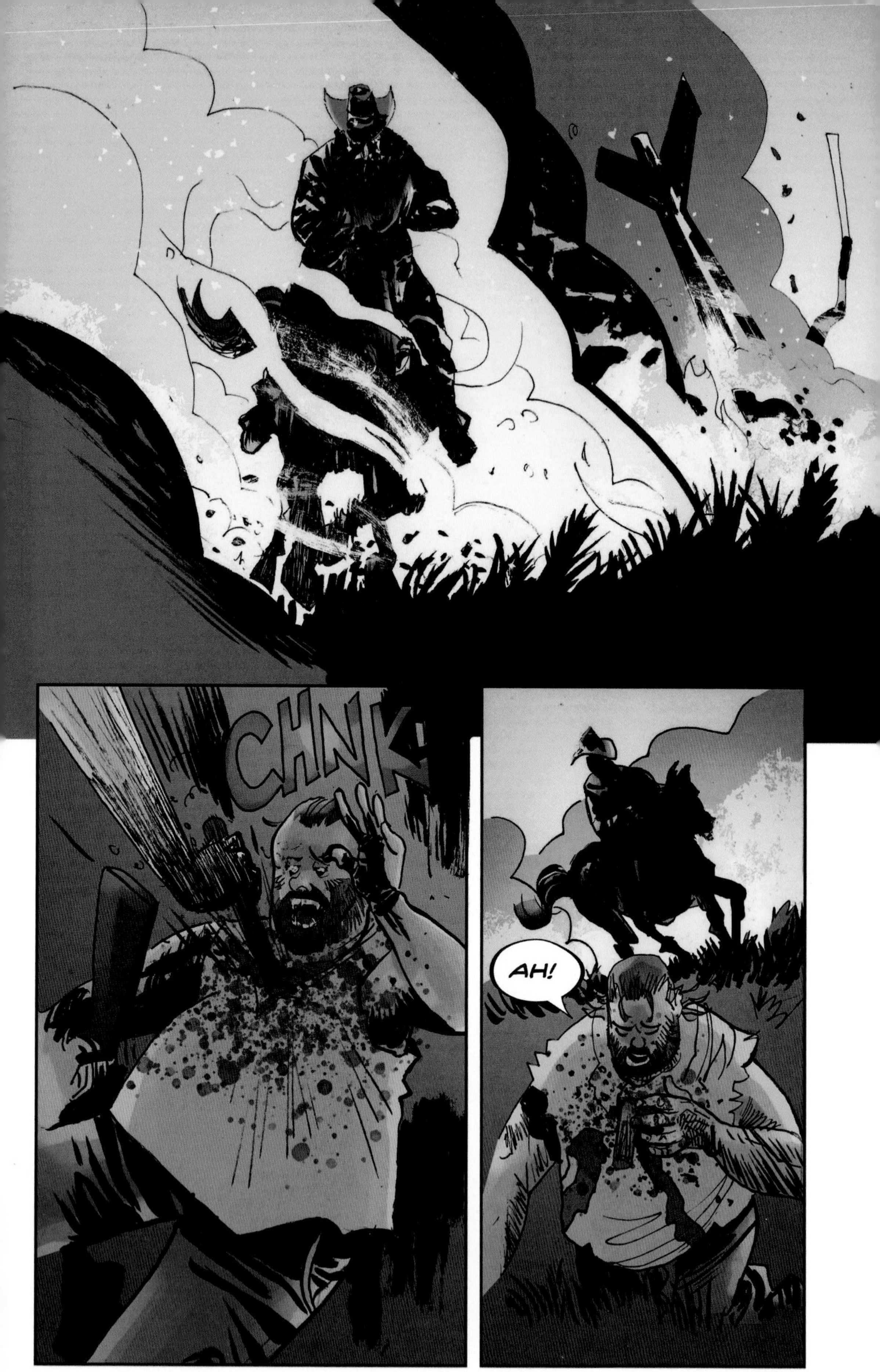
CHNK!
AH!

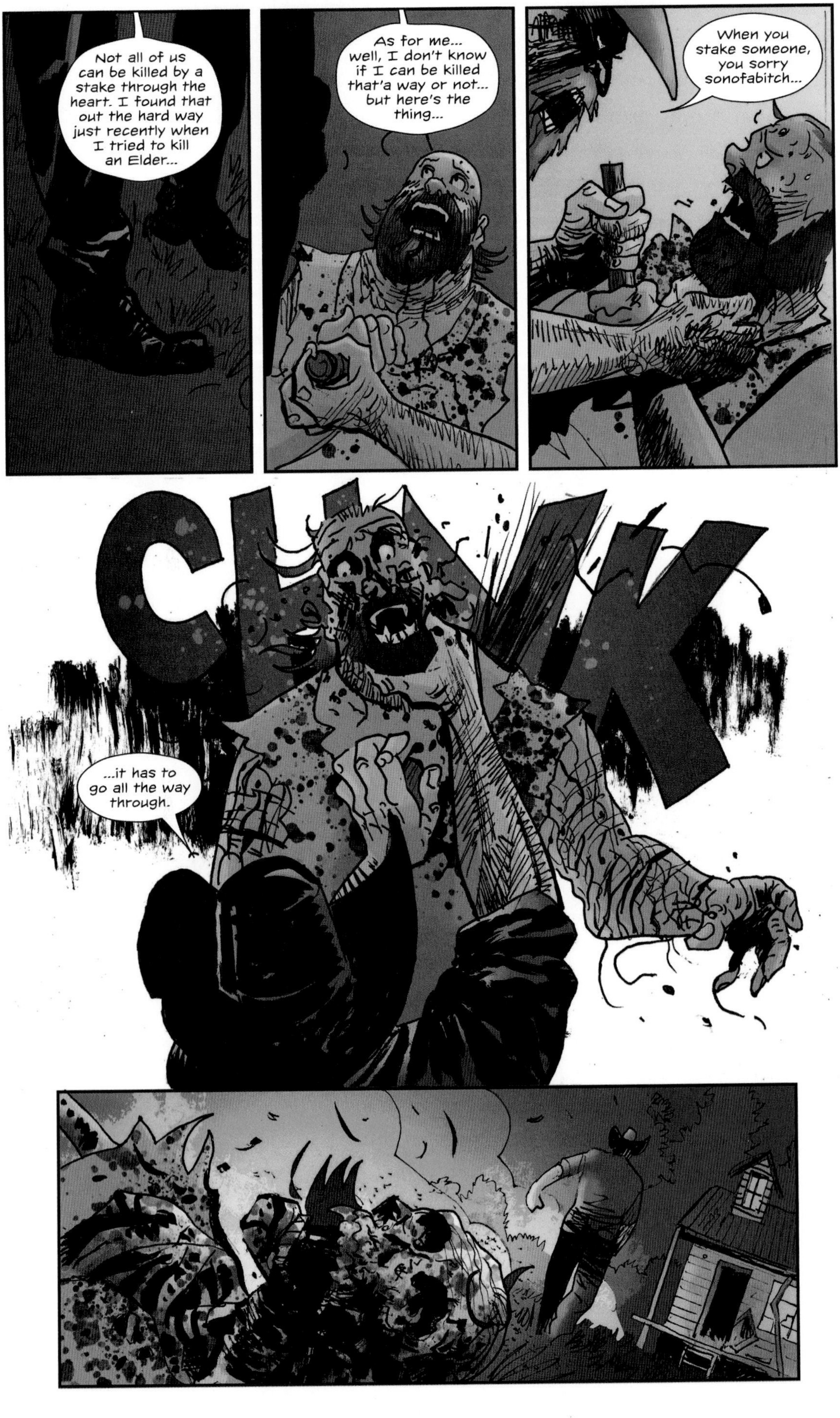
Not all of us can be killed by a stake through the heart. I found that out the hard way just recently when I tried to kill an Elder...
As for me... well, I don't know if I can be killed that'a way or not... but here's the thing...
When you stake someone, you sorry sonofabitch...
CHUNK
...it has to go all the way through.

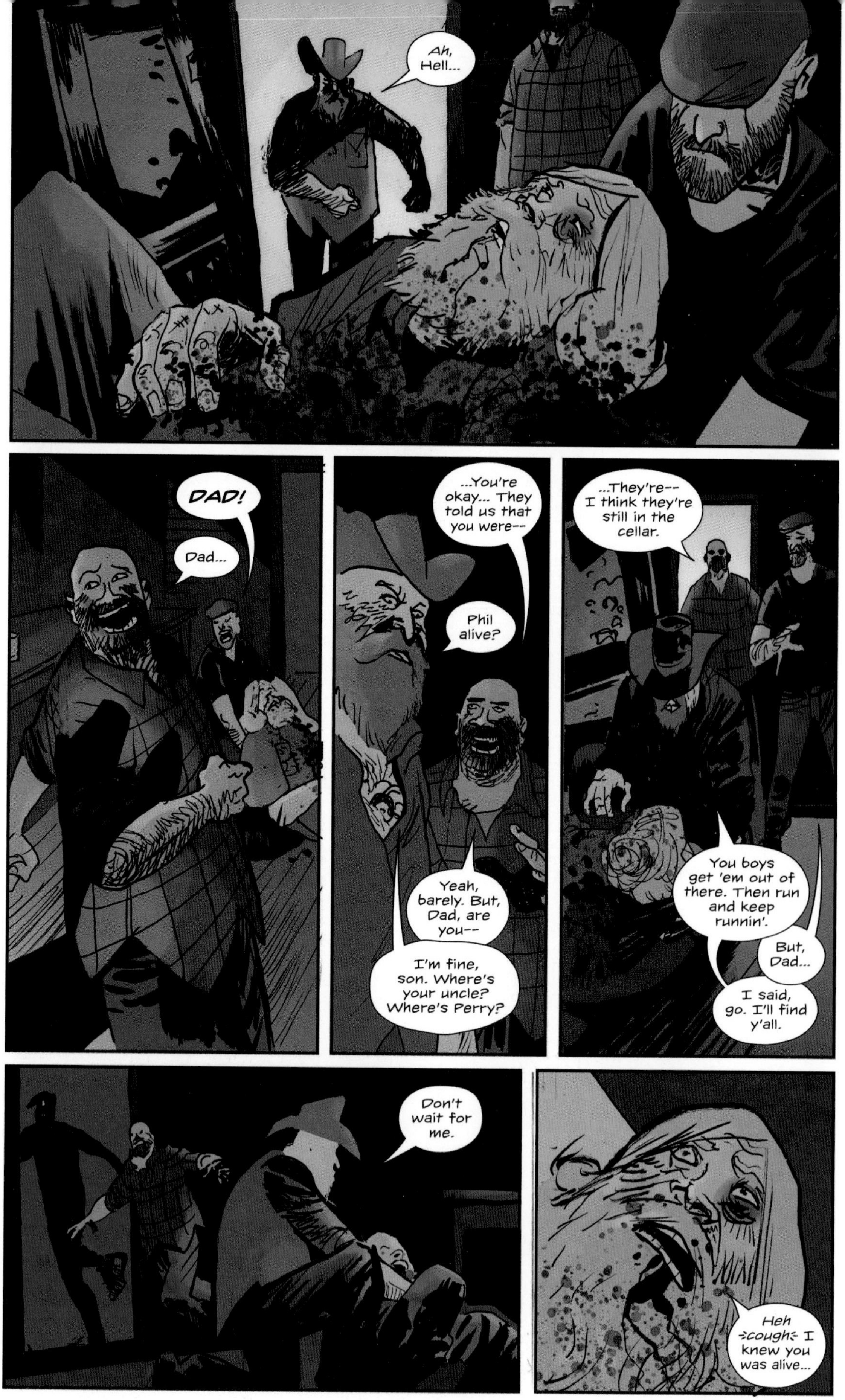
Ah, Hell...
DAD!
Dad...
...You're okay... They told us that you were--
Phil alive?
Yeah, barely. But, Dad, are you--
I'm fine, son. Where's your uncle? Where's Perry?
...They're-- I think they're still in the cellar.
You boys get 'em out of there. Then run and keep runnin'.
But, Dad...
I said, go. I'll find y'all.
Don't wait for me.
Heh -cough- I knew you was alive...

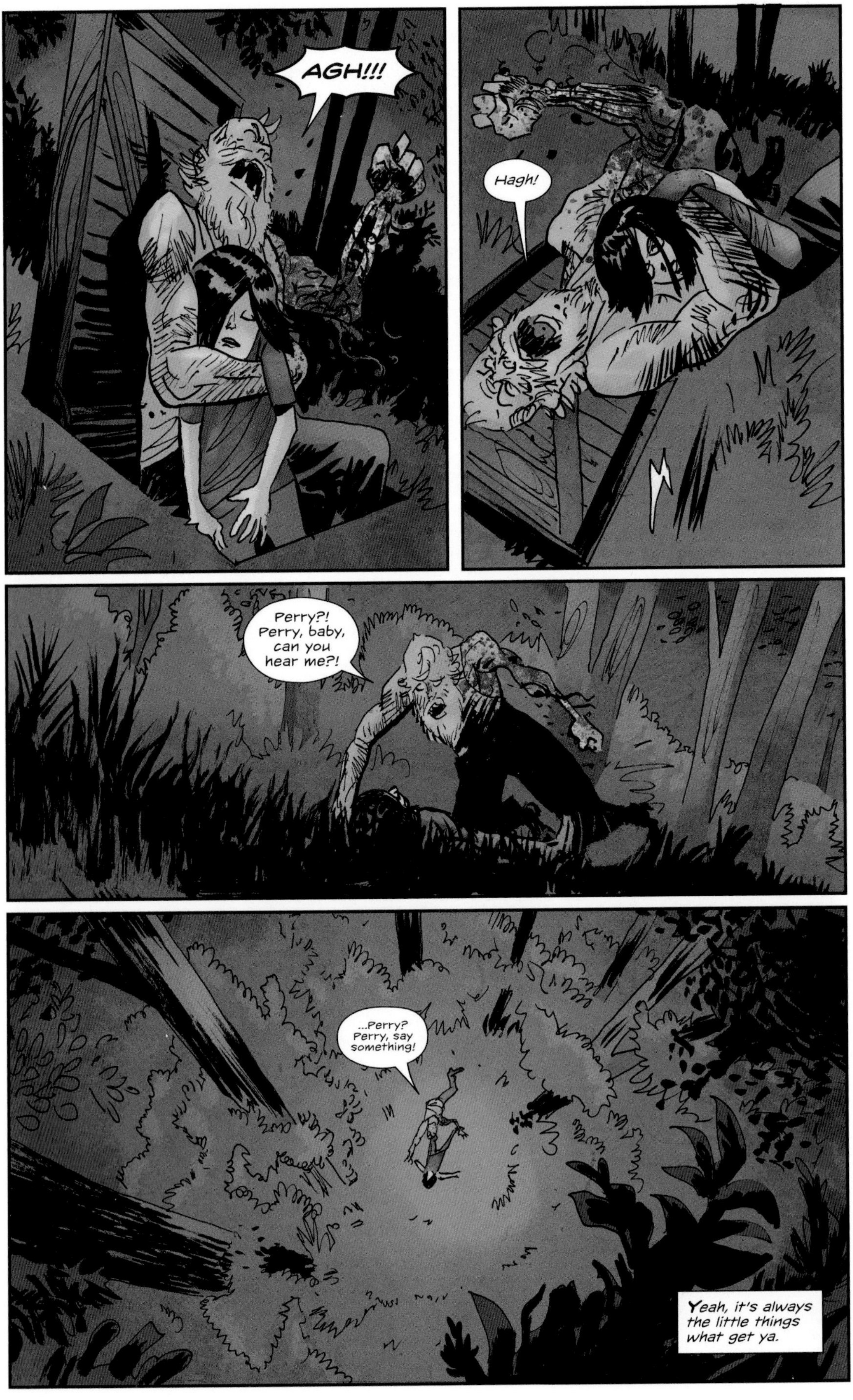
AGH!!!
Hagh!
Perry?! Perry, baby, can you hear me?!
...Perry? Perry, say something!
Yeah, it's always the little things what get ya.

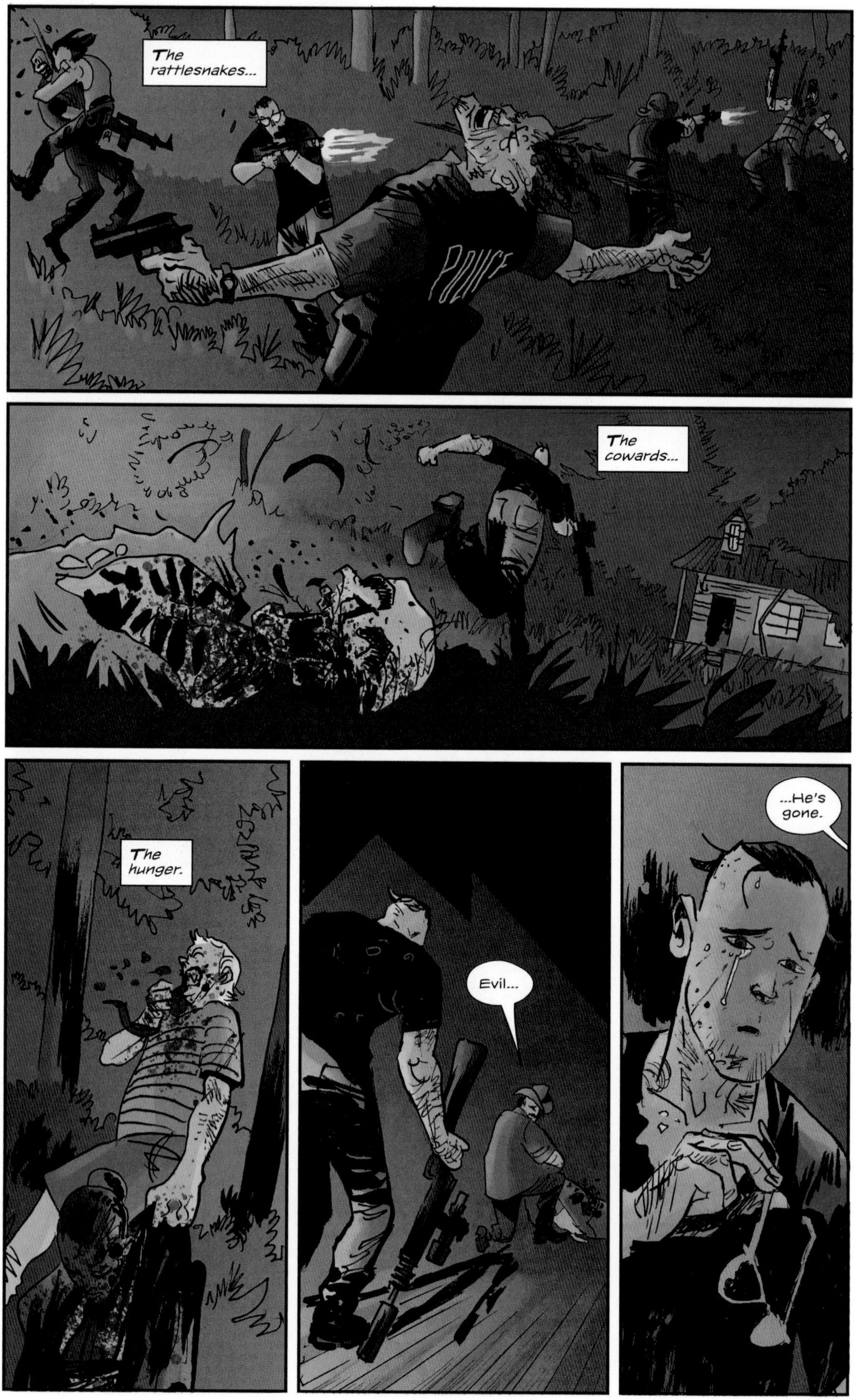
The rattlesnakes...
The cowards...
The hunger.
Evil...
...He's gone.

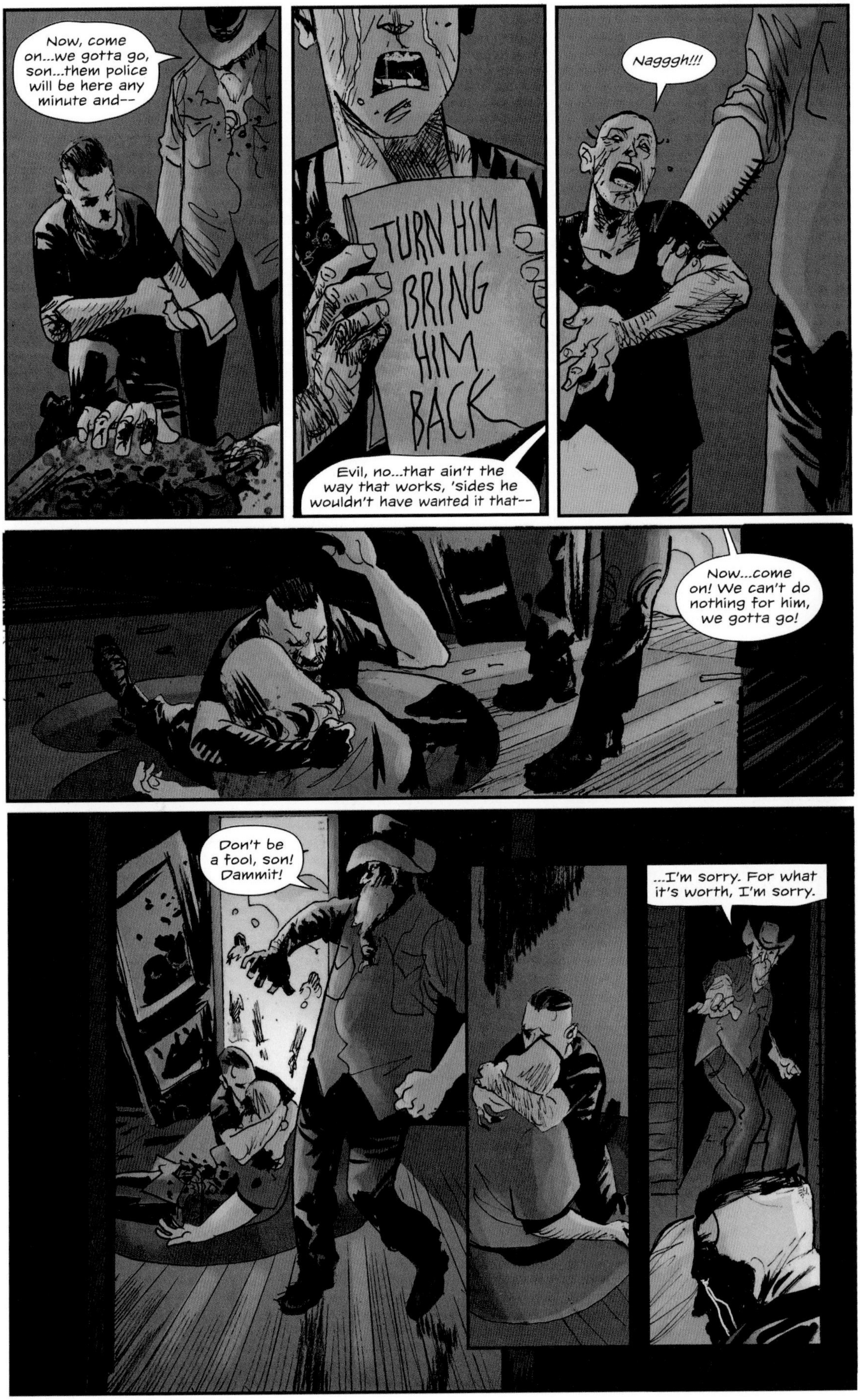
Now, come on...we gotta go, son...them police will be here any minute and--
TURN HIM BRING HIM BACK
Evil, no...that ain't the way that works, 'sides he wouldn't have wanted it that--
Nagggh!!!
Now...come on! We can't do nothing for him, we gotta go!
Don't be a fool, son! Dammit!
...I'm sorry. For what it's worth, I'm sorry.

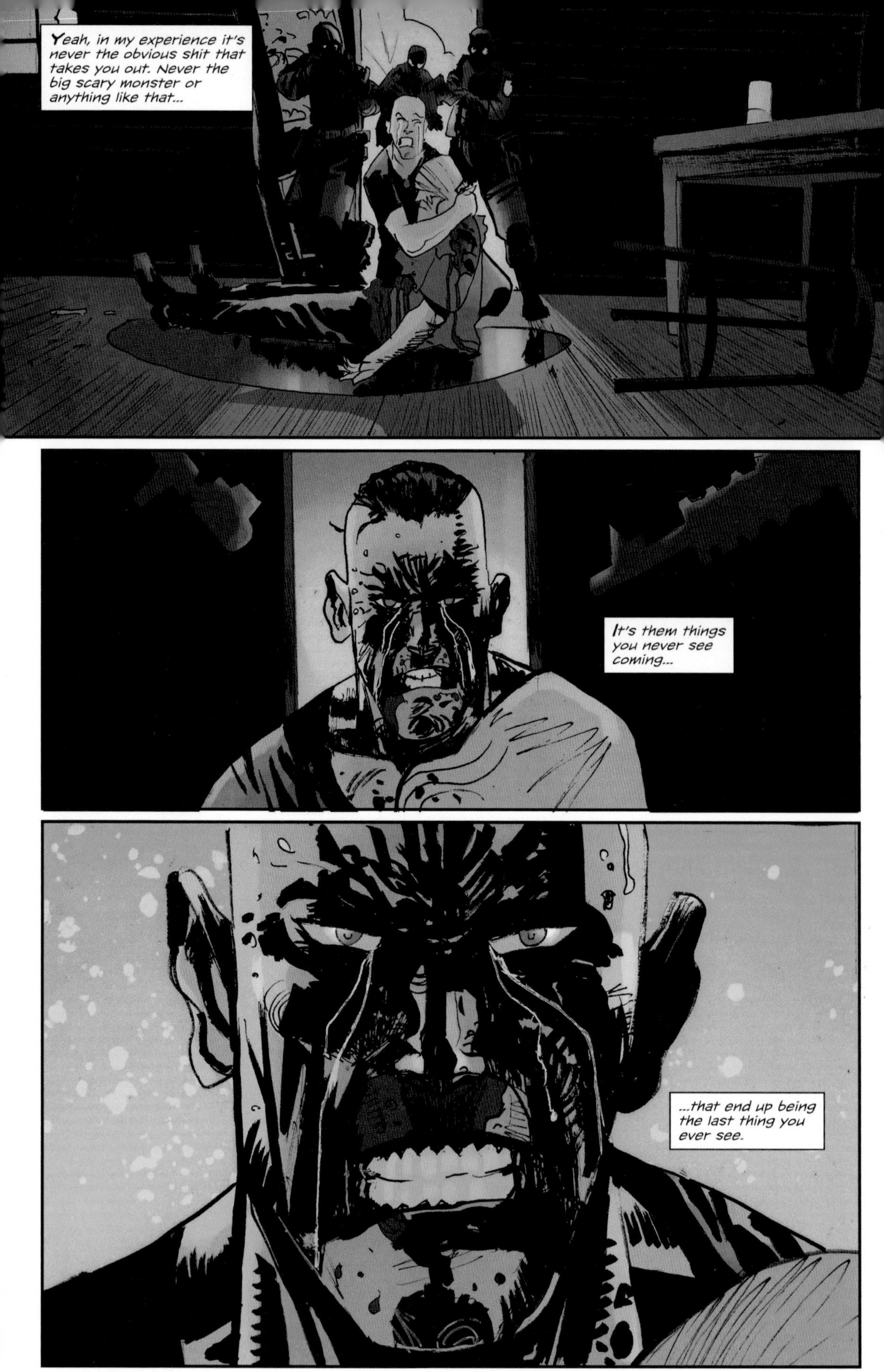
Yeah, in my experience it's never the obvious shit that takes you out. Never the big scary monster or anything like that...
It's them things you never see coming...
...that end up being the last thing you ever see.

To be continued...

"There's no such thing as hope.

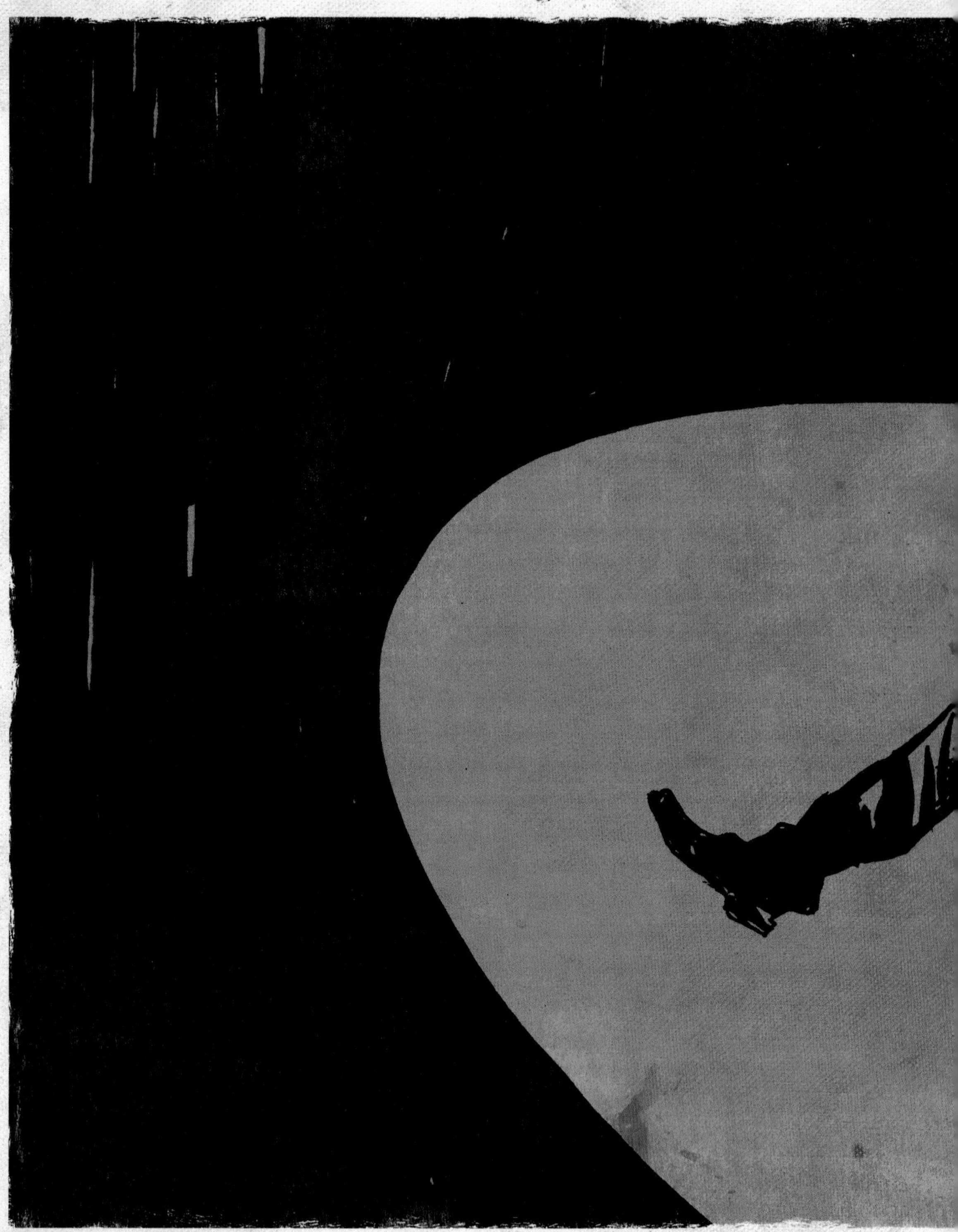